'I am disappoint[ed] rush away befo[re] chance to discuss my proposal. Perhaps we can arrange to meet again at a more convenient time?'

She licked her dry lips and told herself she was imagining the predatory gleam in his eyes. 'Your Highness…' Her voice sounded strangely breathless.

'Please call me Kadir, Lexi.'

The way he said her name, with that soft huskiness in his voice, was too intimate—as if he had stroked each syllable with his tongue.

Lexi felt as though she was drowning in his molten gaze, but a tiny part of her sanity remained and asked why she was letting him get to her. He was a notorious womaniser, and in the past when other men like him had tried to come on to her she'd had no trouble shooting them down.

Of course she would not allow herself to be seduced by the Sheikh. But she could not deny that his interest was flattering, and a salve to her wounded pride. Without conscious thought she swayed towards Kadir, bringing her mouth even closer to his. Her heart pounded and her eyelashes swept down as she waited, tense with anticipation, for him to brush his lips over hers.

Dear Reader,

Sisters often share a special bond of love and friendship—as I do with my own sister. I am fascinated by this unique relationship, and decided to write a duet featuring two sisters.

However, when I thought of Lexi, the heroine of *Sheikh's Forbidden Conquest*, I realised that her relationship with her younger sister Athena was complicated because Lexi was adopted. A year later her adoptive parents had a much longed for daughter of their own, and made it clear to Lexi that they preferred Athena.

Lexi has demonstrated her bravery as an RAF pilot, flying rescue missions in Afghanistan, but sparks fly when she goes to work for Sultan Kadir Al Sulaimar in his desert kingdom of Zenhab. The cultural differences between them are just one barrier they face, and they know they must resist the sizzling chemistry that ignites whenever they are near each other!

In my second book, shy Athena wishes she was as confident as her fiery sister. Athena has been named after the Greek goddess of wisdom, but she feels she is a disappointment to her academic parents, who hoped she would follow them into a medical career.

At least her parents are pleased that she is engaged to English aristocrat Charles Fairfax. But mysterious Italian playboy Luca De Rossi has other plans for Athena!

I hope you enjoy reading about the sisters' journeys to finding true love!

Best wishes

Chantelle

SHEIKH'S FORBIDDEN CONQUEST

BY
CHANTELLE SHAW

MILLS &
BOON

Published in Great Britain 2015
by Mills & Boon, an imprint of Harlequin (UK) Limited,
Eton House, 18-24 Paradise Road, Richmond, Surrey, TW9 1SR

© 2015 Chantelle Shaw

ISBN: 978-0-263-25065-7

Harlequin (UK) Limited's policy is to use papers that are natural, renewable and recyclable products and made from wood grown in sustainable forests. The logging and manufacturing processes conform to the legal environmental regulations of the country of origin.

Printed and bound in Spain
by CPI, Barcelona

Chantelle Shaw lives on the Kent coast, and thinks up her stories while walking on the beach. She has been married for over thirty years and has six children. Her love affair with reading and writing Harlequin Mills & Boon® began as a teenager, and her first book was published in 2006. She likes strong-willed, slightly unusual characters. Chantelle also loves gardening, walking and wine!

Books by Chantelle Shaw

Mills & Boon® Modern™ Romance

To Wear His Ring Again
A Night in the Prince's Bed
Captive in His Castle
At Dante's Service
The Greek's Acquisition
Behind the Castello Doors
The Ultimate Risk

The Bond of Brothers

His Unexpected Legacy
Secrets of a Powerful Man

Irresistible Italians

A Dangerous Infatuation

After Hours with the Greek

After the Greek Affair

Visit the author profile page at millsandboon.co.uk for more titles

For my sister Helen, with love.

CHAPTER ONE

'WHAT LUNATIC DECIDED to go sailing in this atrocious weather?' Lexi muttered into her headset as she piloted the coastguard rescue helicopter over the south coast of England and out across the Solent.

The narrow strait which separated the mainland from the Isle of Wight was a popular area for water sports and on a summer's day, when the sea was calm and blue, it was an idyllic sight to watch the yachts skim across the water with their sails tugging in the breeze. But October had blown in on a series of ferocious storms that had swept away the last remnants of summer and whipped the sea into mountainous waves which crashed against the chalk cliffs, spewing foam high into the air. The white horses reared up in the glare of the helicopter's searchlight but Lexi knew that an even greater threat lay beneath the sea's surface, where dangerous currents eddied and swirled, ready to drag the unwary and unwise down into the depths.

She heard the co-pilot, Gavin's response through her headphones. 'The yacht which has made an emergency call for assistance was competing in a race. Apparently the skipper thought they would be able to run ahead of the storm, but they've hit a sandbank and the boat is taking in water.'

Lexi swore beneath her breath. 'The skipper took a dangerous gamble to win a race. Jeez, I love the male ego!'

'To be fair, the storm is stronger than the Met Office predicted,' Gavin said. 'The complex tidal patterns of the Solent have caught out many experienced sailors.'

'The problem is that too many sailors *don't* have enough experience and fail to appreciate how unpredictable and dangerous the sea can be, like the man on holiday with his son who we were called to assist two days ago. The boy was only ten years old. He didn't stand a chance when their boat started to sink in rough seas.'

'We did all we could,' Gavin reminded her.

'Yeah, but we couldn't save the boy. He was just a kid with his whole life in front of him. What a bloody waste.'

Lexi struggled to bring her emotions under control and concentrated on flying the helicopter in the strong wind and driving rain. She prided herself on her professionalism. The first rule of working for the rescue service was not to allow your mind to linger on past events—even something as traumatic as the death of a child—but to move on and deal with the next incident.

'The Mayday call confirmed that the three males on the yacht are all wearing life jackets,' Gavin said. 'But they're unlikely to survive for long in these rough seas. The skipper reported that he has received a head injury, but he insisted that he wants his crewmen to be rescued first.'

'It's a bit late for him to be concerned for his crew now. It's a pity he didn't take their safety into account earlier and abort the race.'

Lexi constantly moved her gaze between the flight instrument panel and the window to scan the wild waves below. Three massive chalk stacks known as the Needles rose out of the sea like jagged teeth. The famous landmark was iconic but the strong currents around the rocks could be treacherous.

An orange glow suddenly flashed in the sky.

'Did you see the flare?' Gavin peered through the windscreen as Lexi took the chopper lower. A few moments later he gave another shout. 'I've got a visual—on your right-hand side.'

Lexi spotted the yacht. It had been tipped onto its side by the strong sea swell, and she could make out three figures clinging onto the rigging. She kept the helicopter hovering in position as Gavin went to the rear of the aircraft and prepared to lower the winchman, who was a paramedic, onto the stricken vessel. The buffeting wind made Lexi's job almost impossible, but she was a highly experienced pilot and had flown Chinook helicopters over the deserts of Afghanistan. A cool head and nerves of steel had been necessary when she had been a member of the RAF and those qualities were required for her job with the coastguard rescue agency.

She spoke to the paramedic over the radio. 'Chris, once you're aboard the vessel, remind the crew that the coastguard agency are in charge of the rescue and everyone is to follow your orders, including the skipper. If his head injury looks serious we'll winch him up first, whether he likes it or not. This is not the time for him to decide he wants to be a hero,' she said sardonically.

CHAPTER TWO

THE SEARING PAIN that felt as though Kadir's skull had been split open with an axe was the result of being hit on the head by the sail boom of the *White Hawk*—his brand-new racing yacht that was now residing at the bottom of the sea. However, his immediate concern was not for the loss of his boat but the welfare of his crew, who were being stretchered off the helicopter that had just landed at a hospital on the mainland.

The rescue had been dramatic—and just in time. Once Kadir had realised the yacht was sinking, everything had happened so quickly. He hadn't had time to feel fear, but for a few seconds he had pictured himself galloping across a golden desert on his black stallion Baha', and his heart had ached for what would become of the kingdom his father had entrusted to him.

But, like a miracle, out of the dark sky had appeared a shining light, and he had heard the distinctive *whump-whump* of helicopter rotor blades. Kadir had flown in a helicopter many times, and as he'd clung to the rigging of his wrecked yacht being battered by forty-foot waves he had recognised the skill and bravery of the pilot flying the coastguard rescue chopper in the worsening gale.

He knew that he and his crew had been lucky to survive. But the two young sailors who had crewed for him since the start of the race in the Canary Islands were suffering from hypothermia and were in a bad way. As Kadir watched them being wheeled across the helipad, frustration surged through him. His clothes were wet and stiff with sea salt and the wind whipping across the helipad chilled him to his bones. He lifted a hand to his throbbing head and felt a swelling the size of an egg on his temple.

The coastguard paramedic gave him a worried look. 'Sir, please lie down on the stretcher and one of the medical staff will take you down to the A&E department so that your injuries can be treated.'

'I'm fine; I can walk,' Kadir said impatiently. 'It's my crew who I'm concerned about. I wish you had followed my instructions and rescued them first. They got too cold because they were in the sea for so long. You should have winched them up onto the helicopter before you rescued me.'

'I was under instructions to rescue injured casualties first and it was obvious that you had sustained a possibly serious head injury,' the paramedic explained.

'My crew were my responsibility,' Kadir argued. He was interrupted by another voice.

'I hardly think you are in a position to question the professional judgement of a member of the coastguard team when it was *your* poor judgement in deciding to sail in atrocious weather that put your crew in danger.'

Frowning, Kadir turned towards the person who had jumped down from the helicopter cockpit. Like the other members of the rescue team, the figure was wearing a bulky jumpsuit, but as they removed their flight helmet Kadir's confusion grew.

'Who are you?' he demanded.

'Flight Captain Lexi Howard. I was in charge of the rescue operation. The helicopter crew acted under my instructions, which were to winch up injured casualties first.'

'You're…*a woman*!'

The instant the words left his lips Kadir realised he had made a crass fool of himself. There was a crowd of people standing on the helipad—medical staff and a team of firemen, who were required to be present whenever a helicopter landed at the hospital, and everyone fell silent and stared at him.

He could blame his shocked reaction to the female helicopter pilot on his recent trauma of nearly drowning, and also on the fact that—despite the new laws and policy changes he was gradually trying to introduce—gender equality was still a relatively new concept in his country, the isolated desert kingdom of Zenhab. But it was obvious from the pilot's icy expression that any excuse Kadir might offer for his tactless comment would not be well received.

'Full marks for observation,' the Flight Captain said drily. 'If the fact that I'm a woman bothers you so much I could always drop you back in the sea where I found you and your crew.'

The reminder of the two injured sailors reignited Kadir's sense of frustration that he was not in charge of the situation. He was used to making decisions and having them obeyed without question, and he was struggling to accept that in this instance the female Flight Captain was in control. It didn't help matters that his head felt as if it was going to explode. He gritted his teeth, fighting the nausea that threatened to overwhelm him and destroy what was left of his dignity.

'As the yacht's skipper, it was my duty to ensure the

safety of my crew,' he insisted. 'I was in a better posi-tion to judge their physical condition than you were and I could see that they were both exhausted.'

'It was my duty to ensure the safety of *all* the casual-ties in need of rescue, as well as the safety of my flight crew,' the Flight Captain said coldly. 'How dare you ques-tion my authority?'

How dare he? No one had ever dared to address Kadir with such insolence, least of all a woman, and certainly not in public. The knowledge that he was indebted to this self-assured young woman for saving his life made him feel emasculated. The fact that she was the most beauti-ful woman he had ever seen only made him feel worse.

In the nightclubs and casinos—the playgrounds across Europe of the rich and bored—Kadir had met countless beautiful women, and in his youth he had bedded more of them than he cared to remember. For the past decade he had lived his life in the fast lane and played hard, but at thirty-two he felt jaded. It was a long time since his curiosity had been aroused by a woman, but Flight Cap-tain Lexi Howard intrigued him.

Beneath the floodlights on the helipad, her complexion was flawless and so fair that the skin stretched over her high, slanting cheekbones was almost translucent. Her long braid of ash-blonde hair suggested possible Nordic ancestry and the impression was further enhanced by her light blue eyes that reminded Kadir of the cool, clear skies above the Swiss Alps where he skied every winter.

He found he could not look away from her and he felt a sudden tightness in his chest as if a fist had gripped his heart. Heat surged through his veins. He tried to con-vince himself that the fire inside him was a natural response after his recent brush with death, but deep in his core something hot and hungry stirred.

'Surely you checked the Met Office shipping forecast and realised that a storm was approaching?' Lexi glared at the yacht's skipper, infuriated that he'd had the cheek to criticise how the rescue operation had been carried out. She guessed he was an inexperienced sailor, and his failure to respond to the worsening weather conditions had compromised the safety of his crew.

Her mind flew back to the incident the coastguard helicopter had attended two days ago and the young boy they had been unable to save. 'Not every rescue can be successful,' the coastguard station commander had reminded Lexi at the debriefing afterwards. 'Part of the job is to accept that you can't save everyone.'

Lexi's RAF commanding officer of the Medical Emergency Rescue Team in Afghanistan had said the same thing. Many of the things she had seen, the terrible injuries received by soldiers caught in landmine explosions and sniper fire, had been harrowing, but if she had gone to pieces she wouldn't have been able to do her job. The same was true working for the coastguard rescue. Her common sense told her she must not allow one tragedy to haunt her, but in her heart she had taken the failure to save the boy hard.

The tragedy two days ago and the incident today could have been avoided if the yacht's skipper in each case had acted more responsibly, she thought grimly. She was tempted to tell the man standing in front of her what she thought of him, but something about him made her swallow her angry words. Despite his dishevelled appearance and the large purple swelling above his right eye, he had an aura of power about him that set him apart from other men.

He was looking at Lexi in a way that no man had looked at her for a long time. *Too long*—the treacherous thought slid into her head. She tried to push it away but a picture flashed into her mind of the man's strong, tanned hands on her body, dark against pale, hard muscle pressed against soft yielding flesh.

Shocked by her wayward imagination, she narrowed her eyes to hide her thoughts as she studied him. He was sinfully attractive, with exotic olive-gold skin and over-long, thick black hair that curled at his nape and fell forward onto his brow so that he raked it back with an impatient flick of his hand. Lexi's gaze was drawn to his dark brown eyes—liquid pools of chocolate fringed by ridiculously long, silky lashes and set beneath heavy black brows. The gleam in his eyes unsettled her, and the blatantly sensual curve of his lips made her wonder how it would feel if he pressed his mouth against hers.

She shook her head, trying to break free from the disturbing effect he had on her, praying he hadn't noticed that she had been staring at him. She did not understand her reaction to him. It had been a long time since she had looked at a man and felt a quiver in her belly. Too long, she acknowledged ruefully.

'You should have waited for the weather to improve, instead of putting your life and the lives of your crew at risk.' She spoke sharply, desperate to hide her confusing awareness of the yacht's skipper. 'Your behaviour was irresponsible. Offshore sailing is not for inexperienced sailors.'

The man arrogantly threw back his head, drawing

Lexi's attention to his broad shoulders. She assessed him to be several inches over six feet tall.

'I'm not a fool,' he said curtly. 'Of course I checked the marine forecast and I was aware of the storm. The *White Hawk* could easily have run ahead of the bad weather, but we must have hit something in the water that ripped the keel from the hull and resulted in the yacht capsizing.'

He broke off abruptly. Following the direction of his gaze, Lexi saw two men hurrying towards them. The helipad was strictly out of bounds to the public but, as she stepped forward to ask the men to leave, they halted in front of the *White Hawk*'s skipper and, to Lexi's astonishment, bowed to him. She had learned enough Arabic during her tours of duty in the Middle East to recognise the language they spoke. After a brief conversation with the men, the skipper swung away from Lexi without giving her another glance and strode across the helipad, followed by his two companions.

'A word of thanks for saving his life would have been nice,' she said disgustedly, not caring if her words carried across the helipad to him. She glanced at the coastguard paramedic. 'Did you see how those men bowed to him as if they were his servants? He actually clicked his fingers for them to follow him! Who the hell does he think he is?'

Chris gave her an amused look. 'I take it from the way you ripped into him that you didn't recognise him? That was His Royal Highness, Sultan Kadir Al Sulaimar of Zenhab, and I'm guessing that the men who came to collect him *are* his servants. Not only is he a Sultan, he was the skipper of the Zenhab Team Valiant who won the America's Cup in the summer.' He grinned at Lexi's startled expression. 'I got the feeling that he didn't take kindly to you calling him an inexperienced sailor.'

'I still think he was irresponsible to have sailed when he knew that a storm was coming,' Lexi argued. 'But I guess he couldn't have known his yacht's keel would fail,' she conceded reluctantly. She knew enough about sailing to be aware that catastrophic keel failure was uncommon but not unheard of, and it was the main cause of yachts capsizing quickly, giving the crew little warning or time to radio for assistance.

She winced as she remembered how she had accused the man of being an inexperienced sailor. Now that she thought about it, he *had* seemed vaguely familiar, she mused as she climbed into the helicopter cockpit and prepared to take off from the helipad. During the summer there had been extensive news coverage of the famous America's Cup yacht race held in San Francisco, when the Zenhabian Team Valiant had beaten Team USA to win the prestigious trophy. Sultan Kadir Al Sulaimar had been interviewed on live television by an overexcited female presenter who had clearly been overwhelmed by his exotic looks and undeniable charm.

Lexi told herself that it wasn't surprising that she had failed to recognise the Sultan when he had been battered, bruised and dripping wet after being rescued from his sinking yacht. To her annoyance, she could not stop thinking about him. At the end of her shift she went back to the old coastguard cottage that had been her home for the past year but, instead of finishing packing up her belongings ready to move out, she wasted an hour looking up Sultan Kadir Al Sulaimar on her laptop.

She had no trouble finding pictures of him, mostly taken at social events in Europe. He was invariably accompanied by a beautiful woman. Blonde, brunette or redhead, it seemed that the Sultan had no particular preference but, from the dizzying number of different women he was photographed with, it appeared that he liked variety. According to the press reports, he was a playboy with a personal fortune estimated to be in the billions. He owned a luxury chalet in St Moritz, penthouses in New York and London's Mayfair and an English country estate where he kept racehorses.

There was some information about the country he ruled. Zenhab was an independent Arab kingdom in the Arabian Sea. Kadir had succeeded his father, Sultan Khalif Al Sulaimar, who was credited with establishing peace in Zenhab after years of fighting between rival tribal groups. But while the previous Sultan had rarely travelled abroad or courted the attention of the world's media, his son was frequently spotted by the paparazzi at nightclubs in Paris, or at Ascot, where he owned a private box and entertained celebrities and members of the British royal family, or driving his attention-grabbing scarlet sports car around Belgravia.

In short, the spoiled Sultan was the absolute antithesis of the kind of man Lexi admired. When she had served in Afghanistan, she had met men who were brave and loyal and utterly dedicated to carrying out the missions they had been assigned even though their lives were often at risk.

The memory of how the Sultan had looked at her with a predatory gleam in his eyes slid into her mind and her stomach muscles clenched. Sexual attraction followed its own rules and ignored common sense, she thought ruefully. Or maybe it was just her body reminding her that it was perfectly normal for a twenty-nine-year-old woman to feel sexual desire.

It was over a year since she had broken up with Steven—

or, to be more precise, since he'd informed her in a text message hours before their engagement party that he couldn't marry her because he had a girlfriend and a baby daughter who he had failed to mention when he and Lexi had grown close while they had been stationed together at Camp Bastion. Rejection hurt as much at twenty-eight as it had when she had been eighteen or eight, Lexi had discovered. She had dealt with Steven's betrayal the same way she had dealt with all the disappointments in her life, by pretending that she did not give a damn and hiding her feelings from a world that had proved too often that people were unreliable.

Perhaps the women in the newspaper photographs, clinging like limpets to the Sultan of Zenhab, had the right idea, she brooded. At least if you were a playboy's mistress you would have no expectations that he might commit to the relationship or fall in love with you. And no doubt the sex was amazing!

As Lexi visualised Sultan Kadir Al Sulaimar's arrogantly handsome face, heat unfurled in the pit of her stomach. She would never be tempted to sacrifice her hard-won pride and self-respect for five minutes in the sexy Sultan's bed, she assured herself. An hour on the treadmill followed by a brisk shower left her physically spent, but when she flopped into bed she was kept awake by the memory of the sensual promise in his molten chocolate eyes.

Two days later, Lexi donned her coastguard agency uniform for the last time, checked the gold buttons on her jacket were gleaming and adjusted her cap, before she walked into the station commander's office.

'I'm sorry to lose you,' Roger Norris told her. 'You've done a fantastic job over the past year.'

'I'm sorry to go,' Lexi said honestly. 'I'm going to miss everyone on the team, but I knew when I came here that the contract for a second helicopter pilot was only for one year.'

'The number of rescues you have carried out has proved the need for a second rescue helicopter, but unfortunately the funding for the coastguard agency has been cut.' Roger's frown cleared. 'However, I have received a piece of good news. A private donor has offered to pay for a permanent second helicopter and crew. The details will still have to be ironed out over the next few months but, if the offer goes ahead, would you be interested in resuming your role of Flight Captain?'

Lexi's eyebrows rose. 'I'd certainly consider it. Whoever the private donor is must be very wealthy.'

'He's a billionaire, by all accounts. You met him two nights ago—' Roger chuckled '—although I heard from Gavin and Chris that you didn't recognise him. In fact you're the reason that Sultan Kadir of Zenhab has made his incredibly generous offer after you rescued him and his crewmen from his capsized yacht. He has asked to see you so that he can thank you personally. He's staying in the Queen Mary suite at the Admiralty Hotel and requested for you to meet him there at six o'clock this evening.'

Lexi's heart collided painfully with her ribs at the mention of the Sultan. She flushed as she recalled the shockingly erotic dreams she'd had about him for the past two nights. She was behaving like a schoolgirl with a crush on a member of a boy band, she thought disgustedly.

'I'm afraid it won't be possible for me to meet him,' she told Roger. 'I'm going to my sister's engagement party this evening and it's a couple of hours' drive to Henley, where Athena's fiancé's parents live. Can't Chris or Gavin go instead of me?'

Roger shook his head. 'Chris is on duty. Gavin is at the hospital with Kate, and it looks as though her labour pains aren't a false alarm this time. Anyway, the Sultan particularly asked to see you.

'I'll be honest, Lexi. It is vital that the coastguard agency secures his donation. This part of the south coast is a busy area for shipping, and the rescue service needs a second helicopter. Perhaps you could phone the hotel and arrange to meet His Highness this afternoon instead of this evening?' Roger gave her a level look. 'It might also be a good idea to apologise to him. I understand that you had a heated exchange of words with him the other night.'

Lexi frowned at the reminder that she had behaved less than professionally when she had argued with the skipper of the capsized yacht, unaware that he was the Sultan of Zenhab and an experienced sailor. But the coastguard commander's words tugged on her conscience. The Sultan's offer to make permanent funds available for a second helicopter was astonishingly generous and could mean the difference between life and death for accident victims on the south coast who needed to be urgently transferred to hospital.

She stood up. 'I suppose I could stop off at the Admiralty Hotel and meet him before I drive to the party,' she said reluctantly.

'Good. And Lexi, be nice to him.'

She turned in the doorway and gave Roger a puzzled look. 'I'm always nice, aren't I?'

'Certainly—' the commander smiled '—but you can be intimidating. You have an outstanding war record and demonstrated your exceptional bravery, both in the RAF and as a civilian rescue pilot. Sometimes people, men especially, are in awe of you.'

Lexi visualised the Sultan of Zenhab's haughty features and gave a snort. She couldn't imagine His High and Mightiness had ever felt intimidated.

Driving back to the cottage, Roger's comment played on her mind. Did people really find her intimidating? She had always been a popular member of her RAF squadron and, since coming to work for the coastguard agency, she had quickly established her place in the team. The guys treated her as one of them, yet she sensed a faint reservation in their attitude. She had thought it was because she was the only female rescue pilot. But it had been the same when she had been at boarding school. She'd got on well with the other girls but she had never made close friendships.

She telephoned the Admiralty Hotel, and when a vague-sounding receptionist told her that the Sultan was unavailable to take her call she left a message explaining that she could meet him at five o'clock rather than six.

The rest of the day was spent packing up her car with bags and boxes. Closing the door of the cottage for the last time, she felt an unexpected pang. After ten years in the RAF, constantly moving to wherever in the world her squadron was deployed, she had enjoyed making the cottage into a home—even though it had not been the home she had imagined she would share with Steven.

He had talked about them buying a house together. They had even visited an estate agent to discuss the kind of property they wanted, Lexi remembered. Just for a while she had bought into the daydream of a happy marriage, children—a family that was truly her own and a sense of belonging, after a lifetime of feeling that she did not belong anywhere. She should have guessed it was too good to be true. Steven's betrayal had reminded her of the sense of rejection she had felt when her parents had made it obvious that they preferred their own daughter, Athena, who had been born to them a year after they had adopted Lexi.

At five minutes to five, Lexi walked across the foyer of the Admiralty Hotel, praying that she would not slip in her stiletto heels on the polished marble floor. Usually she lived in jeans and running trainers, but because she was on a tight schedule she had changed into a black silk jersey dress that was suitable for a cocktail party and wouldn't crease while she was sitting in the car.

The hotel receptionist looked flustered as she dealt with a coach party of tourists who had just arrived. Lexi checked in the lounge and bar, but there was no sign of the Sultan. She glanced at her watch and decided she would have to take charge of the situation. Abandoning the idea of trying to catch the receptionist's attention, she walked over to the lift and asked a porter for directions to the Queen Mary suite.

CHAPTER THREE

KADIR WALKED INTO his hotel suite and took a moment to appreciate the rare luxury of being completely alone. At the royal palace in Zenhab he was always surrounded by courtiers and government ministers, and a retinue of staff and security personnel accompanied him when he visited his various homes in Europe. Even while he had been staying here in a tiny village on the south coast of England he'd given in to pressure from his chief adviser and brought two security guards with him, as well as his private secretary and his manservant Walif, who, despite his seventy-one years, insisted on serving the Sultan as he had served Kadir's father.

Since his yachting accident two days ago, his staff had driven him mad with their concern for his well-being and, fond as he was of Walif, he had struggled to control his irritation when the manservant had flapped around him like a mother hen. Earlier today, Kadir's patience had finally snapped and he had sent everyone to his house in Windsor to wait for him.

The sense of freedom reminded him of how he felt when he raced his stallion Baha' across the desert with the cool wind whipping his face and a million stars studding the purple sky. Free from Walif's anxious concern for his health, he had spent two hours working out in the hotel gym.

The swelling above his eyebrow had almost disappeared, he noted, glancing in the bathroom mirror before he stepped into the shower cubicle. He had been lucky that the blow to his head from the sail boom had not knocked him unconscious, and even luckier that he had escaped from the capsized yacht with his life. Although it had not been luck, but the skill and bravery of the coastguard rescue crew, and especially the Flight Captain who had flown the helicopter in atrocious weather conditions.

Kadir pictured Lexi Howard's face. Her delicate features—the finely arched brows, defined cheekbones and perfect Cupid's bow lips—reminded him of the exquisite porcelain figurines in his grandmother's collection, which were displayed in a glass cabinet at Montgomery Manor. But the Flight Captain's fragile appearance was deceptive. He frowned, remembering her sharp voice and the dismissive way she had flicked her frosty blue eyes over him.

Immediately after he had been rescued from his doomed yacht, Kadir's pride had stung worse than his cracked skull. But now, with his equilibrium restored, he found Ms Howard's attitude refreshing. It had been a novelty to meet a woman who did not fawn on him or flirt with him. Too often he had found it too easy to persuade women into his bed. When he had been younger he had enjoyed being spoiled for choice, but a life without challenge was boring.

Lexi Howard was definitely a challenge. Desire kicked in Kadir's groin as he thought of the cool blonde beauty. He imagined teasing her mouth open with his tongue and tasting her. How long would it take to break through her reserve until she responded to him? he wondered, picturing her creamy complexion suffused with the rosy flush of sexual arousal.

Closing his eyes, he leaned back against the shower wall and visualised the icy, uptight Flight Captain melting beneath his hands. Slowly, he slid his hand down his body and stretched his fingers around his erection. He pictured Lexi Howard's capable hands on him, caressing him, stroking him lightly and then not so lightly... gripping him hard...

With a groan, he gave in to temptation and the urgent demands of his arousal. The cords in his neck stood out as he tipped his head back and the fire inside him became a furnace. His release came swiftly, awarding him momentary satisfaction that felt somehow incomplete.

But pleasuring himself was his only option, after the decision he had taken six months ago when his future bride had turned twenty-one and under Zenhabian law had become of marriageable age. Out of respect for Haleema, Kadir had ended his affairs with his European mistresses.

In the ten years that he had been Sultan of Zenhab he had been careful to avoid personal scandal in his desert kingdom, and had earned the support and respect of the population. It had been suggested to him by some of his advisers that monogamy was not a requirement of his arranged marriage as long as he was discreet, but he had every intention of fulfilling his role of husband to the best of his ability, to honour the promise he had made to his father.

Kadir had only been sixteen when Sultan Khalif had suffered a stroke that had left him a prisoner in his body—unable to walk, and with limited speech. Under Zenhabian law, the Sultan's brother had been made an interim ruler until the rightful heir came of age. But when Kadir had turned twenty-one, Jamal had been reluctant to hand over the Crown to his nephew, and he'd had support from tribal leaders in the mountain territories.

In order to claim the Crown from his uncle, Kadir had been forced to agree to marry the daughter of Jamal's strongest ally, Sheikh Rashid bin Al-Hassan. At the time he had signed the agreement, Haleema had been a child of eleven. But now she was twenty-one and, since the death of Sheikh Rashid two months ago, Kadir had come under increasing pressure from his uncle to set a date for his wedding. He knew he could not put if off for much longer. Haleema's family would consider a lengthy delay to be an insult to the princess of the mountain tribes, and Jamal—the most poisonous snake in Zenhab—would waste no time stirring up trouble that could threaten the stability of the country.

For the sake of Zenhab and for the love he felt for his father, Kadir would honour his duty. But there was a part of him that rebelled against the old ways of his kingdom. He had been educated in England and at university he had felt envious of his peers, who were free to live their lives without the burden of responsibility that had always been his destiny.

He had never even seen his future bride, but that would soon change. On his return to Zenhab he would travel to the mountains to meet Haleema's brother Omar, the new leader of the northern tribes, and begin formal proceedings for his marriage. He might even be permitted to meet Haleema, but according to the old customs he would not have an opportunity to be alone with her until she became his wife.

Kadir's thoughts turned once again to Flight Captain Lexi Howard. She had proved when she had rescued him and his crew that she was a highly skilled pilot, hence his decision to offer her a job as his private pilot in Zenhab. He knew it might be viewed as controversial to appoint a woman in what was considered by traditionalists to be a male role, but he fervently believed that his kingdom needed to modernise and accept that women were equal to men. The helicopter he had recently purchased would allow him to travel to Haleema's home in the mountainous northern territories more easily. And with that last thought of Haleema, his future had been decided for him ten years ago, he felt a sense that prison bars were closing around him.

Abruptly he switched off the shower, dried himself and pulled on a pair of trousers. Midway through shaving, he heard a knock on the door of the suite, which he ignored, forgetting that he had sent his staff away. Three impatient raps followed, and he cursed as the razor slipped in his hand and the blade nicked his chin. Grabbing a towel, he strode out of the bathroom and across the sitting room to fling open the door.

'Ms Howard! This is a surprise!'

Lexi frowned. 'Is it? I left a message with reception saying that I would be here at five.'

Kadir recalled that the phone had rung as he'd been on his way out of the door to go to the gym, but he hadn't bothered to answer it. 'I'm afraid I didn't receive any message,' he murmured.

How could his smile be so wickedly sexy? Lexi jerked her eyes from the sensual curve of his mouth and tried to ignore the fact that Sultan Kadir Al Sulaimar was half naked and had obviously just taken a shower. Droplets of water clung to the whorls of black hairs that grew thickly on his chest.

When she had rescued him, his body had been hidden beneath a bulky waterproof sailing suit. But now Lexi was faced with rippling muscles, gleaming olive-gold skin, broad, satin-smooth shoulders and his tight-as-a-drum abdomen.

Her eyes were drawn to the fuzz of black hairs that arrowed down from his navel and disappeared beneath the waistband of his trousers, which sat low on his hips. Her mouth suddenly felt dry. She lifted her gaze back to his face and her stomach swooped when she discovered that he was even more gorgeous than she remembered from their first meeting.

The combination of his lean, chiselled features and deep-set dark eyes was mesmerising. His mouth was full-lipped, and curved into a sultry smile that sent a tingle through Lexi's body. Her breath seemed to be trapped somewhere between her lungs and her throat. She needed to say something, anything to break the prickling silence that became more intense with every passing second so that she was sure he must be able to hear the loud thud of her heart.

She said the first thing that came into her head. 'You're bleeding…on your chin. No, closer to your lip…' She pointed, trying to direct him as he lifted the towel he was holding and pressed it against his face.

'I started shaving when I was fourteen. You'd think I'd be better at it by now,' he said ruefully. He thrust the towel at her. 'Will you play nurse?'

His voice was as sexy as his smile—deep and rich, caressing her senses and conjuring up images in her mind that were shockingly inappropriate.

'I should go,' she muttered. 'This is obviously not a convenient time…' Not when her heart was beating painfully fast. Lexi did not understand why he affected her so strongly. For ten years she had worked in a predominantly male environment and had met her fair share of good-looking men. *But none like him*, whispered a voice inside her head. Even his title—Sultan of Zenhab—was exotic and made her think of a desert oasis beneath a starry sky, a tent draped with silks, and him, naked, his bronzed, muscular body sprawled on satin cushions and his dark eyes gleaming as he beckoned to her to come to him.

Lexi swallowed. What on *earth* was the matter with her? She felt as though her body was on fire.

'You're not bothered by the sight of blood, are you?'

The amusement in his voice pulled her back from her erotic fantasy. Thank goodness he couldn't possibly have known what she had been thinking. His question jolted her mind back to her experiences of a real desert— the dry, unforgiving landscape, clouds of choking sand stirred up by the downdraught of the Chinook's rotor blades, the screams of wounded men, the smell of blood and dust and vomit.

'No, blood doesn't worry me,' she told him calmly, in control once more. The cut near to his bottom lip was still bleeding. She pressed the corner of the towel against his face and somehow, without her being aware that either of them had moved, she found herself inside his suite and he shut the door.

She immediately became conscious of how close they were standing. His warm breath whispered across her cheek and the mingled scents of soap, his spicy cologne and something more subtle—the sensual musk of maleness—stirred her senses. Her breasts brushed against his bare chest and the contact with his body sent a ripple of awareness through her.

Panic was an unfamiliar emotion for Lexi, but she was shaken by her reaction to the Sultan. She lifted the towel to see if the cut had stopped bleeding and saw that her hand was trembling. In Afghanistan, when she had flown behind enemy lines to pick up casualties, her nerves had been as steady as her hands on the helicopter's control stick. Why did this pampered playboy prince who had probably never done a day's work in his life disturb her?

Thankfully, the cut on his chin had closed up. She handed him the towel and stepped back from him. 'You'll live. I'm sure legions of women will be relieved,' she said drily.

His smile remained fixed, but Lexi sensed a sudden stillness in him that made her think of a panther about to pounce on its hapless prey. She reminded herself that the playboy was also a powerful Sultan who had kept peace in Zenhab despite the often volatile situation in other parts of the Middle East.

'Your sailing accident was widely reported in the press, Your Highness,' she murmured. In fact the tabloids had only carried a paragraph or two about his capsized yacht and had been more interested in reporting stories of his affairs with supermodels and actresses.

It wasn't as if she was in the least bit interested in a promiscuous womaniser, Lexi thought. She had only agreed to meet the Sultan because Roger Norris had asked her to.

'I understand that your yacht has been retrieved from where it sank in the Solent and it was discovered that the keel had been ripped from the hull.' She hesitated. 'I'm afraid I was rather hasty the other night when I jumped to the conclusion that you had ignored the reports of an approaching storm. I…apologise if my attitude was less than professional.'

Kadir just managed to stop himself from laughing out loud at Lexi Howard's grudging apology. She had spoken politely, but he sensed her reluctance to be here. It was obvious that she had been sent to see him, and it was easy to guess the real reason for her visit. Her next words confirmed his suspicion.

'Roger Norris explained that you have made a very generous offer to finance a second rescue helicopter.'

Kadir idly wondered if the coastguard commander had told Lexi to dress up for their meeting and perhaps try to persuade him to donate even more funds. Catching the cool expression in her eyes, he dismissed the idea. No one would dare tell Lexi Howard what to do—which made her choice of outfit interesting.

He ran his eyes over her, noting how the stretchy fabric of her dress moulded her toned figure and emphasised the shape of her firm breasts. The dress stopped at mid-thigh-level and below the hemline her slender legs, sheathed in sheer black hose, looked even longer with the addition of three-inch stiletto heels. Recalling his erotic fantasies about her while he'd been in the shower, Kadir felt the simmering heat in his gut burn hotter.

'The least I can do is to make a contribution to the rescue agency responsible for saving my life and the lives of my crew,' he said abruptly. 'I must also apologise, Captain Howard, for not thanking you for your skill and bravery after the rescue the other night. I am conscious that I owe you a huge debt of gratitude.'

'I was simply doing my job,' she muttered.

'I understand from Roger Norris that you no longer work for the coastguard agency.'

'My contract was only for a year. Although, if there is to be a second rescue helicopter, I might get my job back.'

'But you don't have another job to go to at the moment?' Kadir knew he was staring at Lexi but he could not help himself. She was so damned beautiful! He cleared his throat. 'I asked you to meet me because I have a proposition I want to discuss with you.'

'What kind of proposition?' The gleam of sexual interest in his eyes, and memories of the stories in the newspapers about his playboy lifestyle, sent Lexi's imagination into overdrive.

Kadir was irritated that Lexi obviously believed the garbage which had been written about him in the tabloids. But she was not nearly as composed as she would like him to think. Her breathing was shallow and the downwards sweep of her long eyelashes was too late to hide her dilated pupils. He roamed his eyes over her in a slow, deliberate appraisal, and was rewarded when the hard points of her nipples became clearly discernible beneath her clingy dress.

Suddenly he understood, and a feeling of satisfaction swept through him. He had seen her scornful expression when she'd referred to the reports of his alleged playboy lifestyle. Most of the stories about his private life, which had been printed alongside the news of his yachting accident, were either rehashed from years ago or greatly exaggerated. Kadir had felt no inclination to defend himself to Lexi, but he'd been annoyed by her readiness to judge him.

Now, as he watched her cross her arms defensively

over her breasts, he realised that the waves of antagonism she had been sending out were a frantic attempt to disguise the fact that she was attracted to him. Perhaps she hoped that her frosty attitude disguised her sexual awareness of him, but Kadir *knew*—just as he always knew when a woman was interested in him. He had played the game of chasing women who wanted to be caught too often, he thought cynically.

But this time the rules were different. When he returned to Zenhab he would honour the promise he had made to his father and marry the bride who had been chosen for him. Although he desired the Flight Captain, he had no intention of actually catching her. But Lexi did not know that!

'Why don't we sit down,' he murmured, 'and make ourselves comfortable?'

Lexi swallowed as she watched the Sultan lower himself onto the sofa. He stretched his arms along the back, drawing her attention to his bare torso. His broad shoulders gleamed like burnished copper in the golden autumn sunshine slanting through the window, and his chest and forearms were covered in a fine mat of silky black hairs that accentuated his raw masculinity.

Conscious that her heart was thudding uncomfortably fast, she made a show of checking her watch. 'I really must be going. I expect you want to finish getting dressed,' she said pointedly, 'and I have to be somewhere at seven-thirty, and I want to hit the motorway before the evening traffic builds up.'

'Do you have a date this evening? And there I was thinking you had worn that very sexy dress especially to meet me,' Kadir drawled.

Lexi flushed. 'It is not a sexy dress,' she said tightly.

'It's a cocktail dress suitable for a cocktail party to celebrate my sister's engagement.' The idea that the Sultan
assumed she'd dressed up for him was infuriating but, to
her shame, she felt a frisson of awareness shoot through
her when his dark eyes gleamed with a hard brilliance.

'Surely you don't have to leave just yet if the party
doesn't start for another two hours?' To Lexi's conster-
nation, he sprang up from the sofa and walked over to
her, moving with the speed and grace of a jungle cat. He
was too close and towered over her so that she had to tilt
her head to meet his intent gaze. Heat radiated from his
body, or maybe the heat came from her, making her feel
flushed and flustered and acutely aware of her femininity.

Desperate to hide the effect he had on her, she launched
into an explanation. 'The journey to Henley-on-Thames,
which is where my sister's fiancé's parents live, will take
over an hour, and I daren't risk being late and upsetting
Lady Fairfax.'

Lexi frowned as she recalled how tense her sister had
sounded on the phone. Athena had confided her worry
that Charles's parents did not approve of their son's choice
of bride because they had hoped he would marry someone with a similar aristocratic pedigree to the Fairfaxes.
'The engagement party is my chance to prove that I can
be a good wife to Charlie and a sophisticated hostess
when he invites business clients to dinner,' Athena had
said earnestly.

Lexi had struggled to picture her accident-prone sister
as a sophisticated hostess, but she had kept her doubts
that Charles Fairfax was the right man for Athena to
herself.

Her thoughts scattered when Sultan Kadir spoke. His
deep, dark voice curled around her like a lover's caress.

She caught her breath as he lifted his hand and brushed the back of his knuckles oh-so-lightly down her cheek. It was a blatant invasion of her personal space but her feet seemed to be rooted to the floor and she could not step away from him.

'I am disappointed that you must rush away before we've had a chance to discuss my proposal. Perhaps we can arrange to meet again at a more convenient time?'

She licked her dry lips and told herself she was imagining the predatory gleam in his eyes. 'Your Highness...' Her voice sounded strangely breathless.

'Please call me Kadir, Lexi.'

The way he said her name, with that soft huskiness in his voice, was too intimate, as if he had stroked each syllable with his tongue.

Lexi felt as though she was drowning in his molten gaze, but a tiny part of her sanity remained and asked why she was letting him get to her. He was a notorious womaniser, and in the past when other men like him had tried to come on to her she'd had no trouble shooting them down.

Of course she would not allow herself to be seduced by the Sultan, she assured herself. But she could not deny that his interest was flattering and a salve to her wounded pride after Steven's betrayal. Without conscious thought, she swayed towards Kadir, bringing her mouth even closer to his. Her heart pounded and her eyelashes swept down as she waited, tense with anticipation, for him to brush his lips over hers.

'You've been a long time in the shower. I've been getting bored waiting for you.'

Lexi froze and jerked her head towards the petulant female voice. Shock slithered like an ice cube down her spine when she saw a woman standing in the doorway that connected the sitting room and bedroom. Through the open door she could see a big bed with rumpled sheets. The woman—girl—was no more than seventeen. Lexi recognised she was Tania Stewart, daughter of the local yacht club president Derek Stewart, who also owned the Admiralty Hotel.

Tania frowned at Lexi. 'What are you doing here?' She turned her wide-eyed gaze to the Sultan and allowed the sheet that was draped around her body to slip down, revealing her bare breasts. 'Don't keep me waiting any longer, Kadir,' she murmured in a sex kitten voice that somehow emphasised how painfully young she was.

'Go and put some clothes on, Tania.' In contrast, Kadir spoke in a clipped tone that was as coldly regal as his expression, Lexi noted, when she looked at him.

She instantly grasped the situation—it didn't take a genius to work out what was going on—and she felt sick at her stupidity. How could she have almost been taken in by the playboy prince's charisma? It stung her pride to realise that she had no more sense than the silly girl who had just crawled out of his bed.

She glanced at Tania and back to Kadir. The reason he was half undressed in the afternoon was now abundantly clear and she supposed she should be thankful that he had pulled on a pair of trousers before he'd opened the door to her.

'Forgive me, Your Highness, for not staying around to discuss your proposition, but I'm not into threesomes,' she said, her voice as biting as a nuclear winter.

His only response was to lift his eyebrows as if he found her reaction amusing.

Lexi's temper simmered. She looked at Tania, who

had at least draped the sheet more strategically around her naked body, and back at Kadir. 'You bastard. She's just a kid. Is that how you get your kicks?'

His eyes glittered with anger, but Lexi did not give him a chance to speak. She despised him, and at that moment she despised herself for her weakness. Dear heaven, she had actually wanted him to kiss her! Even now, as she wheeled away from him and marched across the room, her legs trembled and she had to fight the urge to turn her head and look at him one last time, to imprint his outrageously gorgeous facial features on her mind. Pride prevailed and she walked out of the door, closing it with a decisive snap behind her.

CHAPTER FOUR

KADIR WATCHED LEXI HOWARD across the ballroom and felt a slow burn of desire in the pit of his stomach. She was startlingly beautiful, and he noticed that many of the other party guests glanced at her more than once. There was something almost ethereal about her ash-blonde hair, swept up into a chignon tonight, and her peaches and cream complexion. Her fine bone structure, with those high cheekbones, was simply exquisite. She was an English rose, combining cool elegance with understated sensuality in her short black dress and her endlessly long legs and high-heeled black shoes.

If he was a betting man he would lay money that she was wearing stockings. Kadir's nostrils flared as he visualised her wrapping her legs around his back, wearing the stockings and stilettos—and nothing else!

He frowned and altered his position in an effort to ease the hard throb of his arousal. It was a long time since he'd felt so intensely turned on by a woman, especially by a woman who clearly disliked him. In fact it had never happened to him before. Since his youth, women had thrown themselves at him.

Perhaps it was simply the novelty of Lexi Howard's frosty attitude that intrigued him. His mind flew to those few moments in his hotel room when he had nearly kissed her. What had started out as an amusing game had quickly and unexpectedly turned into something darker and hotter when he'd seen the invitation in her eyes.

He wondered what would have happened if the teenager Tania Stewart, who had followed him around like a lovesick puppy while he had been staying at her father's hotel, had not made her spectacular appearance. Kadir knew he would have covered Lexi's mouth with his and tasted her—and she would have let him. Instead, she had treated him like a pariah. His jaw clenched. The scalding fury that had been responsible for him gunning his sports car up the motorway still simmered inside him like the smouldering embers of a fire.

'I see you're looking at my future sister-in-law.'

Kadir's bland expression gave away none of his thoughts as he turned his head towards the man standing beside him. Charles Fairfax's face had the ruddy hue of a man who was on his fifth gin punch, even though it was still early in the evening. 'I'd better warn you, old man. You won't get any joy there. A couple of my friends have tried and reported that Lexi Howard is a frigid bitch. It's no surprise her fiancé dumped her. The guy was lucky the ice queen didn't freeze his balls off.' Charles laughed, evidently finding his schoolboy attempt at humour funny.

Charles had always been a pain in the backside when they had been at school, Kadir mused, fixing a smile on his lips to disguise his temptation to rearrange Charles's nondescript features with his fist. In truth, he was puzzled by his violent reaction to the Englishman's crude comments, and his desire to defend Lexi Howard. At Eton College he had never considered Charles Fairfax to be a close friend but, thanks to social media, he had remained in touch with many of his fellow students from his school days. Networking was always useful, and when Lexi had mentioned her sister's engagement party Kadir had known that there was only one Lord and Lady Fairfax living in Henley-on-Thames.

His eyes strayed across the room to where Lexi was chatting to a petite woman with a mass of dark brown hair and wearing a dress in an unflattering shade of acid-yellow. It was curious that the Howard sisters were so unalike, he thought.

He saw Lexi glance around the room and stiffen when she noticed him. From across the ballroom he felt waves of hostility emanating from her, challenging him, exciting him. Kadir felt his heart jolt against his ribs. He held Lexi's gaze as he raised his glass to her, before he sipped his Virgin Mary, feeling the peppery warmth of the drink heat his blood.

'Do you think I look fat in this dress? I wish I could wear black like you but it makes my skin look sallow.'

Lexi forced her mind from the humiliating spectacle that had taken place in Sultan Kadir of Zenhab's hotel suite earlier and concentrated on her sister. 'You look lovely,' she said, in what she hoped was a convincing voice.

Athena's face brightened. 'Lady Fairfax helped me to choose my dress. She said the colour suits me.'

'Did she?' Lexi suspected that Charles Fairfax's mother had her reasons for persuading Athena to wear the ghastly yellow satin dress. Charles was her only son and would eventually become the next Lord Fairfax, and Lexi had overheard several party guests comment that

Charles's parents wished him to marry a woman with a title.

Athena fiddled with the large satin bow on her shoulder. 'I wish I looked elegant and sophisticated like you,' she blurted. 'You would be a much better wife for Charlie than me. You would know how to talk to people at dinner parties, and you'd never spill your wine or drop your spoon into the soup. I'm so clumsy. Sometimes I think Charlie finds me an embarrassment.'

Lexi frowned. 'You can't help being short-sighted. Charlie should be more supportive. Presumably he asked you to marry him because he loves you, not because he wants you to be his unpaid social hostess.' She gave her sister an exasperated look and was tempted to ask Athena why she had agreed to marry Charles, who was a wimp with a distinctly spiteful side to his nature. 'To be honest, I'm not convinced that he's the right man for you.'

'Maybe you're jealous that I'm getting married and you're not.' Athena bit her lip. 'I'm sorry, Lexi. That was a horrible thing to say. It's just that since you broke up with Steven you've pushed people away more than ever, including Mum and Dad…and me.'

'I was over Steven a long time ago,' Lexi said curtly. 'I don't push people away.' She remembered the coast-guard commander Roger Norris's comment that she came across as intimidating. 'I admit I'm independent, but I had to be when I was growing up. I always knew I had been adopted, but you are Marcus and Veronica's own daughter and it was natural that they doted on you.'

Athena looked as though she was going to cry and Lexi silently cursed her runaway tongue. It wasn't her sister's fault that she had been the favourite child.

'Mum and Dad are really proud of you, and they're

always telling people that you were a pilot in the RAF and received an award for bravery for your work in Afghanistan. They wanted to catch up with you tonight, but they couldn't make the party because their cruise was booked ages ago.

'I'm sure Mum and Dad wish I was as clever as you,' Athena admitted. 'They are both doctors and I suppose they naturally assumed I would be academic like them. They even named me after the Greek goddess of wisdom, for heaven's sake! I know they were disappointed when I failed to get the grades to go to university. At least they're pleased that I'm going to marry Charlie and I'll be Lady Fairfax one day.'

'You can't marry him just to win parental approval.'

'I'm not... Of course I love him,' Athena insisted, too earnestly, in Lexi's opinion. But she did not voice her concerns. Her sister was an adult and perfectly able to decide who she wanted to marry. In truth, Lexi was surprised that Athena had confided in her. The close bond they had shared as children had faded when Lexi had been sent away to boarding school.

She looked around the room. 'Where is Charlie, anyway? This is your engagement party but I haven't seen him all evening.'

'Oh, he's with one of his old school friends from Eton. Charlie was so surprised when Earl Montgomery phoned out of the blue earlier this evening and said he would like to catch up on old times. Naturally, Charlie immediately invited him to the party. I think they must still be in the library.' Athena squinted around the room. 'Oh, look, they're over by the bar. The Earl is very good-looking, don't you think? But don't tell Charlie I said so, will you?' she said worriedly.

Lexi could not reply. She felt as though her breath had been squeezed out of her lungs as she stared across the room and saw Sultan Kadir Al Sulaimar's mouth curl into a mocking smile. What the hell was he doing here at her sister's engagement party, pretending to be a member of the British aristocracy? She frowned. He couldn't be an imposter because Athena had said he had been at Eton with Charlie. But it was too much of a coincidence that the Sultan, or Earl or whatever he was, had decided to call up his old school friend tonight of all nights.

It was impossible not to compare the two men as they approached. Charles, sandy-haired and weak-chinned, was at least five inches shorter than his companion. But it wasn't only Sultan Kadir's height that set him apart from every other man in the room. He was like an exotic bird of paradise among a flock of pigeons, Lexi thought. His olive-gold skin gleamed beneath the sparkling chandeliers, and his hot chocolate eyes were slumberous and sensual, promising wicked delights that turned Lexi's insides to liquid. The last time she'd seen him he had been half-undressed, but he was no less devastating wearing a black dinner suit that had been expertly tailored to sheath his muscular body.

She hid her fierce tension behind a cool smile as Charlie made introductions, but the glint in Sultan Kadir's eyes told her he was aware of her reluctance to shake his hand; he clasped her fingers for a fraction too long and watched with interest the jerky rise and fall of her breasts as she sucked in a breath.

Lexi could not bring herself to allude to their earlier meeting at his hotel. She shuddered at the memory of how she had swayed towards him and practically begged him to kiss her. She wanted to believe that even if Tania had not interrupted them she would have come to her senses before anything had happened, but her pounding heart mocked that idea.

She affected a puzzled expression. 'I'm sure I recognise you from the newspapers and have read of your many exploits, but your name is not familiar.'

Charlie was quick to explain. 'Earl Montgomery is His Royal Highness Sultan Kadir Al Sulaimar of Zenhab.'

Lexi ignored her future brother-in-law as her eyes locked with the Sultan's. 'Should I address you as Your Royal Highness or My Lord?' she asked, mockingly deferential. She saw amusement and something darker and more dangerous in his intent gaze. The air between them was charged with an electrical current that made every nerve ending on Lexi's body tingle.

'I insist that you call me Kadir, Lexi.' His sexy accent lingered on each syllable of her name. He smiled, showing his white teeth, and a quiver shot through Lexi as she imagined him nipping her throat and the soft flesh of her earlobe. 'I find it is unwise to believe everything printed in the newspapers,' he murmured. 'So often, stories are reported incorrectly or are blatantly untrue.'

'That's a little unfair to journalists. I'm sure most press reports are properly researched and presented.' She thought of all those women who had revealed intimate details of their affairs with His Royal Hotness. Some of the stories must be true.

The sound of a gong rang through the ballroom, shattering the tense atmosphere.

'Charlie and I are supposed to lead everyone into the dining room for the buffet,' Athena explained. She slipped her arm through her fiancé's and promptly tripped on the hem of her long skirt, earning an impatient tut from Charles Fairfax.

Kadir offered his arm to Lexi. 'May I escort you to dinner?'

It was impossible to refuse without causing a scene, but she glared at him as she placed her hand stiffly on his arm and he drew her closer so that her thigh brushed against his as they walked into the dining room.

'How dare you...*infiltrate* my sister's engagement party,' she hissed.

His wide shoulders shook with laughter. 'It would have been bad manners to refuse an invitation from an old school friend.'

'You didn't worry about manners when you came on to me while your girlfriend—with emphasis on the word *girl*—was in the next room.' That wiped the smug smile from his face, she noted with satisfaction.

He dipped his head close to hers. 'Let's get something straight.' His voice was suddenly harsh. The charismatic playboy prince had disappeared and Lexi had a sense that Sultan Kadir Al Sulaimar was a powerful man and a dangerous threat to her peace of mind. 'I did not invite Tania Stewart to my suite and definitely not into my bed. I was as surprised as you were when she walked out of the bedroom.'

Lexi wondered why she believed him. 'Not that I care how you conduct your private life, or with whom, but, out of curiosity, how was Tania in your room if you didn't invite her in?'

'She admitted she'd taken the pass key from the cleaner's office. Her father owns the hotel and she knows where things are kept. When you saw her you immediately leapt to the conclusion that she and I were lovers.'

'She *was* naked under that sheet,' Lexi defended herself. She found she was unable to tear her eyes from Kadir's smouldering gaze.

'Forget Tania. This is about you and me.'

'There is no *you and me*!' She wished she could control her racing pulse. 'I'm not the slightest bit interested in you, Earl Montgomery, or Sultan of Zenhab, or whatever other fancy title I'm supposed to call you.'

'Kadir,' he said softly. 'Why are you uptight about saying my name?'

'I'm *not* uptight.' Glancing around her, Lexi flushed when she realised that her raised voice had attracted curious glances from the other guests.

The amused gleam in his eyes told her he was aware that she felt churned up inside and quite unlike her usual self. 'Perhaps later tonight we will have a chance to discuss my proposition.'

'I've told you I'm not interested in your proposition.'

'How do you know, when you don't know what it is?'

'Knowing of your reputation as a playboy, I have no qualms about turning down your proposition without hearing any of the sordid details,' Lexi said tartly.

Satisfied that she'd had the last word, she turned her back on him and began to select food from the buffet even though her appetite had disappeared. To her relief, Charlie returned to monopolise Kadir's attention and she was able to slip away to a quiet corner and forced down a couple of vol-au-vents filled with a cream cheese mixture that tasted overpoweringly of chopped herbs.

She brooded on her conversation with her sister. Athena—like the coastguard commander, Roger Norris—had accused her of putting up barriers to prevent people getting too close to her. It wasn't deliberate, but subconsciously, perhaps, her wariness of being rejected *did* make her appear remote and self-contained, Lexi acknowledged. She had learned from a young age that the only person she could rely on, the only person she could trust, was herself. When she had served with the RAF she'd learned to trust the professionalism of the people she worked with. But when she *had* lowered her guard with Steven Cromer and followed her heart instead of her head, his rejection had been hurtful and humiliating; she was in no hurry to experience either of those emotions again.

Waiters were circling the room offering glasses of champagne to toast the newly engaged couple. Lexi opted for iced water, hoping she would soon be able to slip away from the party and drive to West London, where she had arranged to stay at a friend's flat while she looked for another job. She sipped the water, but her throat still felt dry and scratchy and the headache that had started five minutes ago was rapidly becoming worse.

Lord Fairfax called for silence and proceeded to give a lengthy speech about how delighted he and his wife were to announce their son's engagement. Lady Fairfax's delight was not apparent on her haughty features, Lexi noted. Charlie looked bored and Athena was tense and had spilled something down the front of her dress.

'What does your sister see in an oaf like Charles Fairfax, apart from his money and title?' The husky drawl close to her ear brought a flush of heat to Lexi's face. She shot Kadir a glowering look and winced as the sudden movement sent a shooting pain through her skull.

'Athena isn't like that,' she said curtly, not about to admit to a stranger her own doubts about her sister's choice of husband. 'She loves Charlie.' She frowned. 'I thought he was your friend. Why else would you accept an invitation to his engagement party?'

'I knew you would be here.'

He was serious, Lexi realised. The smouldering sensuality in Kadir's eyes made her catch her breath. She looked away from him and tried to control her frantic heartbeat. But her chest felt constricted and her shortness of breath was not entirely down to her acute awareness of him. In the last few minutes she had begun to feel nauseous and strangely light-headed, as if she was drunk, except that she hadn't had a drop of alcohol all evening. She swayed on legs that suddenly seemed unable to support her.

'Are you all right? You've gone a strange colour.' Kadir's voice sounded from a long way off. Lexi closed her eyes to stop the room from spinning. She could feel beads of sweat on her brow, and she suddenly knew what was wrong with her. To her horror, she realised that she was going to be sick in front of a room full of onlookers.

She blinked and Kadir's handsome face swam before her eyes. He was the last person she would turn to for help, but she was feeling worse by the second and she had no choice but to abandon her pride. 'Please,' she muttered. 'Please…get me out of here.'

He gave her a sharp look and growled something beneath his breath, then the room spun, Lexi's head spun, as he scooped her up into his arms. She sensed everyone was watching them as Kadir strode past the curious guests and she heard Charlie Fairfax say loudly, 'She's obviously had too much to drink.' Kadir tightened his arms around her and Lexi, who had never been carried by a man in her entire adult life, rested her head on his chest and listened to the steady thud of his heart.

Athena dashed into the hall after them, looking anxious. 'Lexi… Lady Fairfax has just told me that the vol-au-vent filling contained prawns. You didn't eat any, did you?'

'Unfortunately, your warning is too late,' Lexi muttered drily. Noticing Kadir's puzzled expression, she explained, 'I have a shellfish allergy.' Her voice became urgent. 'I need to get to a bathroom—*quickly.*'

At first, when Lexi opened her eyes and did not recognise her surroundings, she wondered if she was in a bedroom at the Fairfax home, Woodley Lodge. Vague snatches of memory floated into her mind of sitting in a car and travelling very fast. She remembered that the car had stopped at least once and she had been ill by the side of the road. There were other memories of strong arms around her, supporting her while she had been sick, a cool hand stroking her hair back from her hot brow.

Where the hell was she? Ignoring the fact that she felt like a limp rag, Lexi sat up and froze as she pushed back the sheets and discovered that someone had removed her dress, leaving her in her sheer lace black bra and matching thong.

Kadir had rescued her from the ignominy of being ill in front of the guests at her sister's engagement party. Had he driven her to wherever this place was—a hotel, perhaps—and undressed her? She glanced around the bedroom, noting the floral wallpaper and an oil painting of a horse hanging above the antique dressing table. The décor of slightly old-fashioned elegance did not feel like she was in a hotel.

Her legs felt weak when she made the short journey into the en suite bathroom and a glance in the mirror revealed that she looked as washed out as she felt. There was a toothbrush among the toiletries on the vanity unit and she felt marginally better once she'd brushed her teeth and pulled a comb through her hair. Walking back into the bedroom, she stopped dead and stared wordlessly at Kadir.

'I knocked but you didn't answer, so I thought I'd better check on you.' His dark eyes drifted over her, bringing a tinge of colour to Lexi's wan face. 'How are you feeling?'

Vulnerable, but no way would she admit it to him. 'Better.' She instinctively crossed her arms over her breasts, wishing she had pulled on the towelling robe that she'd noticed hanging on the bathroom door. 'At the risk of sounding like a corny line from a film, where am I?'

'My English home, Montgomery Manor. Windsor is less than half an hour's drive from Henley-on-Thames, although it took longer to get here last night because you needed me to pull over a couple of times.'

Lexi felt mortified that he had seen her at her most undignified, throwing up in a gutter.

'Did you undress me?' she asked curtly. She had a hazy recollection of being carried up a flight of stairs and placed on a bed, and she remembered feeling her zip being drawn down her spine and the sensation of cool air on her body as her dress was removed.

'There you go, jumping to conclusions again, like you did about Tania,' Kadir said mockingly, but Lexi heard anger in his tone. 'You were so ill you couldn't even walk. Do you think I took advantage of your defenceless state to strip you...and do what—look at you, touch you?'

She bit her lip. 'I had a particularly bad reaction to shellfish last night. I don't remember much after you carried me out of the Fairfaxes' house. All I know is that someone took my dress off. I recall that someone stayed with me and gave me some water.' Someone had slipped an arm around her and held a glass of water to her lips. She remembered gentle hands wiping a cool flannel over her feverish brow.

'My housekeeper put you into bed and took your dress away to be cleaned.' He shrugged. 'I called my doctor and explained your symptoms, and he advised me to stay with you until you'd stopped being sick.' His jaw hardened. 'Believe me, helping you to the bathroom a dozen times did not send me into a frenzy of sexual excitement.'

Kadir watched a stain of colour run along her high cheekbones and some of his anger abated. There were dark circles beneath her eyes and she looked fragile, but he sensed she would hate showing any sign of weakness. He had never met a woman who infuriated and intrigued him as much as Lexi Howard did.

It was a long time since he had been so turned on by a woman, he acknowledged. He was even beginning to question his plans to employ the Flight Captain as his private pilot. But the truth was that she was exactly what he needed and he would have to ignore his inconvenient throb of desire and try to forget that the uptight Ms Howard had a penchant for skimpy, sexy underwear.

Last night, when she had been sick for hour after hour, he had been more concerned about persuading her to take sips of water to prevent her from becoming dehydrated, as the doctor had instructed, and he'd barely noticed that she was almost naked.

But he noticed now.

When she had emerged from the bathroom, his eyes had been drawn to her nipples, clearly visible through her bra, and the shadow of blonde hair beneath the tiny triangle of semi-transparent material between her legs. He had been right about her wearing stockings. They were held up by wide bands of black lace around the tops of her thighs. Kadir's pulse quickened and he dragged his eyes from her, feeling like a voyeur, or an excited teenage boy seeing a naked woman for the first time.

In a bid to ease the throb of his arousal he walked over to the window and pretended to be fascinated by the view of Windsor Great Park. 'Your dress isn't ready yet,' he said abruptly, 'so I brought one of my shirts for you to wear. It's on the bed.'

'Thank you.' Lexi hurried across the room and snatched up the shirt. It was much too big, and as she did up the buttons she felt marginally less exposed now that her underwear was hidden. She had only worn a seamless bra and thong so that they wouldn't show under her clingy dress. Kadir would have completely the wrong idea about her. She wasn't a flighty, flirty type of woman who dressed to impress men. She was sensible, serious—*boring*, taunted a little voice inside her head.

'As a matter of fact, all my clothes are in the boot of my car. After the party, I'd planned to drive to London to stay at a friend's flat.'

'I sent a couple of my staff over to Woodley Lodge to pick up your car.'

'Thank you,' Lexi repeated stiffly. 'I'm sorry to be such a nuisance.'

She looked across the room to where he was standing, half turned away from her so that she could see his proud profile. A weakness invaded her limbs that had nothing to do with her being ill the previous night. Dressed in faded jeans that moulded his firm thighs and buttocks and a cream cashmere sweater that accentuated his exotic olive-gold skin, he was the epitome of masculine perfection. Any woman would find him attractive, she consoled herself. Nevertheless, it was irritating to realise that she was no different to those women in the tabloids who had proudly described every intimate detail of their affairs with the playboy prince of the desert.

She thought about how he had stayed with her during the previous night and taken care of her when she had been ill. Perhaps there was more to him than his reputation as a jet-setting philanderer gave him credit for.

'Thanks for rescuing me from the party last night,' she said awkwardly. 'I guess that makes us even.'

'It's hardly the same thing. You saved my life.' Kadir swung round and gave her a brooding look. 'In fact, events have worked in my favour because now you are trapped here in my home, which gives us an opportunity to discuss my proposition.'

Needing a distraction from the realisation that without her car or clothes she could not leave Montgomery Manor, Lexi asked curiously, 'How are you an English Earl *and* the Sultan of Zenhab?'

'My mother is English. She met my father when he came to England to buy a racehorse from the Montgomery stud farm, and after a whirlwind courtship she married him and went to Zenhab as his Sultana. Unfortunately, my mother wasn't cut out for life in a remote desert kingdom far away from Bond Street,' Kadir said drily. 'My parents split up when I was seven and I continued to live with my father, but I visited my mother and grandparents regularly and went to school in England. When my grandfather, the tenth Earl, died, the title and estate passed to me. However, I do not spend as much time here as perhaps I should. It was my destiny to rule Zenhab.'

But there was a price to his destiny, Kadir thought heavily. To claim the Crown from his uncle, he had been forced to agree to an arranged marriage. His jaw clenched. It was time for him to honour his promise. This trip to Europe would be his last as a single man, and on his return to Zenhab he would set a date for his wedding.

The prospect felt like a lead weight inside him. He tried telling himself that most men faced with imminent marriage, even to a woman they loved, would feel a sense of panic. He did not love his future bride; he had never met her. But until three days ago he had been resigned to fulfilling his duty.

Why was it that since he had met Lexi Howard he had felt a sense that prison bars were closing around him, sealing his fate? Perhaps it was because she was off-limits. He had never denied himself a woman before, he thought derisively. Maybe the knowledge that he could not allow the simmering sexual chemistry that existed between them to ignite was the reason for the raw feeling inside him, the curious longing for something he could not define or explain.

He stared unseeingly out of the window while he struggled to bring his emotions under control. His desire for Lexi was irrelevant. It had occurred to him that it would be a good idea to employ a female helicopter pilot to fly his future bride around Zenhab. He knew that Haleema would only be permitted to travel to the palace accompanied by a chaperone, meaning that he would have no chance to meet privately the woman with whom he must spend the rest of his life.

Employing a female helicopter pilot would negate the

necessity for Haleema to have a chaperone, and perhaps there might be an opportunity for him to establish a rapport with the princess of the mountain tribes who would rule Zenhab with him and bear his children.

He swung round, and his eyes were as hard as his heart as he stared at Lexi. 'The proposition that I want to discuss with you is this. I want you to come to Zenhab and work for me as my private helicopter pilot.'

CHAPTER FIVE

HE WANTED HER to be his pilot! Lexi's face grew warm as she recalled how she had put a very different interpretation on Kadir's proposition. In her wild imagination she had even thought that he might suggest that they become lovers. Desperate to hide her embarrassment, she said crisply, 'Why me? You must have pilots in Zenhab.'

'Of course, but none of the military pilots who belong to the royal household are trained to fly the model of helicopter that I have bought. What I'm proposing is a six-month contract, during which time you will be my personal pilot and driver, and you will also instruct pilots from the Zenhabian air force on how to fly the AgustaWestland.

'You are ideal for the job,' Kadir insisted. 'Initially, when you joined the RAF, you were a chauffeur for the Commanding Officer of an air force base before you went on to train as a pilot. You flew an AW169 for the coastguard agency and know the helicopter inside out. In Afghanistan you were awarded a Distinguished Flying Cross for rescuing injured soldiers under fire.'

'You've certainly done your homework,' she said drily.

More than she knew, Kadir mused. Apart from her impressive military record, his security team had dug up a few other interesting facts about her, including the fact that she owed a significant amount of money to various credit card companies. The first time he had met her, he had formed the opinion that Lexi Howard liked to be in control. The news that she had money problems had surprised him, but it worked in his favour.

'Naturally, the salary I am prepared to pay will reflect your flying experience and expertise.'

The figure Kadir named made Lexi blink. Her job with the coastguard agency had been well paid, but she hadn't earned in a year what Kadir was offering for six months' work. The money was tempting, she acknowledged, because it would allow her to pay off the debts that her birth mother had accrued.

Lexi thought of the woman who had given her away when she had been a few days old. Ten years ago, with the help of the adoption agency, she had found her birth mother. But her dream of an emotional reunion had been disappointing. Cathy Barnes had bluntly admitted that she had been a teenager when she had given birth to Lexi, but she hadn't wanted a baby. *'I don't know your father's name. I didn't ask names. I just met clients in hotel rooms and they paid me for what they wanted. They were mostly businessmen with fat expense accounts to blow.'*

Lexi still remembered how shocked she had felt when Cathy had revealed that she had been working as a prostitute when she had fallen pregnant.

A few years after she had given Lexi up for adoption Cathy had married, but to this day she had never told her husband that she had a daughter.

It was painful for Lexi to know that she was her birth mother's shameful secret. She met Cathy sporadically and their relationship was friendly rather than close. But six months ago Cathy had revealed that she had terminal cancer and had broken down as she'd explained that her husband was unaware that she owed a fortune on credit cards. Seeing her mother's distress had tugged on Lexi's heart, especially as Cathy did not have long to live. To spare her mother further worry, she had arranged for the debts to be transferred onto her own credit card.

'What is your answer? I don't believe you will find a better job offer than mine.' Kadir's voice tugged Lexi's mind back to the present.

She couldn't disagree with him—it was a darned good job offer, and she needed a job. So why was she hesitating?

She had a sudden flashback to those moments in his hotel suite when he had almost kissed her. The spicy scent of his aftershave had intoxicated her senses, just as it was doing now, she thought. Her nerves jangled as she watched him walk towards her, and her heart thudded erratically as her eyes were drawn to his mouth and she remembered the taste of his warm breath on her lips.

A quiver of sexual desire shot through her body, so intense that it took her breath away. She did not want to want him, and she certainly did not want him to finish what he had started at his hotel, she assured herself.

'My new helicopter was manufactured here in England and is ready for collection,' Kadir explained. 'I plan to be in Europe for another week to attend a number of business meetings before I return to Zenhab.'

'The AW doesn't have the range to fly long-haul.'

'A plane from my Royal Fleet will transport the chopper to Zenhab. I assume you are able to start work immediately?'

'I haven't actually agreed to take the job,' Lexi reminded him.

He assumed way too much, she thought as she watched his heavy brows snap together in a frown. It seemed safe to assume that the Sultan was used to having his own way. 'What about accommodation in Zenhab?' she asked abruptly. 'Where would I live?'

'At the royal palace. I will need you to be available at all times.'

Lexi was annoyed when she felt herself blush, and she wondered if Kadir was deliberately playing with words to make her feel flustered.

'You will be allocated a suite of rooms at the palace with access to a private garden and pool, and my staff will do their utmost to fulfil all your needs. All you will have to do is fly my helicopter, and spend a lot of time relaxing in the Zenhabian sunshine. You know, I can't help thinking that maybe we got off to a bad start,' Kadir murmured.

Lexi's brows lifted. 'Whatever gave you that idea?' she said drily.

His mouth crooked into a sensual smile that caused the heat inside Lexi to burn hotter.

'Can we start again—as friends? I've seen that you are an excellent pilot, and I would very much like you to work for me, Lexi.'

She would be a fool to turn this job and high salary down. All she had to do was spend six months in his desert kingdom—at a royal palace. How hard could it be compared to a dusty military camp in Afghanistan? Lexi asked herself. A traitorous thought slid into her head that the palace staff could not fulfil *all* her needs—followed by the even more treacherous thought that undoubtedly the playboy Sultan *could*!

But she would never be any man's plaything. She would never be a rich man's whore like her birth mother had been.

Whatever had happened in the past, Cathy needed her now, Lexi reminded herself. Had she offered to help her birth mother because she subconsciously hoped that Cathy would love her enough so that she would publicly recognise the daughter she had kept secret for nearly thirty years? Deep inside Lexi there was still the little girl who had studied a family photograph and wondered why she looked so different to her parents and baby sister. That had been the day she had learned she was adopted, and even at the age of five she had understood that she was on her own.

She lifted her head and met Kadir's deep brown gaze, determined not to melt beneath his charismatic smile.

'I'm confident that we can have a mutually respectful relationship, Your Highness,' she said coolly. 'I accept your offer.'

A week later, as Lexi lowered herself into the turquoise pool on the rooftop of Kadir's luxury penthouse apartment in Monaco, she reflected that there were certainly benefits to working for a billionaire. The view of the Mediterranean sparkling in the early morning sunshine was breathtaking, and at this time of the day she had the pool to herself. Not that any of the other members of Kadir's entourage were likely to use the pool, she mused. His two bodyguards kept themselves to themselves, and the elderly manservant Walif, when he was not attending to his master's needs, or viewing Lexi with deep suspicion, was often to be found dozing in an armchair.

She wondered what time Kadir had returned to the

penthouse, or whether the party he had attended aboard a Russian oligarch's yacht had gone on all night. Lexi frowned, remembering the gorgeous bikini-clad women who had been gathered on Boris Denisov's super-yacht moored in Monaco's harbour. Like the other 'business meetings' Kadir had attended at the Folies Bergère in Paris and the prestigious Caves du Roy nightclub in St Tropez earlier in the week, she doubted he had spent much time discussing commercial deals when he'd been surrounded by all that naked, nubile flesh.

'There's no need for you to wait for me,' he had told her last night as he'd stepped out of the car onto the jetty and waved to the eager reception committee on the Russian's yacht. 'I'll make my own way back to the penthouse.'

'Are you sure you'll have the energy?' Lexi had murmured drily, earning her one of Kadir's outrageously sexy smiles that had a predictable effect on her heart-rate. Her gaze had been drawn to the girls on the yacht, with their golden tans and itsy-bitsy bikinis, and she had felt staid and inexplicably angry with herself, life and, top of the list, His Royal Rake—prince of the one-night stand!

It was partly her own fault she felt a frump, Lexi acknowledged. Before they had left England Kadir had chosen a pilot's uniform out of a catalogue for her to wear, which had consisted of an eye-wateringly short skirt and a tight-fitting jacket.

'I presume you're joking,' she'd said disgustedly. 'I'm a pilot, not a *Playboy* centrefold.' She had ordered a smart grey suit with a sensible mid-calf-length skirt, much to Kadir's amusement. He seemed to find her a joke and the more she treated him with icy politeness, the more he teased her and tried to draw a reaction from her. Over the past week a battle of wills had developed between them, and Kadir's weapons of choice were his laid-back charm and his sexy smile that Lexi suspected he was fully aware turned her insides to marshmallow.

She did not understand why she was letting him get to her, or why the wicked gleam in his eyes and his husky laughter when she gave him a withering look bothered her so much. She realised he was playing a game and she had no intention of taking his flirtatious behaviour seriously. But that did not stop her heart from thudding whenever he was near—and as he insisted on sitting next to her when she flew the helicopter, and he occupied the front passenger seat when she chauffeured him in the limousine, her nerves seemed to be permanently on edge.

Forcing her mind away from the man who disturbed her equilibrium, Lexi checked the strings of her halterneck bikini were securely tied. The silver bikini had been a crazy impulse buy after she had dropped Kadir at the marina. The three tiny triangles of material revealed more of her body than she was comfortable with, and the bikini was not as practical to swim in as the navy one-piece she usually wore. Cursing her stupidity, she struck out through the cool water and swam twenty lengths of the pool, hoping that strenuous exercise would ease the restless ache in her limbs.

She surfaced after completing the final length and shook her wet hair back from her face.

'You look like a water nymph.'

The husky drawl caused her heart to collide with her ribcage and she sucked in a swift breath as she looked up and saw Kadir sprawled on a sun lounger. His bow tie was undone, and so were several of his shirt buttons, affording Lexi a glimpse of his naked chest covered in whorls of black hairs. The night's growth of dark stubble shading his jaw accentuated his lethal sensuality. She had no idea how long he had been watching her. He moved with the silent stealth of a jungle cat, she thought irritably.

She arched her brows. 'Have you met many nymphs? I would have thought that you'd have your hands full with real women, without concerning yourself with mythological ones.'

He laughed softly and the sound sent a curl of heat through Lexi. 'What a delightful picture you paint. I can visualise myself with my hands full of women.'

One woman, if he was truthful, Kadir mused. He had been on his way to bed, and had stepped onto the rooftop patio for some much needed fresh air after the fug of cloying perfume and cigar smoke that had filled Boris Denisov's yacht. But the sight of Lexi wearing a sexy bikini, with her long blonde hair streaming down her back, had made him forget that he was tired after many hours of negotiations, during which he had persuaded the Russian oligarch to invest in a business venture worth billions of pounds to Zenhab's economy.

Kadir let his gaze drift over Lexi's slender body and her high, firm breasts, and the slow burn of desire that had simmered in his gut since he had first set eyes on her grew hotter and more intense. For the past week, she had driven him mad with her frosty attitude and sharp, often sarcastic, wit, her lack of deference for his royal status. Oh, she was polite, but he had a sense that she had judged him and found him wanting, and Kadir was finding it increasingly hard to resist the challenge in her cool blue gaze.

'I trust your business meeting was successful?' she murmured. 'By the way, you have lipstick on your collar.'

'The night was very satisfactory.' Kadir tucked his hands behind his head, thinking of the agreement he'd got from Boris to build a luxury hotel complex which would attract tourists to Zenhab.

Lexi pursed her lips. Had he had sex with the strumpet who had left a scarlet imprint of her lips on his white shirt? Maybe he'd had more than one woman last night. Probably—knowing his reputation. Acid burned in her stomach and she told herself she must have swallowed some of the chlorine in the pool. Kadir was lying back on the lounger, watching her through half-closed eyes. He looked indolent and beautiful and Lexi had never been more aware of a man in her life. *Why him—a man she did not even like, let alone respect?*

'I wonder what the Zenhabian people think of their Sultan who, as far as I can tell, spends more time partying and living up to his playboy reputation than trying to improve the lives of many of the population who live in poverty?' she said tartly. 'I've heard that your father devoted his life to establishing peace and security in the kingdom, but clearly you don't share his sense of duty.'

'What do you know about my country, and why do you care about my people?' Kadir demanded, stung by her comments. Duty and the desire to ensure long-term stability in Zenhab had made him agree to an arranged marriage with a girl who his weasel of an uncle had chosen for him, he thought bitterly. Lexi had overstepped the mark this time.

He was tempted to point out that many of the best business deals were made through networking and at social events. More deals were arranged over drinks at a bar than around a boardroom table. But he could imagine the response he would get if he told Miss Prim and Proper that he had been hard at work at last night's party.

'I've been reading about the history of Zenhab,' Lexi told him. 'After all, I am going to be living and working in the kingdom for a few months.'

'You would do well to remember that I am your employer,' Kadir said curtly, 'and I suggest you keep your opinions to yourself.'

'I'll try to remember that, Your Highness.' Lexi did not recognise the devil inside who seemed hell-bent on antagonising Kadir. She could tell she had angered him. His lazy smile had disappeared and the sensual gleam in his chocolate-brown eyes had been replaced with a hard stare that riled her, even though she acknowledged that she'd had no right to criticise him.

'While we are on the subject of your employment, I have a special assignment for you.' Kadir got to his feet and walked to the edge of the pool, meaning that Lexi had to tilt her head to look at his face. 'Later today you will fly us to Lake Como in Italy, to the home of a good friend of mine, Conte Luca De Rossi. Luca is hosting a business dinner and an American entrepreneur who I am hoping to do business with will be there.' Kadir hesitated for a nanosecond. 'I want you to be my companion for the evening.'

Lexi stared at him. 'I know nothing about business.'

'You don't have to know anything.' Again he paused and, to Lexi's surprise, he appeared almost awkward. 'I need you to be my date.'

'Your *date*?' Her eyebrows almost disappeared beneath her hairline.

'It's not difficult to understand,' Kadir said impatiently.

'Excuse me, but it is when I bet that any of the women you met last night would be gagging to be your date. Why is it important for you to take a partner to the dinner, anyway?'

He exhaled heavily. 'The American businessman, Chuck Weinberg, is bringing his nineteen-year-old daughter. I met Danielle a few months ago when I visited Chuck's home in Texas.' Kadir grimaced. 'Danielle is a very determined young woman who is used to getting what she wants…and she made it clear that she wants me. To be frank, I want to concentrate on discussing my business proposition with Chuck without having to fend off his daughter.'

'Yes, I can see how annoying that would be,' Lexi said in a cool tone that failed to disguise her boiling anger. She gave in to the childish impulse and splashed water over Kadir's designer suit, before she dived beneath the water and swam to the far end of the pool.

He had a nerve! She was so furious that she could feel her heart jumping up and down in her chest. *Why was she so stupid?* Lexi's anger was partly directed at herself. For a moment, when Kadir had asked her to be his date, she'd thought it was a serious invitation and he genuinely wanted her to accompany him to the dinner party.

Glancing over her shoulder, she saw him stride into the penthouse. She had conveniently forgotten that he'd said he wanted her to carry out an assignment. Now she knew that he wanted her to be his paid escort. She rested her arms on the side of the pool and stared over the rooftops at the sea in the distance. The bright sparkle of the sun on the waves made her eyes water—at least that was what she told herself. With an impatient gesture she dashed her hand over her damp eyelashes.

Her birth mother had been an escort. *It sounds classier than call girl*, Cathy had told Lexi when she had spoken about how she had been drawn into prostitution to fund her drug habit.

Lost in her thoughts, Lexi gave a startled cry when a muscular arm curled around her waist and she was half lifted out of the water as Kadir turned her round to face him.

'What's the matter with you?' he growled. 'I made a simple request…'

'You asked me to pretend to be your mistress. I don't call that a simple request; I call that a darned cheek!' With her face mere inches from his naked bronzed chest, Lexi numbly realised that while he had been inside the apartment he had changed into his swimming shorts.

Her heart kicked into life as she jerked her eyes back to his face to find him watching her intently. She licked her dry lips and his dark gaze focused on the tip of her tongue. The cool water lapped her hot breasts and she felt her nipples harden to taut peaks that chafed against her clingy bikini bra. She was standing with her back against the wall of the pool and Kadir placed his arms on either side of her body, caging her in.

'Nowhere in my contract does it state that one of my duties is to masquerade as your mistress to protect you from the clutches of women who want to climb into your bed,' she said fiercely. 'I don't want to pretend to be your dinner date and I doubt I could convince anyone that we have an intimate relationship.'

'Intimate,' Kadir murmured, his voice suddenly as sensual as molten syrup. 'I like the way that sounds. Don't underestimate yourself, Lexi. I'm sure you could be a very convincing mistress.'

Too late, Lexi recognised the danger she was in. 'Take your hands off me.' In a distant corner of her mind she knew she sounded like a Victorian maiden. What had happened to her military training? she asked herself impatiently. She brought her knee up swiftly between Kadir's legs, but he was quicker and trapped her leg between his thighs. Tension thrummed between them and the only sound was her own quickened breathing.

Deep down, Lexi acknowledged that she had been goading him since he'd arrived at the pool; since the moment she'd first met him, if she was honest. Now, as he lowered his head his eyes reflected the challenge in hers.

'It's not my hands you need to worry about,' he drawled. And then he brought his mouth down on hers and the world exploded.

He was merciless, taking advantage of her cry of protest to thrust his tongue between her lips and explore her with mind-blowing eroticism. Lexi had never been kissed like that in her life, hadn't known that a kiss could be so hot and dark and shockingly wicked. Any idea she'd had of trying to resist him was swept away by his shimmering sexual hunger. He crushed her mouth beneath his and demanded everything: her soul, her secret fantasies, her total capitulation to his mastery. She had dared to challenge him with her cool blue eyes and Kadir would show her that the desert king *never* refused a challenge.

Lexi's body burned with an intensity of need that made a mockery of her belief that she did not have a high sex drive. She had assumed that she was not a particularly sensual person and, although she was not a virgin, her previous sexual experiences had left her with a vague sense of disappointment and bemusement that sonnets had been written about something frankly so mundane.

Everything she thought she knew about herself was shattered by the white-hot desire that ripped through her. Kadir was not touching her body, only her mouth, as he crushed her lips beneath his and deepened the kiss, and Lexi sank into darkness and heat and danger. Compelled by an instinct as old as womankind, she pushed her hips forward, urgently seeking contact with his pelvis.

He should not have started this. The realisation drummed a warning in Kadir's brain. What had begun as a lesson designed to show Lexi that *he* was in command was rapidly becoming a test of his will power. She was so responsive, so hungry, meeting his demands with demands of her own and with a boldness that he should have expected from the strong woman he knew her to be. But he could not take what he so desperately wanted. He should not have made the ice maiden melt and he could not allow himself to burn in her fire. The temptation to sink into her yielding softness and rest his thighs on hers nearly broke his resolve.

Who would know if he enjoyed one last fling before he returned to Zenhab and the life of duty that awaited him?

He would know, Kadir thought grimly. He heard his father's voice inside his head. *To cheat others requires you to cheat yourself first, and who can respect a cheat?*

He wrenched his mouth from Lexi's, feeling ashamed of his weakness and his inability to resist her. She had responded to him, he reminded himself. He was not solely to blame. But the best way he could ensure that the situation never happened again was to fire up her hot temper.

'Remember, when we are sitting at the dinner table tonight with Luca and his guests, I'll be remembering how your tongue felt inside my mouth. Remember that I know your secret, Lexi.'

'What secret?' Lexi dragged oxygen into her lungs and forced her lips, stinging from Kadir's kiss, to form the question.

Kadir deliberately dropped his gaze to her pebble-hard nipples jutting provocatively through her bikini top and his satisfied smile made Lexi's skin prickle with shame. 'We both know I could have you. Did you buy your tiny bikini and imagine me untying the straps that hold it together? Perhaps I should take you here and now, and at the dinner party there will be no need for you to pretend that you are my mistress?'

Heat blazed on her cheeks. 'I don't have to listen to this. I certainly don't have to put up with being mauled by my employer. I resign,' Lexi told him furiously.

'You would walk away from the best-paid job you are likely to find because your pride has taken a knock? I didn't have you down as a coward, Lexi. I thought you had more guts.'

'I am *not* a coward.'

He shrugged. 'There is also the matter of a financial penalty if you break your contract.'

She had signed a contract which had made her a member of the royal staff, and she would owe him three months' salary if she left before completing six months' service. Lexi knew she could not afford to take on any more debt. 'A few thousand pounds is nothing to you,' she said bitterly.

She dragged her eyes from his exquisitely chiselled features and stared at his hands gripping the edge of the pool on either side of her. She had accused him of mauling her, but he had not actually touched her body. The knowledge that he had set her on fire simply with a kiss compounded her humiliation.

Kadir's knuckles were white, and Lexi had the strange sense that he was holding on to the edge of the pool as if his life depended on it. The muscles of his forearms and shoulders were bunched as if he was under intolerable tension and he was breathing hard, his big chest rising and falling jerkily, matching the frantic rhythm of her own heartbeat. She looked into his eyes, expecting to see mockery, but the hard brilliance in his gaze revealed a hunger that shocked her. The realisation that this was not a game to him scared her as much as it excited her.

'Release me from my contract. Let me go before this gets out of hand,' she pleaded in a low, shaken voice.

Logic told Kadir she was right. Taking Lexi to Zenhab would be madness now that he had tasted her. What had started out as a challenge—to melt her ice—had changed irrevocably now that he had discovered her heat and softness and incandescent sensuality.

But the fact remained that he wanted to employ a female helicopter pilot to fly his intended bride around Zenhab. His desire for Lexi was an inconvenience that he would have to deal with, Kadir told himself firmly. His life was mapped out and the path he must take had been plotted by his uncle Jamal. For stability in Zenhab, and for the promise he'd made to his father, he would marry the bride who had been chosen for him.

'We will leave for Italy at two o'clock,' he said abruptly, dropping his arms to his sides, his fists clenched as if he couldn't trust himself not to reach for Lexi's slender body and pull her into the heat of him, the need that burned bright and fierce in his gut.

In a dignified silence that somehow simmered with fury, she climbed the steps leading out of the pool, water streaming from her limbs and her long white-gold hair.

Kadir watched her walk into the penthouse and cursed savagely before he ducked beneath the surface of the pool and powered through the water.

Lexi did not look round, did not even stop to snatch up her towel as she ran inside and almost collided with Kadir's manservant. Walif—as she had come to expect—did not speak to her, but she sensed his disapproval and, when she hurried into her bedroom and glanced in the mirror, the sight of her swollen lips, reddened from Kadir's kiss, brought a flush to her face and strengthened her resolve to keep her relationship with the Sultan of Zenhab on strictly professional lines from now on.

CHAPTER SIX

HIS LAST NIGHT of freedom!

It was not quite as dramatic as that, Kadir acknowledged, the corners of his mouth lifting in a wry smile of self-derision. A royal wedding would take months to arrange, and technically he was free until he led his new bride into his private bedchamber and they were alone for the first time.

But this evening would be his last in Europe for many months, until after his wedding to Haleema had taken place. What better place to be than at Conte Luca De Rossi's breathtaking villa on the shores of Lake Como?

Kadir was grateful to his old school friend for arranging the dinner party and inviting Chuck Weinberg. The American businessman had seemed enthusiastic about investing in the developing telecommunications industry in Zenhab during initial discussions that had taken place in Texas. Tonight, Kadir planned to utilise all his persuasive skills to hopefully secure a deal that would bring his desert kingdom fully into the twenty-first century.

There was only one problem—and she was making a beeline for him across the magnificent entrance hall of the Villa De Rossi. Danielle Weinberg had big hair, a big smile and big breasts that Kadir, who had a certain amount of hands-on experience of the female anatomy, was certain owed more to a cosmetic surgeon's skill than to genetics.

'Kad*eer*, I've been looking all over for you.'

She reminded Kadir of an over-enthusiastic puppy. As he gently but firmly unlocked Danielle's hands from around his neck, he was struck by the thought that his future bride was a similar age to the young American. His jaw clenched. In Zenhab a life of duty awaited him, but tonight he was determined to enjoy his last few hours of freedom.

Despite what he had told Lexi, he knew he could handle Danielle with the same diplomacy that he dealt with her father. But when he had asked Lexi to partner him at the dinner party he had lost his nerve—something that had *never* happened to Kadir before. Citing Danielle as an excuse had seemed like a good idea, but it had backfired spectacularly, and had led to him kissing Lexi in what had started out as a punishment and ended in searing passion that he knew he should not have allowed to happen. His behaviour had been inappropriate, and Lexi had made him aware of that fact on the helicopter flight from Monaco to the Villa De Rossi, when she had been as cold as a Siberian winter.

Kadir glanced at his watch. She was late coming down for dinner. His mouth tightened with annoyance as he remembered her excuse that she had nothing suitable to wear to a grand dinner party. Would she wear the evening gown he had arranged to be delivered to her room? He would give her five more minutes before he went to find her, and if necessary he would put the damned dress on her!

His attention was drawn to the top of the sweeping staircase, and his frustration with his stubborn, insubordinate pilot changed to white-hot desire as he watched her walk gracefully down the stairs. The dress was a Luca De Rossi creation, an elegant floor-length sheath of silk the colour of a summer sky that matched exactly the blue of Lexi's eyes. Her pale gold hair had been left loose and fell past her shoulders like a silken curtain, framing a face as beautiful and serene as a Raphael virgin.

Kadir was aware of every painful beat of his heart as he strode across the hall.

'Am I late?' Lexi gave him a rueful look. 'I couldn't reach the zip on my dress.'

'Why didn't you call one of the maids to assist you?'

She shrugged. 'It didn't occur to me to ask for help. I made a hook out of a coat hanger and managed to pull the zip up with it. I served in the armed forces for ten years and I'm used to working out solutions to problems,' she reminded Kadir.

'Did you often wear evening gowns in Afghanistan?' He did not know whether to be exasperated or amused by her fierce independence.

'Of course not...' She hesitated. 'I've never worn a House of De Rossi dress before, or any other designer dress, for that matter. It's beautiful, and obviously I will pay for it.'

'Fortunately, we have been called in to dinner,' he murmured, offering her his arm, 'so we'll have to save the argument until later.'

'We don't need to argue. You simply have to accept that I won't allow you to pay for my clothes.'

His eyes glittered. 'You always have to have the last word. Stubbornness is not an attractive quality in a woman.'

Lexi flashed him a cool smile that made Kadir grind his teeth. 'I'm not hoping to attract you, Your Highness. Unlike just about every other woman here tonight,' she added drily.

When she had first caught sight of him, dressed in a white tuxedo that looked stunning against his olive-gold skin, she had been blown away by his good looks and smouldering sensuality, and a glance around the room revealed that she was not the only woman who could not take her eyes off him.

They had reached the dining room, and Kadir held out a chair for Lexi to sit down. He was aware of the subtle and, in some cases, not so subtle glances directed at him from the other female party guests. Lexi was the only woman he wanted, but he could not tell her and he could not allow their mutual attraction to ignite. However, as she sat down, he was compelled by a force beyond his control to lower his head so that he could inhale the evocative scent of her perfume.

Lexi was suddenly conscious that Kadir had leaned closer to her and his face was almost touching hers. She held her breath as the close-trimmed stubble on his jaw scraped against her cheek, and only released it when he lifted his head and moved to sit down on the chair beside her. She took a sip of water and waited for her racing pulse to slow before she dared to look at him. His lazy smile did peculiar things to her insides. She wished she had not come down to dinner. She felt so tense that the thought of putting food into her stomach made her shudder. It had only been the thought that he was very likely to come to her room and force her to obey him that had persuaded her to put on the dress that she had discovered wrapped in tissue on the bed.

Heat stained Lexi's cheeks as it occurred to her that she had never in her life allowed a man to force her to do anything she did not want to do. And why did the idea of being made to obey Kadir conjure shockingly erotic images in her mind? What was happening to her? she wondered grimly. Tomorrow she would be going to Zenhab. Pulling out was not an option; she could not afford to pay the penalty clause in her contract. But, more than that, it was a matter of pride that she learned to deal with His Royal Hotness and prove that she had not been fazed when he had kissed her in the pool in Monaco.

Kadir was charming and entertaining during dinner, but it was his unexpected gentleness when he spoke to the over-eager Danielle that surprised Lexi. His charisma and sexual magnetism she could handle, just, she thought ruefully. But the discovery that he could be kind and, dare she even think it, sensitive, was an element to him she had been unaware of until now. Heavens, if he carried on being Mr Nice Guy she might even grow to like him!

'I understand you are a helicopter pilot and flew rescue missions in Afghanistan.' Chuck Weinberg's strong Texan drawl dragged Lexi from her thoughts. 'Is your father a military man?'

'My father...' Lexi's hesitation fired Kadir's curiosity. "He's a doctor. Actually, both my parents are in the medical profession; my father is a heart surgeon and my mother is a neurologist.'

'They must be clever people! It's curious that you didn't inherit an interest in medicine from your parents,' Chuck commented.

God knew what genes she had inherited from her biological parents, Lexi thought bleakly. Her mother had provided sexual favours for a living, and her father had been one of Cathy's clients. The man whose blood ran through her veins was nameless, faceless, and the knowledge that she would never know his identity made her feel incomplete.

After dinner the party moved into the orangerie, where there was dancing to a five-piece jazz band. Lexi withdrew to an alcove and watched Kadir work his way around the room. No female between the ages of eighteen and eighty was safe from his magnetic charm, she thought as he finished dancing with Danielle Weinberg and swept a white-haired lady onto the dance floor.

'I should have expected Kadir would try to seduce my grandmother, and that Nonna Violetta would adore him.'

Lexi glanced at Luca De Rossi, who had come to stand beside her. 'He's certainly the life and soul of the party,' she said drily.

An amused smile crossed Luca's handsome face. Similar in height and build to Kadir, he possessed film star looks, with jet-black hair, classically sculpted features and an air of polished sophistication that marked him out as a European aristocrat.

'Don't be fooled by Kadir's playboy image,' Luca murmured. 'He plays hard but he works harder and he is prepared to devote his life to Zenhab.'

Lexi restrained herself from asking what kind of work the Prince of Pleasure had ever done. 'I understand you became friends with Kadir at Eton? Did you also know Charles Fairfax at school?'

'He was in the year below Kadir and I.' The Italian shrugged an elegant shoulder. 'I can't say Charlie was a close friend. Why do you ask?'

'He's going to marry my sister.'

Luca looked surprised. 'How curious,' he murmured.

Lexi wanted to ask him what he meant, but her thoughts scattered as Kadir appeared at her side. 'You have monopolised my pilot for long enough,' he told Luca lightly, but beneath his easy tone was a possessiveness that made Lexi bristle. 'Dance with me,' he commanded.

She shook her head. 'I can't dance, and you are hardly short of partners. Every woman in the room is hoping it'll be her turn next to be swept onto the dance floor by the Arabian version of Fred Astaire.'

Kadir laughed softly as he clamped his hands on her waist and whisked her around the room. 'There's no need for you to be jealous. I only have eyes for you, angel face.'

'I am *not* jealous!' She knew he was teasing her, playing a familiar game that he had played all the past week, so why was her heart thudding painfully fast beneath her ribs? She brought the tip of her stiletto heel down on his toe and gave him a look of wide-eyed innocence. 'Oops. I warned you I can't dance.'

His eyes glittered with an unspoken challenge that sent a frisson of excitement down Lexi's spine. 'Be careful, or I might be tempted to expose your secret right here while we are dancing in front of all these people.'

'What secret...?' She snatched a sharp breath, remembering how he had kissed her in the swimming pool and she had arched her body towards him in an unmistakable offer that had revealed her desire. The memory of that kiss made Lexi feel vulnerable and exposed—to him. The hunger in Kadir's eyes—no trace of teasing now—caused molten heat to flood through her veins.

Confused by her reaction to a man she knew to be a playboy, she stumbled and Kadir immediately tightened his arms around her, drawing her closer so that her hips came into searing contact with his. The hard ridge of his arousal pushed against her pelvis. She did not dare meet his gaze but she knew from the harsh sound of his breathing that he was in as much danger of bursting into flames as she was.

Why him? she asked herself bitterly. Why had she never felt this intensity of need, this overpowering desire for any other man, including the man she had planned to marry? She had never come close to losing control with Steven. Until she had met Kadir she hadn't known what it was like to ache in every part of her body, or for her breasts to feel heavy and her nipples hot and hard, so that she knew without glancing down that they were visibly outlined beneath her silk dress.

'Excuse me...' She did not care that the tremor in her voice betrayed her tension as she pulled out of his arms and walked swiftly across the dance floor. She was simply desperate to regain control of her wayward body and wanton thoughts.

Kadir watched Lexi's slender figure weave through the other dancers, and it took every bit of his will power not to go after her, sweep her up into his arms and carry her off to—where? he asked himself derisively. Taking her to bed was not an option. It had to end now, this madness, the longing for something he could not have—and quite possibly he wanted all the more because Lexi was off-limits.

He saw Chuck Weinberg beckoning to him from the library, where they had arranged to discuss the business deal that would be hugely beneficial to Zenhab. His last night of freedom ended here, Kadir told himself as he strode towards the library.

* * *

Lexi checked her watch and saw that it was past midnight. The party was winding down and the guests were leaving. She was due to fly the helicopter to Milan Airport in the morning so that it could be loaded onto a transporter plane for the journey to Zenhab. It would be an early start to what promised to be a long day and she knew she should go to bed, but she had never felt less like sleeping in her life.

She wondered where Kadir was. He had disappeared from the party a couple of hours ago and Lexi had not seen him, or the attractive redhead who was almost wearing a daringly low-cut dress, since. He was not her responsibility, she reminded herself. She was employed as his pilot and his personal life was none of her business.

Hadn't he made it his business when he had kissed her? whispered a voice inside her head. She frowned. The kiss had meant nothing to him. He had been playing with her like he had done all week, but tonight he had obviously grown bored of the game and turned his attention to the well-endowed redhead.

Feeling restless and refusing to admit that Kadir was the cause, she stepped outside onto the long terrace that ran along the back of the house. The Villa De Rossi's magnificent formal gardens were dappled in silver moonlight but, as Lexi slipped like a shadow along the path leading down to the lake, the moon was partially obscured by clouds racing across the sky. She drew her pashmina tighter around her shoulders. Autumn in northern Italy was much warmer than in England but, as she stood at the edge of the lake, raindrops began to bounce onto the surface, falling faster and faster until the water seemed to dance.

A wooden summer house further along the path was the only place to shelter from the rain shower, and luckily she found the door was unlocked. Inky darkness greeted her as she stepped inside and an even darker voice demanded, 'What do you want?'

'Kadir?' Lexi's yelp of fright turned to shock and her heart leapt into her throat as a faint yellow light filled the cabin and she saw that Kadir had lit a gas lamp on the wall. 'What are you doing here?' Her eyes flew to an old sofa piled with cushions and realisation dawned. She guessed the redhead was hiding somewhere. 'I'm sorry if I've interrupted something.'

His heavy brows drew together. 'What do you mean?'

'I assume you are here with someone.'

'By someone I suppose you mean a woman?' Kadir growled. 'Why do you always jump to the worst conclusion based on rubbish the paparazzi have written about me in the past?'

Lexi flushed as it became apparent that there was no one else in the summer house. 'What was I supposed to think? Why were you sitting here in the dark?'

He shrugged. 'I went for a stroll because I needed some air and ended up at the summer house. I used to come here with Luca when we were teenagers; I stayed with him sometimes during the school holidays. He taught me to sail on the lake.'

They had been halcyon days, Kadir brooded, before his father had suffered the stroke that had left him paralysed and unable to rule, before his uncle Jamal had seized power, and before he had been forced to agree to an arranged marriage in a bid to maintain peace and stability in Zenhab.

Lexi glanced out of the window. Through the darkness, the twinkling lights of the villages strung around the shores of Lake Como revealed the vast size of the lake. 'I imagine sailing is popular on the lake.' She remembered that he had skippered the Zenhabian team that had won the America's Cup. 'Why did you decide to take up offshore sailing?'

'There are no lakes in Zenhab,' he said drily. 'Away from the coast, most of the land is desert and rock. How do you feel about returning to a desert environment?'

'I'm interested to see a new country and, unlike Afghanistan, there isn't a war in Zenhab so I might get a chance to see the beauty of a desert landscape without having to worry about avoiding landmines.'

Kadir exhaled heavily. His father had ended the civil war in Zenhab and established peace between the tribes two decades ago. With his last breath Sultan Khalif had begged his son to maintain unity in the kingdom. Kadir had vowed to carry out his father's wish, for it was his wish too. He loved the kingdom that he had been destined from birth to rule. It was a small sacrifice to give up his right to fall in love and marry a woman of his choice. Perhaps it was even a blessing. He had learned from his parents that love was a precarious base for marriage. His father had been broken-hearted when Kadir's mother had returned to England for good.

Lust, on the other hand, was easy to understand. It was nothing more than chemistry, and it was a bitter irony, Kadir mused, that the chemical reaction between him and Lexi was blistering.

In the semi-dark summer house he was so aware of her that every skin cell on his body tingled, and he could feel the thunderous drumbeat of his desire pounding in his veins. He had never met anyone like her before, never admired any woman as much as he admired Lexi. She was beautiful, brave, intensely annoying, utterly intriguing—his brain told him to move away from her, but his body wasn't listening. His eyes locked with hers and his heart flipped a somersault when he saw that fire had replaced the ice in her bright blue gaze.

Was it so wrong to want to taste her one last time? To capture a memory that must last him a lifetime. *One kiss*… He lowered his head and watched her pupils darken, heard the soft catch of her breath as he grazed his lips across hers and felt them tremble and open like the velvet-soft petals of an English rose.

One kiss, he assured himself.

She was sweetness and fire, his delight and quite possibly his destruction. When he had kissed her in the swimming pool he had not dared allow their bodies to come into contact, but now she melted into him, soft and pliant against his hard musculature. With a groan, he wrapped one arm around her waist and threaded his other hand into her long silky hair. Her perfume—a blend of crisp citrus and sweet jasmine—so appropriate for her, he thought—wrapped around him and he closed his eyes and sought her mouth blindly, his other senses, of touch and taste, heightened so that the feel of her lips beneath his was beyond pleasure.

The first time Kadir had kissed her in Monaco, Lexi knew that his intention had been to prove a point and show her that he was in control. She had understood that he had been angry because she had challenged him. But there was no anger now. They had not been having one of their verbal sparring matches and, rather than trying to show her who was boss, Kadir seemed to have seduction in his mind. His lips were firm on hers and he

kissed her with demanding hunger, yet there was an unexpected tenderness in his passion that answered a need
deep within her. The bold thrust of his tongue into her
mouth shattered her resistance and destroyed the mental
barriers she *always* kept in place.

She could not control the tremor that ran through her
as he trailed his lips over her cheek, her throat, and found
the pulse beating frantically at its base. Distracted by him
sliding the strap of her dress over her shoulder, she felt
something hard at the back of her knees and belatedly
realised it was the sofa.

He eased her down onto the cushions and knelt above
her. The fierce glitter in his eyes was a promise and a
warning of his intent. Lexi held her breath as he slipped
his hands beneath her and ran her zip far enough down
her spine to allow him to peel away the top of her dress.
The air felt cool on her breasts; his palms felt warm on
her bare flesh. Glancing down, the sight of his darkly
tanned hands on her creamy pale breasts was incredibly
erotic, and when he rubbed his thumb pads across her
tender nipples the sensation was so exquisite that she
could not restrain a soft moan.

'You are more beautiful even than I imagined.' His
voice, roughened with desire, broke the intense silence
of the dimly lit cabin.

Reality pushed, unwelcome, into Lexi's thoughts. She
wasn't a novice when it came to sex; she was an independent woman, free to do as she pleased. She could no
longer deny that she wanted to make love with Kadir,
but choice also meant taking responsibility for herself.
'I'm not on the Pill,' she murmured. 'Do you have anything with you?'

Lexi's words were as effective as a cold shower. Once

again Kadir acknowledged the irony of bad timing. If she had asked him the same question six months ago he would have been able to assure her that he always carried condoms with him. But he had made a commitment to himself to end the playboy lifestyle, in preparation for his marriage.

His desire for Lexi was blazing out of control, but in his heart burned the need to prove to himself that he was an honourable man like his father had been, a man fit to be Sultan of Zenhab and fulfil the destiny of a desert king.

Ignoring the painful throb of his arousal, he got up from the sofa and tugged Lexi's dress back over her breasts. She caught her breath as the silk grazed her nipples, and the evidence of how sensitive her breasts were almost shattered Kadir's resolve to end what he should never have begun.

'We must go back to the house,' he said abruptly as he thrust her pashmina into her hands, and felt relieved when she wrapped it around her so that he could no longer see the hard points of her nipples jutting beneath her dress.

'Shouldn't we wait until it stops raining?' Lexi hesitated when Kadir opened the cabin door and she saw the torrential downpour. But he had already stepped onto the porch. He slid out of his jacket and draped it around her shoulders before he grabbed her hand and practically dragged her along the path.

'We need to go back now.'

His urgency filled Lexi with anticipation. In the cabin she had been aware of his hunger, the need for sexual fulfilment that had almost overwhelmed both of them. But safe sex could not be ignored and Kadir was clearly impatient to take her to his bedroom, where presumably he had contraceptives and they could make love with peace of mind.

Was she out of her mind? demanded a voice inside her head. It defied common sense to sleep with a playboy. But she was tired of being sensible. Her job as a helicopter pilot in the RAF and then with the coastguard agency had required her to take risks, but on a personal level she had played it safe for far too long. Why shouldn't she enjoy everything the Prince of Pleasure had to offer?

Lexi's heart was thumping as Kadir ushered her into the villa through a side door and up a back staircase used by the servants to the third floor, where the guest bedrooms were.

Her smile faltered and she gave him a puzzled look when he stopped in the corridor outside her bedroom and said brusquely, 'Goodnight.'

Goodnight! 'I…I don't understand. I thought…'

The memory of his barely restrained passion ten minutes earlier made her abandon her usual diffidence. She ached for him and she had been certain that he wanted her with the same white-hot need. His chiselled features gave no clue to his thoughts and some of Lexi's certainty faded as she stared into his eyes that were the colour of dark umber, without the teasing glint she was used to seeing. 'I assumed we were going to spend the night together,' she said huskily.

In his wilder days Kadir had slept with more women than he could remember, but he had never felt as much of a bastard as he did now for not sleeping with Lexi. The irony would be laughable if he felt like laughing, but he doubted that he would ever laugh again. There was no good way to handle the situation and only one thing he could say.

'I'm sorry. I should not have let things get out of hand the way they did.'

Lexi's racing heart juddered to a standstill. Oh, no, not sorry, she thought bitterly. Let him be mocking, sarcastic—anything but pitying. She heard Steven's voice inside her head.

I'm sorry, Lexi. I shouldn't have allowed our relationship to develop when I knew that my girlfriend and baby were waiting for me back in England. It felt like you and I were in another world in Afghanistan. But the truth is that I'm not free to marry you because I already have a family.'

Rejection was hurtful and humiliating. After Steven had dumped her she had vowed never to put herself in such a vulnerable position again.

So what was she doing hovering outside her bedroom in the vain hope that Kadir might change his mind and take her to bed? *How much more vulnerable could she feel?* Kadir had been playing games with her ever since they'd met, Lexi thought grimly.

'Good manners prevent me from telling you what you can do with your apology,' she said, her voice so tightly wound that it shook with the strain of retaining her last dregs of pride. She opened her bedroom door and gave a cynical laugh. 'I should thank you for stopping me from making the worst mistake of my life.' Something in his darkly beautiful face made her insides twist. 'Everything is a game to you, isn't it?'

'*Damn it*, Lexi. Of course I don't think this is a game.'

To Lexi's astonishment, Kadir drove his clenched fist against the door frame, and it was a testament to the solidness of the wood that it did not splinter beneath the powerful blow. 'The situation is complicated,' he said savagely. 'I want to spend the night with you and make love to you. But I am not free to do what I want.'

'But…you are a Sultan. You can do whatever you like.'

'I wish that were true.'

Lexi felt a curious sense of déjà vu. Steven had admitted that he wasn't free to be with her because he had a long-term partner and a child. She lifted her chin and stared into Kadir's eyes. 'Why are you not free?'

An indefinable emotion flickered in his dark gaze. 'I am betrothed to the princess of the mountain tribes in Zenhab.'

'You're engaged to be *married*?' Her shock rapidly turned to anger. 'Then what the hell were you doing coming on to me when presumably you are in love with your fiancée—you…cheating *louse*?'

A nerve jumped in Kadir's cheek. 'I am not a cheat. Nor am I in love with Princess Haleema. I've never even met her.' He saw the confusion in Lexi's eyes and his tone softened. 'We are not engaged as you would understand the word. A marriage arrangement was made by our families, and I had to agree to it to keep peace in Zenhab. After his stroke, my father was convinced that the marriage would forge stronger ties with the mountain tribes and ensure stability in the kingdom that had once been torn apart by civil war.'

Lexi stared at him. The story of an arranged marriage sounded convenient, but she sensed that Kadir was telling her the truth. 'I didn't realise that arranged marriages took place in Zenhab.'

'*Forced* marriages will not be allowed under the new law I have introduced. And in fact they are rare. Many families believe in arranged marriages where sons and daughters are introduced to a potential spouse, but marriage can only take place if it is the choice of the bride and groom.'

'Did you have a choice about becoming engaged to the princess?'

'No,' Kadir said heavily. Agreeing to marry Haleema had been the only way he could claim the Crown—his birthright—from his uncle. 'It was my father's dying wish that I should ensure the future stability and safety of our country. Haleema was only a child at that time, but I gave my father my word that I would honour my promise and take her as my bride when she was old enough to marry. When I return to Zenhab I intend to fulfil my duty.'

Lexi guessed it was a duty that weighed heavy on Kadir's shoulders. She remembered Luca De Rossi had said that Kadir was prepared to devote his life to his kingdom and she felt a grudging respect for his determination to honour the promise he had made as a young man. But he had not treated her honourably, she thought with a flash of anger.

'You should have been honest with me from the start. You had no right to…to flirt with me.' She felt sick when she remembered his sexy smile and the gleam of sensual promise in his eyes. The realisation that it had all been a game to him was humiliating. Just like Steven, Kadir had not considered her feelings, she thought painfully. He had kissed her and started to make love to her, knowing that he was promised to another woman. To both men, she had been unimportant, and the realisation opened up the raw feelings of rejection that had haunted her for years.

'I know it was wrong of me to kiss you,' Kadir growled. 'I cannot deny that I desire you. From the moment we met, we were drawn to each other.' He held her gaze and dared her to deny it. 'But I give you my word that I won't kiss you again, and when we are in Zenhab I will treat you with courtesy and respect.'

'I can't go to Zenhab with you now! How can we forget what nearly happened between us tonight?'

'We have to forget,' Kadir said harshly. 'I still need a helicopter pilot.'

'You could release me from my contract and employ another pilot.'

He shook his head. 'I chose you especially because one of your duties will be to fly Haleema between her home in the mountains and the palace. Her family are very traditional and she will only be permitted to travel with a female pilot.'

'You want me to chaperone your fiancée?' Lexi was tempted to tell him what he could do with his damned job, but hot on the heels of her temper was the realisation that she still had to repay her mother's debts and she could not afford the financial penalty if she broke her contract with Kadir. It was also a question of pride. Kadir had guessed that she found him attractive, but if he could forget their passion that had almost blazed out of control in the summer house then so could she.

She stepped into her bedroom and forced her lips into a dismissive smile. 'Fine, I'll come to Zenhab as per our agreement,' she told him coolly. 'I'm sure I'll have no problem forgetting the regrettable incident that took place tonight, and from now on I will expect our relationship to be purely professional, Your Highness.'

CHAPTER SEVEN

LEXI STARED OUT of the plane window at the seemingly unending expanse of saffron-coloured sand that had been wind-whipped into towering dunes and sinuous ridges which resembled a giant serpent writhing across the land. In the far distance she could see craggy grey mountains, beyond which, according to her guidebook, lay Zenhab's wild and barren northern lands where a few ancient Bedouin tribes lived.

Looking in the other direction, she saw the outlines of modern skyscrapers alongside elegant minarets and curving mosque roofs. Zenhab's position in the Arabian Sea made it an important trading route, and its rich cultural history and architecture reflected the periods in time when the country had been under Portuguese and, later, Persian rule.

As the plane flew over the capital city, Mezeira, Kadir's chief adviser, Yusuf bin Hilal, pointed out places of interest. 'There is the royal palace. You see how the pure white walls sparkle in the sunshine as though the stones are mixed with diamonds? They are not, of course,' Yusuf explained. 'The bricks contain a special kind of sand that gives the jewel effect.'

'It looks like a fairy tale palace from *Arabian Nights*

with all those towers and spires. It reminds me a little of the Taj Mahal in India.'

'The people of Zenhab believe that *our* Sultan's royal palace is the most beautiful building in the world,' Yusuf said proudly.

'I understand that in the past there was unrest in the mountain territories of Zenhab,' Lexi commented.

Yusuf nodded. 'There was a terrible civil war. But the present Sultan's father, Sultan Khalif, established peace in the kingdom and for the past decade his son has introduced a programme of liberalisation and modernisation that has resulted in economic growth for the country. Sultan Kadir works tirelessly to attract foreign business and investment to Zenhab and he is regarded by the majority of the population as an inspired leader.'

Yusuf pointed to another building. 'That is Zenhab's first university, opened by Sultan Kadir five years ago and partly funded by him personally. His advancement of education for rich and poor alike, and especially for women, has gained him much support, and sadly a few enemies. The Sultan has received death threats, but he still insists on walking among his people whenever he can. He is a truly great man,' Yusuf said reverently.

Every member of Kadir's staff that Lexi had spoken to seemed to share Yusuf's opinion. Her own opinion of him as a playboy prince was changing since she had discovered that he was willing to sacrifice his right to choose a wife and had agreed to an arranged marriage because he believed it was best for his kingdom. She respected his determination to put his duty to his country above his personal desires, and she knew she should be grateful to him for being honest with her in Italy instead of taking her to bed. But she had lied when she'd told him that she would easily forget the passionate moments they had shared in the summer house. He dominated her thoughts, day and night, but now that they had arrived in Zenhab he would soon marry his Princess, she thought dully.

She had not seen Kadir since they had boarded the plane and he had walked past his entourage of staff in the main cabin on his way to his private suite at the front. Once the plane had landed, she'd expected him to reappear, but there was no sign of him as she'd followed Yusuf down the steps and onto the tarmac. To her surprise, the members of Kadir's staff who had travelled abroad with him stood with the plane's crew, forming what appeared to be a reception committee, and Lexi had no option but to stand in line with them. 'What's happening?' she whispered to Yusuf.

'By tradition, when the Sultan returns home, glorious from his conquests and battles abroad, although, of course, he has business meetings now rather than battles,' the adviser hastily explained, 'he is escorted through the streets of the city to the palace by horsemen.'

Yusuf's voice was drowned out by the sound of thundering hooves and Lexi turned to see a great dust cloud, through which appeared thirty or so horsemen wearing traditional Zenhabian clothes—white robes with brightly coloured short-sleeved jackets on top and white headdresses which billowed behind them as the horsemen raced along the runway.

Glancing up at the plane, Lexi's heart lurched as Kadir appeared in the doorway and stood on the top step. Like the horsemen, he was dressed in a white robe, and his jacket was exquisitely embroidered in red and gold. At his waist he wore a wide leather belt and a terrifying-looking ceremonial knife in a jewelled holder. His white head-dress, which Lexi knew was called a *keffiyeh*, was held in place by a circle of black and gold rope. He looked regal and remote, the powerful ruler of his desert kingdom, and far removed from his alter-ego of an English Earl.

Even from the distance that separated Lexi from him, she could see the dark brilliance of his eyes. She could not stop herself from staring at him, riveted by his handsome face, and she felt the same curious ache in her heart that she had felt in Italy when he had admitted that he was not free to make love to her.

He descended the steps and walked past the line of staff. Lexi found she was holding her breath as he came closer. She willed him to turn his head and notice her, but he strode straight past, leaving in his wake the spicy tang of his cologne that hung in the hot, still air and teased her senses.

She closed her eyes, assailed by memories of when he had kissed her in the summer house at Lake Como. She remembered the heat of his body through his silk shirt, the feel of his hands on her skin when he had pulled her dress down and caressed her breasts. Frantically, she tried to block out the erotic images in her mind as she reminded herself that Kadir should not have kissed her because he was engaged to another woman. She felt as if a knife had sliced through her heart, and she swayed on her feet.

'Miss Howard?' Yusuf sounded anxious. 'Are you going to faint? The heat of the desert can take some getting used to, especially for someone as fair-skinned and delicate-looking as yourself,' the adviser murmured sympathetically.

Lexi's eyes snapped open. 'I assure you I am not in the least delicate,' she told Yusuf tersely. She was furious with herself for reacting to Kadir the way she had. It could not happen again. She was not a silly lovestruck girl, wilting beneath the desert sun and a surfeit of hormones. She had come to Zenhab to do a job and she *must* forget those passionate moments she had spent in the Sultan's arms, as it appeared that he had forgotten her.

Kadir had reached the group of horsemen and a huge black horse was brought to him. He swung himself into the saddle and reached behind his shoulder to withdraw a long curved sword from a jewelled scabbard that Lexi saw hanging down his back. The horsemen did likewise, and held their swords aloft, the steel blades glinting in the fierce sun as their Sultan gave a loud victory cry.

The scene could have taken place centuries ago, when the great Islamic leader Saladin had fought the English King Richard in the Crusades, Lexi thought. This was the real Kadir Al Sulaimar, she realised. There was no sign of the charismatic playboy she had met when they had been in Europe. The Sultan of Zenhab looked stern and forbidding, yet she could not forget how his mouth had felt on hers when he had kissed her, his unexpected tenderness as he had teased her lips apart and explored her with his tongue.

Her breath caught in her throat as Kadir turned his head and stared directly at her. Lexi had the strange sense that he was remembering the moments when they had fallen into each other's arms in the summer house. But the gleam in his eyes must have been sunlight reflected off his sword. He turned away and gave a blood-curdling cry before he galloped his horse down the runway, pursued by the thirty horsemen, in a cloud of dust and flashing horses' hooves and white *keffiyeh's* streaming behind the cavalcade.

* * *

She could not ask for a better place to work, Lexi conceded a few days later. She had been given a luxurious apartment at the palace with her own private terrace and pool, and she had access to the beautiful royal gardens, where it was pleasant to sit by the ornamental fountains and feel the cool spray on her face.

Kadir had a busy schedule and attended meetings and functions most days, requiring Lexi to fly him by helicopter to towns across the kingdom. The previous day she had flown him along Zenhab's stunning coast so that he could inspect the site of a new hotel complex, which his adviser Yusuf had said was going to be built by the Russian businessman Boris Denisov.

Apart from bidding her good morning, Kadir had not spoken to her, and he'd sat in the rear of the helicopter. He obviously intended to keep their relationship strictly professional, but Lexi had been aware of his brooding gaze burning between her shoulder blades during the flight.

She was lonely at the palace, and missed the sense of camaraderie she'd had with her friends in the coastguard agency and the RAF. From one of the tallest towers she was able to look out over the desert, and remembering the dusty military base at Camp Bastion in Afghanistan and the other pilots she had flown missions with increased her sense of isolation.

As was her habit, she turned to physical exercise to relieve her frustration, and went running every morning before the sun rose high in the sky and the temperature soared. She'd also discovered an air-conditioned gym in the palace where Kadir's bodyguards worked out. Ashar and Nasim were reasonably fluent in English, and Lexi spoke some Arabic. Once they had got over their initial hesitancy at sharing the gym with a woman, the two young men were friendly and their company went some way to alleviating her loneliness.

'I'll grant you that men are physically stronger than women, but in a test of stamina and endurance women can equal, or even beat their male counterparts,' Lexi argued one afternoon.

Nasim stepped off the treadmill. 'Okay, prove it. Push-ups until one of us gives up.'

Determination gleamed in Lexi's eyes. 'You're on. Ashar, you can act as judge.'

Kadir frowned as he walked down the corridor to the gym and heard voices from behind the door. He had been busy with matters of state since he had returned to the palace, and this was his first chance for a workout. He had hoped to find the gym empty but, as he opened the door, he came to an abrupt halt at the sight of one of his bodyguards and his private pilot stretched out on gym mats, pumping their bodies up and down in a series of push-ups.

From where he was standing he had a perfect view of Lexi's pert bottom covered in bright pink satin shorts—lifting and lowering, lifting and lowering in a steady rhythm that had a predictable effect on his pulse rate. He visualised her slender body arched above him, the tips of her bare breasts brushing his chest as she slowly lowered herself onto him... His arousal was instant and so hard that he hastily held his towel in front of him and cursed beneath his breath.

'What is going on?' He knew it was a stupid question, but the sound of his voice had the desired effect of making Lexi and the bodyguard stop what they were doing and jump to their feet. The guilty expression on Nasim's face heightened Kadir's anger. Why did the bodyguard look guilty, unless the push-ups were a prelude to another form of exercise? he thought grimly.

'Do you not kneel before your Sultan?' he demanded to Nasim and Ashar.

'Your Majesty!' The men immediately dropped down onto one knee, but Lexi remained standing and met Kadir's hard stare with a challenge in her eyes as she placed her hands on her hips.

'Is there a problem, Your Highness?'

You're damned right there's a problem, Kadir thought to himself. But he was not going to admit that his body felt as if it was about to explode, or that he was unbearably tempted to dismiss the bodyguards and make love to his feisty helicopter pilot right there on the gym mat. He was shocked and, if he was honest, ashamed of his ferocious desire for Lexi. No other woman had ever made him feel so out of control. He was a powerful Sultan, but she reminded him that he was also just a man with an inexplicable hunger clawing in his gut.

'My bodyguards owe you an apology. They should have respected your privacy and departed from the gym while you were exercising.'

Lexi shrugged. 'They offered to leave, but I don't have a problem with them being here. I was used to training alongside men when I was in the RAF.'

Kadir's jaw tightened. 'You must understand that we have different ways here than in England.'

Lexi knew that although Zenhab was one of the more liberal countries in the Middle East, there were rules regarding men and women socialising together. 'I understand that I wouldn't be allowed to mix with men in a public gym, but this is a private facility and surely the same rules don't apply? After all, the palace is your home, and you make the rules.'

'That's right,' Kadir said in a dangerously soft voice intended to warn Lexi that she was close to overstepping the mark, 'and my rule is that from now on you will be allocated separate times to use the gym when the men are not allowed in.'

Lexi could see that further arguing would be pointless. The Sultan had spoken. She glanced at the bodyguards, who were still kneeling, their heads bowed. Usually Kadir had an easy-going relationship with his protection officers and she did not understand why he was so annoyed. She did not want to lose her friendship with the two bodyguards. They were her only companions at the palace and if she was banned from spending time with them she knew she would feel even more isolated.

'Please don't blame Nasim and Ashar. It was my fault if any rules were broken.'

Her defence of the two men further fuelled Kadir's temper. He held the door open for Lexi to leave. 'I will deal with them as I see fit, before I deal with you.'

'*Deal* with me?' The vague threat was like a red rag to a bull. 'What are you going to do, send me to bed with no tea? Put me across your knee?'

'Would you like me to spank you?' Kadir murmured dulcetly. He had followed Lexi out into the corridor so that the bodyguards could not hear their conversation.

A shockingly erotic image of him holding her face down over his thighs while he chastised her flashed into her mind and fiery colour flooded her cheeks. 'Of course not,' she said sharply.

His husky chuckle warned her that he had read her

thoughts, and Lexi's embarrassment became more acute. But she wondered why he was clutching his towel in front of his hips as if his life depended on it. Her senses, acutely attuned to him, detected the undefinable essence of male pheromones, the scent of sexual arousal.

'Why does it matter to you if I hang out with Nasim and Ashar in my free time?' she burst out. 'There is no one else I can socialise with and I realise that it is not possible for me to go out in the city in the evenings on my own. I feel like I'm trapped at the palace.'

'You have been provided with excellent accommodation and leisure facilities; I did not realise you expected to have a full social calendar. The palace is hardly a prison,' Kadir said drily.

Lexi gave up trying to make him understand that she craved the company of other people. When she had served in the RAF she'd had a wide group of friends and had felt a sense of belonging that had been missing with her adoptive parents. Being alone gave her too much time to think, and stirred up her old feelings of loneliness and inadequacy she had felt as a child.

But Kadir knew nothing about her troubled background, and she had no intention of telling him. A dignified retreat seemed her best option but, as usual, she was determined to have the last word.

'Perhaps hard physical exertion in the gym will relieve some of your tension,' she murmured, before she turned and marched down the corridor, leaving Kadir fighting the temptation to go after her and kiss her sassy mouth into submission. There was only one kind of physical exertion that he knew was guaranteed to relieve his sexual frustration, but he could not make love to Lexi, no matter how much he wanted to.

* * *

Lexi had hoped that a punishing fifteen-kilometre run through the palace grounds would expend her anger with Kadir for criticising her friendship with his bodyguards. But when she returned to her apartment her temper was still simmering, and to cool down she dived into the pool and swam twenty lengths. Breathless at last, she hauled herself onto the poolside and shook her wet hair back from her face.

She stiffened when she saw Kadir was standing watching her. 'I assume you have no objection to me swimming in my private pool?' She hoped her cool tone disguised the heat that surged through her as she drank in the sight of him in cream chinos and a black polo shirt. His eyes were hidden behind designer shades and he was so outrageously attractive that Lexi almost jumped back into the pool to hide her body's reaction to him. Her nipples were as hard as pebbles and she hastily dragged the towel around her shoulders to hide her traitorous body from view.

He gave her a lazy smile, no hint now of his earlier bad mood. 'None at all,' he assured her, 'although I am wondering why you aren't wearing your silver bikini.'

She shrugged. 'A one-piece is more comfortable for swimming. But another reason is that I *do* appreciate the cultural differences in the Middle East. Although the pool is for my private use, the palace staff are around and out of respect for them I chose to wear a swimming costume. It's more demure than a bikini.'

Demure! Kadir wondered if Lexi had any idea how sexy she looked in her sleek navy costume, which clung to every dip and curve of her superbly toned figure. He could not forget the image of her taut buttocks covered in tight pink shorts pumping up and down when she had been doing push-ups in the gym. Fire heated his blood and he altered his position to hide the evidence of his arousal beneath his trousers, which suddenly felt uncomfortably tight.

'Anyway, there is no point in me wearing my bikini when I'm not allowed to socialise with anyone at the palace, or get a chance to meet a guy who I would like to untie the strings,' Lexi said defiantly.

Kadir's eyes narrowed. 'Always you challenge me, Lexi. You want to be careful that I do not rise to your bait.'

Her gaze did not waver from his. 'You have already demonstrated that that isn't going to happen. I made a fool of myself in Italy,' she said bitterly. She hated herself for the way she had responded to him like a gauche teenager on a first date. He was the only man who had ever made her lose control and the level of her desire had shocked and shamed her.

She suddenly became conscious of how close they were standing. The air between them throbbed with tension and every nerve ending on her body tingled with sexual awareness that she knew he felt too.

'I was the fool, for kissing you when I knew I was not free to make love to you,' Kadir said harshly. He picked up her robe and handed it to her. 'Put this on, before I forget my good intentions.' He gave a wry smile that did not reach his eyes, and Lexi had a sudden sense of how lonely his role as Sultan must be. His father was dead, his mother lived abroad and he was destined to marry a woman he had never met who had been chosen for him.

If he had not been contracted to his arranged marriage, she knew that they would be lovers by now. His desire for her smouldered in his dark eyes, but the firm set of his jaw told her that he would put his duty to his kingdom before his personal desires.

She pulled on the robe and tied the belt tightly around her waist. 'Why did you want to see me?'

Because he could not keep away from her, Kadir thought grimly. She was like a drug in his veins and even the knowledge that his desire for her was forbidden did not stop him thinking about her constantly.

'I came to apologise for my behaviour earlier. I appreciate that you might feel cut off from your friends and family. I have come with an invitation to tea from someone who I believe you could become friends with.'

Lexi eyed him suspiciously. 'Who?'

His grin made him look suddenly younger. 'I'm taking you to meet the most important woman in my life.'

'I'm seventy-six,' Mabel Dawkins told Lexi as she poured tea into bone china cups and nodded towards a plate of scones. 'Help yourselves. I always make scones when Kadir comes to tea. When he was a boy he could eat a plateful all to himself.'

Lexi settled back on the chintz sofa in Mabel's pretty apartment at the palace and bit into a feather-light fruit scone. 'So you were Kadir's nanny when he was growing up?'

'Lady Judith hired me when her son was born. After she left the palace and returned to England, Sultan Khalif asked me to remain here to give Kadir stability because it was a difficult situation for a young boy to grow up in two very different cultures, here in Zenhab and at Montgomery Manor in England.'

Lexi glanced at Kadir. 'It must have been strange to move between Western culture and Middle Eastern traditions. Do you think of yourself more as an English Earl or an Arab prince?'

'I love my mother and I was close to my grandfather, the tenth Earl. But I am my father's son, from an ancient line of desert kings, and my heart and soul belong to Zenhab,' he said without hesitation.

Recalling how, when they had arrived in Zenhab, Kadir had wielded a fearsome-looking sword and given a battle cry to rouse his horsemen, Lexi was learning that beneath his playboy image reported in the European press there was a far more serious side to the Sultan of Zenhab that the paparazzi never saw.

She was agonisingly conscious of him sitting next to her. The two-seater sofa was made even smaller because it was stuffed with Mabel's many crocheted cushions and, however stiffly Lexi held herself, she could not prevent her thigh from touching Kadir's. She could feel his hard muscles through her thin skirt, and the spicy tang of his cologne wove a seductive spell around her.

'What made you decide to join the RAF?' Mabel's voice dragged Lexi's mind away from her wayward thoughts.

She shrugged. 'I wanted an exciting career, the opportunity to travel.' She did not explain that one reason why she had joined the air force had been because she had been looking for somewhere where she felt she belonged. Her adoptive parents had not really wanted her, and she had been hurt that her birth mother had insisted on keeping her a secret from her husband, as if Cathy was ashamed of her.

'It must have been an exciting life, but dangerous too,' Mabel said. 'I expect your parents must have worried about you when you were stationed in Afghanistan.'

'I don't think so,' Lexi said wryly. 'My parents are busy with their own lives.'

'Kadir told me that you will be staying in Zenhab and working as his helicopter pilot for six months. That's a long time to be away from home, although I suppose when you were in the RAF you got used to living away from loved ones. Do you have a sweetheart back in England?'

Lexi was amused by the elderly nanny's curiosity. 'No, I don't.'

'I'm surprised. You're such a pretty girl. Are you gay?' Mabel asked bluntly.

Lexi choked on a mouthful of scone and hastily washed it down with a sip of tea. 'No, I'm not.' Realising that Mabel had no qualms about prying into her personal life, she murmured, 'Actually, I was engaged but it didn't work out.'

'Mabel, it's unfair to interrogate Lexi,' Kadir interrupted. He had felt the sudden tension that gripped her and forced himself to ignore his own curiosity about her love life. He recalled Charles Fairfax had mentioned that she had been engaged but her fiancé had ended the relationship. Was she still in love with the guy she had hoped to marry? he mused, wondering why he disliked the idea.

His phone rang and he glanced at the name of the caller. 'I'll have to take this, I'm afraid,' he said apologetically. 'Lexi, please stay and finish your tea. If you think Mabel's scones are good, wait until you try her sponge cake.'

'He works so hard,' Mabel sighed when Kadir had left. 'He told me that his latest trip to Europe was very successful and he managed to secure several big deals with companies who will invest in new businesses in Zenhab.'

Lexi remembered that Kadir's adviser, Yusuf bin Hilal, had said that the Sultan worked hard to attract foreign investment to his kingdom. 'The European press seem more interested in Kadir's private life and his reputation as a playboy.'

'Oh, the press!' Mabel gave a snort. 'Most of what is written in the foreign newspapers is rubbish. The paparazzi don't know the man that I know Kadir to be. He vowed as his father lay dying that he would devote his life to Zenhab and continue Sultan Khalif's work to maintain peace and bring prosperity to the kingdom.'

'Was Kadir close to his father?'

'Very. Father and son adored one another.' Mabel's lined face softened. 'Kadir was heartbroken when Khalif died but at the same time he was relieved that his father was spared any more suffering.'

Lexi felt strangely unsettled at the thought of Kadir being heartbroken. She had been too ready to believe the stories in the tabloids about him leading a charmed life of hedonistic pleasure, she acknowledged guiltily. But she was discovering that he was a man of deep emotions who had grieved for his father and vowed to rule Zenhab with the same devotion to duty as Sultan Khalif had done. 'Why did Sultan Khalif suffer? Was he ill before he died?' she asked curiously.

'He suffered a stroke when Kadir was sixteen, which left him completely paralysed and barely able to speak. Obviously, Khalif could not continue to rule the country,' Mabel explained, 'and Kadir was too young to become Sultan, so Khalif's younger brother, Jamal, became the interim ruler until Kadir came of age.'

'And Jamal handed the Sultanate to Kadir when he was twenty-one?'

'Unfortunately, it wasn't quite as simple as that. Jamal wanted to remain as Sultan, and he had followers who believed that he should rule Zenhab and who were opposed to Kadir's plans to modernise the country. Before Jamal would agree to step aside and allow Kadir to take his rightful place as Sultan, he insisted that Kadir sign a contract to marry the daughter of Jamal's great ally, Sheikh Rashid bin Al-Hassan. Since Rashid died two months ago, Kadir has been under pressure to go ahead with his wedding to Princess Haleema to unite the country.

'Jamal and his followers are against change and want Zenhab to return to feudal isolation as it was in the past,' Mabel said grimly. 'There have been plots to overthrow Kadir, and two years ago he survived an assassination attempt. A gun was fired by someone in a crowd, but fortunately the bullet narrowly missed him.'

The conversation turned to other matters, but later, as Lexi walked in the palace gardens, she could not forget Mabel's revelation that an attempt had been made on Kadir's life by his enemies. Far from being the playboy prince she had believed him to be, he was a dutiful Sultan who had dedicated his life to his kingdom.

The sun was sliding below the horizon, staining the sky flamingo-pink, and the fiery hues were reflected in the ornamental pools and many fountains in the formal gardens. Lexi strolled along an avenue of palm trees, but a familiar voice drew her from her thoughts, and her heart gave an annoying flip when she watched Kadir get up from a bench and walk towards her.

He had changed into a traditional white robe which skimmed his powerful body. As he came closer, Lexi could see the shadow of his black chest hairs beneath the fine cotton. He halted in front of her and smiled, revealing his perfect teeth, as white as his *keffiyeh* which framed his darkly tanned face.

'The gardens are so beautiful,' she said, looking around her because she dared not look at him, searching for something to say while she frantically tried to control her racing pulse.

'My father had them landscaped as a gift for my mother. She fell in love with the gardens at Versailles on their honeymoon and *Baba* wanted to re-create them at the palace. Unfortunately, the project took longer to complete than my parents' marriage lasted,' Kadir said drily.

He indicated a carving on the trunk of a palm tree, and Lexi saw the shape of a heart inscribed with the words *Judith will love Khalif for ever.* 'My mother made the carving. After she left, my father used to come and sit beneath this tree every day. He loved my mother until the day he died. When I look at the inscription I am reminded that people often do not mean what they say.'

'How true,' she said flatly, thinking of the many times people had let her down.

The emptiness in her voice stirred Kadir's curiosity. 'Why did your engagement end?'

For a moment Lexi did not answer. She rarely opened up about her private life. She did not understand the connection she felt with Kadir, but for some reason she felt drawn to confide in him.

'I met Steven when we were serving with the RAF in Afghanistan. Living in a war zone is a strange experience,' she explained ruefully. 'Your emotions are heightened by the constant threat of danger. When Steven proposed, I accepted because I longed for a settled life, a home and a family. We planned to marry as soon as we finished our tour of duty, but he had failed to mention that he had a girlfriend and a baby in England. He told me by text message on the evening that we were supposed to be holding our engagement party that he wasn't free to marry me.'

Beneath Lexi's tough exterior was a vulnerable woman who had been badly hurt, Kadir realised. He felt guilty that while they had been in Europe he had succumbed to the sexual chemistry between them and kissed her, knowing that he wasn't free to have any kind of relationship with her.

'Mabel reminded me that six months is a long time to be away from home,' he said abruptly. 'You are welcome to invite your friends and family to the palace. I thought you might like to ask your parents to visit.'

'They wouldn't want to come. But thanks for the offer.'

He was puzzled by her offhand response. 'It sounds as though you don't have a close relationship with your parents.'

Lexi shrugged. 'It's true that we're not close. I'm adopted. My parents believed they couldn't have a child but, after they adopted me, my mother fell pregnant and gave birth to a daughter, which rather made me redundant.'

Once again Kadir heard a note of hurt in her voice and he felt an unexpected tug on his heart. 'I'm sure your parents did not think that.'

'As a matter of fact I overheard Marcus tell another relative that he and Veronica—my adoptive mother— would not have adopted a child if they had known they could have a child of their own,' Lexi said flatly. 'From the age of eight I knew I was an inconvenience when my parents packed me off to boarding school so that they could concentrate on Athena.'

'I wondered why you and your sister do not look alike.

Did you resent Athena because your parents gave her more attention?'

Lexi thought of her awkward, accident-prone sister and gave a rueful smile. 'It would be impossible to resent Athena. She has the sweetest nature, and actually I think she has struggled to meet Marcus and Veronica's expectations.' She frowned as she recalled her misgivings about Athena's intention to marry Charles Fairfax.

While she and Kadir had been talking, day had turned into night as quickly as Lexi remembered from the desert in Afghanistan, and a sliver of silver moon was climbing the sky accompanied by the first stars. She wondered what he was thinking. His hard-boned face was impossible to read, but she seemed to be acutely sensitive to his emotions and sensed that his mood had darkened.

'Tomorrow I will require you to fly me across the desert to the old city of Sanqirah in the mountains,' he said tersely. 'The northern territories are much hotter and drier than here, where we are closer to the coast. You will probably be more comfortable wearing appropriate clothing rather than your pilot's uniform.'

Lexi's stomach plummeted as if she was riding a big dipper at the funfair. She knew that Princess Haleema lived in the mountains. And Mabel had said that Kadir's uncle Jamal had been pushing for him to honour his marriage agreement. Pride demanded that she kept her voice unemotional. 'What time do you want to leave?'

'Early, and we won't return until late.' Kadir's jaw tightened. Since he had received a phone call from Haleema's brother, Omar, to confirm their meeting tomorrow he had sensed that his freedom was ending.

He felt no joy at the prospect of taking a girl he had never met as his bride, but it was necessary to prevent his detractors and Jamal's supporters from challenging his rule and creating civil unrest in the kingdom. The time had come for him to honour his promise to his father. But the future seemed bleaker since he had been plucked from the sea by a woman who challenged him at every opportunity and made his blood run faster through his veins.

'Lexi...' Kadir watched her walk away from him and could not prevent himself from uttering her name in a low, driven tone.

She turned to him, her face serenely beautiful. Her long blonde hair seemed to shimmer in the moonlight. 'Yes.'

Her voice was not quite steady, and Kadir knew then that the night air, thick with the scents of jasmine and orange blossom, was bewitching her senses as it beguiled his. He saw wariness in her eyes as well as a hunger that she could not hide, and he knew he should walk away from her.

She had been hurt by her ex-fiancé and by her adoptive parents. He had no right to play with her emotions when he knew that it could only lead to him hurting her too. But she was so lovely. He had never wanted any woman as fiercely as he wanted her and he could not stop himself from walking towards her.

'Was there something else you wanted?' she asked innocently.

'Just...this...'

'No.' Lexi's soft cry was crushed by Kadir's mouth as he pulled her into his arms and claimed her lips. Her protest was carried away on the breeze that stirred the fronds of the palm trees. She had not expected him to kiss her and she had no time to muster any resistance, or so she tried to kid herself. But she was already lost to his magic, swept into his sensual spell as he swept her hard against him so that she was conscious of every muscle and sinew in his body, every beat of his heart.

His lips sipped from hers as he kissed her with a hunger that matched her own. Desire blazed white-hot, but underlying their passion was something indefinable, a connection between two souls as their two hearts thundered in unison.

Lexi gasped as Kadir skimmed his lips down her throat. The stubble on his jaw grazed her sensitive skin and the exquisite pleasure-pain sent a shudder through her. She arched her neck as he threaded his fingers into her hair and almost purred with pleasure when he cradled her head, angling her face so that he could plunder her mouth again and again until she felt boneless.

She could feel the solid ridge of his arousal pushing against her pelvis, and the evidence of his need excited her. But it was *wrong*. He had promised to marry another woman.

'No!' She tore her mouth from his, noting that he made no attempt to stop her. 'No more games,' she said quietly, proud that her voice was steady, even if her legs were not. Somehow she forced her feet to move, although it felt as if she had severed a limb when she stepped away from him. 'What do you want from me, Kadir?'

'Everything.'

The single word detonated between them as his harsh voice resonated with a depth of emotion that shocked Lexi. His eyes were black in the darkness. Kadir clenched his hands into fists to prevent himself from reaching for her. She could never be his and the knowledge felt like a knife blade through his heart. 'But I cannot take your beauty and your fire. And I can offer you nothing. I should not have brought you to Zenhab.'

The tortured expression on his face made Lexi's insides twist with a shared pain, and she suddenly knew that if she stayed in Zenhab they would destroy each other.

'Then let me go,' she whispered. 'This situation is unbearable for both of us. And it will be unfair on your young bride. Haleema may have led a sheltered life but she will notice the way we look at each other.' She swallowed. 'Steven made me an unwitting accomplice when he cheated on his girlfriend who was waiting for him in England. Our desire for one another is wrong, and the only way we can end it is for me to leave Zenhab and we will never see each other again.' The thought was agonising, but Lexi knew it would be even more painful to remain at the palace and watch Kadir marry his Princess.

Lexi was right. He had to let her go, Kadir acknowledged heavily. His duty to his kingdom and his promise to his father must come before his personal desires. 'I still need you to fly me to Haleema's home in the mountains tomorrow. My meeting with her brother, Sheikh Omar, is arranged and it will be seen as a great insult if I fail to attend. But after that I will release you from your contract…and you will be free to leave Zenhab,' he said harshly.

It was for the best, Lexi told herself. The madness had to end. Without a word, she turned and fled from Kadir, her chest aching with the leaden weight of her heart. As she ran through the dark gardens she did not notice one of the palace staff watching her from the shadows.

CHAPTER EIGHT

THE SULTAN WAS dressed in his robes of state, although he was not carrying a sword or a ceremonial knife in his belt, Lexi noted. The embroidered jacket he wore over his white robe was encrusted with dark red rubies which reminded her of droplets of blood.

She gave herself a mental shake, impatient with her fanciful imagination. But she could not tear her gaze from Kadir as he walked across the palace courtyard to the helipad, and she was conscious of his gaze skimming over her desert boots, khaki combats and vest top. She had tied her hair into a ponytail and the peak of her baseball cap cast a shadow over her face which she hoped disguised the dark circles beneath her eyes, evidence of her sleepless night.

'You said I didn't need to wear my pilot's uniform,' she reminded him, taking his silence as censure.

'You should bring a jacket. The temperature in the mountains can drop twenty degrees once the sun sets in the evening.'

Silence stretched between them, tightening Lexi's nerves. She could still taste him on her lips from when he had kissed her the previous night. 'Is it safe for you to go to the mountains?' she burst out. 'Mabel said that the

northern tribes are your enemies and there has already
been one attempt made on your life.'

His brows rose 'Why, Lexi, would you care if someone took a pot shot at me?' he drawled.

In her mind, she was back in Helmand province in
Afghanistan, watching her co-pilot Sam jump out of the
helicopter and run to the aid of an injured soldier. The
sniper's bullet seemed to come from nowhere. One second Sam was running, the next he was lying lifeless on
the desert sand. Death had been delivered in the blink
of an eye. Lexi would always remember Sam's cheerful
grin and zest for life.

She stared at the blood-red rubies spattered over Kadir's jacket and pictured a faceless figure in a crowd,
aiming a gun and pulling the trigger. 'Of course I'd care,
damn you,' she said thickly.

'Lexi.' Kadir swore beneath his breath.

She turned away from him, afraid he would see the
raw emotions he evoked in her. 'Why do you have a different bodyguard?' She glanced at the man sitting in the
front passenger seat of the helicopter. 'Where are Nasim
and Ashar?'

'Ashar is away visiting his family. Nasim called in
sick this morning.'

Lexi frowned. 'What's wrong with him? He seemed
fine in the gym yesterday.'

Kadir closed his eyes and tried to dismiss the vision
of Lexi's bottom in tight pink shorts moving up and
down as she performed push-ups in a competition with
his bodyguard. 'Your concern for Nasim is touching,'
he said curtly. 'But no doubt you will strike up a friendship with Fariq.'

'I'm not so sure.' Lexi couldn't explain why she had

not warmed to the replacement bodyguard, or why her
nerves felt on edge. She looked around the empty courtyard. 'Where are Yusuf and your other advisers who usually accompany you?'

'I am going to the mountains alone, and I am not carrying my ceremonial weapons to show my host, Sheikh
Omar, that I come in peace.' By the end of today he would
be officially engaged to Haleema and Zenhab would be
looking forward to a royal wedding, Kadir thought with
grim resignation.

Lexi held open the door of the helicopter and was
gripped by an inexplicable sense of dread. 'I've got a bad
feeling about this trip.' She shrugged helplessly. 'I wish
we weren't going today.'

For a split second, emotion flickered in Kadir's dark
gaze, a look almost of pain, before his thick lashes swept
down like curtains hiding the windows to his soul.

'I have to go,' he said harshly. 'This is my destiny.'
He glanced at the gold watch on his wrist. 'It's time we
were on our way.'

The AgustaWestland was a dream to fly, and once
Lexi had taken off she turned the helicopter towards the
desert and prepared to enjoy the spectacular view. Beside her, the new bodyguard seemed restless and ill at
ease and although the cabin was air-conditioned he was
sweating profusely.

Lexi glanced at him. 'Are you nervous about flying,
Fariq?' she asked him, speaking into her headset.

'No. *I'm* not afraid, but you should be.'

Puzzled, she turned her head to look at him and her
heart catapulted against her ribs when she saw a gleam
of grey metal and recognised the barrel of a pistol partly
concealed in the bodyguard's jacket. 'Don't make a fuss,'

Fariq said softly. 'Fly the helicopter to these new coordinates.'

Lexi glanced at the piece of paper he placed on her knee. On the video screen she could see Kadir in the rear of the helicopter, putting on his headphones, and she guessed he was unaware of the situation. Her eyes jerked to the pistol that Fariq was aiming at her ribs. Her mouth felt dry, but her military training kicked in and she suppressed her fear by forcing herself to think logically and remain calm.

Moments later, Kadir's voice came though her headphones. 'Why are you heading towards the coast? You're flying in the wrong direction.'

The bodyguard turned around and pointed the gun at Kadir. 'There has been a change of plan, Your Highness. Hand over your cellphones, both of you.'

Kadir froze, and his first thought was that he should have questioned, as Lexi had, the fact that Nasim had unexpectedly been taken ill. Clearly, someone had wanted his protection officer out of the way and he prayed that Nasim had not been killed.

'Whatever it is you want, there is no reason for you to involve my pilot.' He spoke calmly to Fariq. 'Let Lexi land the helicopter. You can keep me as a hostage, or kill me if that is your plan. But let her go.'

'*No!*' Lexi felt a rush of emotion at Kadir's attempt to protect her. 'You can't kill the Sultan,' she told the gunman. 'You'll never get away with it. If you allow him to go free, I'll fly you to wherever you want to go and no one will know about this incident.'

Fariq laughed. 'Your determination to protect each other is touching,' he sneered. He stared at Kadir. 'The rumour that the western woman is your mistress is obviously correct. Nobody will get killed as long as you do as I tell you. Continue flying to the coordinates I gave you,' the gunman ordered Lexi, 'and don't try anything clever because I swear I will pull the trigger and we'll all go down.'

She could tell he meant what he said, and she could also tell he was nervous, which made him volatile and likely to panic. There was nothing Lexi could do but fly to the new destination. After fifteen minutes, during which time the mounting tension seemed to suck the air out of the cabin, they flew over the coast.

The sea was sapphire-blue and sparkled in the early morning sunshine. Did the world seem more beautiful because she had a gun aimed at her? Lexi wondered. She was conscious of her heart beating hard and fast in her chest as adrenalin pumped through her veins. On the video screen she could see Kadir sitting behind her. What if the gunman did actually intend to kill him?

Fear stole her breath. *She could not bear to lose him!* She couldn't bear to kneel by his lifeless body as she had knelt beside her best friend, Sam, desperately searching for a pulse but knowing it was too late.

Kadir is not yours to lose, whispered a voice in her head. And in a heartbeat she discovered that she wished he was.

Below them, a small island came into view, white sand and green palm trees rising up out of the sapphire sea. 'Land the chopper down there on the beach,' the gun-man instructed.

Would they be ambushed by more gunmen once they were on the ground? Supremely conscious of the pistol barrel inches away from her, Lexi took the helicopter down and landed it on the beach.

'Now get out, both of you, and put your hands above your heads.'

Lexi jumped down onto the sand and raised her arms, and seconds later she was joined by Kadir. The gunman seemed to be working alone. She scanned the line of trees at the top of the beach and saw no sign of anyone else.

'I reckon we could take him,' she muttered to Kadir. 'We're two against one.'

'But the one has a gun,' he hissed back. 'Don't be stupid.'

His words had the desired effect, Kadir noted with relief as Lexi's eyes flashed him a furious look. She was as courageous as a tigress, but no way would he allow her to risk her life. He was confused by their location. Nothing made sense, and the situation became even more bizarre when the gunman locked the helicopter and pocketed the key.

Fariq ran down the beach, and it was then that Lexi noticed a motorboat half hidden behind some rocks. She watched Fariq push the boat into the sea before he leapt aboard and started the engine.

'He's leaving us here!' Her brain finally clicked into gear. Events had happened so quickly, but now Lexi stared at the boat as it sped away. *'Hey...'*

She spun round to Kadir. 'Terrific, we're stranded. From the air, the island looked uninhabited. But why would the gunman leave us here? Surely when you fail to arrive for your meeting with Haleema's brother, an alert will be raised that you are missing and people will search for you? What can anyone hope to gain by kidnapping us and dumping us on a deserted island?'

Kadir racked his brain for an explanation. Someone did not want him to meet Omar bin Al-Hassan to discuss his marriage to Princess Haleema, but who, and why? The only reason he could think of was that the person behind the kidnap plot did not want him to make peace with the leader of the northern tribes. Someone wanted to stir up trouble in Zenhab, and the most obvious suspect was his uncle. He dragged his mind from his confused thoughts as Lexi started to stride along the beach. 'Where are you going?'

She glanced over her shoulder. 'To find somewhere for us to shelter; it's the first thing I learned to do in RAF survival training. From the air I saw some cliffs on the other side of the island, and there might be a cave. We'll also need to find food, and collect firewood.'

Kadir hid his irritation that his pilot was too bossy for her own good and sat down on a rock. 'It sounds exhausting,' he drawled.

Lexi put her hands on her hips, her slender body practically quivering with impatience. 'Are you just going to sit there? You might be a Sultan, but if you think I'm going to wait on you like your staff at the palace do, think again.'

She marched away from him, her temper fizzing. But she recognised that her anger was a release of her pent-up emotions. She felt sick with relief that the gunman had not hurt them. Fear had churned in her stomach when the gun had been pointed at her, and she'd been terrified when the gunman had aimed at Kadir. Now, for some reason, she felt stupidly tearful and she was fighting a strong urge to run back to Kadir and throw herself into his arms.

The island was bigger than it had looked from the air and it took Lexi almost two hours to follow the coastline round to the other side, where she found a few low cliffs and no caves. She continued walking for another hour before completing a circuit of the island and finally ended up back at the helicopter. There was no sign of Kadir and, after dumping the driftwood she had collected to make a fire, she walked up the beach and into the shade of the palm trees. The ground was littered with branches and palm fronds that could be used to construct a shelter, she decided.

Pushing through the trees, she found herself at the edge of a desert plain. Beyond a line of dunes she could see more palm trees and the glint of water—an oasis, and next to it…a tent!

What on earth? Ignoring the fact that she was hot and tired from hours of walking in the burning sun, Lexi scrambled over the dunes, her progress hampered by her feet sinking into the soft sand. She was breathless when she arrived at the huge tent and stared in disbelief at Kadir lying on a hammock strung between two palm trees.

'Where *are* we?' She was beginning to feel as if she had fallen into the pages of *Alice in Wonderland.*

Kadir propped himself up on one elbow and regarded her lazily. He had changed out of his royal robes into a pair of frayed denim shorts that sat low on his hips and displayed his muscle-packed abdomen. Beneath the glare of the desert sun, his bare chest was the colour of burnished bronze overlaid with whorls of silky black hairs.

Lexi licked her parched lips, conscious that her pounding heart was not the result of walking over the dunes.

'We're on Jinan, which means beautiful garden,' he told her. 'It is a private island belonging to me personally, rather than to the Sultanate of Zenhab.'

'Why did the kidnapper bring us to your private island?' Lexi frowned as the meaning of his words became clear. 'You must have known where we were when I landed the helicopter. Why did you let me traipse around the island looking for a place to shelter when you knew that this—' she waved towards the tent '—was here?'

He shrugged and his powerful shoulder muscles rippled beneath his satiny skin. 'You were determined to demonstrate your survival techniques and it seemed a shame to spoil your fun.'

In truth, Kadir had felt relieved when she'd stormed off along the beach. He had needed some time alone to control his emotions in the aftermath of seeing a gun being aimed at Lexi. When her life had been threatened on the helicopter he had been consumed with rage, but his desperation to protect her had been tempered by the bitter realisation that the kidnapper was quite literally calling the shots.

Lexi glared at him, her temper flaring as quickly as tinder set alight with a match. 'Bastard!' Her blue eyes blazed as she walked towards him and Kadir tensed as he watched her pull a penknife from the pocket of her combats. Without uttering another word, she sliced through the rope which tied one end of the hammock to the tree trunk and watched him land in an ignominious heap on the sand before she strode into the tent.

It was the size of a marquee, Lexi realised as she looked around the interior of the tent. Camping on Dartmoor on military exercises with the RAF had *never* been like this! She pulled off her boots and walked barefoot across the richly patterned rugs covering the floor. In place of chairs and sofas there was a raised platform covered with brightly coloured fabric and sumptuous silk cushions. Drawing aside a curtain, she discovered a bedroom with a huge, low bed draped with satin sheets in vibrant jewel shades. Behind a partition was a bathroom with a walk-in shower and at the far end of the tent was a kitchen area complete with a working fridge.

'Solar panels provide electricity, and the oasis is a source of fresh water,' Kadir explained as he followed her into the kitchen and opened the fridge to take out a bottle of drink. 'I keep a satellite phone here, but the kidnappers have taken it so we can't call for help,' he said in answer to Lexi's questioning look.

He watched her gnaw her bottom lip with her teeth and the giveaway sign of her vulnerability touched him more than it had any right to. 'I don't believe that whoever is behind the kidnap plot intends to harm us, because they would have done so by now. For some reason, someone wants me out of the way for a while.' He frowned. 'I have an idea who is behind this.' Jamal's weasel features came into his mind. 'But at the moment I don't understand why.'

'What if we are left stranded here for weeks?'

'That won't happen. My staff come to the island regularly to check on the place, and there is always a supply of non-perishable food here, certainly enough to last us for a few days before we have to go hunting for our meals.'

The amusement in his voice was the last straw. 'I can't believe I was actually worried that the kidnapper might hurt you,' Lexi snapped. 'I walked around the island for three goddamned *hours* while you were lazing here in luxury.' As she spoke, she swept her arms around the tent. 'I could *kill* you!'

Her hand collided with the glass Kadir held out to her, showering him in pomegranate juice. 'Oh, I'm sorry.' She stared at the rivers of red liquid running down his face and chest. The dark red juice looked like blood.

If the kidnapper had fired the gun at Kadir... The thought made her feel ill. 'I...I didn't mean that.' Her voice shook. She tried to firm her trembling mouth, but her lips wouldn't stop wobbling. 'I was scared on the helicopter,' she admitted.

'You, scared?' Kadir's voice sounded strained. 'Never. You are the bravest, craziest woman I've ever met.'

Suddenly Lexi did not care if she was revealing too much of herself. 'I was scared the kidnapper would kill you.'

'I would have ripped the gunman apart with my bare hands if he had tried to harm you,' Kadir said roughly. The shimmer of tears in her eyes tore him apart. His self-control exploded and he muttered a savage imprecation as he hauled her into his arms, crushing the air from her lungs as he lifted her and held her so tightly to him that Lexi felt the urgent thud of his heart beating in time with her own.

The threat of death had brought home to Lexi the immeasurable value of life. She had been running from the truth and trying to hide her feelings for Kadir, but she could not run or hide any longer.

She felt detached from reality, cast adrift in a world where only the two of them existed. The feel of his warm skin beneath her hands heated her blood, and the feral hunger glittering in his eyes evoked an ache in the pit of her stomach. She curled her arms around his neck and buried her fingers in his silky dark hair as he lowered his head and captured her mouth, kissing her urgently as if he was slaking his thirst after being stranded in the desert without water for many days.

His lips tasted of pomegranate juice, and the sticky juice running down his chest transferred to her. But Lexi did not care; all she cared about was that he should not stop the sensual sorcery he was creating with his tongue inside her mouth. She was only vaguely aware of him striding across the tent into the bathroom, and she gasped as he turned on the shower and stepped beneath the spray with her in his arms.

'I've still got my clothes on,' she muttered against his lips.

'Not for much longer,' he promised.

He let her slide down him so that she was standing on her feet, and whipped her vest top over her head. 'No bra,' he growled in satisfaction, cupping her firm breasts that he had bared.

'It's too hot to wear one.' She caught her breath as he rolled her nipples between his fingers until they hardened to turgid points and starbursts of sensation arrowed from her breasts to the pit of her stomach. His tanned hands splayed over her creamy pale breasts, caressing their rounded shape before he lowered his head and closed his lips around one nipple, suckling her strongly until she gave a moan of pleasure. He judged the exact moment when she could withstand no more of the exquisite caress, and moved to her other nipple, lashing the taut peak with his tongue, back and forth, tormenting her so that she gripped his hair and held his head to her breast in a silent plea for him to ravish her eager flesh.

'You are so damned beautiful, you're driving me crazy,' Kadir said harshly. 'When I thought the kidnapper might kill me, all I could think was that I was going to die without ever knowing the sensual promise of your body.'

In those seconds when he had faced his mortality the only person in his mind had been Lexi, and she consumed his thoughts now, making Kadir forget his responsibilities as Sultan, his duty to his kingdom and the promise he had made to his father. Time had halted, the universe had stopped spinning, and nothing mattered but the woman who had haunted his thoughts and dreams since he had met her.

His hands shook as he fumbled with the zip of Lexi's combats and pushed them over her hips. While she was stepping out of her trousers he hooked his fingers in the waistband of her briefs and dragged them down her thighs, his impatient fingers skimming over the neat triangle of blonde hair to part her and probe her silken heat.

'You want me.' His dark eyes gleamed with triumph, but Lexi could not deny her need when the wetness of her arousal betrayed her. Kadir gave a soft laugh as he slid one finger deep inside her, stretched her a little and inserted a second finger, swirling them in an erotic dance that drew a husky moan from her.

He handed her a bar of soap and Lexi smoothed it over his chest to wash away the sticky pomegranate juice. Now it was her turn to feel triumphant as she dragged her knuckles down his stomach and felt his body shudder. With deft fingers she opened the fly of his shorts and tugged the wet denim down his thighs before repeating the action with his black silk boxers. The size of his erection caused her a moment's panic. He was beautiful, and *huge*, and her insides turned to liquid as she imagined taking him inside her.

Kadir gritted his teeth as Lexi stroked her fingers lightly up and down his shaft, teasing him with butterfly caresses that increased the blood flow to his swollen tip. In retribution he circled his thumb pad over the tight bud of her clitoris and simultaneously circled his tongue around a dusky pink nipple.

The effect was electric; she trembled and gave a keening cry which he caught in his mouth as he lifted her up and claimed her lips in a slow, sweet kiss that made his gut ache. Her unguarded response stirred his soul. Something about this strong woman coming apart so utterly in his arms humbled him and at the same time he felt like a king who had captured a thousand kingdoms.

She wrapped her legs around his waist as he carried her out of the shower. The drumbeat of desire pounded harder in his veins. 'I can't wait,' he groaned, feeling the storm inside him building to a crescendo.

Lexi smiled against his mouth. Nothing mattered but that they were alive and she wanted to celebrate life in the most fundamental way, by making love with the man who had captured her heart. 'I can't wait either,' she whispered. She could feel his arousal nudging her belly and she wanted him inside her now, *now...*

Kadir stood her on her feet and turned her around so that her back was against his chest. There was a chair in the bathroom. He placed it in front of her and gently pushed her forward so that her body formed an arch over the wooden backrest and her hands rested on the seat. She was still wearing her baseball cap, and he pulled it from her head so that her long blonde hair cascaded around her shoulders like a river of silk.

'Hold on,' he murmured and felt a quiver run through her as he smoothed his hands over her perfect peachy bottom. The memory of her doing push-ups in a pair of tight satin shorts shattered the last vestige of his restraint and with a harsh groan he eased her buttocks apart and thrust deep into her moist heat, where his fingers had aroused her moments earlier.

Sweet heaven... Lexi could not hold back a cry of pleasure as Kadir entered her. Nothing had prepared her for the incredible eroticism of stretching forwards over the chair while he stood behind her and drove his powerful erection into the heat of her femininity. Nor had she been prepared for the intensity of emotions she felt as their bodies joined and became one.

He leaned forward and kissed the tip of her ear. She turned her head and sought his mouth and he kissed her with passion and a heart-shaking tenderness that answered a deeper need inside her.

He began to move, slowly at first to allow her to accommodate his size. Lexi gripped the edge of the chair as he increased his rhythm, each measured stroke building her excitement and her anticipation that the best was yet to come.

She spread her legs wider, encouraging him to drive deeper and harder. He wrapped his arms around her waist, cocooning her with his big body, and drew gasps of delight from her when he played with her nipples, heightening her sensual pleasure until she trembled and shivered with each new sensation created by his skilful mastery.

It couldn't last. The fire of their mutual passion swiftly became a furnace that blazed out of control. Lexi was vaguely aware of panting breaths and realised it was the sound of her breath being torn from her lungs as she strove to reach the pinnacle. Kadir held her there for breathless seconds, making her wait for the rapture of release. And then he thrust into her the hardest yet and sent them both tumbling over the edge into ecstasy. She cried his name and he soothed her with soft words in Arabic, his voice deep as an ocean as emotions he had not expected to feel, knew he should not feel, rolled over him.

As Kadir withdrew from her, Lexi's legs gave way and he swept her up in his arms and carried her into the bedroom. The satin sheets felt cool against her burning skin as he laid her on the bed. She stared up at him and held her hand to his cheek, traced the shape of his beautiful mouth with her fingertips. His smile stole her breath and the sultry gleam in his eyes warned her that he had by no means finished.

'Already?' She could not hide her shock as he knelt above her and pushed her legs apart. 'You're insatiable.'

'Insatiable for you,' he whispered against her lips before he kissed her deeply and made love to her again with such exquisite care that Lexi felt a sense of belonging she had been searching for her whole life.

CHAPTER NINE

SOMETHING WAS BRUSHING softly across her face. Lexi opened her eyes and discovered the mosquito net draped around the bed was fluttering in the breeze wafting into the tent. She was alone in the semi-dark. The luminous dial on her watch revealed that it was early evening, which meant that she had slept all afternoon. It was not surprising after her energetic sex session with Kadir, she thought. Her face warmed as she recalled how he had made love to her bent over the chair in the bathroom, and twice again in a variety of erotic positions on the bed.

Where was he? Fear gripped her as she wondered if the kidnapper had returned and taken Kadir away at gunpoint. *Perhaps the gunman had killed him?* Heart hammering, she slid off the satin sheets. There was a shirt draped over the arm of the chair; she assumed it belonged to Kadir and slipped it on before she stepped cautiously out of the bedroom, wishing she had a weapon to defend herself with if the kidnapper had indeed returned.

She walked noiselessly into the living area and found it empty. The tent flap had been tied back and through the opening she saw Kadir standing next to the oasis, staring up at the sky that was rapidly darkening as the sun completely disappeared. The heavens were filling with silver stars, like pins on a velvet pincushion. The wondrous beauty of the cosmos was displayed in breathtaking magnificence and, standing in the vast desert beneath the vast sky, Lexi thought how insignificant the human race was.

'My father loved to watch the stars.' Kadir turned as Lexi approached, sensing her presence although she made no sound. 'Many nights when I was a boy we sat outside the tent and *Baba* taught me the constellations.'

'You came to Jinan with him?'

'Yes, it was a special place for both of us, away from the palace and the many duties of a Sultan. Here we were simply father and son, and we used to go fishing and cook what we caught. My father taught me to enjoy the simple things in life.'

'Everyone I've spoken to says that Sultan Khalif was a great ruler of Zenhab,' Lexi said softly.

'He was the salvation of the kingdom.' Kadir's voice was fierce with pride. 'Before my father became Sultan, Zenhab was riven by civil war. He worked hard to establish peace and he gave hope for the future, but only if the population were willing to embrace change and welcome ideologies from the outside world.' His jaw clenched. 'There are still some people in Zenhab who want to return to the old ways.' Always he came back to the thorn in his side—Jamal—he brooded.

'You loved your father.' Lexi's voice pulled Kadir from his dark thoughts about his uncle. 'It's sad that he died when you were a young man and you did not have more time with him.' She felt a tug on her heart, remembering how Kadir's old nanny, Mabel, had said his heart had been broken by Sultan Khalif's death. 'At least you had a loving father while you were growing up. Mabel said the Sultan adored you.'

Kadir heard the wistful note in her voice and pictured her as a little girl whose adoptive parents had sent her away to boarding school so that they could concentrate on their own daughter.

'How old were you when you were adopted?'

'Four.'

He frowned. 'So, did you spend the first years of your life with your real parents?'

'No, I was placed into social services' care soon after I was born. Apparently I was fostered by a couple who planned to adopt me, but some time during the adoption process they changed their mind and I went back into care until the Howards adopted me two years later. I was too young to remember any of those experiences, of course.'

As an adult, Lexi had read various articles about attachment issues which could affect adopted children and the psychological problems resulting from negative early life experiences which could last into adulthood. The first failed adoption, followed by her failure to bond with the Howards was likely to be the reason why she was fiercely independent, yet deep down she wished she'd had a close, loving relationship like Kadir had enjoyed with his father. She'd been accused of pushing people away. It was true that she was wary of allowing anyone too close, she acknowledged. And when she *had* lowered her barriers with Steven, he had betrayed her trust.

Caught up in her thoughts, Lexi had only been partly aware that Kadir had led her back inside the tent. 'I thought you must be hungry,' he said, indicating the trays of food set out on the raised platform. He dropped down onto the piles of cushions and indicated that she should do the same. 'It's only crackers and dried fruits, I'm afraid.'

Lexi scanned the picnic and realised she was starving. 'It looks wonderful,' she assured him, biting into a plump dried fig. 'It reminds me of the midnight feasts we used to have at boarding school, only we had to eat in the dark because if we were caught by the housemistress it meant a week of detentions.'

Kadir thought of his own generally happy years at Eton College. The only downside had been that he had hated being separated from his father. 'What did you think of boarding school?'

'It was hard at first, but I got used to sleeping in a dormitory and only going home for the school holidays. In many ways it toughened me up.'

'Did you need to toughen up? You were eight years old,' he said softly. With her pale blonde hair falling around her beautiful face she looked fragile and ethereal, but he knew she had a backbone of steel.

She shrugged. 'It helped. After a while I stopped caring that my adoptive parents didn't love me.'

'What about your biological parents? Have you ever tried to trace them?'

'No,' she said abruptly. She did not want to tell him that her birth mother had been a prostitute when she had conceived Lexi.

She wondered how the Sultan of Zenhab would react if she told him he had spent the afternoon having sex with the daughter of a whore. Keen to turn the subject away from her private life, Lexi focused on the meal he had prepared.

'This is *baklava*, isn't it?' she said, picking up a little pastry. 'Layers of dough stuffed with pistachio nuts and honey. I tried them once before when I was serving in the Middle East and I remember they were delicious.'

'They're even better if you dip them in honey,' Kadir told her, pushing a bowl of thick golden liquid towards her.

She dipped the pastry into the honey and popped it into her mouth. A rapturous expression crossed her face. 'Mmm, I admit I have a weakness for sweet things.'

Kadir watched the tip of her pink tongue dart out to capture a crumb of pastry. She reminded him of a contented kitten, and her sensual enjoyment of the cake aroused a barbaric need in him to push her back against the cushions and thrust his throbbing erection deep inside her welcoming heat. He knew she would be ready for him. Her blue eyes—no longer chips of ice, but smoky-soft—had been issuing an invitation since she had stood beside him at the oasis.

'You've got honey on your chin,' he murmured as he lowered his head towards her. 'And as there are no napkins I'll have to lick it off you.'

Her impish smile tugged on something deep inside him. For a few seconds he glimpsed the child who had grown too serious too soon.

'I would be grateful if you would,' she murmured, as demure as a Victorian maiden. But Kadir had a vivid memory of earlier, when she had pushed him down on the bed and positioned herself above him, deliberately tormenting him as she had slowly, oh-so slowly, lowered herself onto his erect shaft before riding him hard and fast.

His breath hissed between his teeth as he struggled to control his hunger. His hand was already untying the belt of his silk robe, revealing his swollen manhood, and her little gasp when she saw how aroused he was drove him beyond rational thought.

It was impossible to rationalise anything that had happened since they had flown away from the palace that morning, Kadir brooded. Those moments on the helicopter when he had looked at death down the barrel of a gun had evoked a feeling of urgency to reaffirm life. He was aware that this was one stolen night. For a few hours, the past and the future did not exist and there was only now, with this woman. He could not fight his need for Lexi.

He brushed his lips over hers and his heart kicked when he felt her instant response. 'You taste sweet,' he growled, sliding his tongue into her mouth to explore her with mind-blowing eroticism that left them both shaking.

Lexi tasted salt on his skin when she kissed his throat. In the glow from the oil lamp his broad shoulders gleamed like polished gold, and his dark chest hairs felt abrasive against her palms as she ran her hands down his body, over his flat stomach and lower to clasp the rigid length of his erection.

His hands were no less busy opening the buttons down the front of her shirt and sliding the material from her shoulders so that she was naked beneath his glittering gaze. She made a startled protest when he dipped his fingers into the bowl of honey and trickled the sticky syrup over her breasts. He laughed at her surprise before closing his lips around one honey-coated nipple and suckling her until she sobbed his name.

'Sticky and sweet,' he murmured, transferring his mouth to her other honey-anointed breast and curling his tongue around its taut peak. 'From now on I will always be addicted to the taste of honey.'

It was sensuality taken to another level and before long Lexi was squirming and arching her hips in mute supplication for him to assuage the ache between her legs.

'Patience, *habibi*,' he teased. 'Let me discover if you taste sweet here, too.'

She shivered with anticipation as he hooked her legs over his shoulders and slid his hands beneath her bottom, lifting her as he lowered his head and pressed his mouth against her to taste her molten heat with his tongue.

The intimate caress felt unbelievably good. Lexi was lost from the first lick of Kadir's tongue up and down her moist opening, as he delicately but determinedly probed and delved and finally thrust into her feminine heat. Her body arched like a bow under intolerable tension, quivering as the pleasure inside her built. She curled her fingers into the satin cushions beneath her as he curled his tongue around her clitoris and created a storm of sensations that were too exquisite for her to withstand.

She exploded in a frantic orgasm, her hips jerking towards his wicked mouth, her breath forced from her lungs so that her gasps of pleasure filled the tent. It was impossible that anything could be better than what he had just done to her, but then he lifted his head and stood between her spread thighs to drive his powerful erection deep inside her, and Lexi began the delicious journey to nirvana all over again.

Lexi turned her head on the pillow and studied Kadir while he slept. The chiselled angles of his face looked softer, and his thick black lashes made crescents on his cheeks. Last night he had called her *habibi*, which she knew was an Arabic term of endearment, and when he had made love to her she had sensed tenderness as well as passion in his caresses. Had they simply had sex, she mused, or was it possible that he cared for her a little?

Dear heaven! What had they done?

She jolted fully awake, and the dreamy smile on her lips disappeared. Last night had been no dream. Of course he could not care for her. She and Kadir had had sex, but their passion was forbidden and they should not have become lovers. She glanced around the tent, filled with warm golden sunlight, and a chill spread through her body as cold reality hit her.

She had been flying Kadir to meet his fiancée when they had been kidnapped and stranded on the island. It was true that Kadir's arranged marriage was no love match. He had never even met Haleema. But he was contracted to marry the Princess, and they should not have allowed themselves to be swept away by passion, Lexi thought bleakly.

Her heart was beating so hard that she was sure she could hear it. She frowned when she realised that the sound came from a long way off and she recognised the low throb of a motorboat's engine. *Perhaps the kidnapper had returned to the island.* Their lives could once again be in danger.

'Kadir.'

His lashes lifted, and his smooth chocolate eyes regarded her slumberously. 'I thought I was dreaming.' He cupped her breasts in his hands and gave her a sinful smile. 'But these feel real.'

Fear made Lexi momentarily forget her feelings of guilt. 'I can hear a boat engine,' she said urgently.

He dropped his hands from her body and leapt out of bed, frowning as he heard a faint thrumming sound. 'Stay here,' he ordered, dragging on his shorts. 'Find somewhere safe to hide while I go and see what's happening.'

'You must be joking!' It took seconds to pull on her combats, but longer to wriggle her feet into her boots and tie the laces. 'Wait for me!' She cursed as he strode out of the tent, but common sense warned her not to run across the desert in bare feet and risk being bitten by a highly venomous death stalker scorpion.

Adrenalin pumped through Kadir as he hid behind a palm tree and watched a motorboat land on the beach. No doubt the kidnapper was still armed with a gun. He glanced around for something he could use to defend himself with. A tree branch would not be much use against a pistol, he thought ruefully, but he had the element of surprise combined with an implacable determination to protect Lexi from the gunman.

Shielding his eyes against the bright sun, Kadir frowned as he recognised the man. 'Nasim!'

'Sir!' The bodyguard tore up the beach and dropped down onto one knee before his Sultan. 'Your Highness, I feared Jamal might have had you killed.'

'I guessed my uncle was behind this,' Kadir said grimly. 'Do you know what he is up to?'

'He intends to depose you and make himself Sultan, and he has a few followers, including Fariq, working for him. I was held at gunpoint but I managed to escape. I overheard that Jamal planned for you and Miss Howard to be kidnapped and brought to the island. Your uncle has gone to the mountains to inform Sheikh Omar that, instead of attending the meeting to discuss your marriage to Princess Haleema, you chose to come to Jinan with your mistress.

'Jamal has spies at the palace, and one of them reported that he had seen you kissing Lexi,' Nasim explained when Kadir frowned. 'Jamal hopes that Sheikh Omar will believe that you have snubbed his sister, and he will incite the mountain tribes to join forces with your uncle to overthrow you.'

Kadir's jaw clenched. 'I must act quickly. It is time I dealt with my uncle once and for all.' He looked round to see Lexi running across the sand. After giving instructions to his bodyguard, he walked up the beach towards her.

'What is Nasim doing here? He's not working for the kidnapper, is he?' she demanded.

'He came to rescue us. As I suspected, my uncle is behind the kidnap plot.' Kadir threw her the helicopter keys. 'I need you to take me to the mountains to visit Haleema, and there is no time to lose. Wait here while I go and shut up the tent.'

Lexi stared after him as he strode up the beach and bit her lip. She did not know what she had expected from him, but his absolute indifference to the fact that they had spent the night together made her feel used and humiliated. His urgency to visit Haleema emphasised how unimportant she was to him, Lexi thought bitterly, just as she had been unimportant to her adoptive parents.

What the hell had he done?

As Kadir ploughed over the soft sand dunes, the sated ache in his groin was a mocking reminder of exactly what he had done to Lexi last night, and what she had done to him. She had made him forget *everything* except the thunder in his blood, his urgent, uncontrollable need to make love to her. But he could not blame Lexi for the fact that he had broken his promise to himself. And, despite the fact that he had just enjoyed the most amazing night of his life with her, he could not break the promise he had made to his father.

He heard Sultan Khalif's voice inside his head.

'The marriage arrangement that Jamal has brokered between you and the daughter of the leader of the northern tribes will ensure stability in the kingdom. The people of Zenhab deserve peace and prosperity after years of war and bloodshed. It is my dying wish, my only son, that when the time comes you will honour your promise to take Princess Haleema as your bride.'

Stumbling into the tent, Kadir sank to his knees and dropped his head into his hands as if he could somehow hold back the tidal wave of emotions rolling over him. Shame tasted as bitter as poison in his mouth. By making love to Lexi he had betrayed his personal code of honour and he had betrayed his father. It was no comfort that he had not technically had sex with Lexi in Zenhab and they had been on his private island, Jinan.

Even worse than letting himself down was the realisation that Lexi hoped, perhaps even expected, that having sex with her had meant something to him. Her soft smile when she had run towards him on the beach just now had made his gut twist, and the look of disappointment on her face when she'd realised that they could leave the island had been more revealing than perhaps she knew.

He cursed savagely, anger and guilt mingling with his shame. *He did not want to hurt Lexi.* The discovery shocked him. His many previous affairs had been with sophisticated European socialites, women who had understood he wasn't looking for a relationship that would continue outside the bedroom. Perhaps he could have been forgiven for believing that a tough-talking ex-RAF pilot knew the score. But he had glimpsed Lexi's vulnerability and heard the hurt in her voice when she had explained how, as a child, she had overheard her adoptive parents say that they wished they had not adopted her.

He was jerked from his thoughts by the *whump-whump* of rotor blades. Dragging himself to his feet, he stepped outside the tent and stared up at the helicopter hovering in the blue sky. *What was Lexi playing at?* He watched her fly a circuit of the island before the chopper dipped below the tops of the palm trees.

The rotor blades had almost stopped spinning when Kadir reached the beach. Lexi jumped down from the chopper onto the sand and watched him walk towards her. He had changed back into his royal robes, and in the breeze his white *keffiyeh* fluttered around his tanned face. His dark eyes were no longer warm but hard and unreadable, and with every step he took closer to her she sensed a widening distance between them.

'Why did you take off without me?'

She shrugged. 'I wanted to make a test flight on my own. Although I'd checked underneath the chopper and didn't find an explosive device, I couldn't be certain that the kidnapper hadn't tampered with the controls before he left us stranded here yesterday.'

Kadir was aware of a curious sensation in his chest, as if a fist was gripping his heart. 'Are you saying you flew the helicopter to check it was safe? What if the kidnapper *had* done something to it that caused it to crash? It's very likely you would have been killed.' His jaw clenched. 'You are the craziest woman I've ever met. You should have waited for me instead of risking your life.'

'It is my duty as a pilot to ensure the safety of my aircraft.' Lexi looked at him steadily. 'Your life is more important than mine. You are the Sultan of Zenhab and your people need you to rule the kingdom and build hospitals and universities and continue the work your father started to maintain peace.'

'Of course your life is as valuable as mine, you little idiot,' Kadir said harshly. He was beginning to realise how much harm her adoptive parents had done by failing to make Lexi feel loved and valued. He frowned as the full implication of what she had just said sank in. The possibility that the kidnapper might have placed explosives on the helicopter hadn't occurred to him, but now he visualised the chopper exploding with Lexi on board and imagined her lying lifeless amid the tangled wreckage of the helicopter.

He stared at her. Wearing army-issue combat trousers, a baseball cap and an attitude, she was beautiful and sexy, brave as a lioness yet vulnerable as a day-old kitten.

She'd been vulnerable in his arms last night as they'd made love over and over and—

Was it possible that she was pregnant with his child?

She had told him in Italy that she wasn't on the Pill, but when he had made love to her last night he hadn't given contraception a thought. He had been too swept up with his selfish need for her to think logically, he acknowledged grimly.

Feeling as though he had been struck by a lightning bolt, Kadir realised that *everything* had changed and nothing could continue as he had planned. He was bound by his duty to his kingdom and the promise he had given his father. But if Lexi had conceived his heir, then his greatest duty was to his unborn child.

The grey mountains of Zenhab were rugged and forbidding, and the Bedouin tribes who lived in some of the most ancient settlements in the world were as hardy as their surroundings.

As Lexi landed the helicopter in the central square of the fortress town Sanqirah, a large crowd of curious on-lookers gathered in front of the market stalls, although most people kept their distance and only a few daring boys surged forward to stare at the chopper.

Kadir's keen eyes noted that there were a couple of armed security guards posted around the square, but he was relieved that Sheikh Omar did not appear to be mustering his forces, which perhaps meant that Jamal's plan to incite the tribes into civil unrest had not yet happened. However, Kadir was aware that the situation could become more volatile after he had discussed his marriage contract to Princess Haleema with her brother.

He jumped out of the helicopter after his bodyguard Nasim, and spoke to Lexi while she was sitting in the cockpit. 'I want you to fly straight back to the palace. I don't know how long my visit will last, but when I return we will need to talk.'

What was there to talk about? Lexi wondered bleakly. Kadir had made it obvious that he was not going to refer to the fact that they had slept together. Presumably he regarded their stolen night of passion as a shameful secret, just as her birth mother regarded Lexi as a shameful secret. Her old feelings of insecurity returned. She had not been good enough for her adoptive parents or Steven, and now she was not good enough for Kadir. How could she have thought that he might want her when he was about to meet the Princess he was going to marry?

She watched him walk across the courtyard towards Sheikh Omar's palace, his robes billowing behind him. He was a regal, remote Sultan, but she pictured him on

Jinan wearing a pair of frayed denim shorts, or wearing nothing but a wickedly sensual smile, and her heart ached.

Sheikh Omar was a young man, and the responsibility of leading the mountain tribes which had been thrust on him after the death of his father, Sheikh Rashid, two months ago showed on his tense face as he greeted the Sultan of Zenhab. Once the servants had poured cups of rich black coffee and placed a plate of sweetmeats on the low table, Omar dismissed his staff so that he and Kadir were alone.

'Welcome to my home, Your Highness.'

'I apologise that my arrival was delayed,' Kadir replied. 'I understand that my uncle Jamal visited you.'

Omar nodded. 'I will speak frankly. Your uncle wishes me to lead the mountain tribes into civil war against you.'

'I know Jamal wants to seize back the Crown and rule Zenhab. Ten years ago he brokered a marriage arrangement between me and your sister, Princess Haleema, because he believed that with the support of your father he would have more power over me and be able to influence my decisions.' Kadir hesitated. He knew what he must do. His duty lay with Lexi, who might be carrying his child, but as he pictured his father's beloved face his heart ached with remorse. *Forgive me, Baba*, he begged silently.

'My greatest wish is for there to continue to be peace in the kingdom,' he told Omar. 'But I must be honest and tell you that I am unable to honour my marriage contract with Haleema. I intend to outlaw forced marriages, and this is one of many changes which I hope will allow all of the population of Zenhab, men and women, to live their lives with greater freedom.'

In the silence that followed, Kadir was aware of each painful beat of his heart. Would his decision lead Zenhab towards civil disturbance? He knew he was taking a great risk. Ten years ago, when he had sought to claim his right to rule the kingdom, he had been forced by his uncle to sign the marriage agreement with a girl he had never met. But he was no longer prepared to be swayed by threats. He was convinced that forced marriages were wrong, not just in his case, but for the whole population. He was determined to stand up for his beliefs, but he had no idea what the new leader of the mountain tribes thought. The old Sheikh Rashid had been a warmonger, much like Jamal. Was his son any different?

Omar stood up and walked across the room to open a door. When he returned to Kadir he was accompanied by a young woman wearing traditional robes and a headscarf. Her expression was calm and intelligent, and her dark eyes observed Kadir with curiosity.

'This is my sister, Princess Haleema,' Omar introduced her.

'I am pleased to meet you after so many years of wondering about you, and I am even more pleased that you do not wish to marry me, Your Highness,' Haleema said with an unexpected frankness that brought a smile to Kadir's lips.

'Haleema and I share your wish that the peace and prosperity which Zenhab has enjoyed under your rule and, before you, your father, Sultan Khalif, will continue,' Omar said quietly. 'We also share your views on forced marriages. My father told my sister when she was just eleven years old that her marriage had been arranged and she would not be allowed to choose her husband. Haleema wishes to go to university and train to be a doctor, and she has my support. It was not possible when my father was alive. He believed in the old ways and would not have understood my sister's ambition to follow a career, a vocation, which will allow her to help the people in our remote part of Zenhab. But my father is dead and I am the new leader of the mountain tribes.' Omar smiled ruefully. 'Your uncle Jamal was not pleased when I told him that I fully support your rule, Your Highness. I ordered my staff to lock him in his rooms, but I am afraid he managed to escape.'

'I'll issue a warrant for his arrest and have security staff at the airports and ports watch out for him. Jamal cannot be allowed to go free after what he has done.' Kadir's jaw clenched as he remembered those moments on the helicopter when the kidnapper had threatened Lexi with a gun.

In the aftermath of being kidnapped, when they had feared for their lives, it was perhaps unsurprising that their desire for one another, which they had tried so hard to suppress, had finally exploded in fierce passion. With his arranged marriage ended, he had resolved one problem only to face a new one, Kadir brooded, thinking of the possibility that Lexi might be pregnant.

CHAPTER TEN

KADIR COULD NOT fail to notice Lexi's suitcase standing in the middle of the sitting room when he followed her into her apartment at the palace. She had refused to meet his gaze when she'd opened the door, and he could feel the tension emanating from her slender frame as she stood on the opposite side of the room from him.

'Are you going somewhere?' he murmured.

'I'm going back to England. You agreed to release me from my contract after I had flown you to the mountains to visit Haleema,' she reminded him.

'The situation has changed. I agreed to you leaving before we became lovers.'

'We are not lovers!' She whirled round to face him, her blue eyes flashing. 'We spent one night together but we shouldn't have done. We should both have been stronger and not given in to desire.'

Lexi turned away from Kadir and cursed her traitorous heart for leaping when she sensed him walk across the room towards her. The familiar scent of his aftershave stole around her and she dared not look at his handsome face. The moment she had opened the door and seen him, dressed in black jeans and a polo shirt, she had struggled to maintain her composure. She wished she had left the palace before he'd returned, as she had originally planned to do. But she could not leave Zenhab without saying goodbye.

'I think it was inevitable that we would make love.' His deep voice broke into her thoughts. 'We were attracted to each other from the moment we first met.'

How could he sound so matter-of-fact about the most incredible night of her life? Perhaps because for him it had just been sex, Lexi thought bleakly. And, having satisfied his inconvenient desire for her, he had hurried to meet his future bride.

'I take it that you met Haleema? So, when is the wedding?'

Kadir heard the hurt in her voice and guilt washed over him because he knew he was to blame. Lexi might be acting like a spitting wildcat, but he had discovered on Jinan that she was so vulnerable.

'I did meet her and her brother. I told them that I wished to break the marriage arrangement, and Haleema and Omar supported my decision.'

'You broke your marriage contract!' Lexi's heart gave another painful lurch. 'But I thought you had to marry Haleema in order to keep peace and avoid civil war.'

'That was true when Sheikh Rashid was alive. My uncle Jamal could count on Rashid's support. But Omar is not like his father. He wants peace in the kingdom and welcomes changes to some of the old traditions.'

'So Jamal's plan to cause trouble backfired.'

'Yes, thankfully. My uncle is now in custody after he was arrested trying to leave the country.'

Lexi shivered as she remembered those terrifying moments when she had feared that the kidnapper might kill them. On the island her emotions had been raw, and she had been unable to resist Kadir because facing death had forced her to face up to the truth—that she was halfway to falling in love with him.

But even though he had ended his marriage arrangement with Haleema, she had no expectation that he wanted a relationship with *her*.

She picked up an envelope from the table and thrust it at him. 'It's my letter of resignation. You agreed to forget the financial penalty if I end my contract early, but if you've changed your mind I'll send you the money I owe when I'm back in England.'

Kadir opened the letter and skimmed his eyes over the terse two lines Lexi had written. 'How will you repay me when you have other debts?'

She stiffened. 'How do you know about my private life?'

'You know I had a detailed security check run on you before I employed you as my helicopter pilot.'

'It's a pity you didn't run a more detailed check on Fariq. It would have saved a lot of trouble.' If they hadn't been kidnapped and stranded on Jinan, their heightened emotions wouldn't have exploded in frantic passion and they would not have made love.

Lexi grimaced. Love hadn't been involved. They'd had sex, and just because it had been amazing, mind-blowing sex she had stupidly hoped that she meant something to Kadir. But the truth was she meant nothing to him and now that he was free from his arranged marriage he could choose who he wanted to marry. No doubt he would want a beautiful socialite to be his bride, she thought dully. In England he was Earl Montgomery and one of the most eligible bachelors in Europe.

Kadir slipped the letter into his pocket. 'The finan-

cial penalty clause in your contract does not apply because it is not your fault that you have to resign.' Kadir
paused and took a deep breath before taking a step towards Lexi. 'Have you considered the possibility that
you could be pregnant?'

Lexi's eyes widened.

'The Civil Aviation Authority's advice to female pilots is that they should not fly in the early stages of pregnancy,' Kadir continued.

Lexi bit her lip, wondering how he could sound so
calm about something so potentially life-changing. But
if she *was* pregnant it was not his life that would change,
she thought grimly.

'It's unlikely I'm pregnant. It was the wrong time of
the month for me to have conceived.'

He gave her an impatient look. 'We both know that
can't be predicted. We will need to know for sure.'

'Well, since I'm boringly regular, I'll tell you in just
over a week.' She hated herself for blushing, thinking
how ridiculous it was to feel embarrassed about discussing such a personal issue when Kadir had seen, touched
and kissed every centimetre of her body. 'I'm certain
there's nothing to worry about, but if there are any repercussions from our irresponsible behaviour I'll let you
know,' she told him with a forced airiness.

The situation felt surreal. She *couldn't* be carrying
Kadir's baby, Lexi assured herself. But the stark fact
was that pregnancy *was* a possibility after she'd had unprotected sex. Actually, she felt a bit sick, but she was
probably imagining it, she told herself. What she definitely felt was a fool. She was a sensible, responsible
twenty-nine-year-old and she had no excuse for risking
an unplanned pregnancy. But when Kadir had stripped

her naked in the tent on Jinan her only thought been how desperately she wanted him to hold her, to feel safe in his arms and for him to make love to her.

She picked up her suitcase and opened the drawer in the bureau to retrieve her passport. 'I'll phone you from England once I have any news.'

'If you are pregnant you will marry me.'

Her head whipped round, and the fact that the drawer was empty did not register in her brain at first. 'Don't be ridiculous.'

'You have a better suggestion?'

He was serious? Lexi laughed shakily. '*If* I'm pregnant, which I am quite sure I'm not because I can't believe fate would play such a ghastly joke, then it will be my problem and I'll deal with it.'

He swore. 'If by *deal with it* you mean what I think you mean…'

Something in his voice, an indefinable emotion, made her pause, and she paled as *his* meaning sank into her dazed mind. 'I would never do that.' Shocked beyond words, her hand shot out before she had time to think and she struck his cheek, leaving a red imprint of her fingers on his olive skin.

His eyes glittered dangerously and he caught hold of her arm as if he thought she might slap him again. But Lexi was horrified by her loss of control and her mouth trembled, betraying her intense hurt.

'My biological mother admitted that she wanted to abort me,' she said thickly, 'but by the time she found out it was too late to get rid of me.' She swallowed. 'If it turns out that I have conceived your child I will take care of it and…and *love* it, because I know better than most what it's like for a child not to feel loved.'

'And I know what it feels like for a child to *be* loved.' Kadir's dark eyes burned into hers. 'My father showered me with love and affection, and I have every intention of doing the same with my child. The baby that is possibly already developing inside you will be my heir, and if you are carrying my son he will be the future Sultan of Zenhab. But, more important, our child has the right to be brought up by both its parents. Far from being ridiculous, marriage is the only option I will consider.'

Lexi felt as if an iron band was squeezing her lungs. Kadir's words and, even more, the fierce emotion in them, filled her with a strange sense of relief that if the unthinkable had happened and she was actually pregnant, he would accept responsibility for his child.

He would be a wonderful father, she thought. In her mind she pictured a baby with olive-gold skin and dark curls and thick black eyelashes. She imagined Kadir cradling his son in his arms and she felt a sudden acute longing to be part of the tableaux, for Kadir to look at her with the same love in his eyes that he felt for his child.

What was she thinking? 'There are other ways that we could both be parents to our child without a sham marriage that neither of us wants,' she said stiffly.

'Not in Zenhab there aren't. The kingdom is becoming more progressive, but the Zenhabian people will not tolerate their Sultan fathering an illegitimate child.'

Kadir suddenly smiled and the sexy curl of his lips evoked a purely physical longing in the pit of Lexi's stomach. 'If we have to marry, it won't be a sham, certainly not in the bedroom. I already have proof that we are sexually compatible.'

Lexi saw determination stamped on his hard-boned features and panic gripped her. He was deadly serious that if she was pregnant he would insist on them marrying for the sake of their child. He had been freed from his arranged marriage, only to be faced with a marriage of convenience and she would be his unwanted wife, just as she had been her adoptive parents' unwanted daughter once they'd had a daughter of their own.

'I doubt the Zenhabian people would support a marriage between us if they knew the circumstances of my birth,' she said tautly. She had never revealed to anyone the truth of her background, but once Kadir learned the facts she was sure he would drop the crazy marriage idea. 'And they *would* find out about me. Your press may not be as intrusive as the European paparazzi, but someone will dig up the dirt about me.'

His eyes narrowed. 'What do you mean?'

'A woman named Cathy Barnes is my biological mother. During the early years of her life she worked as a prostitute, selling sex to fund her drug habit. My father was…' she shrugged helplessly '…one of her clients, a stranger who went to a hotel room and paid for sex with a woman he would never see again, much less know that his sordid transaction had resulted in a child. Me.'

'You told me you knew nothing about your real parents.'

'My background is hardly something to be proud of,' she said drily. She sighed. 'Like many adopted children, I imagine, I was curious about who had brought me into the world and, without any facts to go on, I created a fantasy that my real parents had been forced by tragic circumstances to give me away, but they had always loved me and were desperate for us to be reunited.'

The unconsciously wistful note in her voice evoked a pang of sympathy in Kadir but he knew she would hate any suggestion of pity. He strolled across to the window overlooking the palace courtyard where the helicopter was parked on the pad.

He remembered the night his yacht had capsized off the south coast of England and his relief when he had looked up and seen the coastguard helicopter piloted by Lexi which had come to his rescue. It was due to her fearlessness that his life had been saved. And she had demonstrated her bravery again when she had calmly flown the helicopter while the kidnapper had stuck a gun in her ribs. But, beneath her tough exterior, Kadir knew she hid a vulnerability that touched something inside him.

'How did you learn the truth about your biological mother?'

'When I was eighteen the adoption agency helped me to trace her. But my hope that I would feel an instant bond with her was quickly shattered. Cathy agreed to meet me, but there was no emotional reunion,' Lexi said wryly. 'She told me that she hadn't wanted a baby and had handed me to a social worker immediately after I was born. When I finally met Cathy, she had sorted her life out and was married, but her husband had no idea of her past life or that she'd had a child and, because she is ashamed of her past, she has never told anyone about me.'

'Do you keep in contact with her?'

'We meet a few times a year, always in secret,' Lexi said bitterly. 'Six months ago Cathy learned that she has cancer which is untreatable. She broke down when she told me that she had built up huge debts on credit cards that her husband did not know about. She knew he would be worried about the money she owed and she was upset that their last few months together would be spoiled, so I offered to pay the debts for her.'

'It was good of you to help her when she doesn't seem to have been much of a mother to you.'

'She's my mother,' Lexi said flatly. 'She was in a desperate situation when she gave birth to me, and I think she tried to do her best for me by having me adopted. Surely you can understand now, why, even if I am pregnant, you can't marry me. The Zenhabian people were expecting you to marry a princess and I doubt they would accept a whore's daughter for their Sultana.'

Kadir caught hold of her chin when she looked away from him as if she was embarrassed to meet his gaze. 'Lexi, whatever your mother was and however she lived her life has no bearing on who you are. No one could fail to be impressed by your courage and your compassion. If you are pregnant I can't think of anyone who would be a better mother to my child, and as my wife you would be a great role model to young women in Zenhab.'

Lexi swallowed. He sounded as if he meant what he had said, but a voice of caution inside her head warned her that she would be a fool to trust him. The truth was that if she had conceived Kadir's baby he was prepared to marry her *only* because he wanted his child.

She dragged her eyes from the molten warmth in his and spun away from him. 'This conversation is premature and almost certainly pointless. I'm sure I'm not pregnant. There's a flight leaving Zenhab for Dubai, from there I can catch a direct flight back to London, and I intend to be on it.'

She stared at the empty drawer in the bureau. 'I know I put my passport in here.' She suddenly remembered that the maid who cleaned her apartment had opened the drawer and quickly shut it again when Lexi had entered the room earlier. 'One of the staff wouldn't have taken it, would they?'

'Yes, on my instruction,' Kadir said coolly. 'But don't worry. I have it safely locked away in my study and if you are not pregnant I'll return it to you.'

Her shock turned swiftly to fury. 'You *stole* my passport?'

'Borrowed,' he drawled.

'That's *outrageous*. How *dare* you? I *demand* you return it immediately.' Lexi could feel her blood pounding through her veins, but her anger was mixed with apprehension when she realised that she was effectively a prisoner in Zenhab and probably at the palace, she thought, remembering the guards who protected the perimeter walls and gates. Kadir could not force her to marry him, she reminded herself.

As if he could read her mind, he said inexorably, 'If the news is positive, we will marry without delay before word gets out that you are carrying the Sultan's child.'

Kadir's jaw hardened. Taking Lexi's passport had been a panic reaction to prevent her from leaving, and he acknowledged that she had every right to be angry. But if she left she might refuse to return to Zenhab. And if she was pregnant she might decide to bring up her child—*his* child—on her own in England. He knew she was fiercely independent, and it was possible that she wouldn't want to spend her life in a remote desert kingdom.

He remembered how his mother had hated Zenhab and the restrictions of being the wife of the Sultan. Judith Montgomery had abandoned her husband and seven-year-old son to live at the Montgomery estate in Windsor, but whenever Kadir had visited his mother she had put emotional pressure on him to live in England with her.

Kadir grimaced as he remembered his mother's tears when he'd said goodbye to her at the end of each visit. He had loved both his parents and had felt torn between them. His mother had made him feel guilty for choosing to live with his father and he had spent his childhood shuttling back and forth between his parents and the two very different cultures in Zenhab and England.

If Lexi was pregnant, he would not want his child to go through what he had as a child, to feel torn loyalties and guilt, as he had done. Somehow he must try to convince Lexi that their child, if there was a child, deserved to be brought up by both of them in a stable family unit. But he could not abandon his duty to his kingdom. He was a Sultan and his child would be heir to the throne. Marriage to Lexi was the only option.

But what if, after a few years of marriage, she left him like his mother had left his father? How would he feel if she decided that life in the desert kingdom was not for her? Sultan Khalif had been heartbroken by his wife's desertion, Kadir remembered. As a teenager, he had watched his father sitting alone in the gardens that had been created for Judith, and he had vowed that he would never lose his heart to a woman. Love had been his strong father's one weakness, but Kadir knew better than to risk his emotions on something as unreliable as love.

Lexi stared at Kadir's chiselled features and wondered what he was thinking. He had insisted that if she was pregnant he would marry her, and she supposed she should feel relieved that her child would have a father. But the harsh truth was that his child was all he was interested in. He had proved that he was not interested in her when he had virtually ignored her after the night they had spent together on Jinan.

She tried to hold on to her anger. She needed to be strong to stand up to him and not allow him to push her into a loveless marriage that would be convenient for him but heartbreaking for her. But her fire and her temper had deserted her and she felt empty and alone, just as she had been all her life. No one had really wanted her or loved her, she thought bleakly. Memories of her childhood, when she had been made to feel a nuisance by her adoptive parents, still hurt. How could she marry Kadir, knowing that he did not want her—apart from for sex? she thought, remembering how he had said that they were sexually compatible.

'I wish none of this had happened,' she said in a choked voice.

An odd expression flared in Kadir's eyes. 'Do you regret making love with me?'

How could she regret the most beautiful night of her life? 'Do you?' she countered.

'No.' The night they had spent together on the island had been magical—a stolen night of pleasure when he had been able to forget the responsibilities of being a Sultan.

The molten warmth in Kadir's eyes sent a warning shiver through Lexi. She dared not soften towards him. When had he moved closer to her? The heat of his body and the evocative masculine scent of him tugged on her senses. If he touched her she would be lost! Suddenly scared of what she might reveal, Lexi tried to twist away from him, but he settled his hands on her shoulders and pulled her to him.

His body was all hard muscle and sinew, and the feel of his erection nudging her thigh made her insides melt.

'I will never regret the pleasure and the passion we shared on Jinan,' he said softly.

'Don't...' she pleaded as she watched his head descend. She struggled against the strength of his arms holding her, but her real battle was with herself and her body betrayed her the moment he claimed her lips and kissed her with the ruthless mastery of a desert warrior.

It was sweet rapture to be in his arms, to lay her hand on his chest and feel the erratic thud of his heart, to know that his arousal was as swift and all-consuming as her own. She had thought he would never kiss her again, that their stolen night was all she would ever have of him. She had no protection against his sorcery, no defence against the bone-shaking tenderness of his kiss as he eased the pressure of his mouth on hers and traced the swollen contours of her lips with the tip of his tongue.

'Do you still doubt we could make our marriage work?'

Lexi swept her lashes down to blot out the satisfied gleam in Kadir's eyes. Of course he looked triumphant when she had capitulated so utterly and responded to him so shamelessly, she thought bleakly. Her mouth was stinging from his hungry passion, and she told herself she must have imagined an underlying tenderness in his kiss that had tugged on her frayed emotions.

'It's just sex,' she muttered. 'I don't deny the chemistry that ignites whenever we're within a few feet of each other, but it's not a basis for marriage.'

She assumed he would step away from her, and was unprepared when he framed her face in his hands and murmured, 'Was it *just sex* we had on Jinan? I have never experienced such intense pleasure as when we made love, and I can't help feeling that we shared something more than merely physical satiation.'

On the island Kadir had tried to dismiss the surpris-

ing feelings that had swept over him in the languorous
aftermath of making love to Lexi. He had been aware
that he could not allow himself to feel anything because
he was bound by duty to honour his arranged marriage.
But since he had ended his marriage arrangement with
Haleema he could not stop thinking about the sex with
Lexi, which had been amazing. But he also remembered
that when she had fallen asleep in his arms he had remained awake to protect her if the kidnapper returned;
he had held her close to him and studied how her long
eyelashes curled against her cheeks.

'You're just saying that because if it turns out that I
am pregnant you want me to stay in Zenhab so that you
can be a father to your child.'

Kadir saw the mistrust in her eyes and understood it
all the more now that she had told him how her biological mother had rejected her.

'I don't deny I would want custody of my child,' he
admitted, determined to be honest with her. 'I would be
prepared to seek a legal ruling if necessary.'

He wanted much more, he acknowledged. He had told
Lexi once that he wanted everything, and he knew with
sudden insight that it was true.

She paled. 'Do you mean you would fight for custody
if I have a baby?'

For the first time since the nightmare had begun, Lexi
considered the real possibility that she was pregnant. Sup-
posing she had a baby, a tiny, vulnerable scrap of life, utterly dependent on her, that she could love and who would
love her unconditionally? Unconsciously, she placed her
hand over her stomach, the instinct of maternal protec-
tiveness kicking inside her.

'I would *never* give up my child. I've told you how

my birth mother gave me away. How could you think I would do the same?'

The glimmer of tears in her eyes got to Kadir. 'I know you wouldn't,' he said roughly. 'So I suggest we stop the talk of fighting and custody and spend the next week or so getting to know each other better because, if you are carrying our child, then, like it or not, we will be spending the foreseeable future together.'

His suggestion of calling a truce made sense, Lexi acknowledged reluctantly. Nothing would persuade her to give up her child. Even if she managed to leave the palace and return to England, Kadir would find out if she was pregnant and he would use his wealth and power to claim his heir. In a strange way she was glad of his determination to be a devoted father, unlike the faceless man who had accidentally fathered her.

He took her silence as agreement. 'We'll start by having dinner tonight. Unfortunately, we won't be alone because Yusuf reminded me that the French ambassador is coming to dinner at the palace this evening, but it will be good practice for you if you become Sultana of Zenhab.'

She did not return his smile. 'The idea is laughable, isn't it?' she said in a low voice full of self-doubt, 'considering my genes. I don't know how to talk to an ambassador.'

'Just be you,' Kadir advised. He glanced at his watch. 'I'm expecting a phone call. Dinner will be at eight.' On his way out of the door, he glanced back at her. 'I've taken the liberty of ordering some clothes for you. I will be hosting several social functions over the coming week and you'll need evening dresses,' he explained quickly when he saw the battle gleam in her eyes.

'I don't want you to pay for my clothes...' Lexi stared

at the door as Kadir closed it after him. The snick of the catch made her feel trapped; although he had not locked her in her apartment and presumably she could walk around the palace and gardens, she was not at liberty to leave the kingdom—at least, not until they knew if she was pregnant or not.

If she *hadn't* conceived his child then, no doubt, she would find herself on the next flight out of Zenhab, and Kadir would be free to marry a woman of his choice.

She bit her lip and pushed away the crazy idea that she secretly hoped she was pregnant. She had spent her whole life hoping to find love, but she knew with painful certainty that her heart's desire would not be granted here in the Sultan's palace.

The evening was less of an ordeal than she had expected. The French ambassador had been invited to the palace, ostensibly to discuss opportunities for business investment in Zenhab but, with typical Gallic charm, he flirted with Lexi throughout dinner so that she soon relaxed and chatted away to him, earning her several hard stares from Kadir. Until her possible pregnancy was confirmed he had no right to look at her with brooding possessiveness in his eyes that in the flickering candlelight were the colour of bitter chocolate, she thought indignantly.

But once again the devil inside her enjoyed goading him, and she could not deny a sense of satisfaction when she met his gaze across the table and watched streaks of colour flare along his cheekbones. He might not love her, but he desired her.

She was glad she had abandoned her pride and worn one of the dresses that had been delivered to her apartment. The full-length black velvet gown had a modest neckline, in respect for Zenhabian culture, but it was expertly designed to show off her slim waist, and the colour was a perfect foil for her pale blonde hair that she had left loose so that it fell smooth and sleek to halfway down her back.

Kadir walked beside her as the party moved from the dining room outside to the terrace, where coffee was to be served. 'I commend your efforts to encourage Zenhabian-French relations,' he said curtly, 'but I would prefer you not to flirt with Monsieur Aubrech.'

Lexi gave him an impatient look. 'I was simply being friendly, and I have to say it wouldn't have hurt you to have been a bit more amenable during dinner instead of scowling at Etienne. What's wrong with you tonight?'

Where did he start? He had never experienced jealousy before, but every time Lexi had laughed at one of the ambassador's jokes Kadir had felt corrosive acid fizzing in the pit of his stomach, and he had spent the entire dinner fighting the urge to ignore social niceties and carry her off to have hot, hard sex with her on the nearest available flat surface.

Aware that he was scowling as she had accused him of doing, he muttered something about her pushing his patience and strode onto the terrace, determined to keep the over-friendly French ambassador away from Lexi.

At the end of the evening, Lexi's temper was still simmering over Kadir's unfair accusation that she had been flirting with the French ambassador. She walked into her bedroom and smiled as she dismissed the maid who had turned down the sheets on her bed. Picking up her hairbrush from the dressing table, she heard a faint sound behind her and whirled around with a startled cry as the bathroom door opened and Kadir appeared.

'What are...?' She broke off when he put a finger to his lips, warning her to be quiet.

'Has the maid gone?' he murmured. 'Go and lock your bedroom door.'

She marched across the room and turned the key in the lock before she turned to face him, and immediately wished she hadn't when she realised he was naked apart from a towel knotted dangerously low on his hips. He was rubbing his damp hair with another towel. Lexi forced her eyes up from his naked, bronzed chest to his face and felt her stomach dip as she studied the sensual curve of his mouth and the sexy stubble that covered his jaw.

'Why didn't you want the maid to see you?'

He shrugged. 'It's better not to publicly advertise our relationship just yet, at least until we know if you are pregnant. It is against Zenhabian custom for men and women to share a bedroom before marriage.'

'So instead you are skulking around the palace and visiting me in secret.' She welcomed her temper to disguise her hurt that once again she was a shameful secret. 'I have no intention of sharing my bedroom with you,' Lexi told him furiously. 'You said we should spend time getting to know one another better, but you obviously thought I would provide ten nights of sex. I don't suppose I'll even see you in the daytime.'

'On the contrary; I've arranged for us to spend tomorrow at the coast. I thought you might like to learn to sail my yacht, and we could anchor in a secluded little bay I know of and swim or even snorkel. There are some beautiful fish and the water is crystal-clear.'

'Oh...well, I guess that does sound fun.' She bit her lip, unable to drag her eyes from the sensual gleam in his, and her heart suddenly began to hammer. 'But that doesn't explain why you are here.'

'Why do you think?' he said softly.

The dangerous glitter in his eyes as he walked towards her had her hurriedly backing up against the door.

'I don't want to sleep with you.' She was aware that now he was free from his marriage contract there was nothing to stop them being lovers, but she did not dare have sex with him again. Not now she had revealed intensely personal things about herself and her background that she had never told anyone else. She had made herself emotionally vulnerable to Kadir. Damn it, she had fallen in love with him. But he did not love her, and she did not trust herself to make love with him without giving away how she felt about him.

'That's okay because sleep is the last thing I had in mind, too.' Lexi's spine was jammed against the door and Kadir trapped her there by placing his hands on either side of her head so that his body was almost touching hers. 'Shall I tell you what *is* in my mind, *habibi*?'

'Don't...call me that.' She turned her head so that he wouldn't see the tears that stung her eyes. Her emotions were see-sawing all over the place. Perhaps it was a sign she was pregnant? Distracted by the mental picture of holding her baby in her arms, she had no time to defend her heart against the sweet seduction of Kadir's mouth as he claimed her lips in a kiss that stirred her soul.

'I want you to trust me. I don't want to hurt you, Lexi,' he said softly.

But he would, she thought with a flash of despair. If she was carrying his baby he would insist on marrying her, but she would be his unwanted wife, and if she wasn't pregnant, his desire for her would fade as quickly as it had with his other mistresses.

Her brain urged her to resist his sensual foreplay, but he had lowered her zip and tugged the top of her dress down, baring her to his hungry gaze. His hands were exquisitely gentle as he cupped her breasts in his palms and rubbed his thumb pads over her nipples until they hardened and tingled and the pleasure was too intense for her to bear.

'Let me love you,' he said in his deep, dark voice that wrapped around her like a velvet cloak. She knew he meant *make love to you*, and she knew she would be a fool to succumb to his sorcery. But for the next few days and nights he would be hers, whispered a voice inside her head. Her future was on hold until she found out if she was pregnant so why not enjoy what he was offering now?

Anticipation licked like scorching flames through her as he swept her up in his arms and carried her over to the bed. Entranced by the magic he was summoning with his mouth and hands, she had no recollection of him removing her dress and knickers, and she was unaware of the savage kick of desire Kadir felt in his gut as he stared at the erotic contrast of her ash-blonde hair and creamy pale limbs spread against the black silk sheets.

Spread for his pleasure, Kadir thought as he pushed her legs apart and knelt above her. He had never known any other woman to be as responsive and generous a lover as Lexi, and he had never felt such powerful thunder in his heart as he felt with her. He wanted everything, he acknowledged. And the desert king always took what he desired.

CHAPTER ELEVEN

'WELL—ANY NEWS?' Kadir demanded the moment Lexi emerged from the en suite bathroom.

'Nothing yet,' she murmured. She slid back into bed and Kadir curled his arm around her and drew her into the warmth of his body. His spicy cologne teased her senses and the whorls of black hairs on his chest tickled her cheek. These moments in the early morning when they lay together, half dozing, muscles aching pleasurably after long hours of lovemaking the previous night, were dangerously intoxicating, she thought ruefully as she snuggled up to him.

'You're late.'

'It's not an exact science,' she said drily. But actually her monthly cycle was as regular as clockwork. Lexi felt a heart-thumping mixture of dread and excitement. She had never been even one day late before. She might be imagining it, but she was sure her breasts looked a bit fuller when she'd glanced in the bathroom mirror.

She couldn't be pregnant, she assured herself. And of *course* she did not want to be. She could never forget that she had been an accidental pregnancy, unwanted by her mother. It shamed her that she had made one stupid mistake and it would be better for everyone if there were no consequences.

She bit her lip as Kadir placed his hand on her flat stomach. What if his baby was inside her? For years she had been absorbed in her career and had never really had any maternal feelings. But when she had left the RAF, and with her thirtieth birthday on the horizon, she'd begun to feel wistful whenever she held one of her friends' newborn infants. For the past eleven days she had found herself scrutinising every tiny symptom that might mean she was going to be a mother.

'You had better do a test. And if it confirms what we both suspect I'll start making arrangements for our wedding.' Kadir rolled onto his back, taking Lexi with him, and slid his hand into her hair, urging her mouth down onto his. The kiss was slow and sweet, drugging her senses and stealing her heart as she sensed tenderness in his passion.

The past week and a half had been wonderful, she thought dreamily. Kadir had spent every day with her, only popping into his office briefly to deal with any urgent matters that his chief adviser deemed to require his attention. He had given her sailing lessons on his yacht, and they had swum in a turquoise sea that was as warm as a bath. Lexi enjoyed their trips to different parts of Zenhab, including driving out to the desert in a four-by-four, but, for all Kadir's determination to spend a few carefree days, he was still the Sultan and they were always accompanied by bodyguards. Only within the palace walls were they able to be completely private, and several times he had instructed the staff not to disturb them before making love to her on a sun lounger by the pool.

'What would you like to do today?' His voice was indulgent as he stroked her hair back from her face. 'Perhaps you had better not do anything too energetic in case the pregnancy test is positive.'

Kadir was growing increasingly convinced that Lexi had conceived his baby. The very real possibility that he was going to be a father made him miss his own father, and he wished Sultan Khalif could have seen his grandchild. Thoughts of fatherhood had also brought back memories of his childhood, when he had felt torn between his parents, and he was more determined than ever to persuade Lexi that they should marry and stay together for the sake of their child.

He traced his hands over her slender figure and imagined her belly swollen with his baby. Skimming lower, he began to stroke her buttocks in rhythmic circles. 'We could spend the day in bed?'

'I thought you said I shouldn't do anything too energetic,' she said breathlessly, instantly turned on by the sensuous motion of Kadir's hand caressing her bottom.

He gave a wickedly sexy smile as he flipped her onto her back. 'You won't have to do anything. I'll do all the work and you can just lie back and enjoy me pleasuring you.'

Oh, God! She curled her fingers into the silk sheet as he kissed his way down her body from her breasts to the sweet spot between her thighs and flicked his tongue over her clitoris until she moaned and pressed her feminine heat against his mouth. He took her with his tongue and then drove his rock-hard arousal deep inside her and took her to the peak again so that her first orgasm had barely ended when the next one began.

His passion seemed wilder, more uncontrolled, and when he came the cords on his neck stood out and he groaned her name as if it had been torn from his soul. Overwhelmed by the feelings that overspilled her heart, Lexi wrapped her arms around him and hugged him tightly, uncaring at that moment that her tender smile betrayed her.

'You know I have to leave tomorrow, and I'll be away for a week?' he said later when they had showered together and were eating a very late breakfast on the balcony. 'Sheikh Omar has organised meetings with the mountain tribes; I am hoping I can persuade them to swear their allegiance to the Crown.'

Kadir looked across the table at Lexi and thought that she had never looked more beautiful, with her long blonde hair falling around her shoulders and her bright blue eyes sparkling like precious gems. She seemed softer somehow, and he had noticed a dreamy expression in her eyes that made him wonder if his patience was paying off and she was beginning to trust him.

The rest of the day and night passed too quickly, and Lexi sensed an urgency in Kadir's caresses when he made love to her in the cool grey light of dawn, before he slid out of bed and headed into his dressing room to prepare for his trip to the northern territories. He emerged dressed in his robes of state, his *keffiyeh* held in place on his head by a circle of gold.

'I've left a pregnancy test kit in the bathroom. Try to call me if you have any news, but communication in the mountains is limited—something I will be working with Omar to improve in the future.' He dropped a brief fierce kiss on her mouth. 'I wish I didn't have to go,' he groaned. 'Why don't you do the test now?'

Butterflies leapt in Lexi's stomach. What if the pregnancy test gave a positive result? *What if it didn't?* Either way, her relationship with Kadir would be affected. She suddenly wished the past eleven days could last for ever.

'It will be better to wait a few more days to make sure the test gives a correct result.'

'All right.' He kissed her again, softer this time, his lips clinging to hers as if he really did not want to leave her, almost making her believe that he cared for her a little.

She missed him the second he strode out of the bedroom and closed the door behind him. An inexplicable sadness filled her, a feeling that the days they had spent together had been a golden time that had slipped through her fingers like the desert sand and now had disappeared for ever.

The hours without Kadir dragged, and the huge bed was a lonely place without him lying next to her.

Next morning, a trip to the bathroom revealed that the niggling stomach ache she'd had during the night was not indigestion as she had thought—as she had hoped, she acknowledged dully.

There seemed no point doing the pregnancy test now she had evidence that she had not conceived Kadir's baby. She ordered herself to feel relieved but her heart disobeyed and an unexpected torrent of grief ripped through her. Faced with reality, she admitted the truth. She would have loved to be a mother, loved to have Kadir's child—loved him, she thought painfully.

She'd felt so close to him recently that she had even started to believe that, if they were going to be parents, perhaps they could have a successful marriage. A few times she had caught Kadir looking at her in a way that had made her heart leap. But now reality brought her crashing back down to earth. He did not love her, and when he learned that she was not expecting his baby he would send her away from Zenhab and search for a suitable bride to be the mother of his heir.

The strident ring of her phone made her jump. She stared at the handset, wondering if Kadir was calling her. If it was him, shouldn't she break the news that he wasn't going to be a father?

Athena greeted her cheerfully. 'How is everything in Zenhab? I was thinking about you, and I had a funny feeling that something's wrong.'

Lexi forced an airy tone. 'You and your funny feelings!' Actually, she recalled her sister had had a 'feeling' when she had phoned Lexi in Afghanistan the day that her co-pilot had been killed. 'Everything is fine; couldn't be better, in fact.'

Afterwards, she did not know what made her confide in Athena, but she felt more alone than she had felt in her life and her sister's gentle voice reached out to her. The whole story of being kidnapped with Kadir and stranded on his island came tumbling out, along with the fact that she'd had unprotected sex with him, and his insistence that if she was pregnant he would marry her.

'But you're not pregnant,' Athena repeated what Lexi had just told her. 'What a shame. You would be a wonderful mother, and a great wife for the Sultan.'

'Of course it's not a shame,' Lexi said sharply. 'You're such a daydreamer, Athena. The fact that I'm not pregnant is good news. It means I can carry on with my career. I couldn't be happier...' she choked, and suddenly she couldn't hold back her tears. It was as if a dam had burst and her grief for the baby she had imagined holding in her arms poured out, along with a lifetime of pain and hurt at feeling rejected and unloved. Her secret hope that she would spend the future with Kadir and their child was over, and now she had nothing.

'Why don't you tell Kadir you love him?' Athena asked softly. 'What have you got to lose?'

'Apart from my pride, dignity and self-respect, you mean?' Lexi's chest hurt from crying so hard. She had never lost control of her emotions so violently before and she felt scared that loving Kadir had changed her, weakened her, and she would never be tough-talking, no-nonsense Lexi Howard again.

'I wish I was with you in Zenhab to give you a hug,' her sister said. 'I wish I could help. You know I love you, Lexi.'

Lexi swallowed. She *did* know that Athena cared for her, but she had always struggled to show her own emotions. 'You're a great sister. I…I love you too,' she said huskily.

She sensed Athena's surprise. 'You've never said it before. I think you should tell Kadir how you feel about him and give him a chance to explain why he seems so determined to marry you.'

'It was only because he wanted his child. But there isn't going to be one. He's the Sultan of Zenhab and needs to marry a woman of royal blood, not someone whose genes come from a very murky pool.'

'What will you do?'

'Come home, look for a job.' She still needed to pay off Cathy's debts, Lexi thought wearily. She remembered that Kadir had taken her passport and she would have to stay on at the palace until he returned from his trip to the mountains. It was only fair to tell him her news in person rather than leave a message on his phone.

Memories of the past days they had spent exclusively

in each other's company pushed into her mind. Had she imagined that they had had fun together, shared laughter, *friendship*? Could she do what her sister had suggested and tell Kadir she had fallen in love with him?

Her stomach swooped at the idea of risking his rejection. Kadir had only wanted her when he had thought she could be carrying his baby, and the traditions of his kingdom meant he could not allow his child to be born illegitimate, she reminded herself. She was certain he would be relieved not to be forced into a marriage he did not want.

The helicopter buzzed above the palace before dropping down to land in the courtyard. Kadir had hired a new pilot, an Australian guy called Mitch, who Lexi assumed would continue to work for the Sultan after she had gone.

She had carried her suitcase down to the entrance hall and as she watched Kadir walk up the palace steps she pulled the peak of her cap lower over her eyes. The clothes he had bought her were hanging in the wardrobe in the apartment she had first occupied when she had arrived in Zenhab. She had applied for a job in the UK, flying workers out to oil rigs in the North Sea, and she doubted there would be many opportunities to wear designer evening gowns in the cold winter in Aberdeen.

Wearing her pilot's uniform made her feel more like herself. A grey skirt and jacket teamed with a crisp white blouse, and her hair swept up beneath her cap, gave the impression of cool professionalism and hid the truth that her heart was breaking. Through a window, she studied the Sultan in his traditional robes and tried to feel distanced from him, but memories of Kadir, naked, beautiful, lowering his body onto hers, threatened to shatter her composure.

She took a few steps forward as he swept through the great palace doors, halting when his dark eyes immediately shot to her suitcase.

His smile faded. 'Do you have news for me?'

'I'm sure you will be as relieved as I am to hear that I'm not pregnant.' Her jaw ached as she flashed him a brittle smile. 'Our worries were needless, but now we can both get on with our lives.'

Kadir's eyes narrowed and he fought the urge to whip Lexi's damn cap off her head so that he could see her face. She sounded so cool and in control, reminding him of the ice queen who had rescued him from his capsized yacht and ripped into him for risking the lives of his crew.

He absorbed her words. There was to be no child. No son to love, as his father had loved him. No daughter to adore, with silvery-blonde hair and eyes the colour of mountain skies. No requirement under Zenhabian tradition to marry Lexi. She had said she was relieved not to be pregnant. Maybe she was right, he brooded.

'It's probably for the best.' He glanced around the entrance hall, suddenly aware of the presence of several palace staff. Ignoring his chief adviser who was hurrying towards him, he caught hold of Lexi's elbow and steered her into his study, shutting the door and locking it to ensure their privacy.

'Was it necessary to manhandle me?' she complained, rubbing her arm. 'Why have you brought me in here?'

He countered her question with one of his own. 'Why are you leaving?'

'I've told you why. I'm not carrying your baby. You

have hired a new pilot so there's no reason for me to stay in Zenhab.' It took all Lexi's will power to keep her voice steady. Kadir had said it was for the best that she wasn't pregnant. Of course he was pleased, she told herself. Of course he did not want a whore's daughter to be the mother of his heir. Of course he did not love her because no one, apart from her sister, ever had.

'You can't think of any reason to stay?' Kadir's jaw hardened when she shook her head. 'I thought you had enjoyed the days we spent together, and I know I gave you pleasure every night, just as you captivated me with your sensuality. We're good together, Lexi.'

Pride forced her chin up to meet his gaze. 'I don't deny we had some fun. But it didn't mean anything, did it? Now we know there is no baby it's time to move on.'

She was leaving him. Kadir's heart gave a painful jolt. In his mind he was seven years old, running down the palace steps after his mother, tears running down his face. *'Why do you have to go back to England, Mama? Why don't you want to stay here with me and Baba?'*

'I'll still see you, darling, when you come to stay at Montgomery Manor. But I don't belong in Zenhab. I can't live with the restrictions of being the wife of the Sultan.' Judith had bent down and kissed his cheek. Kadir still remembered the scent of the perfume she had worn that day. *'The truth is that I want to be free to live my own life.'*

Was that why Lexi had decided to leave him? Did she care more about her freedom and her career than him? 'I suppose you want to continue flying helicopters,' he said tersely.

'Yes, I love being a pilot.' Lexi made a show of checking her watch. 'Look, I really need to go if I'm going to catch my flight. You still have my passport,' she reminded him.

He was silent for a few moments before he gave a shrug. 'I'll tell Yusuf to bring it to you. The helicopter will take you to the airport but you'll have to wait while it's being refuelled.'

He moved suddenly and Lexi gave a startled cry when he pulled her cap off, freeing her hair so that it tumbled around her shoulders. Kadir slid his hand beneath her chin and tilted her face up, subjecting her to an unsparing appraisal that took in the dark circles under her eyes and the tears sparkling on her lashes. A fierce emotion stirred inside him but he ruthlessly suppressed it.

'Goodbye, angel-face,' he murmured before he strode out of the room, leaving Lexi with the exotic scent of his cologne and a heart that felt as though it had splintered into a thousand shards.

Her plane was due to leave Zenhab's main airport in less than an hour, Lexi fretted. She had been delayed at the palace because apparently there had been a problem with the fuel pump for the helicopter, and once that had been sorted out she'd still had to wait for Yusuf, who had eventually appeared with her passport and a rambling explanation about how it had not been where he had thought it was and he had spent ages looking for it.

In half an hour it would be dark. She was used to the way the sun set quickly over the desert. Right now, the sun was a huge ball of fire that was turning the sea orange.

The sea!

Frowning, she turned to the helicopter pilot and spoke into her headset. 'Mitch, you're going the wrong way. The airport is in the opposite direction.'

'This is the direction I was told to fly. I'm just following the Sultan's orders.'

Below them, Lexi saw the black silhouettes of palm trees rising up from a desert island, and her heart gave a jolt as the chopper swooped lower over an empty beach. *Jinan.* 'Why have you brought me here?' she asked Mitch fiercely.

The pilot landed the chopper on the sand. 'This is where the Sultan told me to bring you.' Reaching under his seat, he handed her a jar of honey. 'He said to give you this.'

Thankfully, the fading light hid her scarlet face from the pilot. Memories of Kadir's unconventional use of honey when they had been trapped on the island flooded Lexi's mind. Was he playing some sort of cruel mind game with her? She made a muffled sound in her throat and curled her hand around the jar. 'It'll make a useful missile to throw at him,' she muttered.

'The Sultan said you'd probably say that.' Mitch grinned. 'It seems like Sultan Kadir knows you pretty well.'

What the devil was Kadir playing at? Lexi's heart was pounding as she marched up the beach. She scrambled over the sand dunes and saw the oasis and next to it the tent, illuminated by glowing lamps that cast shadows onto the canvas.

Pushing through the flaps, she stopped dead and stared at Kadir, sprawled on a pile of silk cushions. He was wearing a black robe tied loosely at the waist and revealing his bare chest. In the lamplight his body gleamed like polished bronze, and as he propped himself up on one elbow Lexi's eyes were drawn to his hard abdominal muscles and the line of dark hairs that arrowed lower. She remembered that the very first time she'd met him she had imagined the Sultan lying on silk cushions, beckoning to her to join him.

'Good, you brought the honey,' he drawled.

She gripped the heavy glass jar. 'Have you any idea what I'd like to do with this?'

'Show me,' he invited softly.

'Don't tempt me.'

'Why not?' He sat up and stared at her intently. 'You tempt me constantly. I think about you all the time.'

'Don't say things that aren't true.' She stared at the patterned rug on the floor, willing herself not to cry.

'I never took you for a coward, Lexi.'

'I'm not a coward, damn you.'

'Then look at me.'

Something in his voice, a tremor of emotion that felt like an arrow through her heart, made her slowly raise her head. His eyes were darker than she had ever seen them—dark with pain, she realised with a jolt. His teasing smile had disappeared and he looked serious and tense, almost— *nervous*. But that was ridiculous. What did the powerful Sultan of Zenhab, the desert king, have to fear?

'You really would have gone back to England, wouldn't you?' he said harshly. 'After everything we shared, the most beautiful time of my life, I thought, hoped you were starting to trust me.'

He couldn't sound hurt, Lexi told herself. She must be imagining the raw expression in his eyes. 'You said it was for the best that I'm not pregnant.' Her voice shook. 'You said goodbye at the palace and let me go.' Only now did she acknowledge she had been testing him, hoping at the eleventh hour for a miracle.

'I was hurting,' he shocked her by saying, 'and I was angry with myself for failing to do enough to convince you that we have something special. I went into the gardens and sat on my father's favourite bench. Remembering how much he loved me, the confidence I gained from my happy childhood, made me understand why trust is such a difficult concept for you. I understand why you are scared of emotions because you were rejected by your birth mother and your adoptive parents failed to make you feel loved.'

He stood up and walked towards her, stealing Lexi's breath with his masculine beauty, his powerful body all satiny skin and strong muscles.

'I do think it is better that you didn't fall pregnant the last time we were on Jinan.' He tipped her face towards him when she tried to look away to hide her pain and confusion. 'I can't imagine you would be happy to have an accidental pregnancy after what you told me about your biological mother,' he said with an intuition that touched a chord inside Lexi. 'When you conceive my baby I hope it will be an event we have planned, and our child will be longed for and loved from the moment of conception.'

Her heart was thumping so hard she could barely breathe. 'I don't understand,' she whispered. 'Why did you bring me here?'

He brushed her hair back from her face with gentle fingers. 'Jinan is where it began, although that's not quite true because it started when you hauled me out of a stormy sea and promptly wiped the floor with me.' He smiled. 'No one had ever spoken to me like that before. I was furious but at the same time all I could think of was how badly I wanted to kiss you. But I knew I couldn't. I had to honour my arranged marriage, and my desire for you was forbidden.

'I thought I would have no trouble resisting you,' he said roughly. 'Ever since I was a young man, I had resigned myself to the prospect that I must marry for duty, not love. And in some strange way it was a relief to know I would not suffer the heartbreak my father felt when my mother left him. My emotions would never be at risk, or so I believed. But when the kidnapper threatened you with a gun the truth hit me like a bullet through my heart.'

Kadir closed his eyes for a few seconds, haunted by the memory of the fear that had churned in his stomach when he'd thought she might be killed.

'I realised that if I lost you, my life would not be worth living. I also knew that I could not keep the promise I had made my father and marry Haleema. I could not marry without love, even though my decision meant I might lose my kingdom and my role as Sultan of Zenhab.'

Lexi was stunned by his revelation. 'I know how much it would have hurt you to break your promise to your father. You loved him so much.' She did not know what to think, and she was afraid to trust the expression in Kadir's eyes. He had told her he'd realised he could not marry without love, but that didn't mean that he loved her.

For some reason she thought of her sister. Athena had always been patient and loving, never asking Lexi for anything in return. She felt ashamed that it had taken her so long to tell her sister she loved her.

She remembered the magical days she had spent with Kadir and knew she hadn't imagined their friendship that had grown stronger every day. He had been kind and caring, patient and *loving*, but she had listened to her insecurities and been afraid to listen to her heart. She *had* been a coward, Lexi acknowledged.

But a lifetime of feeling rejected was not easy to overcome, and her voice caught in her throat when she spoke. 'The days and nights we spent together while we waited to find out if I was pregnant were the most beautiful of my life too. I didn't want them to end but I knew they couldn't last and I was sure you couldn't feel anything for me.'

'Why couldn't I?' he demanded.

'You are the Sultan of Zenhab,' she said as if it explained everything, 'and my mother was a whore.'

'I don't give a damn if your mother is a Martian.' Kadir seized hold of her shoulders and stared down at her startled face. 'Will you marry me, Lexi Howard?'

She so desperately wanted to trust the fierce emotion blazing in his eyes. Her bravery had never been put to such a defining test, not even when she had risked her life flying rescue missions in war-torn Afghanistan.

'There's no reason for you to marry me,' she reminded him.

He moved his hands up to frame her face and captured the tears clinging to her eyelashes on his fingers. 'I love you, Lexi. That's the only reason why I want you to be my wife and the mother of my children that, fate willing, we will be blessed with in the future. I want you as my lover and my best friend, and I hope you will be my Queen and help me rule my kingdom.'

He could not catch all her tears as they slipped down her cheeks, and he tasted them on her lips when he covered her mouth with his and kissed her with such beguiling tenderness that Lexi's heart felt as though it would burst.

'I love you,' she whispered, and suddenly the words weren't hard to say because they came from her heart. She said them over and over in a husky litany that moved Kadir unbearably because he knew the demons she had faced and beaten to give him her trust.

He lifted her into his arms and carried her over to the pile of silk cushions, where he removed her skirt and blouse with hands that visibly shook. 'I will tell you every day for the rest of our lives how much I love you,' he promised. 'You are my heart's desire, the love of my life, *habibi*.'

From somewhere he produced a small box, which he opened to reveal an exquisite oval blue diamond ring.

'I knew the colour would be a perfect match for your eyes. Blue diamonds are rare and precious, just as you are to me, my angel.' He looked intently into Lexi's eyes. 'You haven't given me an answer. Will you make me the happiest man in the world and marry me? Will you love me for eternity, as I will love you?'

Lexi wiped away her tears and met his gaze, her blue eyes sparkling as bright as the diamond he slid on her finger. 'Yes, my Sultan, my love. I never knew I could feel this happy,' she whispered, shivering with anticipation as he removed her underwear and knelt over her.

'Tomorrow we'll start planning our wedding,' he promised. 'Luca De Rossi guessed how I felt about you when we stayed at his villa in Italy, and he will be my best man. Who will you choose for your chief bridesmaid?'

'My sister,' Lexi said instantly. 'Athena suggested I should tell you I love you.'

'Why don't you show me?' Kadir murmured.

'With pleasure, my Sultan.' She took him by surprise, pushing him back against the cushions and straddling him at the same time as she unscrewed the lid of the jar of honey.

'*Habibi*…where are you going to pour that honey?'

Kadir groaned when she showed him.

* * * * *

"What is this? Where are we?"

"This is an airport," Rihad told her, in the same lecturing way she'd used when she'd ordered him not to use his mobile as he drove out of Manhattan. "And that is a plane. *My* plane."

Sterling went so white he thought she might topple over where she sat. Her hands moved at once to the round swell of her belly, as if she was trying to protect the child within from him, and he hated it that there was some part of him that admired her for so futile a gesture.

"Who are you?" she whispered.

He suspected she knew. But he took immense satisfaction in angling closer, so he could see every faint tremor on those sinful lips. Every shiver that moved across her skin. Every dawning moment of horrified recognition in her deep blue gaze.

"I am Rihad al Bakri," he told her, and felt a harsh surge of victory as her gaze went dark. "If that is truly my brother's child you carry, it is my heir. And I'm afraid that means you'll be coming with me."

Scandalous Sheikh Brides

And the powerful men who claim them!

In their rival desert kingdoms the word of Rihad al Bakri and Kavian ibn Zayed al Talaas is law.

Nothing and no one stands in the way of these formidable and passionate sheikhs.

Until two exceptional women dare to defy them and turn their carefully controlled worlds upside down.

These men will do whatever it takes to protect their legacies—including claiming these women as their brides before a scandal ensues!

Read Rihad's story in
Protecting the Desert Heir
June 2015

And look out for Kavian and Princess Amaya's story, coming soon!

PROTECTING THE DESERT HEIR

BY
CAITLIN CREWS

MILLS & BOON

Published in Great Britain 2015
by Mills & Boon, an imprint of Harlequin (UK) Limited,
Eton House, 18-24 Paradise Road, Richmond, Surrey, TW9 1SR

ISBN: 978-0-263-25065-7

Books by Caitlin Crews

Mills & Boon® Modern™ Romance

At the Count's Bidding
Undone by the Sultan's Touch
Not Just the Boss's Plaything
A Devil in Disguise
In Defiance of Duty
The Replacement Wife
Princess from the Past

The Chatsfield

Greek's Last Redemption

Vows of Convenience

His for Revenge
His for a Price

Royal and Ruthless

A Royal Without Rules

Scandal in the Spotlight

No More Sweet Surrender
Heiress Behind the Headlines

Self-Made Millionaires

Katrakis's Last Mistress

Bride on Approval

Pure Princess, Bartered Bride

CHAPTER ONE

THE LAST TIME she'd run for her life, Sterling McRae had been a half-wild teenager with more guts than sense. Today it was more a *waddle* for her life than anything approaching a run —thanks to the baby she carried and had to protect no matter what, now that Omar was dead—but the principle remained the same.

Get out. Get away. Go somewhere you can never be found.

At least this time, twelve years older and lifetimes wiser than that fifteen-year-old who'd run away from her foster home in Cedar Rapids, Iowa, she didn't have to depend on the local Greyhound bus station to make her getaway. This time, she had limitless credit cards and a very nice SUV at her disposal, complete with a driver who would take her wherever she asked to go.

All of which she'd have to ditch once she got out of Manhattan, of course, but at least she'd start her second reinvention of herself with a little more style.

Thank you, Omar, Sterling thought then. The heels she refused to stop wearing even this late into her pregnancy clicked against the floor of the apartment building where she and Omar had shared his penthouse ever since they'd met while he'd been a graduate student. A wave of grief threatened to take her feet right out from under her, but Sterling fought it back with grim determination and clenched her teeth tightly as she kept on walking.

There was no time left for grief or anything else. She'd seen the morning news. Rihad al Bakri, Omar's fearsome older brother and now the ruler of the tiny little port country on the Persian Gulf that Omar had escaped at eighteen, had arrived in New York City.

Sterling had no doubt whatsoever that he would be coming for her.

There was every chance she was already being watched, she cautioned herself as she hurried from the elevator bank—that the sheikh had sent some kind of advance team to come for her even though the news had broadcast his arrival barely a half hour ago. That unpleasant if realistic thought forced her to slow down, despite the hammering of her heart, so she *appeared* nothing but calm. It forced her to smile as she moved through the lobby, the way she might have on any other day. There would be no honoring Omar if she let herself—and more important, her baby—fall into the clutches of the very people he'd worked so hard to escape. And she knew a little bit about the way predators reacted when they saw prey act like prey.

The more fearful you acted, the harder they attacked. Sterling knew that firsthand.

So instead, she walked. She *sauntered*.

Sterling walked like the model she'd been before she'd taken her position at Omar's side all those years ago. Like the notorious, effortlessly sensual mistress of the international playboy Omar had been in the eyes of the world. She strolled out into the New York

City morning and didn't look around to savor the great sprawl of the city she'd always loved so much and so fiercely. There was no time for goodbyes. Not if she wanted to keep her baby—Omar's baby—safe.

And she might have lost Omar, but God help her, she would not lose this baby, too.

Sterling was glad the summer morning was bright and warm, giving her an excuse to hide her thick grief and her buzzing anxiety and the too-hot tears she refused to let fall behind a pair of oversize sunglasses. It took her longer than it should have to realize that while that was indeed Omar's gleaming black SUV pulled up to the curb on the busy Upper East Side street, that was not Omar's regular driver standing beside it.

This man lounged against the side of the vehicle looking for all the world as if it was some kind of throne and he its rightful king. His attention was on the cell phone in his hand, and something about the way he scrolled down his screen struck Sterling as insolent. Or maybe it was the way he shifted and then looked up, his powerfully disapproving dark gaze slamming into hers with the force of a blow.

Sterling had to stop walking or fall over—and this time, grief had nothing to do with it.

Because that look felt like a touch, intimate and lush. And despite all the work Sterling had put into her image as a woman who wallowed neck-deep in the pleasures of the flesh, the truth was she did not like to be touched. Ever.

Not even like this, when she knew it wasn't real.

It *felt* real.

This driver was too much. Too tall, too solid. Too damned *real* himself. He was dressed in a dark suit,

which only served to make his lean, intensely dangerous body seem *lethal*. He had thick black hair, cut short
as if to hide its natural curl, rich brown skin and the
most sensual mouth Sterling had ever seen on a man
in her life, for all that it was set in a grim line. He was
astonishingly, noticeably, almost shockingly beautiful, something that should have been at odds with that
knife-edged form of his. Instead, it was as if he was a
steel-tempered blade with a stunningly bejeweled hilt.

He was either the last person she should want driving her to freedom, or the first, and Sterling didn't have
time to decide which. She didn't have any time at all.
She could feel her phone buzzing insistently from the
pocket where she'd stashed it, and she knew what that
meant.

Rihad al Bakri. The king himself, since his and
Omar's father had died a few years back. He was finally here, in Manhattan, as she'd feared. Both Omar's
friends and hers were texting her warnings, calling to
make sure she was aware of the impending threat. Because no matter what else happened, no matter what
might become of Sterling now without the man who
had been everything to her, Omar's older brother could
not know about this baby.

It was why she'd taken such pains to hide the fact that
she was pregnant all these months. Until today, when it
didn't matter any longer, because she was running away
from this life. She'd do what she'd done the last time.
A far-off city. Hair dye and/or a dramatically different
cut. A new name and a new wardrobe to go along with
it. It wasn't hard to pick a new life, she knew—it was
only hard to stick to it once you'd chosen it, because

ghosts were powerful and seductive, especially when you were lonely.

But she'd done it before, when she'd had much less. She had even more reason to do it now.

All of this meant that Sterling certainly didn't have time to ogle the damned driver, or wonder what it said about her that the first man she'd noticed in years seemed to have taken an instant dislike to her, if the strange driver's expression was any guide. It said nothing particularly good about her, she thought. Then again, maybe it was just her grief talking.

"Where is Muhammed?" she asked crisply, forcing herself to start forward again across the sidewalk.

The new driver only stared at her and as she drew closer she found herself feeling something like *sideswiped* by the bold, regal line of his nose and the fact that those dark eyes of his were far more arresting up close, where they gleamed a dark gold in the bright morning light. She was breathless and fluttery and she couldn't make any sense of it, nor understand why he should look something like *affronted*. Her phone kept vibrating, her breath was ragged and she was *this close* to bursting into tears right there on the street, so she ignored the odd beauty of this strangely quiet and watchful man and wrenched open the door to the SUV herself.

"I don't actually care where he is," she threw at him, answering her own question as her panic started to bang inside her like a drum. "Let's go. I'm sorry, but I'm in a terrible hurry."

He leaned there against the driver's window, his expression startled and thoughtful all at once, and he only studied her in a leisurely sort of way as Sterling slung her oversize shoulder bag inside. And she had never been much of a diva, no matter how much money Omar had given her to throw around. But today was a terrible day after a week of far worse, ever since she'd gotten that call in the middle of the night from the French police to tell her that Omar was dead after a terrible car crash outside Paris. And she had none of the social graces she'd worked so hard to learn left inside of her after that. Not even a polite word.

Not for a man like this one, who stared at her as if he would decide when and where they went, not her. Something snapped inside of her and she let it—hell, she welcomed it. A surly driver was a far better target than herself or Omar's terrifying brother, who, Sterling was well aware, could show up at any moment and destroy everything.

As far as she'd ever been able to tell from reading between the lines of Omar's staunchly loyal stories, that was pretty much all the sheikh did.

"How did you get this job?" she demanded, focusing her temper and her fear on the stranger before her. "Because I don't think you're any good at it. You do realize you're supposed to open the door for your passengers, don't you?"

"Yes, of course," he said then, and Sterling was so startled by that rich, low, deeply sardonic voice that she curled a hand around her big, low belly protectively even as her throat went alarmingly and suddenly dry. "My mistake. It is, of course, my single goal in life to serve American women such as yourself. My goal and my dream in one."

Sterling blinked. Had he said that in another way, she might have ignored it. But the way he *looked* at her.

As if he was powerful and hungry and *ferocious* and was only barely concealing those things beneath his civilized veneer. It arrowed into her, dark and stirring.

It reminded her, for the first time in a very long while, or maybe ever, that she was a woman. Not merely mother to her best friend's child, but entirely *female* from the top of her head, where that look of his made her feel prickly, all the way down to her toes, which were curling up in her shoes where she stood on the curb.

And entirely too many places in between.

The baby chose that moment to kick her, hard, and Sterling told herself *that* was why she couldn't breathe. *That* was why her entire body felt taut and achy and very much like someone else's.

"Then yours must be a life of intense disappointment," she told him when she could breathe again, or anyway, fake it. "As you fall so far short."

"My apologies," the driver replied at once, his voice smooth, but with that hard undercurrent in it that made Sterling's head feel light. "I forget myself, clearly."

He straightened then and that didn't make it any better. He was tall and broad at once, a sweep of black that took over the entire world, and she wouldn't have been at all surprised if he'd snatched her up, belly and all, in one powerful fist—

But he didn't. Of course he didn't. He reached over and wrapped his hand over the top of the door instead, then inclined his head toward the SUV's interior as if it was his car and he was the one doing her a great favor.

Impossible images chased through her head then, each more inappropriate and embarrassing and *naked* than the last. What was *wrong* with her? Sterling didn't

have thoughts like that, so yearning and wild. So…
unclothed. She didn't like to be touched at all, much
less…*that*.

"Well," she said stiffly after a tense, electric moment
she could feel everywhere, even if she couldn't understand it. She felt weak and singed straight through and
she couldn't seem to look away from him when she
knew that he was causing this. That it was *him*. "Try
not to do it again."

His dark gold eyes got more intense, somehow, and
that stunning mouth of his shifted into something that
could only be described as *mocking*. She ordered herself not to shiver in response, but she felt it wash over
her anyway, as if she had.

"But we really do have to get moving." She made her
voice softer then. Placating, the way she'd learned to
do with all kinds of men—all kinds of *people*, come to
think of it—over the years. She'd made it her art, and
no matter that her life with Omar had tempted her to
believe she wouldn't have to live like that any longer.
That she could turn it on or off for fun, as she wished.
There's no such thing as a happy ending, she reminded
herself harshly. *Not for you.* "I have a long way to go
and I'm already behind schedule."

"By all means, then," he said invitingly, the way a
wolf might have done, with the suggestion of claws and
the hint of fangs yet nothing but that sardonic smile on
his shockingly sensual, infinitely dangerous mouth.
"Get in. I would hate to inconvenience you in any way."

Then he reached out and took her hand, ostensibly
to help her into the SUV.

And it was like fireworks.

It was pure insanity.

Sensation galloped through her, shooting up from that shocking point of contact like wildfire, enveloping her. Changing her. Making the city disappear. Making her whole history fall out of her own head as if it had never happened. Making her body feel tight and restless and dangerously loose at once. Making her wonder, yearn, *long*—

She wanted to jerk her hand away from his, the way she always did when someone touched her without her permission, but she didn't. Because for the first time in as long as she could remember, Sterling wanted to *keep touching him* more than she wanted to stop.

That astounding truth pounded through her like adrenaline, a sleek and dizzying drum.

"I cannot serve you if you do not enter the vehicle," the driver said after a moment, his gaze narrowing in on hers in a way that made her breath go shallow. And his voice seemed to stoke the fires that raged in her, as if the way his hand wrapped around hers was a sexual act. A whole lot of sexual acts. "And that would be a tragedy, would it not?"

Sterling couldn't breathe. She couldn't *breathe*—and she was terribly afraid that the edgy feeling swamping her just then wasn't panic at all. She knew panic. This was deeper. Richer.

Life-altering, she thought in a kind of awe.

But the only thing she could let herself think about right now was her baby, so she shoved all the confusing sensations away as best she could—and tried to get into the car and get away from him before her legs simply gave out beneath her.

Or before she did something she'd truly regret, like moving closer to this strange man instead of away.

* * *

There were a number of things Rihad al Bakri—reigning sheikh, Grand Ruler and King of the Bakrian Empire—did not understand.

First, how his late brother had neglected to mention that he had impregnated his mistress and quite some time ago, if her current condition was any guide. Or how this one delicate American woman had managed to elude his entire security force and was now sashaying out into the city as if she was still on the sort of catwalks she'd frequented when she'd been, by all accounts, a feral teen. Finally, he was arrogant enough to wonder how on earth she could possibly have mistaken him—*him*—for a livery driver, of all things.

And that was not even getting into his unending grief that his brother was gone. That after wasting so many years of his life gallivanting about with this unsuitable woman, Omar could have disappeared so senselessly in the space of a single evening.

Rihad could not come to terms with it. He doubted he ever would.

Yet all of that faded when Rihad took her hand, meaning only to help her into the SUV as any decent servant might. He had enough of them. He should know.

The loud, brash, concrete city all around them seemed to skip its groove like an old-fashioned record, and go still.

So still it was like a quiet agony, reverberating inside of him.

Her hand was delicate and strong at once, and Rihad didn't like that. Nor did he like the way her mouth firmed as she looked at him, as if she was pressing her lips together to disguise the way they trembled, because he had the wild, nearly ungovernable desire to taste that theory.

Surely not.

Her strawberry blond hair should have appeared messy, twisted back in a riot of smooth gold and copper strands, but instead made her look fresh. She wore a stretchy sort of tunic dress over skinny jeans and absurdly high heels, quite as if she wasn't so heavily pregnant that it looked as if she'd shoved a giant ball underneath her clothes. Worst of all, she was remarkably graceful, moving easily from the sidewalk into the vehicle, making him wonder exactly how she might move when not pregnant.

Or better yet, beneath him.

Rihad did not want to wonder about this woman in any capacity at all and much less that one. He'd wanted nothing more than to eradicate the stain of her from the memory of his brother's life, erase her taint from the Bakrian royal family once and for all. That was why he'd come here himself, straight from Omar's funeral, when he could easily have sent agents to eject her from this property.

Enough scandal. Enough selfish, heedless behavior. Rihad had spent his life cleaning up his father's messes, Omar's messes, even his half sister Amaya's messes. Sterling McRae was the emblem of his family's licentiousness and Rihad wanted her—and all the remnants of his brother's lifetime of poor decisions—gone.

So naturally she was pregnant.

Hugely, incontestably, irrevocably pregnant.

Of course.

CHAPTER TWO

"YOU ARE WITH CHILD," Rihad said grimly as his brother's mistress settled herself in the SUV, pulling her hand from his as she sat—and perhaps, he thought, with a certain alacrity that suggested that simple touch had affected her, too.

He opted not to consider that too closely.

"You are very observant." Was that…sarcasm? Directed at *him*? Rihad blinked. But she continued, her voice now coolly imperious. "And now if you'll close the door and *drive*?"

She was giving him orders. She expected him—*him*—to obey these orders. To obey *her*.

That was such an astonishing development that Rihad merely stepped back and shut the door while he processed the situation. And thought about how to proceed.

All Rihad could hope for was that the child this woman carried was not Omar's—but he was not optimistic. His brother's obsession with his regrettable mistress had spanned the better part of a decade. Omar had famously scooped her up when she'd been a mere seventeen. He'd installed her in his apartment within the week, not caring in the least that she was little more than an ignorant guttersnipe with a made-up name who wasn't even of legal age at the time.

The paparazzi had all but turned gleeful cartwheels in the streets.

"Omar will tire of her," their late father had said after scanning one such breathless and insulting article, back in the Bakrian palace.

The old sheikh had been a connoisseur of flagrantly inappropriate women. He'd stopped marrying them after the mercenary Ukrainian dancer—the mother of the deeply disobedient Amaya, who was chief among Rihad's many problems these days while she evaded her responsibilities and the fiancé she'd decided she didn't want on the eve of her engagement party—had taken off and proceeded to live off the telling of her "my life in the evil sheikh's harem" story for decades. The old man had gone off matrimony after that, but not women. If anyone knew how men treated their mistresses, it would be his father.

"Perhaps a refresher course in your expectations of Omar might not go amiss," Rihad had suggested drily. "His time in New York City appears to have affected his memory, particularly where his duties to this country are concerned."

His father had only sighed, as Rihad had known he would. Because while Rihad was his father's heir, he had never been his father's favorite. And no wonder. Omar and the old sheikh were peas in a deeply selfish pod, stirring up scandals left and right as they did exactly as they pleased no matter the consequences, while Rihad was left to quietly clean it all up in their wake.

Because somebody had to be responsible, or the

country would fall to its enemies. That somebody had been Rihad for as long as he could remember.

"No man is without his weaknesses, Rihad," his father had said, frowning at him. "It is only regrettable that Omar is making his so public."

Rihad had no idea if he had weaknesses or not, as he'd never been given any leave to indulge them. He'd never kept mistresses, inappropriate or otherwise. He'd known full well that as his father's successor he'd been promised in a political marriage since birth. And he'd dutifully married the woman picked out for him when he'd finished his studies in England, in fulfillment of that promise.

Tasnim might not have been a flashy model type, with masses of shining copper-blond hair and a sinful mouth like the woman Omar had holed up with all these years. But she'd been as committed to their marriage as Rihad had been. They'd worked their way to something like affection in the three short years before she'd been diagnosed with cancer at a routine doctor's appointment. When she'd died five years ago this past summer, Rihad had lost a friend.

Maybe that was what moved in him then, on the side of a New York City street as his brother's worst and most public embarrassment sat waiting for him to drive her away from the comeuppance Rihad had planned to deliver upon her, in spades. Fury that Tasnim, who had kept all her promises, was gone. The same old mix of fury and bafflement that Omar had broken all the rules, as usual, and gotten this plaything of his big with child anyway—and then abandoned a Bakrian royal child to fate, its mother unmarried and unprotected.

That or the fact her hand in his, her skin sliding

against his in even so simple and impersonal a touch, had made him burn. He could feel it now. Still.

Unacceptable.

If he'd been anyone else, he thought, he might have been shaken by that astonishing burst of heat. Altered, somehow, by that fire that roared through him, making him feel bright and needy, and suggesting all manner of possibilities he didn't wish to face.

But Rihad was not anyone else. He did not acknowledge weakness. He rose above it.

He pulled out his mobile, made a call and snapped out his instructions as he climbed into the driver's seat, his decision made in an instant. Because it was the most expedient way to handle the crisis, he assured himself, not because he could *still* feel her touch as if she'd branded him. He could see Sterling in the back via his mirror—such a fanciful, ridiculous name—and the frown she aimed at him. It had nothing to do with the things that coursed through him at the sight of her, none of which he'd expected. He was a man of duty, never of need.

"You can't talk on your phone while you drive," she told him. *Scolded him*, more like. "You know that, don't you?"

As if he was extraordinarily dim. It occurred to Rihad then that no one he was not related to by blood, in all his years on this earth, had dared address him with anything but the utmost respect—if not fawning deference.

Ever.

For a moment he was stunned.

He should have been outraged. He couldn't under-

stand why instead there was a part of him that wanted
only to laugh.

"Can I not?" he asked mildly, after a moment, his
tone an uneasy balance between the two. "I appreciate
the warning."

"Aside from the fact it's against the law, it's not safe,"
she replied in that same irritated way he'd never in his
life had directed at him before, her voice tight. *Annoyed*,
even. He saw her shift against the leather seat and put
her hands over her swollen belly, in a way that suggested she was not quite the soulless, avaricious harlot
he'd painted her in his head. He ignored that suggestion.

"I don't think I'd care if you ran this car into the side
of a building if it was only me, but it's not."

"Indeed it is not." Rihad slid his phone into the interior pocket of his jacket and then started the vehicle.
"Yet your husband would miss you, surely?"

He was needling her, of course, and he couldn't have
said why. What could he possibly gain from it? A glance
in the rearview mirror showed him her profile, however,
not that cool frown he found he very nearly enjoyed.
She'd turned her head as if to stare back at the building
as he pulled the car into traffic. As if leaving it—this
place she'd lived with his brother, or *off* his brother if
he was more precise—was difficult for her.

Rihad supposed it must have been. It would be much
harder to find a patron now, no doubt. She was older,
for one thing. Well-known—infamous, even—for her
role as another man's prize possession, across whole
years. Soon to be a mother to another man's child, which
the sort of men who regularly trafficked in mistresses
would be unlikely to find appealing.

Because you find her so unappealing even now, when

she is huge with your brother's child, a derisive voice inside chided him. *Liar.*

Rihad ignored that, too. He could not find himself attracted to his brother's infamous leftovers. He would not allow it.

"The father of my child is dead," Sterling said, her voice so frozen that if he hadn't stolen that glance at her, he'd have believed she really was utterly devoid of emotion.

"And you loved him so much you wish to follow him into that great night?" He couldn't quite keep the sardonic inflection from his own voice, and her head swung back toward him, her lovely brow creasing again. "That seems a rather desperate form of tribute, don't you think? The province of the cowed and the cowardly, in my opinion. Living is harder. That's the point of it."

"Am I having an auditory hallucination?"

That was obviously a rhetorical question. Still, Rihad shrugged as he turned onto the narrow highway that clung to the east side of the city and led out of town, and replied, "I cannot answer that for you."

"Or are you quizzing me—in a snide manner—about the death of someone I loved? You're a *driver.*"

And her tone was withering, but there was something about it that spoke of repressed emotions, hidden fears. Or perhaps he was the one hearing things then.

"I don't care what you think about my life or my choices or my feelings, in case that's not clear. I want you to drive the damned car upstate, no more and no less. Is that all right with you? Or do you have more unsolicited opinions to share?"

Rihad smiled as he merged onto a different highway and headed toward the top of the island and the stately bridge that would lead to the airfield where his jet should be waiting, refueled and ready, upon his arrival. Or heads would roll.

"Where are you going?" he asked her with deceptive casualness. "Upstate New York is lovely in the summer, but it is not possible to outrun anything in your condition. Surely you must realize this."

"My condition." She repeated the words as if, until she sounded them out, she couldn't believe she'd heard them correctly. "I beg your pardon?"

"You look as if you're used to being kept well," Rihad continued. Mildly. "That will be hard to replicate."

She swiped those huge, concealing sunglasses off her face, and Rihad wished she hadn't. She was nothing less than perfection, even in a quick glance in the rearview mirror of a moving vehicle, and he felt as if he'd been kicked by a horse. Her eyes were far bluer than the sky outside and she was more delicate, somehow, than she appeared in photographs. More vulnerable, he might have thought, had she not looked so outraged.

"Does it make you feel good to insult people you don't know?" she demanded, also in a tone he'd never heard directed at him before. This woman seemed to be full of such tones. "Is that the kind of man you are?"

"What kind of man I am or am not is hardly something you will be capable of ascertaining from the backseat of this vehicle."

"Yet you feel perfectly comfortable shredding my character from the front, of course. What a shock."

Rihad didn't like the tightness in his chest then. "Were you not kept well? Please accept my condolences. Perhaps you should have found a better patron before you permitted such a shoddy one to impregnate you."

He didn't know what he expected. Floods of tears? But Sterling sat straighter in her seat, managing to look both regal and dignified, which only made that constriction around his chest pull tighter.

"Let me guess," she said after a hard pause, her tone so scathing she was clearly nowhere near tears of any kind. "This is some kind of game to you. You intrude upon people's lives, insult them, and then what? Is causing pain its own reward—or are you hoping they'll do something crazy to get away from you, like demand you leave them by the side of the road? Exactly what do you get out of being this nasty?"

Rihad's teeth were on edge, his body tense. He left the bridge behind him and headed west, wanting absolutely nothing at that moment but to get to his plane and get the hell out of here, back to his own land. His throne. The familiarity of his country, his rule. Before the tension in him exploded into something he couldn't control.

That such a thing had never happened before—that he had never been quite this tense in the whole of his life before he'd laid eyes on this woman—did not bear thinking about.

"I have no intention of leaving you by the side of the road," he assured her, and there was possibly too much dark intent in the comment, because she scowled at him in response. "Not yet anyway."

"You're a true gentleman. Clearly."

And Rihad laughed then, because it was funny. All of this was funny, surely, however little familiarity he had with such things. He was a king pretending to be a driver. She was the mistress who had ruined his dead brother's life. And he felt more alive trading insults with her than he had in years.

In fact, he couldn't recall when he'd ever felt quite like this, for any reason.

He'd obviously gone mad with guilt and grief.

"I want us both to be very clear about who you are," Sterling said then, leaning forward in her seat, and her scent teased at him, honey and sugar with the faintest hint of a tropical bloom beneath. It made his hands clench into fists against the steering wheel. It made him hard and needy.

It made him feel like a stranger to himself. Like the hungry, selfish man he'd never been.

Rihad couldn't bring himself to analyze it. He concentrated on the road instead.

"I am perfectly clear about who I am," he told her.

Or perhaps he was telling himself—because he had been. When he'd exited his private jet mere hours before. When he'd arrived at Omar's apartment building, dismissed the driver who waited there and sent his team inside to secure this woman so he could have the pleasure of evicting her himself. He'd known exactly who he was.

And nothing has changed since then, he told himself harshly.

Or would.

"You are a man who thinks it's appropriate to mock and insult a woman, first of all," Sterling said in that precise way of hers that he really shouldn't find so fascinating. It was only that no one had ever dared use a tone like that in his presence before, he assured himself. He was intrigued intellectually, nothing more. "Congratulations. Your mother must be proud."

He laughed again, with significantly less mirth than before. "My mother died when I was twelve years old."

"A great blessing, I think we can agree, so that she might be spared the knowledge of who you've become in her absence," Sterling said, so matter-of-factly it took Rihad a moment to realize how deeply she'd insulted him. And then she kept going, unaware that no one spoke to him like that without consequences. No one would dare. "You are also a man who finds it amusing to speculate about the lives of strangers. Openly and repulsively."

"Are you not a kept woman?" he asked, making no attempt to soften his tone. "My mistake. What is it you do, then, to support yourself?"

"You are ill-mannered and rude, and that was evident at a glance, long before you opened your mouth." She laughed then, an abrasive sound that made his hackles rise. "I've met more honorable pigs."

"Be very careful," Rihad warned her. Because he had limits—even if, he was well aware, anyone who'd ever met him might have thought he'd crossed them a long while back. "A man does not react well to the questioning of his honor."

"Then a man should act as if he has some," she snapped.

"Yes, of course," Rihad snorted. "And how would I prove that I am an honorable man to one such as you, do you imagine? Will you be the judge? A woman who—"

"Is pregnant?" Her voice was icy then, so cold he almost overlooked the fact that she'd interrupted him. Something no one had done since his father had died, and no *woman* had ever done, as far as he could recall. "So scandalous, I know. It's almost as if every single person walking this earth came about their presence here some other way."

"I must have mistaken you for someone else," Rihad murmured as he made the final turn that would lead them to the airfield, which was just as well, because he thought his temper might flip the damned SUV over if he didn't put some distance between the two of them, and soon. "I thought you were the mistress of Omar al Bakri."

"If I were you—" and her voice was very soft, very furious then "—I'd be very, very careful what you say next."

"Why?" Rihad realized he was taking out his aggression on the gas pedal and slowed as he arrived at the gate to find his men already there, which was lucky for everyone involved. They waved him through and he was glad, he told himself, that this little farce was almost finished. He wasn't one for subterfuge, no matter how necessary. It felt too much like lies. "He is dead, as you say. You remain. Is that child his?"

"Ah, yes. Of course." She sounded bored then, though he could still hear the fury beneath it, giving it a certain huskiness that he felt in all the wrong places. "I must be a whore. That's the point of these questions, isn't it? Are you trying to determine whether or not I'm a terrible, no-good, very bad harlot or have you already rendered your judgment?"

"Are you?"

She laughed. "What if I am? What is it to you?"

But Rihad glanced at her in the mirror and saw the truth of things in the way her hands clasped on the shelf of her belly, her knuckles white, as if she was not as blasé as she was pretending.

It would be easier if she was. Easier, but it wouldn't

do much for that thing that still held him in its grip, that he refused to examine any closer.

"I'm only using the proper terminology to describe your role," he said mildly as he pulled up beside his plane out on the tarmac. "I apologize if you find that insulting."

"You decided I was a whore the moment you saw me," she said dismissively. Or he assumed that was what that particular tone meant, having never heard it before. "But virgins and whores are indistinguishable, I hate to tell you."

"It's a bit late to claim virginity, I think."

"Whores don't have identifying marks to set them apart." If she'd heard him, she was ignoring him—another new sensation for Rihad. He was beginning to feel each of them like blows. "Purity isn't a scent or a tattoo. Neither is promiscuity, which is lucky, or most men like you who love to cast stones would reek of it."

"I am aware of only one case of a virgin birth," he pointed out as he put the SUV into Park. "Everyone else, I am fairly certain, has gone about it the old-fashioned way. Unless you are on your way to notify the world's religious leaders of the second coming of Mary? That would explain your hurry."

"How many people have you slept with?" she asked, sounding unperturbed.

He laughed as much to cover his astonishment at her temerity as anything else. "Are you petitioning to be the next?"

"If you've slept with anyone at all and you're unmarried, you're a hypocrite."

"I am widowed."

A typical female might have apologized for his loss,

but this was Sterling McRae, and she was not, he was already far too aware in a variety of increasingly uncomfortable ways, the least bit *typical*.

"And you've never touched a single woman in your whole life save your late wife?"

He should not have brought Tasnim into this. He was furious with himself. And Sterling, of course, correctly interpreted his silence.

"Oh, dear," she murmured. "It appears you are, in fact, a hypocrite. Perhaps you should judge others a bit less. Or perhaps you're no more than one of those charming throwbacks who think chastity only matters when it's a woman's."

"The world has turned on its ear, clearly," Rihad said in a kind of wonder, as much to the tarmac as to her, and he told himself that what surged in him then was relief that this was over. This strange interlude as a man people addressed with such stunning disrespect. "I am being lectured to by a blonde American parasite who has lived off of weak and foolish men her entire adult life. Thank God we have arrived."

He turned in his seat, so he saw the way she jolted then, as if she hadn't noticed the SUV had come to a stop. She looked around in confusion, then those blue eyes of hers slammed back to his.

"What is this? Where are we?"

"This is an airport," Rihad told her, in that same patronizing, lecturing way she'd ordered him not to use his mobile as they'd driven out of Manhattan. "And that is a plane. My plane."

She went so white he thought she might topple over where she sat. Her hands moved over the round swell of her belly, as if she was trying to protect the child within from him, and he hated that there was some part of him that admired her for so futile a gesture.

"Who are you?" she whispered.

He suspected she knew. But he took immense satisfaction in angling closer, so he could see every faint tremor on those sinful lips. Every shiver that moved across her skin. Every dawning moment of horrified recognition in her deep blue gaze.

"I am Rihad al Bakri," he told her, and felt a harsh surge of victory as her gaze went dark. "If that is truly my brother's child you carry, it is my heir. And I'm afraid that means it—and you—are now my problem to solve."

CHAPTER THREE

THE SUV SEEMED to close in around her, her heart was a rapid throb in her throat and it was only another well-timed kick from the baby that broke through the panic. Sterling rubbed a hand over her belly and tried to calm herself.

He won't hurt you. He can't. *If this is the heir to his kingdom, you've never been safer in all your life.*

The man she should have realized wasn't the slightest bit subservient to anyone threw open the driver's door and climbed out of the SUV, then slammed it shut behind him. She could hear the sound of that voice of his outside on the tarmac, the spate of Arabic words like some kind of rough incantation, some terrible spell that he was casting over the whole of the private airfield. His men. *Her.*

And she couldn't seem to do anything but sit there, frozen in place, obeying him by default. She stared at the back of the seat he'd vacated and tried to convince herself that despite the panic stampeding through her veins, she really was safe.

She had to be safe, because this baby had to be safe.

But the truth was, there was more than a small part of her that was still holding out hope that this was all a terrible nightmare from which she'd bolt awake at any minute. That Omar would be there, alive and well, with that wry smile of his at the ready and exactly the right words to tease away any lingering darkness. He'd tell her none of this could possibly have happened. That it never would.

And this would be a convoluted, nonsensical story she'd tell him over a long, lazy breakfast out on their wraparound terrace with views of New York City stretching in all directions as if it really was the center of the world, until they both laughed so hard they made themselves nearly sick.

God, what she would do to wake up and find out this was all a bad dream, that Omar had never gotten in that car in France, that it had never spun out of control on its way back into Paris—

But the door beside her opened abruptly then and Rihad stood there before her.

Because, of course, it was him. Rihad. The sheikh. *The king.* The more-feared-than-respected ruler of his fiercely contested little country on the Persian Gulf. The older brother who had consistently made Omar feel as if he was a failure, despite how much Omar had looked up to him. As if he was less than Rihad somehow. As if the deepest truths of who he'd been had to be hidden away, lied about, concealed where no one could see them—especially not the brother who should have loved him unconditionally.

Omar had loved him, despite everything. Sterling had not been similarly handicapped.

"There has been no mention of this pregnancy in any of the papers," Rihad said in his dark, authoritative way. "No hint."

"Guess why?" she suggested, hoping all the pain she'd like to inflict on him was evident in her voice. "Guess who we didn't want to know?"

"You were both fools."

Sterling glared at Rihad as the light wrapped around him and made him look something like celestial. How had she managed to convince herself this man was merely a *driver*? He fairly *oozed* power from every pore. He was the physical embodiment of ruthlessness no matter how the summer sunlight loved him and licked over the planes and valleys of his fascinating face. He exuded ruthless masculinity and total authority in equal measure, and she'd thrown herself directly into his hands.

He stared down at her, that mouth of his in a sardonic curl, his dark gold gaze bright and hot and infinitely disturbing, until Sterling thought she might not be able to breathe normally again. Ever.

"I believe this is the part where a good driver helps a fine, upstanding lady such as yourself from the vehicle," he said in that smooth way of his, like silk and yet with all that steely harshness beneath it. "Without any commentary involving terms she might or might not like."

"I think you mean insults, not terms."

"I think it's time to get out of the car."

Then he held out his hand and there was no pretending it was anything but a royal command.

"I'm not getting on that plane," Sterling told him.

Very carefully and precisely, as if perfect diction might save her here. Save her from him. As if anything could.

"It was not a request."

She could see then how much he'd been *acting* the

part of the supposed servant before, because he wasn't bothering with that any longer. He was a stern column of inimitable power, his will like a living thing coiled tight around both of them and the whole damned airfield besides, and she couldn't understand why he'd played that game with her in the first place. This was not a man who pretended anything, ever, she understood at a glance. Because he didn't need to pretend. This was a man who took what he wanted as he wanted it, the end.

But she was not going to let him take her. Not without a fight.

"Perhaps you're misunderstanding me, Rihad," she said, deliberately using his first name to underscore how little she respected him.

She felt the ripple of that impertinence move through him and then beyond him, through the line of his men, where they stood in a loose ring around him and the SUV, protection and defense. The disapproval washed back over her from all sides, but the gleam in Rihad's dark gold gaze merely edged over into something more shrewd as he considered her.

As if she was an animal in a trap, she thought, and he was deciding how best to put her out of her misery. That was not a restful notion.

Sterling pushed on. "I would rather die than go anywhere with you."

He leaned toward her in the open wedge between the door and the body of the SUV and every single nerve inside of her went wild. Sharp and hot and *alert*— something so much like pain it very nearly toppled her before she realized it wasn't really pain at all. Merely an exquisite reaction—pure sensation, storming all over her—that she didn't recognize and didn't know what to do with.

It was almost impossible to keep herself from reacting, from throwing herself backward across the wide backseat and scrambling for safety—not that there was any available to her, she understood in a shattering instant. Not really. This man might not hurt her, physically, not as long as she was pregnant with the heir to his kingdom—but then, there were worse things.

She'd seen so many of them firsthand.

"Please believe me," Rihad said softly then, so softly, though, that it only made her understand on a deep, visceral level how truly lethal he was. "I would arrange that if I could."

"How charming," she breathed, trying desperately not to sound as panicked as she felt. "I love threats."

He smiled. "I would have done so years ago if I'd believed for one second that it would ever come to this. But let me assure you, any interest I appear to have in you is about the child you carry, not you. Never you."

"This is Omar's child," she snapped back at him, struggling to keep her jangling, shimmering reaction to him to herself. "And since he is gone, that makes the baby my responsibility, not yours."

"That is where you are wrong," Rihad told her, his tone as merciless as that harsh look on his forbidding face. "If that child is indeed my brother's—"

"Of course it is!" Sterling threw at him.

And only realized once she had said it that it was hardly strategic to tell him so. If he thought the child was someone else's, if she could have convinced him of that, he might have let her go. Something in that dangerous dark gold gleam in his gaze told her he'd reached the same conclusion.

"Then, as I have explained, it is potentially next in line to rule my country." He shrugged. "Your wishes would be of less than no importance to me at any time, but in a situation such as this? Which affects the whole of my country and its future?"

He didn't have to finish the thought. That hard, sardonic twist to his lush mouth did it for him.

She tried again. She had no choice. "I refuse to go anywhere with you."

"Get out of the car, Sterling," he ordered her, steel and warning, and there was nothing but sheer power in his gaze. It rolled through her like fire. Or perhaps that was her name in his mouth while he looked at her like that. "Or I will take you out of it myself. And I rather doubt you will enjoy that."

"Wow." Sterling let out a small, brittle laugh. "This has been quite a morning for exploring the dimensions of your character, hasn't it?"

"Hear this now," he replied, his voice a hoarse kind of softness that made her shiver, his gaze dark and so powerful as it held fast to hers. "There is nothing I wouldn't do for my country. Nothing at all."

"How heroic." But she was far more shaken by that than she should have been, when it wasn't even any kind of direct threat. "I think we both know the truth is less noble. You're nothing but a reactionary Neanderthal who is never challenged, never questioned, never forced to face the consequences of his actions."

"You appear to have your al Bakri brothers confused," Rihad replied with a certain soft menace that made her think she'd landed a blow. "I am not the renowned playboy who lived a life of leisure and debauchery. That was Omar. I am the one who cleaned up his messes. Again and again and again."

She wanted to scream. Throw things. But she only curled her hands into fists and glared. "I take it you mean me. I am the mess."

"You are not a mess, Sterling." He sounded kind, but she could see that look in his gaze, and she knew better. "You are a toxic spill. You corrupt and you destroy, and you have been doing it for over a decade. What you did to my brother was bad enough. It appalls me to think you will have your claws sunk deep in the next generation of al Bakris." His perfect lips firmed. "But I am a man of duty, not desire. Which means as much as I would prefer to pretend you and whatever child you carry do not exist, I cannot."

She couldn't breathe for a moment. It was almost too much. It threw her back in time to that terrible house in Iowa and the foster parents who had believed that she was nothing but their personal punching bag. Worthless and dirtied, somehow, by her own tragic history. And their contempt. For a moment she almost tipped back over into all that darkness—but then she caught his gaze again, so bright and hard at once, and it bolstered her. It lifted her.

Because she'd survived far worse than this man and *like hell* would she slide back into that headspace after a few mean words.

"Oh, no," she murmured icily. "You might get this toxic spill all over your sheikhdom. What then?"

"You'll find I am not so easily led astray," he said, his voice as low as hers had been, but layered with a kind of dark heat she could feel within her. Making her too warm in all kinds of places she didn't understand. "And I've had a lifetime of preparation. You're merely one more disaster it falls to me to handle."

"And then, oddly, you wonder why I don't want to go anywhere with you." She squared her shoulders. "I'm not afraid of you, Rihad."

And the strange thing was, she wasn't. He made her anxious, yes—panicky about the future. But that wasn't the same thing as *afraid*. She didn't know what to make of that. It didn't make any sense.

"Go ahead," Rihad suggested, those disturbingly bright eyes of his tearing into her, seeing far too much. "Fight me if you like. Scream loud enough to draw down the sun. Kick and scratch and hurl invective as it pleases you." He shrugged almost lazily, and Sterling's throat felt tight, while far to the south, parts of her she'd always largely ignored bloomed with a mad heat. "But this will still end the same way, no matter what you do. What is Omar's belongs to Bakri. And what is Bakri's is mine. And I will do what I must to protect what is mine, Sterling, even if it means I must kidnap you to accomplish it."

He straightened then, though his gaze never shifted from hers, and Sterling couldn't tell if that lump in her throat was panic or tears or something a good deal more like *fate*.

Don't be absurd, she snapped at herself, but that sensation of foreboding snaked down her back all the same.

"But by all means," he said, daring her in that soft way that danced along her limbs and made her skin prickle with warning, and something much warmer, "try me."

Sterling opted to decline that offer with as much icy

silence as she could muster. She also ignored his offered hand, but she pushed herself out of the SUV and
onto the tarmac anyway, because she'd always been a
realist at heart. Oh, her years with Omar had tempted
her to surrender to optimism, but deep down she'd always known better. She'd always known what lurked
down there beneath the happiest-seeming moments.
She'd always assumed, on some level, that it would all
end badly.

So she stood on her own two feet in front of this terrible man and she made the command decision to keep
playing her role. Sterling McRae, rich man's whore.
Toxic spill, no less. Coveted by many, captured by none
save Omar. She'd gotten very good at it. She reached up
and unclipped her strawberry blond hair, shaking her
head to send it tumbling down around her shoulders.
She shifted position so that her breasts were thrust out
and saw the very male response in his eyes.

All men were the same after all, even when a woman
was as far along as she was. Even kings.

"How long will you be kidnapping me for?" she
asked, so very politely.

"Ah, Sterling," he replied in the same tone, though
his look was far darker, and she had to fight back a betraying sort of flush when he shifted, the lean power of
his body too obvious, too *close*. "Haven't you guessed
yet how this must end?"

She eyed him with sheer dislike. "You dropping dead
where you stand, if there is a God."

He shook his head at her. "You can always take to
prayer, if you feel it will help. It won't change what must
happen, but perhaps you'll approach it all with some
measure of serenity."

"Is that what you call this? 'Serenity'?"

His fine, dark brows lifted. "I call it duty. I doubt you'd recognize it if you tripped over it."

"Says the man who already married a stranger on command once and thought that made him virtuous," she snapped, the past he'd thrown in Omar's face so often coming back to her then in a burst. "I'm more afraid of tripping over your ego than your duty."

"You don't know anything about my first marriage," Rihad told her with a lethal, vicious edge in his voice. "Not one single thing."

"I know that expecting Omar to make the same sacrifice was hideous," she said crisply, as if she wasn't the least bit shaken. Though still...not afraid of him, somehow. "And you can tell yourself any stories you want about me and my past and whatever else, but I had nothing to do with it. *I* was the only thing in his life he liked."

"Sterling."

His face was closed down then, granite and bone. Utterly forbidding.

"If this is where you bore me with self-serving lies about your idyllic arranged first marriage, I think I'll pass." She eyed him. "I'm not as big a fan of stories as you seem to be."

"It is my second marriage that should concern you, not my first."

She stared back at him. Then she understood, in a terrible rush that felt like a tide coming in, crashing over her and rolling her into the undertow, then sweeping her far out to sea. All in that instant.

"Do I know the lucky bride?" Sterling asked, her

voice as sharp as the razor-edged smile she aimed at him. "I'd like to convey my condolences."

"An heir to my kingdom cannot be born out of wedlock," he said, and she couldn't tell if that note in his voice was fury or satisfaction. Perhaps it was both. It thudded in her all the same. "You must realize this."

She jerked up her chin, belligerently. "I'm not marrying you. I'm not getting on that plane, I'm not letting you near my baby, and I'm definitely not *marrying* you. Your heirs are your own damned problem."

And the sheikh only smiled.

"I didn't ask you to marry me," he said softly. "I told you what was going to happen. Resign yourself to it or do not, it won't make any difference. It will happen all the same."

"You can't *tell* me to do anything," Sterling fired back at him, and she couldn't control the way she trembled then, as if he'd already clapped her in chains and carted her away to his far-off dungeon. "And you certainly can't make me *marry* you!"

"Pay attention, Sterling." Rihad's gaze was hotter than the summer sun, and far more destructive. And his will was an iron thing, as if he didn't require chains. She could feel it wrapped around her already, pressing against her skin like metal. "I am the King of Bakri. I don't require your consent. I can do whatever the hell I want, whenever I want. And I will."

CHAPTER FOUR

STERLING MARRIED SHEIKH RIHAD AL BAKRI, King of Bakri, at his royal palace on a lovely terrace overlooking the gleaming Bakrian Sea a mere two weeks later, surrounded by his assorted loyal subjects and entirely against her will.

Not that anyone appeared to care if the bride was willing. Least of all the groom.

"I don't want to marry this man," she told the assembled throng when Rihad walked her through the crowd as the ceremony began. "He is *forcing me* to marry him!"

She didn't expect that anyone would spring into action on her behalf, exactly, but she'd expected... something. Some kind of reaction. Some acknowledgment, however small, of what was happening to her. Instead, the collection of Bakrian aristocrats only gazed back at her. Indifferently.

"They don't speak English," Rihad murmured lazily from beside her, resplendent in his traditional robes in a way Sterling couldn't let herself look at too closely. It made her feel faint. Weak. Or maybe that was the way he held her arm as they walked, too strong and somehow too appealing there beside her, despite everything.

She didn't want to marry him. But she didn't seem to mind him touching her, and that contradiction was making her feel even crazier. "And even if they did, who do you think they would support? Their beloved king or the woman who led my brother down the path of wickedness?"

"Don't they have a problem with the fact you're marrying a woman who's carrying another man's child?"

But no one seemed particularly moved by that, either, when she knew they could hear her. *See* her. Least of all Rihad.

"They think I am a great hero, to protect the family honor in this way." He sounded so at his ease. It made the knot in her belly pulse in response. She told herself that was *dismay*. "To do my duty, a concept I know escapes you, despite the fact it requires I lower myself to marry a known harlot of no pedigree, less education and inadequate means."

He'd reduced her entire life into three cruel phrases. And not as if he was trying to slap at her as he did it, but as if he was merely stating the unsavory, unfortunate facts. Sterling's throat was impossibly dry. She was sure she was shaking. But he still held her arm in his easy grip, giving her the impression she could wrench herself away from him if she wanted. She knew better, somehow, than to test that.

"There's nothing preventing me from throwing myself over the side of that railing over there to escape you and save you from this great act of charity you're performing," she told him then, sounding far away even to her own ears. "What makes you think I won't?"

They stopped walking and stood before the small, wizened man she understood would marry them here, with the sea spread out before them like the promise of eternity—but it felt as much like a prison as the plane that had brought her here days ago had, or the rooms they'd stashed her in since, no matter how well-appointed. Inside of her, something ached. And she felt more than saw that infuriating, indolent shrug of his from where he stood next to her.

"Jump," Rihad invited her, low and dark. It shouldn't have moved in her the way it did, like fire and need, when he was only goading her. "It's a fifty-foot drop to the rocks below and, in truth, the answer to a thousand prayers for deliverance from you and all you represent." A small smile played over his mouth when she glared back at him. "Did you imagine I would beg you to reconsider? I am only so good, Sterling."

He was so certain she wouldn't do it. She could see it as if it was written across his darkly handsome face in block letters—and he was right. She'd survived too much, come too far, to take herself out now, even if there hadn't been a baby to consider.

It wasn't the first time she'd had to grit her teeth to make it through an unpleasant situation, she reminded herself staunchly. With a quick glance at the man taking up too much space beside her, implacable and fierce, Sterling rather doubted it would be the last.

Rihad hadn't hit her. He didn't seem violent at all, in fact, merely unimpressed with her. That was a long way from the worst place she'd ever been. She didn't want this—but it wouldn't kill her, either. So she trained her eyes on the officiant before them and surrendered.

And when there were no further disruptions from her, the wedding went ahead. Sterling felt it all from a great distance, as if she was watching a movie of that enormously pregnant woman in the billowing dress stand next to that darkly beautiful man with the smug expression on his face that indicated he'd had no doubt at all that she would do exactly as he pleased. Exactly what he wanted, as, apparently, everyone did eventually. It didn't seem to matter that she didn't participate in her own wedding ceremony, didn't speak a single word either way. No one asked her to do anything but stand there. The man marrying them merely waved his hands in her direction, Rihad answered him in impenetrable Arabic and that was that.

The crowd cheered when it was done, as if this was a happy occasion. Or, she supposed, as if it was a real wedding.

"I hate you," she told him, and bared her teeth at him. She didn't pretend it was any kind of smile. They stood there in all that distractingly cheerful sunshine, as if there really was some call for celebration in the midst of this disaster. When instead she was married to a man she loathed, trapped here in his world, his palace, his very hands. She told herself that was fury she felt, that low, shivering thing inside her, or the fact she couldn't seem to take in a full breath. Because she refused to let it be anything else. "I will always hate you."

"Always is a very long time, Sterling." Rihad sounded darkly amused. "I find most people lack the attention span for sustained emotion of any kind. Hate, love." He shrugged. "Passion is always brightest when temporary."

"You are an expert, of course."

"My expertise fades next to yours, of course, and all your fabled conquests," he replied, his tone ripe with bland insult.

"You have yet to marry a woman who actually *wants* to marry you," Sterling couldn't keep herself from railing at him, almost as if his insults got to her. Which she refused to allow. "I doubt you have the slightest idea what passion is."

Rihad's smile edged into something lethal, and while he didn't hurt her in any way when he took her arm, she couldn't pull out of his firm grasp, either. His smile deepened when she tried.

"You forget that I did not exactly choose you, either," he said, darkly and too hot and directly into her ear, making her shudder in reaction—and she was all too aware he could feel her do it. That made it worse, like some kind of betrayal. "I executed my duty to this country the first time I was married. Can you truly imagine I wanted to do it again?"

"Then you should have left me in New York."

"No." His voice was firm. Matter-of-fact. She saw the harsh intent in his golden gaze, stamped deep into the lines of his dark, gorgeous face. "That child cannot be born out of wedlock and also be recognized as a part of the royal bloodline. It isn't done."

"Omar said it would be fine," Sterling threw back at him as Rihad's aides corralled the well-heeled courtiers and herded them from their seats, directing them farther down the terrace. "He said it was the only child he planned to present to you and if you wanted it, or him, you could change the law. After all, you're the king."

"Of course," Rihad growled.

A muscle worked in his lean jaw and she felt his fingers press the slightest bit harder into the flesh of her upper arm where he still held her fast, though, still, it didn't hurt. Quite the opposite—she was astonished at the fact her usual revulsion at the faintest physical contact hadn't kicked in yet. It was her hatred of him, she told herself resolutely. It was shorting out her usual reactions.

"How typical of my brother," Rihad was saying. "Rather than adhere to a tradition dating back centuries, why not demand that the tradition itself be altered to suit him instead? I don't know why I'm at all surprised."

Sterling opened her mouth to argue, to defend Omar, but the dark look Rihad threw at her stopped her. She shut her mouth with an audible snap. And then he began to move, sweeping her along with him whether she wanted to go or not.

He led her back through the glorious royal palace to the suite of rooms she'd been installed in when she'd arrived, and Sterling was glad he did it in that fulminating, edgy silence of his. She felt utterly off balance. Shaken down deep. She couldn't tell if it was because the wedding had actually happened precisely as he'd warned her it would. Or because he kept *touching* her in a thousand little impersonal ways that were nonetheless like licks of fire all over her body and none of it because of fear.

Or because when he leaned down and spoke so close to her ear she'd felt it everywhere. *Everywhere.* Like the most intimate of caresses.

She still felt it. And she hadn't the slightest notion what to do about it.

It wasn't until they reached her door that Sterling realized she had no idea what was going to happen next. That she'd resolutely refused to believe this was happening at all, this mockery of a wedding, and had thus not thought about…the rest of it.

Did he expect...? Would he...? Her mind shied away from it, even as her body burst into a humiliating flash of delirious heat that she was terrified he could *see*, it felt so bright and scarlet and obvious. She clutched at her belly, as much to remind herself that she was hugely pregnant as to assuage her sudden spike in anxiety.

But Rihad merely deposited her inside the lovely, spacious suite that was the prettiest prison cell she'd ever seen, then turned as if to leave her there without another word—standing in the middle of the suite's grand foyer in an indisputably gorgeous dress her attendants had insisted she wear today, that had made Sterling feel pretty despite herself. Despite *him*.

"That's it?" she blurted out.

She wished she hadn't said anything when he turned back to her. Slowly. He was particularly beautiful then, in his ceremonial robes with that remote, inscrutable expression on his lean face. Beautiful and terrible, and she had no idea what to make of either.

But she didn't think it was fear that made her pulse pick up.

"What were you expecting?" he asked, mildly enough, though there was a dark gleam in those gold eyes of his that made her breath catch. "A formal wedding reception, perhaps, so you could insult my guests and my people with your surly Western attitude? Berate our culture and our traditions as you are so fond of doing? Shame this family—and me—even more than you already have?"

"You're not going to make me feel guilty about a situation all your own doing," she told him, ignoring the hint of shame that flared inside of her anyway, as if he had a point.

He does not have a point. He hurt Omar, kidnapped

you—but she could still feel it inside of her. As if her own body took his side over her own.

"Or perhaps you thought we should address the subject of marital rights. Did you imagine I would insist?" Rihad moved closer and Sterling held her breath, but he only stopped there a breath away from her, his gaze burnished gold on hers, and still too much like a caress. "I hate to disappoint you. But I have far better things to do than force myself on my brother's—"

Sterling couldn't hear him call her a whore on the day she'd married him. He'd come close enough out on the terrace. She couldn't hear him say it explicitly, and she didn't want to consider why that was. What that could mean.

"Don't let me keep you, then," she said quickly before he could say it. "I'll be right here. Hating you. Married to you. Trapped with you. Doesn't that sound pleasant?"

"That sounds like normal life led by married couples the world over," he retorted, and then he laughed. It seemed to roll through her and a smart woman, Sterling knew, would have backed away from him then. Found safer ground no matter if it looked like retreat. But she, of course, stood tall. "And yet there is nothing *normal* about this, is there?"

And something shifted then. The air. The light that danced in from outside her windows. Or, far more disturbing, that shimmering, electric thing that she worked so hard to pretend she couldn't feel there between them. It pulled taut. It gleamed there in his fascinating gaze, dark gold and intoxicating.

Maybe that was why she did nothing when he reached out and slid his hand over her jaw to cup her cheek. Nothing but let him, when she'd never *let* anyone touch her before. She only held that gaze of his and possibly her breath, too, as his hard dark gold eyes bored into her and the heat of his hand *changed* her, from the inside out, telling her things she'd never wanted to know about herself, because she felt so many things, so many wild and intense sensations, and none of them were *revulsion*—

"Damn you," he muttered, as if he was the cursed one. As if he was as lost as she was, as utterly out of control. "Everything about you is wrong."

Then he bent his head and fit his mouth to hers, claiming her as easily as if he'd done so a thousand times before. As if she'd been his forever.

And everything stopped. Then melted.

Sterling braced herself for the kick of panic, of horror, but it never came. There was only the heat of it, the banked fury, the rolling wildfire that swept through her and altered everything it touched.

It was long and hot, slow and thorough.

Astonishingly carnal. Deliriously perfect.

It was nothing like the kisses she'd imagined, locked safely away in her little world, where she was never at risk of having one. Rihad's kiss was possessive and devastating at once, storming through her, making her forget everything but him. Everything but this.

She forgot that she was anything but a woman—*his* woman, however he would have her, whatever it took, to burn in this fire until she was nothing but ash and longing, fire and need.

And his. God help her, she wanted to be *his*—

Rihad pulled away then and she could feel his breath against hers, harsh and stirring. Uneven, just as hers was.

He dropped his hand from the side of her face and stepped back, and it was as if he'd thrown them both out of vivid color and bright hot light into a cool, gray chill in that same instant. They only stared at each other for what felt like an eternity.

Sterling was aware of everything and nothing at once. The fine tapestries on her walls, in pinks and reds and ancient golds. The gilt and marble statuettes that bristled on every surface and the sparkling crystal that adorned the high chandeliers, every inch of which she'd studied in the long days she'd been here. The endless blue sea outside, putting the world right there in front of her yet always out of reach, so high up on the cliff side was the Bakrian royal palace. The baby inside of her, low and painful today, as if even her unborn child was expressing its disgust at what she'd let happen to her.

And Rihad. The king. Her husband. The man who had just *kissed* her. He looked every inch the wealthy sheikh today, in his traditional garments that only emphasized his strength, his power. The sheer intensity he carried with him like a sword, and now she knew he could wield it, too.

His expression was like stone as he gazed back at her, though his dark gold eyes burned the way she still did with the aftereffects of that kiss stampeding all over her, and Sterling couldn't bring herself to look away.

"Whatever you're about to say, don't." Her voice hardly sounded like hers, and she understood that it was far too revealing. That it told him far too much, and in far more depth. But she couldn't seem to help herself. "Not today."

Rihad's nostrils flared as if he was pulling in a deep,

deep breath, or fighting for control. As if he was as thrown by this as she was. As if the addictive taste of that wildfire that still crackled through her was too sharp, too dangerous, in him, too.

"I'm touched," he said, and she understood that was all wishful thinking on her part, thinking this was difficult for him. Nothing was, after all. Not for the king. "I had no idea our wedding meant so much to you, considering how bitterly you complained throughout it."

His voice was rough and sardonic, but Sterling was sick, she understood then, because she still felt the kiss like a caress. Her oversensitive breasts ached as if it had been that faintly calloused palm of his all over her bare skin. A little flicker of sensation skated from the tight peaks of each of them down through the center of her body to pool deep in her core. Then pulsed.

She'd always had a vivid imagination. But now what stormed in her was *need*.

"You don't know anything about me," she said, with what she thought was admirable calm, given the fact she now knew what that hard mouth of his felt like against hers, so hot and so male she might never recover from it.

"The trouble is, I know entirely too much about you," he said after a moment, his tone harsh and cool, while his golden gaze seemed to tear into her. "And despite the temptation, I can't overlook the fact that you were my brother's low-class tramp of a mistress for over a decade."

"And I am now also your wife," she pointed out, amazed that her voice sounded so much calmer than she felt, if not quite as regally cool as his. She tipped up her chin. "Congratulations on your choices."

"Let me be clear about how this marriage will work," he said, and something curled up inside of her at the way he said it. "You will stay here in the palace until you deliver the baby. Will you wish to nurse it?"

"I…" She felt as if he'd tossed her over the side of that terrace after all. One moment he was kissing her, all carnal longing and impossible heat, and the next he was interrogating her about her plans for the baby's feedings?

"I don't care if you do or do not," he said when she only blinked at him. "But if you do, you will stay here until the child is weaned. You will receive all the care and help you could require, of course. For all intents and purposes, that is now my child."

"Never," she said at once. Softly enough, but with feeling. "This is Omar's baby. *My* baby. Nothing you do can change that."

"Yes." And his voice was ferocious. "Omar's baby. Omar's mistress. Omar's many problems. This is nothing new for me, Sterling. I have been cleaning up after my brother all my life—why should it change now that he is dead?"

It was all too easy to remember how much she hated him then, and she clenched her hands so tightly into fists that her nails dug into her palms.

"What happens after the child is weaned?" she asked in a clipped voice as a tsunami of self-loathing crept ever closer, reminding her that she'd not only let this callous man touch her, but she'd also *liked* it. More than liked it.

She'd wanted more. Maybe she really was the whore

Rihad thought she was. Maybe the fact she'd never touched anyone had concealed the essential truth about her.

"That is entirely up to you," he said curtly. "Behave, and I may let you stay here, as long as you do not make a nuisance of yourself. Misbehave, and I will have you locked up in a remote part of the kingdom, a prisoner in fact and deed. I don't care which it is."

"I don't want this," she blurted out, because she was suddenly light-headed, and the thought that this was really her life now, that this had really happened, made the world spin.

He lifted a shoulder, then dropped it in that way of his— the royal sheikh untouched by and uninterested in such lowly concerns.

"Life is filled with sacrifices, Sterling." His voice scraped over her, so harsh she expected it had left marks. "There were always going to be consequences for your relationship with my brother, whether he told you so or not. This is but one of them."

She shook her head, as much to clear it as to negate him. "I don't understand why you won't let me go."

He considered her for a moment, and there was no reason at all Sterling should flush while he did.

"You cannot imagine I would release a member of my blood into your tender care, can you?" He sounded amazed. And that was so insulting it would have hurt, had not everything else hurt that much more already. "The child stays here. And if you have a shred of maternal feeling in you, which I doubt, so will you. A child needs its mother, I am reliably informed. Even if that mother is you."

"Wonderful," she managed to say then, her voice bitter and thick. "That sounds like quite a life sentence. How lucky I am to have been snatched off the street and forced into such an advantageous marriage with the most benevolent and thoughtful dictator around."

"If you weren't so appallingly self-centered, you'd see that you truly are lucky," he retorted, a flash of something dark in those eyes of his. "Far luckier than you deserve. But then, thinking of others is hardly your strong suit, is it? Or you'd have left my brother alone years ago."

"And a happy wedding day to you, too, Rihad," she threw back at him, and it was easier to simply hate him. Cleaner. Less complicated. It felt like a relief, and she didn't question why she felt so free to do it. "You're a terrible man and will no doubt be a worse husband, in much the same way I'm sure you're an awful king. Oh, joy."

Temper cracked over his face then, dark and alarming, and she braced herself for whatever awful thing he might say next—*whore whore whore, wash and repeat, whore whore whore,* she thought with a mental roll of her eyes that suggested an insouciance she didn't quite feel—but instead, he went still. Then frowned.

Not at her, exactly. More at the floor beneath her.

Sterling looked down to find a puddle around her, soaking the hem of her wedding dress and then spreading out across the inlaid mosaic tiles at her feet, and froze in horror. Had she actually humiliated herself to such a degree that she'd—

But then she understood.

The puddle announced what she should have guessed from her mounting discomfort throughout this conversation, but had been too furious and too emotional to face—that her water had broken.

Her baby was coming a few weeks early, whether she was ready or not.

CHAPTER FIVE

SOME THIRTY-SIX HOURS after he'd kissed the new wife he hadn't wanted in an act of dark foolishness that had haunted him ever since, Rihad stood in the shadows of Sterling's state-of-the-art hospital suite in the center of Bakri City and watched her sleep at last.

He didn't know why he was there, lurking about like a spurned lover instead of the king, when they had both been forced into this marriage, him by circumstance and her by his own hand. Instead, he couldn't seem to look away from Sterling, the woman he'd called a toxic spill.

He should not regret that. It was the truth, he knew, at least in terms of his brother's life this past decade. But it was hard to remember that at the moment.

There were the faintest smudges beneath her impossibly long lashes, the only indication he could see on her lovely face of how she'd spent the past day and a half. And she was so beautiful, so very nearly angelic in repose, that it made him realize he'd never seen her like this before—so vulnerable, so soft. Not fighting him, poking at him, insulting him or challenging him. Not plastered across tabloid magazines with her breasts falling out of her neckline and Omar's arm wrapped tightly around her.

Not toxic by any measure.

His chest felt too tight for his own ribs.

And there beside her, lying in a bassinet wrapped up in a swaddling blanket so that only the wisps of jet-black curls on her head poked out above her wrinkled little brown face, was a miracle.

It had been among the hardest things Rihad had ever done, to step aside and let a woman he barely trusted walk across a room to do this work that only she could do. After that scene in the palace, she'd been rushed to the hospital, where the finest doctors in the kingdom had assured them that while the baby was coming a bit early, that didn't mean anything was wrong with either it or Rihad's new bride. And sure enough, when Sterling's exquisitely formed little daughter entered the world at last, she was perfect in every respect. Tiny, perhaps, but utterly, undeniably perfect.

Rihad had been there moments later, to see a woman he'd dismissed as nothing more than callous and calculating beaming down at the scrap of a girl she held in her arms, the look on her face so intimate, so filled with love, it had almost been too much to bear.

He'd had the strangest sensation then—the oddest regret. As if she really was meant to be his. As if this was meant to be his family in more than simply name. As if this was all wrong, somehow—that he should have been there with her, holding her hand, reminding her she wasn't alone, sharing his strength so hers would seem that much more boundless. Not an intruder into these first moments between mother and child, but a part of it. That was all insane, of course. He'd tried to shake it off as he'd approached her, stiff and formal.

She'd glanced up at him, and that look on her face had altered. That wasn't a surprise, but still, Rihad had felt it like a blow. Her mouth had flattened when she'd seen him. She'd hidden that naked joy in her gaze.

He'd hated it.

"Her name is Leyla," Sterling had told him after a moment, as if she'd needed a breath or two to pull herself together before she could speak.

There had been nurses bustling in and out of the birthing suite behind him, doctors being paged incessantly from the intercom out in the corridor, but Sterling had been still. Rihad had had the notion that she'd been waiting for some kind of strike. From him.

As well she should, he'd thought.

It had made that sensation of inexplicable loss yawn open even wider within him. The baby had made tiny noises, more a creaking sound than actual crying, and Sterling had finally relented, her mouth curving into a sweet little smile as she looked down to soothe the little girl that almost undid him. When she'd looked up again, it had almost killed him. He'd never seen that expression on her face before, not even in those happy tabloid pictures of her and Omar. Open. Loving. Soft.

Something like pure.

Even then, at such a tender moment that had nothing at all to do with him, Rihad had wondered what it would be like if that look had been meant for him—and then he'd wondered if he'd utterly lost his mind.

Not if so much as when, he'd told himself then.

"It was Omar's favorite name for a girl," she'd continued after a moment, a faint line appearing between her brows. "That's not… I mean, is there some royal naming tradition I should know about?"

"No." He'd sounded so stiff. So altered. "Leyla is a lovely name."

"She's wonderful," Sterling had whispered then, bending her face back down to the infant, fierce and maternal—and he'd had to leave. Because he hadn't known what to do with that roaring, howling thing inside of him, so threaded through with emotions he didn't know how to process.

Emotions he hardly recognized. What had emotions ever had to do with his life before now? His was a cool world, rational and logical and coldly reasoned. It was his weapon, his strength. The bedrock of his ability to rule his country. He didn't know what the hell to do with all these *feelings*. He didn't know what it made him, that he felt anything at all for this woman or her child. He didn't know what he was supposed to *do* with any of it.

He'd waited until night fell before he returned, and he slipped in only after his security detail assured him she slept at last. He told himself a thousand different reasons why that was the proper, even respectful, thing to do for a woman he hardly knew who'd just given birth—but the truth was, he was completely off balance and he knew it. He wasn't sure he knew *himself*, was the thing—as if he'd been a stranger to himself since Sterling had walked up to him outside that building half a world away. And that alone was enough to give him pause.

Enough to keep him standing there in the shadows.

The child moved in her swaddling then, making that tiny noise again. Part alien, he thought, and part feline, and still it tugged at him. Rihad moved over to the bassinet before he knew he meant to leave his post across the room, seating himself in the chair beside it.

"Hush, little one," he murmured, stroking his fingers down the whisper-soft plushness of one newborn cheek, marveling at it as he did. "Let your mother sleep."

Then he covered the baby's soft little body with his hand, letting the warmth of his palm seep into the rounded swell of her tiny belly, and sure enough, she quieted. Just as he'd done for his half sister Amaya when she'd been an infant. Just as he remembered watching his mother do to baby Omar when Rihad had been a small boy.

Rihad stayed where he was, gazing down at her sweet face, all those dark curls and the eyes that he'd seen earlier were a liquid black that reminded him of his brother, and tried to make sense of the wild tumult within him.

Like an earthquake, when he knew he wasn't moving and neither was the ground beneath him. It tore him apart even so, even while he felt little Leyla's sweet new breaths beneath his hand.

Or perhaps it was because of her.

And he'd been furious for such a long time now. He'd been in a dark, black, consuming rage since he'd gotten that call from the Parisian police. Since he'd had to bury his younger brother so many years before his time. He'd understood it was grief, mixed up somewhere in that terrible rage inside of him, but understanding such a thing hadn't done much to soothe him or stop the fury. His anger—that Omar had been lost so tragically, at this woman who had twisted him into unrecognizable pieces, at the marriage he'd felt he had no choice but to insist upon no matter how little he might have wished it—had been a living flame, hotter by the day, and he'd stopped wondering when or if it might go out.

It had been so easy to focus it all on Sterling. His brother's whore, Rihad's new wife—

But here, now, it was gone. Extinguished completely.

That was what he felt, Rihad realized then. That internal earthquake ripped away his fury and left him with no one to blame. There was only the darkness of fate, the sheer, spinning horror that was his brother's pointless, untimely death.

And this tiny, perfect child was all that remained of Omar on this earth. This little scrap of life, so new she still bore the wrinkles from the womb, was all that was left of the brother Rihad had only ever wished to protect, from his own debauchery as from anything else.

"I will not fail with you, little one," he vowed then. "No matter what."

And it was only when he spoke that he felt the dampness of water on his face. He made no move to wipe it away. Not here in this dark place where no one could see him. Where he could not see himself. Where there was nothing but his grief and this brand-new life he held in his hands.

He felt stretched out taut between the two, the dark and the light. Perhaps he always would.

"I will not fail you again, brother," he whispered into the night. To Omar, wherever he was now. To the little baby that was all that remained of his brother. To the woman his brother had held above his own family, however little Rihad might understand that. None of that mattered any longer. "I will not fail the family you left behind. This I swear."

* * *

Sterling woke that first night again and again, jolted awake by some internal panic that had her jackknifing up in her bed in alarm each time. But she found Leyla right there beside her, more beautiful each time she kissed her sweet cheeks or held her surprisingly hot little body against her own skin.

Those first days were a blurry sort of cartwheel through time, when all she could see or hear or focus on at all was this perfect little creature she'd somehow been chosen to bring into the world, and the astonishingly steep learning curve required to take care of her as she deserved—even in the Bakrian palace, where she had all the help she needed. That didn't alter the weight of the responsibility she felt to this creature she found she loved bigger and wider and better than she'd imagined it was possible to love anything.

Her world shrank down to Leyla, only Leyla, and through her a connection to Omar again, who felt a little bit less lost to her when she held the daughter they'd made in her arms.

Beyond that, there was nothing save the dark, surprisingly quiet man who kept watch over her in his own way, moving in and out of the periphery of all that wasn't Leyla until Sterling was as close to *used to him* as she imagined anyone could be around a man as intense and nerve-racking as Rihad.

She'd even dreamed she'd seen him in her room while she slept, watching over her like some guardian angel. She knew it was absurd. She'd given up believing in guardian angels a long time ago, and Rihad was more warrior than angel anyway, but the notion was warming all the same. It made her feel something like safe—and perhaps a woman who hadn't so recently given birth might have questioned that. Investigated her own feelings, looked for reasons why a man like Rihad felt like safety when she knew perfectly well he was anything but.

As it was, Sterling merely accepted it, forgot about it, and kept her attention on Leyla.

Who, despite that unfurling of love and hope that had swamped Sterling from the moment she'd first seen her, was not gaining the weight she should have in those crucial first days. And for the first three weeks of her life, it was nothing but panic and worry and a terrible battle, no sleep and too many tears, as Sterling tried to breastfeed her and failed.

Again and again, she failed.

All she'd ever wanted was a family of her own, a child she would treat far better than she'd ever been treated herself, and now that Leyla was here she couldn't even manage to *feed* her.

When Rihad found her in the chair next to her bed in her suite in the palace, finally bottle-feeding Leyla on the express and stern orders of the palace's physician, Sterling had finally given up. She couldn't remember the last time she'd taken a shower, or felt like anything but a great, gristled knot of pain and failure.

Everything hurt. Everywhere. Inside and out. Her battered body and her beat-up heart alike.

But her baby girl, who hadn't managed to get anything from Sterling's own breast, was finally feeding hungrily. Almost gleefully. It should have made her feel better, to see that Leyla was obviously going to be fine now that she was able to eat her fill. It did, in a very deep and fundamental way that told her things about how limited her own parents had been.

Yet that had nothing to do with why Sterling was sobbing. Broken into a thousand pieces. Shaking as she held the bottle to Leyla's busy mouth.

"Why are you crying?" Rihad asked, but in a very nearly gentle tone, unlike anything she'd ever heard from him—which might have set off an alarm or two somewhere inside of her, had she had room to process such things. "Has something happened?"

"Are you here to gloat?" she hurled back at him, tears streaming down her face unchecked because her arms were full of baby and bottle, self-recrimination and regret. "Call me more names? Comment on what a mess I am? How toxic a spill I am now, as you predicted?"

And then she was shocked almost out of her skin when the high and mighty King of Bakri simply reached over and took the baby from her with a matter-of-fact confidence that suggested he'd done exactly that a whole lot more often than Sterling ever had. He held Leyla in the crook of his arm and the bottle in his other hand as competently as any of the nurses who'd been in and out these past weeks. He leaned back against the side of the high bed, held the bottle to the baby's sweet mouth and fixed his arrogant stare on Sterling once Leyla started suckling enthusiastically once again.

"What names do you imagine I should call you?" he asked mildly. "Do you have new ones in mind or will the old ones do? You seem to recall them so clearly."

Sterling pulled her legs up beneath her, hugged her knees to her chest in the shapeless, ugly pajamas she'd been wearing for a long time and felt split wide-open with guilt and grief and intense self-loathing.

"Selfish, vain, I don't know." Nothing he could call her was worse than what she was calling herself just then. "If I was any kind of real woman, real mother, I would be able to do the most natural thing in the world, wouldn't I?"

"Give birth?" He sounded completely unemotional, which was maybe why she was able to talk about this at all. The doctor had been so sympathetic it had made Sterling want to scream, then collapse to the floor in a puddle. She didn't want sympathy. She wanted to know *why*. She wanted to know *exactly how much* she was to blame and *precisely how correct* her foster parents had been when they'd assured her she wasn't worthy of a real family. "I believe you already did that, and quite well, if this child is any indication."

Sterling rubbed her palms over her face, somewhat surprised to find herself shaking. "That was the easy part."

"I've never done it myself, I grant you." His voice was so arid then that it made her tears dry up in response. "But I think it's a commonly held truth that while labor is undoubtedly many things, *easy* is not one of them."

"There was an entire hospital wing's worth of doctors and nurses right there, advising me and guiding me. I could have been knocked out and they would have done the whole thing without my input or participation." She knew she was being ridiculous, could tell from the way she felt almost seasick where she sat when she knew she wasn't moving—but that didn't change the way she felt. What she *knew*. She'd told Omar she couldn't do this, much less without him, and here was the proof. "This is what *I* needed to do, all by myself. This is what I'm *supposed* to do and I can't do it."

He didn't respond, that fierce, brooding attention of his on the baby in his arms again—the baby who looked as if she could be his, she realized with a distant sort of jolt. That same rich brown skin, those same fathomless eyes. Because of course a baby of Omar's would look as if she belonged to Rihad, as well. Why hadn't she expected the family resemblance? Another kind of jolt hit her that she couldn't entirely define, so wrapped up was it in all the rest of that storm inside of her.

"At the very least," she made herself say, because if she didn't she would break into sobs, "I'm exactly the useless, selfish bitch you already think I am."

"What I think," Rihad said after it seemed her words had crowded out all the air in the room and simply hung there like suffocating proclamations of inescapable truths, "is that it would be profoundly self-ish indeed to continue to try to do something that isn't working, against all medical advice, when surely the only goal here is to feed the child. No matter how you manage it."

"But everybody knows—" she began, almost angrily, because she wanted to believe him more than she could remember wanting anything else, and yet she couldn't let herself off the hook. She simply couldn't.

They'd told her all those years ago that she was worthless. Useless. She'd always suspected they were right—

"I was exclusively bottle-fed, as was Omar," Rihad said then, smooth and inexorable, his dark brows edg-ing high in a kind of regal challenge. "Our mother never intended to breast-feed either one of us. She never did.

And no one ever dared suggest that the Queen of Bakri was anything less than a woman, I assure you. Moreover, I seem to have turned out just fine." His voice was still so dry, and when she only stared back at him, and her tears became salt against her cheeks, he laughed. "You preferred Omar, I understand. But he, too, was a product of the bottle, Sterling."

Sterling let out a long, slow breath and felt it shudder all the way out, as if he'd picked up a great deal more than simply the baby when he strode in here, and stood there holding all of it off her for the first time in weeks. Maybe that was why she didn't police herself the way she should have. That and the unwieldy mess of guilt and fear and worry that there was something bent and twisted, something rotten that would ruin her child, too, careening around inside of her.

"I want to be a good mother," she whispered desperately, as if this man was her priest. As if he really was as safe as he felt just now. "I have to be a good mother to her."

Because of Omar, yes. Because she owed him that. But it was more than that now. It was also because her own mother had been so useless, so remarkably unequal to the task of having a child. Because Sterling had once been a baby called Rosanna whom everyone had discarded.

And because everything had changed.

She'd been forced across the planet and into a marriage with the last man on earth she'd ever wanted to meet, much less marry. But then she'd given birth to this squalling, angry-faced, tiny demon thing with alien eyes and that fragile little head covered in all those dark curls, and everything had simply...shifted.

She felt twice as big on the inside than she could ever be on the outside, ripped open and wholly altered by a kind of glorious light she hadn't known could exist. Love, maybe. Hope. Both.

As if windows she hadn't known were inside of her had been tossed wide-open, and nothing but sunshine streamed in.

And she'd known the instant she'd held her baby against her own skin that she absolutely had to be a good mother to this little girl. To her daughter. No matter what that meant. No matter what it took.

Her eyes met Rihad's then, over Leyla's dark little head and soft brown cheeks. This man who detested her, who had never thought she was anything but the worst kind of whore, and had said so. And Rihad's dark brows edged up that fine, fierce forehead of his even farther, as if he was astonished that she was in any doubt following his stated opinion on the matter.

It occurred to her that there was something the matter with her, that she should find that so comforting.

"You are a good mother," he replied.

It sounded like one of his royal decrees. And Sterling wanted to believe that, too. Oh, how she wanted to believe it.

"You can't know that," she argued, her palm moving to rub against that ache in her chest she didn't understand, in the very place where Leyla's hot head had first rested. She scowled at him instead, because it was easier. "And the fact I can't nurse my own child certainly suggests otherwise."

"This is the great beauty of living in a monarchy, Sterling." His lips twitched, which on anyone else she might have called the beginnings of a smile, or even laughter—but this was Rihad. "The only opinion on the subject—on any subject, in fact—that matters at all is mine. Are you not relieved? If I say you are an excellent mother, that is not merely a social nicety I am extending to my brand-new wife on a trying afternoon for her. It is an edict, halfway to a law."

"But—"

"Go," he ordered her. He lifted his chin in that commanding way of his when she only blinked back at him as if he'd lapsed into Arabic. "Take a shower. A bath. A walk outside. Sleep as much as possible and let others worry about this one. She will be fine, even if you let her out of your sight. This I promise."

Leyla hadn't been out of Sterling's reach since her birth. Not even once. "But I can't—"

"This is the royal palace," he reminded her gently. Yet still with that implacable steel beneath his words. "I am perfectly capable of watching an infant but I don't have to do that, either, because we have an extensive and very well-paid nursing staff here to tend to her every possible need. Which you might have noticed over the past three weeks had you not been so determined to drive yourself into the ground."

"But—"

"Martyrdom is actually a far less endearing trait than many people seem to imagine, Sterling. And it always ends the same unpleasant and painful way." His voice was all steel again then, and dark command besides. "Let the nurses do their jobs."

"I don't need them," she argued, though she was so tired she thought she might fall off into sleep right where she sat, if she let herself. As if sleep was a cliff and she'd been balancing on the edge of it for weeks now, unsteadily. "Leyla is *my* daughter."

"Leyla is also a royal princess of the House of Bakri," Rihad said, with all that innate power of his she hadn't forgotten, exactly, but had certainly stopped noting in the past few weeks. There was no noting anything else then, not when he sounded like that—as if he truly was issuing edicts he expected her to follow. "There is nothing, no accommodation or luxury or whim, that is not available to her at a moment's notice."

His dark gold gaze moved over hers, seeing things Sterling feared she was too tired to hide the way she should. And she was definitely suffering from sleep deprivation, she told herself, because there was no way Rihad would actually look at her the way he seemed to be then, with an expression that veered far too close to tenderness.

But that was impossible. She was delirious.

"You do not have to do this by yourself, Sterling," he said quietly. "Especially not here in the royal palace. I don't know what you think you have to prove."

She knew exactly what she felt she had to prove, but she couldn't tell him. She couldn't tell anyone, but she especially couldn't tell Rihad—and not only, she assured herself, because this was the nicest, warmest interaction she'd had with the man since she'd met him. But also because he wasn't her confidante. He was her husband, yes, but only in the broadest sense of the term. There was no relationship, no trust. There wasn't even affection, despite that odd light she'd imagined in his gaze just then. There was no intimacy.

Only that one kiss, she thought, the memory prickling over and into her, like gooseflesh rising along her arms. She'd almost forgotten it.

Perhaps she'd wanted to forget it, as there was no making sense of it.

She shoved it away again now, as his too-incisive gaze rested on hers as if he was also reliving those strange, wild moments with his mouth hard on hers. She needed sleep, that was all. Especially before she started thinking about things that made no sense—things she'd been so certain were purely hormonal and would disappear when she was no longer pregnant.

Maybe that kiss was still something she needed to sleep on, she thought then, as a different sort of shiver moved through her. Maybe it was something she needed *at least* a long shower and a good night's rest to consider. Or maybe it was better by far—safer, certainly—to pretend it had never happened.

But either way Sterling stopped arguing and did as he'd told her.

Carrying that image, of the ruthless and terrible Rihad al Bakri cradling her tiny infant daughter in his strong arms, from the long, hot shower and straight on into her dreams.

CHAPTER SIX

"I OWE YOU an apology, Rihad," Sterling said, her voice crisp and matter-of-fact.

She'd worked hard to make it that way. To sound businesslike, which suited this strange marital arrangement of theirs instead of actually apologetic, which did not. *Apologetic* was far too emotional.

They sat out in the fantastical garden that was the king's private retreat in the center of the palace. Lush plants tangled with brightly colored flowers around three separate fountains, while gentle canopies covered the different seating areas tucked into this little bit of wilderness hidden away inside the palace complex. It was possibly the most beautiful thing Sterling had ever seen.

Then again, so was Rihad—not that it was at all smart to let herself think along those lines.

It's like admiring the tapestries in my suite, she told herself today, sitting across from him at the graceful iron table where their breakfast had been laid out for them, the way it was every summer morning. *That he's beautiful is a fact, not an emotional thing at all, and certainly doesn't take away from how terrible he always was to Omar.*

But when he glanced up from the tablet computer where he'd been scrolling through something the way he often did, she felt too hot and looked away, and only partially because his dark gold gaze seemed harsher than usual today. She looked toward the nearest fountain that had been made to resemble a tropical waterfall, gurgling down over slick, shiny rocks to form a small, inviting pool Rihad had once told her she was welcome to make use of whenever she wished.

Yet somehow, despite the fact this man had seen her at her worst, dirty and crazy and sobbing and wild, the idea of him seeing her in anything like a bathing suit—splashing around in front of him or, worse, with him—made her heart thud too hard inside her chest. She chose to ignore that, the way she always did.

She ignored more and more by the day, she knew. And it was only getting worse.

They had taken to having their meals together here in the weeks since Rihad had forcibly removed Leyla from her arms and insisted Sterling take care of herself. Well. It was more that Rihad had decreed that they would take their meals here, whenever it was possible with his schedule, and Sterling hadn't had it in her to object.

You didn't want to object, a voice deep inside of her whispered. *Or you would have.*

"It seems I must keep an eye on you," he'd said when he'd informed her of this new schedule. She'd been fresh from her first full night of sleep since Leyla's birth and had felt drunk with it. Like a different person.

And he had looked at her in a way that had made her breath catch, as if he'd truly wanted nothing more than to take care of her. As if he really was some kind of guardian angel—though she knew better. She did.

Life had shifted all around her in these strange months since Leyla's birth, then settled into a new form altogether. Sterling slept well at last. She spent her days with the baby and the fleet of cheerful, efficient nurses Rihad had acquired and who made Sterling feel like twice the mother she suspected she was. She took long walks around the palace and the surrounding grounds and gardens, sometimes pushing Leyla's buggy and sometimes on her own, enjoying how much more like herself she felt by the day.

How oddly content she felt, here in her forced marriage to a man she'd vowed years ago to hate forever, no matter if Omar had or not. She'd been happy to carry that torch. She'd meant it on their wedding day when she'd told Rihad she hated him.

And then you kissed him.

But she didn't want to think about that.

The presence of the nurses meant she had time to read again, to exchange emails with her friends in New York, to reacquaint herself with the life she'd put on hold when Omar had died. She started to imagine what might come next for her. She got back in touch with the foundation she'd worked with to aid foster children once they aged out of the system and found in the various responses to her marriage that things were very different now.

Omar's friends, perhaps predictably, felt betrayed.

I understand why you'd feel that way, she emailed one after the next, trying hard to hold on to her patience—because where had they all been when she'd tried to run from Rihad? They'd texted, yes. Called. But not one of them had actually shown up that morning to help a heavily pregnant woman escape her fate.

Her entire plan had been to disappear somewhere and hope for the best. That had worked out well enough when she'd been fifteen and on her own—or in any case, she'd survived—but would it have been fair to Leyla? Sterling might have been married against her will, but a little bit of distance and a whole lot more sleep had made her think that having Leyla's future assured was what mattered. That it was the *only* thing that mattered—and no matter that it was Omar's infamously judgmental brother who'd made that possible.

But give me some credit, she'd chided Omar's old friends—*her* old friends, too, not that anyone seemed to remember that while busy picking sides. *Leyla is a princess and Bakri is a part of her birthright she can only access if legitimate. That's all this marriage is: legitimacy for Leyla.*

The charities and foundations she'd worked with who'd known her as Omar's lover, by contrast, were *ecstatic* at the notion of working with the Queen of Bakri—a title Sterling hadn't fully realized was hers to claim now.

Maybe a little bit too ecstatically, she'd thought only that morning, when yet another solicitation had hit her inbox.

It was only then that she realized that Rihad was staring at her across the table, and that she had no idea how much time had passed since she'd last spoken.

"Why are you looking at me like that?"

"You told me you wished to apologize and then lapsed into silence," he replied, mildly enough—though once again, there was a gleam in the dark gold of his gaze that reminded her what a dangerous man he was. That suggested he was *waiting* for something as he watched her. "I thought perhaps you were rendered mute by the enormity of your sins."

"My sins have been widely overexaggerated, I think." It had been two months since that kiss she found herself thinking about much more than she should. It was something about his mouth, crooked slightly in that sardonic way of his that thudded through her. "I wanted to apologize for falling apart the way I did in the first place. It's taken me weeks to realize just how out of it I was."

Rihad shifted in his seat, his strong fingers toying with the steaming cup of rich coffee before him on the table. And though the baby slept happily in her little buggy beside Sterling's chair, Sterling had the sudden, crazy desire to wake her up—so there would be something else to concentrate on, something other than the way this lethal man was looking at her. A distraction from all of this intensity that swirled between them like the desert heat itself.

"And here I thought your apology would be for telling all your American friends that our marriage was a fake."

She blinked. "What?"

A deeper, darker crook of that mouth. "I think you heard me."

"Yes, but…" Had he been reading her email? But even if he had been, and she wasn't sure she'd put it past him, she'd never said that. Never quite that. "I never said that. Not to anyone."

"Were you misquoted, then?" He slid his tablet computer across the table to her. "Show me where, and I will notify my attorneys at once."

Sterling swiped her finger across the screen and

stared down at the page that opened before her, from a famously snide tabloid paper.

Queen of the Rebound screamed the headline. Then beneath it:

Sexy Sterling uses famous wiles to bewitch Omar's grieving brother, the King of Bakri, but tells pals back home: "This marriage is for Baby Leyla. It's all for show."

The worst part, Sterling thought as she glared down at the offensive article and felt her stomach drop to her feet, was that she had no idea *which* of the people she'd thought were her friends had betrayed her.

"You understand that this is problematic, do you not?" he asked, still in that mild tone—though she was starting to see that there were other truths in that hard gleam in his eyes, in the tense way he held that mouth-watering body of his as he sat there in one of those dark suits of his that some artist of a tailor had crafted to perfectly flatter every hard plane, every ripple of muscle. Every inch of sensual male threat that emanated from him, made worse because of the luxurious trappings.

"It's a tabloid," she said dismissively, because she might note that threat in him but for some reason, it didn't frighten her. Quite the opposite. "It's their job to be problematic. It's our job to ignore them."

"I would ordinarily agree with you," Rihad said, so reasonably that she almost nodded along, almost lulled by his tone despite the way her pulse leaped in her veins. "But this is a delicate situation."

She deliberately misunderstood him, sliding the tablet back toward him and returning her attention to the selection of fruit and thick yogurt, flaky pastries and strong coffee, as if that was the most important thing she could possibly concentrate on just then: her breakfast. And so what if she wasn't hungry?

"This is tabloid nonsense, nothing more," she said, as calmly as she could. "Nothing delicate about it, I'm afraid. They like to smash at things until they break, then claim they were broken all along. Surely you know this."

He didn't speak for a moment and she tried to pretend that didn't get to her—but eventually she couldn't help herself and glanced up again, to find Rihad watching her too closely with a narrow sort of gaze, as if he was trying to puzzle her out.

She swallowed hard, and she couldn't tell if it was because she wanted to keep her secrets hidden from him, or if she wanted to lay them all out before him in a gesture so suicidal it should have traumatized her even to imagine it. Yet somehow, it didn't.

"The whole world knows that Leyla is Omar's daughter, not mine, no matter that my name is on her birth certificate," he said, after a moment, when she was beginning to imagine she might simply crack open.

"Did I know that you put your name on the birth certificate?" Sterling asked, shocked and taken aback, somehow, at that little revelation. "I don't think I did."

She remembered his look of dark impatience, though she hadn't seen it in a while. That made it all the more effective today.

"Exactly what sort of legitimacy did you imagine I meant to convey on your child when I married you?"

"I guess the sort where we're not completely erasing Omar from his daughter's life." She reached over and fiddled with the hem of the blanket that drooped over the side of the buggy, though Leyla still slept soundly and no adjustments were needed.

"It is a legal maneuver, nothing more," Rihad said, his tone harsher than it had been in months, but that couldn't be why her chest felt tight. It shouldn't matter to her either way. "But you're making my point for me. Omar has not been erased in any meaningful way. Everyone knows who fathered Leyla. Her place might be assured on paper and in the courts, but in the eyes of the Bakrian people and, more important, our enemies, her legitimacy must come from us."

"Us?"

"Us. Me, their king, and you, my brand-new and deeply controversial queen."

She shied away from that term, scowling at him instead. "I don't like that word."

"Which one?" His voice was so dry then. So dark and compelling. *"Us? Controversial?"*

"Queen." Her scowl deepened. "It's ridiculous. It doesn't fit the situation at all."

She meant it didn't fit *her*, trash dressed up in an unearned crown—and she had the strangest notion he knew exactly what she meant. His dark gold gaze almost hurt against hers.

"And yet it is your title, accorded to you with all due deference two months ago when you married the King of Bakri. That would be me, in case you're not following this conversation, willfully or otherwise."

"But I don't want to be your—"

"Enough," Rihad said then, cutting her off.

He sat back in his chair, never shifting those mesmerizing eyes of his from hers, looking dark and terrible and entirely too fascinating, from that brusque nose of his to his strong jaw and all that rich brown skin in between. She wanted to lean closer to him, explore him—and hated herself.

"I don't care what you call yourself, Sterling. You are my queen either way. I suggest you accept it." When she didn't respond, that light in his gaze sharpened and made it a little too hard to breathe. "I think you understand perfectly well that we cannot allow any speculation that this marriage is fake to fester. It serves no one but our enemies."

She felt oddly fragile. "Why do you keep talking about enemies?"

"The kingdom has been rocked by one scandal after the next and we are weak." His gaze sharpened. "My father's tumultuous love affairs. My wife's death without giving me any heirs. Omar's notorious mistress that he flaunted in the tabloids and his refusal to come back home and do his duty. My sister's betrothal to Kavian of Daar Talaas, which she responded to by running away—"

"I like her already."

"Amaya was a successful runaway, Sterling. She's managed to avoid both my security and Kavian's for months. Kavian will no doubt run out of patience with her, and when he does? Our countries will not unite and if they do not, Bakri will fall. There are too many other powers in the area that want our location and our shipping prowess, and we cannot possibly keep them all at bay alone."

"You're talking about *your* enemies." She lifted her

chin as she held that harsh gaze of his. "The only enemy I've ever been aware of was you."

"I am talking about *our* enemies." He nodded toward the tablet. "Or do you imagine that whatever 'pal' sold that story is your friend? Will they take you in when I am imprisoned and you—if you are lucky—are a royal Bakrian in exile?"

Sterling opened her mouth to argue when something else occurred to her. That wild kiss swelled up in her again, a tactile memory. Searing through her as if it had only just happened. Flooding her with sensory images, with yearning, all over again.

"Is this really because you're worried about how our marriage is perceived?" she asked him. "Because of *enemies*? Or is it because you want to get into my pants?"

He didn't move a muscle. She knew that because she was watching him so closely that she could see it when he breathed. He didn't even tense. And yet he seemed to explode outward, becoming twice his size and a thousand times more dangerous, like some kind of mystical being let loose from its cage at last.

And every single cell in Sterling's body shivered to red alert.

She was flushed with the heat of it. Her skin seemed to ache for his touch. Her breasts felt too heavy and the taut peaks pulled tight. Inside of her, there was a low, hot humming that coiled between her legs and pulsed. Hard and wet. Ready.

It was the most carnal experience of her entire life.

It was the *only* carnal experience she'd ever had, save that last kiss.

And they weren't even touching.

* * *

That he did not turn over the table between them and taste her again right now was, Rihad thought, the only evidence remaining that he had once been a civilized man.

He thought too much about his enemies as it was. He did not want to think about Sterling's pants. He did not want to think about that body of hers that had redefined grace while heavily pregnant and now… She was difficult to look away from.

He found he rarely did.

Rihad did not want to think about the way he fought himself to keep from touching her, because he was determined to make this marriage work in some fashion or another, the way it had with his first wife. He and Tasnim had been friends, after a fashion. They'd eased into the physical aspects of their marriage and had worked on their friendship first. He'd decided at some point during the first days of gorgeous little Leyla's life that he owed her mother no less, no matter how they'd come to find themselves married.

But that did not explain why he took himself in hand each morning in his shower to slake his growing need. And it certainly did not explain the tempting array of images he tortured himself with as he did so.

His voice was quiet when he finally answered her, and it cost him. "Can't I be preoccupied with both the perception of our marriage *and* 'getting in your pants,' as you so charmingly put it?"

"Unlikely. Men are more often focused on the one thing above all else."

"That shows how little you know me. I am not merely a man. I am a king."

"I know you enough, Your Majesty."

Her blue eyes rivaled the summer sun above them, and yet even when she looked straight at him he was certain he could *see* the walls she kept up, high and bolstered. He loathed them more and more each day. He wanted them knocked down. And he was entirely too aware that the urge was not exactly *friendly*.

"And besides," she continued, her voice light, "you don't really want into these pants anyway." She let out a self-deprecating laugh and waved her free hand in the general direction of her midsection. "Everything's gone a little crazy after giving birth."

He snorted. "Self-deprecation does not suit you, Sterling."

She frowned at him, and he saw her ball her hands into fists, then drop them in her lap. "I don't know what that means."

"It means you were gifted with the sort of genetics that make most women green with envy, as I suspect you are aware." He shifted in his chair and let his gaze move all over her, which was not exactly an improvement for that wild hunger battering at him from within. Because she had been so beautiful when they'd met that she'd made Manhattan disappear so he could better admire her. And she grew more beautiful by the day. And the fact that she was no longer big with her pregnancy was the least part of that. "You gained a minimal amount of weight while carrying Leyla, lost most of it while giving birth to her and are probably healthier now than when you got pregnant in the first place. If the fashionably gaunt pictures I've seen of you back then are any guide."

He saw emotions he couldn't name flit across her face, one after the next, and he hated that he couldn't read them. Or her. That she defied him even now, without a single word, by simple virtue of remaining opaque.

Rihad couldn't have said when he'd begun to find that intolerable.

"I'll thank you to keep your comments on my body to yourself."

He smiled, and then wider when he saw the spray of goose bumps rise along her bare arms. "Unfortunately for you, Sterling, you are mine. And I take a keen interest in the welfare of the things that belong to me, whether that means trade prospects in my cities or my wife's form."

She was flushed, he noted, and he was sure that if he mentioned it she would claim it was disgust. Distress. But he didn't believe that.

"How delightfully medieval."

And he enjoyed this, Rihad realized with a thud. He *liked* her sharp tone, her icy wit, even if it was at his expense. Because Sterling was the only person he'd ever met who dared speak to him this way.

Perhaps there was something wrong with him after all, that he should enjoy it—*her*—so much.

"Your body is fine, Sterling," he told her, as much to see her draw herself up in outrage as anything else. He made a show of drinking from his coffee cup, then setting it down, for the sheer pleasure of watching temper crack through those blue eyes of hers like lightning. "You're not a model any longer. You certainly don't need to keep yourself so drawn and skeletal." He smiled again, and he could feel the wolf in it. "If you want to dissuade me from making advances on you, you'll have to come up with something better than that."

Her lips quivered and her gaze flashed dark, with

something he didn't understand. He was fascinated all the same.

"How about this." Her voice was fierce, almost aggressive, but that only deepened his fascination. "Don't make advances on me at all. I don't want you."

He watched her for a moment. He waited, and sure enough, she flushed again, brighter and delightfully redder than before.

"Now, that's just an outright lie," he murmured.

And she looked away, because he was right. And she hated it. And he loved that he could read *that* as easily as the text on his tablet.

"Is this where you force me again?" she asked tightly, her eyes on the pool nearest the table while her body shouted out all the ways she was a liar, again and again, as if it was in collusion with Rihad. "Because that was so much fun when you called it a wedding."

He laughed then and saw her jolt with surprise. She turned back to him, her gaze unreadable again, but he'd come to a decision. The *friendship* angle had been fine these past months. It had been appropriate. The woman had just had another man's child—and lost that man to a tragic accident besides. But it was time to move on.

Rihad stood, aware of the way her eyes clung to him as he moved, very much as if she was finding his body as much a temptation as he found hers.

"We'll have a honeymoon, I think," he said, and watched her shift restlessly in her chair, the truth in the pink bloom on her cheeks. "You and me for two weeks in the desert, with a thousand opportunities for intimacy."

"What?" She sounded panicked, and he was not a

civilized creature, he realized. Not at all, because he liked that. "Intimacy? Why would you want that?"

"Perception." He shrugged. "Of course, it will be widely assumed that you're merely pandering to my base, animal instincts with that famously lush body of yours. Men are beasts, are they not? And I am no better than my brother when it comes to your seductive powers."

"Yes, you are!" Sterling looked alarmed. "You live to resist me! Or you should."

"I am unfamiliar with weakness," he told her, and he didn't care if that truth hit her as arrogance. It didn't make it any less true. "But in this case, succumbing to the practiced charms of a known seductress is a weakness I am prepared to allow the world to dissect at their leisure." He eyed her aghast expression. "Doesn't that sound like a wonderful story for your tabloid-loving friends to sell far and wide?"

Her voice was scratchy when she answered, and her eyes were much too bright with a heat he wanted to bathe himself in. "It sounds heinous. And completely unbelievable anyway."

"Why don't you ask me the question?" He thrust his hands into the pockets of his trousers, because he doubted she'd appreciate it if he put them on her. Yet.

"Why are you so awful?" Sterling asked at once, her voice sharp but with that storm in her blue eyes. "But I already know the answer, of course. Because you can be."

"That's not the question you want to ask."

Sterling stared back at him. He heard the summer breeze high above them, dancing through the plants and the trees, and the running water all around them, like songs. He saw her pulse hammer against the delicate skin of her neck and wanted nothing more than to press his mouth to it, as if he could taste her excitement. He saw her hands open and then bunch into fists again, as if she couldn't control them.

She sat up straighter. Squared her shoulders. Tilted up her chin.

"So we'll simply go out to the desert for a little while. Spend the time out there so people think…whatever they want to think. Call it a honeymoon so the whole world leaps to the same conclusion. That we're together in more ways than one. A unit."

"Yes."

She swallowed, hard. "You won't… I mean, we won't…"

"I have no intention of forcing you to consummate this marriage," he said bluntly, and he told himself it wasn't fair to think she should already know that he was not that kind of man. It didn't help when she sagged in her chair in exaggerated relief. "Have I given you cause to imagine otherwise?"

"You kidnapped me," she pointed out, though what he noticed was how little heat there was in it. "You married me against my will. You'll forgive me if I'm not entirely certain where you draw that line."

He took his time moving around the table. Her eyes widened, but stayed fast to his, and she made a squeaking sort of noise that reminded him of Leyla when he pulled her chair out from the table and then around to face him, so he could brace himself on its arms and put his face directly into hers.

And God help him, but it was sweet.

"Bringing you to Bakri and marrying you before you bore a royal Bakrian child outside of wedlock was my duty," he told her, dark and serious, though he was far more fascinated by the high color on her cheeks than was wise. "Containing the scandal that you represent is my responsibility. But what happens between us now?"

"Nothing is happening! There's no *us* for anything to be between!"

He ignored her. "That has nothing to do with duty." Rihad leaned in closer, so close he could have easily tasted that seductive mouth of hers, yet he held himself back. "That has everything to do with need."

"I have no needs," she said, but then she shivered, and Rihad smiled.

"I won't force you, Sterling," he told her with quiet intent. "I won't need to."

She stared back at him. No snappy comeback. No sharp wit. Wide blue eyes and that pulse of hers a wild staccato in her neck. And he wanted her more than he could recall wanting anything, for all that she was a wild card, a loose woman, a problem to be solved. He accepted all of that.

"But first," he said, "it's time to talk about Omar."

CHAPTER SEVEN

STERLING GAPED AT HIM, her head spinning madly at the sudden shift in conversation and her stomach in a new, hard knot.

"You look at me as if you expect me to transform into a monster where I stand," Rihad pointed out with a certain gruffness, almost as if that wounded him. She told herself she was imagining it. "All fangs and claws and evil intent."

"I'm not sure you haven't already done so."

That mouth of his crooked into something not quite a smile. He reached over and tucked a stray tendril of her copper-blond hair behind one ear, and neither one of them moved for a long, shattering instant.

Then he straightened to his full height, but she could still see that steely glint in his dark gold eyes, the potency of his gaze undiminished.

"I am not going to go on a honeymoon, whether real or for show, with a woman whose head is filled with another man, Sterling. It's time you told me about my brother and your relationship with him."

He didn't object when she pushed back the chair and surged to her feet, hurriedly stepping away from him. He only watched her as she went, and that shattering thing between them seemed to expand into a taut, terrible grip around her heart. But she made herself stand straighter.

"I don't think you really want to have that conversation," she told him as evenly as she could. "You're unlikely to hear anything you like."

Sterling wasn't sure she wanted to have it, either. She felt too guilty, too ashamed. No matter what she might have told their friends or herself, this wasn't what Omar would have wanted. He'd left Bakri for a reason. This—all of this, everything that had happened since the accident—was a stark betrayal of the best friend she'd ever had. The only family she'd ever known.

And that fire inside of her, that terrible flame when she looked at Rihad that she didn't know what to do with, was worse.

"This is not the first time you have insinuated that I harmed my brother in some way," Rihad said darkly. "Why? What is your evidence for this?"

She shook her head, as if she could shake him away that easily, and all his questions, too. "Don't act the innocent, Rihad. It isn't a good fit."

"You mistake innocence for intent, I think. It's time to stop talking in circles, Sterling. If you wish to accuse me of something, do it to my face."

He smiled again then, lethally, and she felt it everywhere.

And she'd forgotten this, hadn't she? She'd been lulled into a false sense of security because there'd been nothing in her head but Leyla and he'd been so encouraging, so supportive, since the day she'd been born. They'd eaten their meals together these past months and talked about a thousand things, like any other civilized strangers who happened to be married to each other. Books, art. The cities they'd seen, the places they'd visited, from Cannes to the Seychelles to Patagonia.

She'd learned that he had been a solemn child and an even more serious young man, studious and focused in all things. She'd discovered that he had played a great deal of soccer and the occasional game of rugby all the way through university, but only for sport, as he'd always known his future. His place.

"That must have been nice," she'd said once. Perhaps too wistfully. "To have no doubt what direction you were headed in, no matter what."

He'd eyed her across their dinner and the candles that had lined the table and she'd shivered, though she hadn't been cold.

"Who can say if it was nice or not?" he'd replied after a moment, as if he'd never thought about it before that instant. "It was all I knew."

She'd started to think of this man as something like *pleasant*. She'd started to imagine that this forced-marriage thing might not be quite so terrible after all. But she'd been kidding herself. This was Rihad al Bakri. He was the most dangerous man she'd ever encountered.

How had she allowed herself to forget that?

"Fine," she said staunchly now, telling herself this had always been inevitable. That they had always been heading straight here. "Let's talk about Omar."

Sterling crossed her arms, wishing she didn't feel so compelled to *dress* each time she knew she would see him, including the airy sundress she wore now that felt a bit unequal to the conversation. She told herself fashion and beauty were armor, the way they had been when she'd been a model and the point was to look at

the clothes, not the woman in them. And they were—
but that wasn't the only reason she did it these days.

The depressing truth was that back then she'd liked
to hide in the glare of any spotlight that might have
been focused on her. But here in this far-off palace that
sometimes felt like a dream over these past months,
she *liked* it when he saw her. When he got that gleam
in his dark gold eyes that told her he appreciated what
he saw. Even now.

She had so many reasons to hate herself that Sterling
couldn't understand why she hadn't started overflow-
ing where she stood. Like a backed-up sewer. That was
precisely how she felt, clogged and *wrong*.

"Wonderful." His gaze was so dark. So intense.
"Let's begin with why Omar persisted in his relationship with you across all these years. He defied his family and his country, abandoned his duties and broke
our father's heart into a thousand pieces. That was un-
accountable enough. Yet he never married you, never
claimed you in the eyes of the world. Never stood up
for you in any way when he knew perfectly well his affair with you was scandalous. Not even when you fell
pregnant."

"You're relentless." But she said that as if it was only
to be expected, without any particular heat. "Omar was
the best man I ever knew. The kindest and the bravest.
He stood up for me in ways you can't imagine."

"My imagination is remarkably vivid." His voice
was cool. "Why don't you try me?"

"Maybe Omar and I didn't want to get married,
Rihad." She sighed when he only gazed at her in arrogant disbelief. "Maybe not everyone is as traditional as
you are. In some places, it's the twenty-first century."

"I have no doubt that you and Omar lived a delightfully modern and unconventional life in every possible way, cavorting about New York City in all that marvelous limelight for so many years." He eyed her in a way she didn't much like then. "But your pregnancy should have snapped him back to the reality that, like it or not, he was a Bakrian royal who owed legitimacy to his own child. Why didn't it?"

"Perhaps he assumed you would swoop in like the Angel of Death and sort it all out to suit yourself," she said coolly. Then threw a smile, sharp and icy, back at him. "And look at that. You did."

"Do you think these little games you seem determined to keep playing will distract me from getting your answer, Sterling? They won't, I promise you. Why didn't he marry you?"

His whole bearing had gotten colder and more regal as he stood there, his gaze a demanding thing that beat at her, and she believed him. She believed that he would keep asking that same question, again and again, until she finally answered it. That he would stand here an eternity if that was what it took. That he was like the great desert that surrounded his country on three sides, monolithic and impassable, and deeply treacherous besides.

"He wanted to marry me," Sterling said after a moment. Then she raised her gaze to meet his again and forced herself not to show him any of the emotion that swirled around inside of her. "I refused."

Rihad laughed. Not at all nicely. It set her teeth on edge, as she imagined it had been meant to do, and she had to order herself to unclench her jaw before she broke something.

"Of course you did." His tone then was so dark, so sardonic, it felt like another one of his disturbingly sensual touches inside of her. "He begged you, I imagine, and you nobly rebuffed him, in the vein of all gold diggers and materialistic mistresses across the ages."

He didn't quite roll his eyes. His derisive tone meant he didn't have to. But Sterling felt sharpened all the same then. Honed into some kind of blade by that dismissive tone of his.

"I know it's hard for you to believe, Rihad. I know it flies directly in the face of all the fantasies you have about social-climbing sluts like me. But that doesn't make it any less true. Omar would have married me in a heartbeat. I was the one with reservations."

"The prospect of becoming a Bakrian princess was too onerous for you? It seemed too much of a thankless chore?" There was that lash in his voice then that should have made her crumble, but she only tilted up her chin and glared back at him. "You were already living off him. Why not make it legal and continue to do so forever?"

"You're such a small man, for a king," she said softly, and had the satisfaction of watching his eyes blaze at the insult. This was the man she'd met in New York. This was the man who had sparred with her in that SUV. It was absurd that some part of her thrilled to see him again, as if she'd missed him. "Or maybe all kings are the same. What do I know? Obsessed with all these tiny details, territories and tabloids, that make them what they are. Life is a great deal richer and more complicated than that."

He studied her for a moment, and Sterling stared right back at him. There was something about the way he was looking at her, about the particular quality of that dark temper she could see inhabiting his gorgeous face just then. If he'd been any other man—if *she'd* been any other woman—she'd have thought it was some kind of jealousy.

But that made absolutely no sense.

"Give me one good reason you wouldn't marry my brother," Rihad growled after a moment or two inched by and still they stood there, faced off like enemy combatants. "You are a woman with no family. No support."

Did he know that was a sore spot for her? Or had he scored a lucky hit? Sterling sucked in a breath and hoped against hope he hadn't noticed.

But his dark eyes gleamed. He noticed everything.

"A marriage to Omar would have changed all that. Even were you to eventually divorce, and even if you'd signed away everything ahead of time as our attorneys would have made certain you did, you would always have remained a part of the kingdom. Your child would always be a member of the royal family. Why would a woman like you turn down that kind of security?"

A woman like you. That phrase rolled around and around inside of her, picking up all the mud and grime of all the other people in her life who had said something like that to her. *No one could want a child like you,* her foster parents had told her. *Girls like you are only good for one thing,* her first, sleazy modeling contact had told her. *I should have known a bird like you would land on her feet,* a British photographer friend of Omar's had sneered in an email only yesterday.

Omar had been the only person she'd ever met who had never, ever, put her in that kind of box. Sterling told herself she had to focus. This was about him, not her.

This was about his life—the one he'd wanted to live, not the one his overbearing brother thought he should have lived.

Maybe there wasn't much *a woman like her* could do to a king, but she could certainly defend her best friend.

"You don't know anything about your brother, do you? You never did."

"I'm growing impatient," Rihad growled. "If you want to continue to talk in circles, that's your prerogative. But I will make no promises about my reaction to that. What I can promise you is that you are unlikely to like it very much."

Sterling took a deep breath.

And then she told him Omar's secret. At last.

"Omar was gay."

If Sterling had reached beneath that maddeningly flowy dress she wore and pulled out a gun, then shot it directly into his heart, Rihad could not have been more shocked.

And for a long, tense moment, it felt as if she'd done exactly that.

The report from her statement echoed so loudly it drowned out the world. It made the breezes still, the far-off noise of the palace and the city beyond fade. Even the water in the fountains seemed to run dry for what seemed like a very long time.

Then she laughed, but it was a bitter, accusing sort of sound. It made him feel worse. Like a monster.

"Is that not what you were looking for, Rihad? I'm so sorry. Not everyone lives according to your narrow standards of behavior."

"Explain this to me." He didn't sound like himself. He sounded like some gruff, autocratic mockery of the person he'd thought he was instead. He knew it. He could hear it. But he didn't care. Not at that moment.

She glared at him. "Sometimes, Rihad, when little princes grow up and want to play with others, they don't want to play with the little princesses as much as the—"

"Explain your relationship with him," he snapped.

"This is ridiculous." She rocked back on her heels and scowled at him. "You didn't grow up beneath a rock. I don't have to explain the world to you. You might choose to act as if it hasn't moved on from the Stone Age here, but you know perfectly well that's a choice you're making, not the truth."

"I don't require that you explain the world to me. Only my brother."

He shook his head, frowning, as every conversation he'd ever had with Omar raced through his head, one after the next. Every time Rihad had brought up Sterling, Omar had shrugged it off.

"She is necessary, brother," he'd said. He'd never explained that assertion any further—and Rihad had thought him besotted. Bewitched. Led about by his most sensitive parts by a scandalous woman. It was a tale as old as time. As old as their own father, certainly.

It had never crossed his mind that this notorious woman, this walking sexual fantasy who had been the torment of thousands the world over in those coyly sensual perfume advertisements that had made her name, could possibly have been Omar's beard.

Yet he believed her, and that meant she'd been exactly that, and he'd fallen for it. To the detriment of his own relationship with his brother.

"I think that if you could see the look on your face right now, you would understand why he felt this was necessary," Sterling said coolly. "Omar didn't dare tell you. He hid in plain sight and used one of the oldest tricks in the book." She raised one hand and made the kind of imperious gesture in his direction that made him all but see red. "That exact expression."

"I have no idea what you think you see on my face," he gritted out. "But let me tell you what's behind it. Shock."

She scowled. "There is absolutely nothing wrong—"

"That he didn't tell me," Rihad threw at her. "That he felt he needed to sever his relationship with his own family. That he felt he needed to keep this secret all these years."

"How could he possibly tell you?" she demanded, and he could see how much she'd cared for Omar in that fiercely defensive light in her blue eyes then, and everything inside him tilted. Slid. Because Rihad had only ever wanted to be that kind of support for his brother, and he'd failed him. "The only thing you ever talked to him about was what a disappointment he was. How he had let you down by not racing off to get married and have babies the way you thought he should. Having Leyla was his attempt to pacify you and *I* wouldn't marry *him* because I thought he deserved more from his life. I thought he could do better than living a lie."

"But this is what I do not understand." Rihad raked his hands through his hair and had the odd notion that he was a stranger to himself. If his brother had been an entirely different man than the one he pretended he was, what else could be a lie dressed up like the truth? He felt cut off at his knees. Adrift in the middle of his own palace, where he had always known exactly what and who he was. "Why go to such lengths to live this lie?"

"I haven't gotten the impression that Bakri is renowned for its open-mindedness," Sterling said in that sharp way of hers that he enjoyed a bit less than usual then. "Much less its king. And I've only been here a few months."

"I can understand why he would not wish to tell our father," Rihad said, as if he was talking to himself. In part, he was. "The old man was harsh, despite his own weaknesses. He was of another time."

"Whereas you are the embodiment of the modern age?" Sterling sniffed. "What with the kidnapping and the ranting about legitimacy and your obsession with al Bakri blood. Very progressive."

"He should have come to me."

"It's not up to you to decide how he should have lived his life," she threw at him, that scowl that twisted her face making her more pretty instead of less, somehow. "What he *wanted* was to live as he pleased. What he *wanted* was not to be nailed down into the things *you* thought he should do. He didn't need your permission to be who he was."

"Perhaps not," Rihad said, and he heard a note he didn't quite recognize in his own voice. Profound sadness, perhaps, that he doubted would ever leave him now. It cracked in him like temper. "But perhaps he could have used my support."

Her lips parted then, her expression confused, as if he'd spoken that last part in Arabic.

"Your support?" she echoed. "What do you mean?"

Rihad was furious. And something that felt a great deal like lost, besides. He had always known precisely what he had to do and how to do it. He had always known his path and how to walk it. He didn't know this. He didn't know how to navigate it—because it was too late.

Omar was dead, and Rihad had loved him—yet never truly known him.

The grief he'd understood would always be with him seemed to triple inside of him with every passing moment. Became darker. Thicker. And woven in with it was guilt. That he hadn't seen. That he hadn't looked. That he'd accepted his own brother at face value, even when doing so had meant thinking the worst of him.

He hated this. He hated himself. He hated all those wasted years.

"None of this explains you," Rihad bit out at Sterling, because she was there. Because she'd participated in this deception. Because she'd known his brother in a way he never would, and he was small enough to resent that, just then. "If he wanted a beard, why did he not marry years ago and cement it? And if he was going to be in a fake relationship with a woman, why did he not choose a woman who would raise no objections? Why you?"

"That seems to be the sticking point," she pointed out, her lovely eyes flashing with something heavier than temper. Darker. He felt another stab of guilt, and hated that, too. "Not so much why he did it, but that he did it with a woman like me."

"Because it's impractical." He wanted to punch something. He wanted to rage. He settled for seething at her instead. "You are a lightning rod of controversy. Why not choose a woman who would have flown beneath the radar?"

"Why don't we conduct a séance?" Sterling suggested in that same sarcastic tone, her pretty eyes narrow and dark on his. "You can lecture him just like this. I'm sure it will have the same effect now as it clearly did when he was still alive."

He didn't know when he'd drifted closer to her, as if she was some kind of magnet. Only that they were much too close then, and he wanted to touch her too much, and that was only one of the reasons he was furious.

It was the easiest reason.

"Don't." Sterling's eyes were glittering yet her mouth was vulnerable and Rihad wanted her. God, how he wanted her.

"Don't what?" he asked. "You were never my brother's lover."

"That doesn't mean I have any desire to be yours."

Yet he could see the faint tremor beneath her skin. He could see the flush across her cheeks. He knew her desire as well as he knew his own.

"Liar." But he said it as if it was very nearly a compliment.

She didn't contradict him, and the world was still so far away. There was only her. Here. And there had already been too many lies. There had been too much hidden and for too long, and Omar was lost.

His brother had never trusted him. Neither did Sterling. And he couldn't have said why he felt both so keenly. So harshly. As if they were the same thing. As if he could no longer trust himself.

"Help me solve the puzzle you present," he urged her in a rough whisper. "Why did he have a child with you? What did he hope to gain?"

She looked confused and slightly bereft. "He imagined that if he had a child, that would show you that he wasn't as irresponsible as you thought he was, even without you knowing the truth."

"That is a fine sentiment, Sterling, but all the reasons I married you held true for him, too."

"I doubt very much it was his intention to die," she threw back at him. "If he hadn't, maybe we would have married. Had he told me the reasons why that would help Leyla, I would have relented. But we'll never know what might have happened, will we?"

"I know that if he'd come to me, if he'd told me, I would not have turned my back on him. That's what I know." Rihad let out a long breath. "I will never understand why he did not."

Sterling made a frustrated noise. "That might have a bit more weight if you hadn't spent all these years acting as if he was a communicable disease."

He made a sound of protest, but she wasn't listening to him. Instead, she thrust one of her fists at him as if she wanted to hit him, but held herself back at the last moment.

"All you did was talk about how you had to clean up after him, as if he was garbage." And her voice was so bitter then. Her blue eyes the darkest he'd ever seen them. "Maybe if he'd thought he could trust you, if you cared about anything besides the damned country, he might have risked coming out to you."

"I loved him."

Again that fist, not quite making contact with his chest.

"Actions speak louder than words, Rihad. Don't blame Omar for your failure to treat him like a person. That's on you. That's *entirely* on you."

And whatever was left inside of him shattered at that.

Leaving him nothing but a howling emptiness, and the uncomfortable ring of a truth within it that he'd have given anything not to face.

"Damn you," he whispered, his tone harsh and broken, and he didn't try to hide it.

Then he reached for her, because he knew, somehow, that Sterling was the only person alive who could soothe that shattered thing in him—

But she flinched away from him and threw up her arms, as if she'd expected him to haul off and hit her.

As if, he understood as everything inside of him screeched to a halt and then turned cold, someone had done so before.

CHAPTER EIGHT

STERLING FLINCHED, WHEN she knew better than that. But she couldn't seem to help herself.

She'd finally pushed him too far. She'd felt safe with him all this time, safer than she'd ever felt with another man, but that was before. She'd gone over the edge at last and she'd seen that broken look on his face.

She knew what it meant. She remembered too well.

She expected the hit. It had been a long, long time, but she thought she could take it. There was no warding off a blow from a man as strong as he was or as close, but if she could take the inevitable fall well, it wouldn't immobilize her. The trick was not to tense up too much in anticipation, and then to curl into a tight ball against the kick—

"Sterling," Rihad said then, in that low, dark way of his that rippled through her, making her want to cry. Making her want him, too, which she thought was evidence that she was deeply sick in the head. Twisted all the way through, the way they'd always told her she was. "What do you think is happening here?"

"Please," she whispered, trying to stand tall, to square her shoulders despite the fact she couldn't stop shaking. "Just don't wake the baby. I don't want her to see."

And she closed her eyes, tried not to brace herself too much and waited for him to hit her.

The way her foster parents always had.

She heard nothing. For one lifetime, then another.

Then, finally, Rihad's voice, but he wasn't speaking to her. He spoke in Arabic, and she didn't have to understand the words he used to know he was issuing orders again in that matter-of-fact, deeply autocratic way of his that was as much a part of him as breathing.

Then again, the quiet.

The breeze above and the water all around, and she kept her eyes shut tight because the quiet was the trick. It was always a trick. The false sense of security had always, always tripped her up. The moment she'd thought it wasn't going to happen and looked to see was the moment they'd laid her flat.

She heard footsteps, then the sound of Leyla's buggy being wheeled away, and her stomach turned over, then plummeted. He was sending the baby off with the nurses, as she'd asked. That meant—

She flinched away from his hand on her arm, making it that much worse. Her eyes flew open and met his, burning dark, dark gold and far too close, and she nearly bit off her tongue.

"I'm sorry," she whispered hurriedly, in a panic she couldn't control, even when he let go of her and stepped back. "I didn't mean to flinch."

He studied her for a long, long time.

"Sterling," he said, very quietly, but somehow with more power behind it than she'd ever heard him use before. "Who hit you?"

And everything inside of Sterling ground to a lurching, nauseating halt. She couldn't risk this. She should never have flinched. Open up that old can of worms and he would *see*. He would *know*.

She didn't think it through, she simply catapulted herself across the wedge of space between them, trusting he would catch her. She didn't ask herself how she knew he would.

But he did.

His arms came around her as her chest collided with his, and all of that panic and all of those old ghosts shimmered into something else entirely.

His seductive heat poured through her. Into her. Chasing away all those old cobwebs she couldn't afford to let him see. *He couldn't know.*

She didn't want to think too much about *why* that was the worst thing she could imagine. The very worst. She only knew, without a shred of doubt, that it was.

"Exactly what do you think you are doing?" he asked, but his voice was as gentle as his hands against her.

And yet she could feel how hot he was, hot and hard and deliciously male against her, everywhere. He wanted her. It was a revelation. He was so hot that she might have thought he was feverish, had she not been looking straight up into those dark gold eyes of his, where she could see he wasn't the least bit unwell.

Dark and beautiful and much too close to all the parts of her she didn't want him to see, perhaps. But not sick.

Sterling was more than a little bit worried that she was the sick one here, but she shoved that thought aside. There was no time left to worry about any of that. About the strange revelations this morning had wrought, much less what they meant or the repercussions they might have. She couldn't let her mind spin out that way. She couldn't see the future, so there was no use panicking about it.

She could only do her best to confuse the present in the easiest and most direct way available to her before Rihad talked them both to the point of no return. Before he saw who she really was and was as disgusted as everyone else had always been.

So that was what she did.

Sterling pressed against him in what she hoped was an excellent show of wanton abandonment, winding her arms around the strong column of his neck, her mouth actually watering as she let her gaze move from that smooth, brown sweep of skin to his marvelous mouth that was now *right there*—

"Sterling," Rihad said repressively, but his hands were flush against her hips and he wasn't pushing her away. And she could feel him against her belly, so hard where she was so soft and yielding. The wild sensation made her shudder all the way through and then arch against him.

As if this wasn't the man she'd tried to run from, so long ago in New York, so sure he would ruin her.

As if this wasn't the man she'd thought was about to haul off and hit her moments before.

Or maybe because it was him. Because she'd snapped into a very old, horribly familiar place and he hadn't hit her after all. He'd looked appalled at the very idea.

And he wanted her. Even with that glimpse of the truth about her, he wanted her.

He wasn't like any other man she'd ever known. And that shattering thing swirled inside her, making her feel something rather more like truly wanton after all. That maddening heat, storming through her limbs and gathering low in her belly, making her feel hot and ripe and *hungry*—

She arched into him, harder this time, then went up on her toes and kissed him.

And everything exploded.

His mouth was divine torture, his kiss insane. Rihad took control almost the second it began, one of his hands moving to wrap itself in her hair, the better to hold her head where he wanted it, the other a hard, wild encouragement at her hip.

He angled his head for a better fit, and then he simply...*took*.

And she loved it.

Rihad kissed like a starving man, as if Sterling wasn't the only one scraped raw and left aching by this hungry thing between them. He kissed as if there was nothing at all for her to do but go along for the ride, wherever he took them. He kissed her until she was shivering against him in uncontrollable reaction, need and longing and the rich headiness of desire making her dizzy. And still so needy it hurt.

She couldn't get close enough. She couldn't taste him deeply enough. She didn't care if she could breathe, if her feet touched the ground, and when he shifted to haul her against him and then lifted her high in the air, the only thing she could think to do was kiss him again.

Harder. Deeper. Longer. Hotter.

He wrapped her legs around his waist and held her there, twined around him with no other support, making her tremble at the strength he displayed so offhandedly— and then he shifted again, so their hips dragged against each other, his hardness against the part of her that was the neediest, and she moaned into his mouth.

She'd never liked being touched. But she found that didn't apply to Rihad, who couldn't seem to touch her *enough*.

And right at that moment, she didn't care why that was. She would die if he knew, she thought. If he comprehended how untouched she truly was.

It wasn't until her back came up against something that she realized it wasn't just that spinning in her head that was making her feel loose and adrift—he'd walked over and laid her out on the table like his very own banquet.

"Reach up," he ordered her, sounding more like a king than she'd ever heard him sound before, and there was probably something deeply wrong with her that she liked it. More than liked it—that hot, dark note in his voice swept over her skin as if he'd used his mouth against her, his mouth and his wicked tongue. "Hold on."

She did as he asked. As he *commanded*. She didn't even think twice about it, and not only because she wanted him to think she was that slut everyone believed she was, but also because that was so much easier than who she really was.

Sterling reached up over her head and grabbed the far edge of the table as he leaned in harder, pressing his hips against hers even as this new position made her back arch, as if she was offering up her breasts to him.

She was. She hoped she looked as if she'd done this a thousand times before—or even if she didn't, that he'd be too interested in her breasts to care.

He smiled dangerously as he looked down at the place their bodies pressed together, and Sterling felt the glow of that sweep over her. Through her, hard and hot and needy, until it settled like a lightning bolt between her legs.

She bucked against him, helpless against these new sensations, and he laughed.

And then he bent down and found her nipple through the gauzy material of her dress with that dangerously clever mouth of his, so hot and so demanding, and sucked it straight into all that heat.

Sterling lost her mind.

There was nothing then, but the fire that rolled through her, one bright flame after the next, building toward something so immense, so impossible, that she would have been afraid of it if she'd been able to catch her breath.

But Rihad didn't allow that.

He pressed the proof of his need hard into the place she hungered for him the most, soft and wet and wild for him even through the trousers he wore, with her ankles locked in the small of his strong back. He set a lazy, mind-melting rhythm, and Sterling could do nothing but meet it, shuddering more with every roll of his lethal hips.

She didn't know what she was doing. But she couldn't seem to stop.

His mouth teased her breasts through her dress while his hands streaked beneath it, testing her shape, her heat. Learning all kinds of things about her. That she rarely bothered with a bra, even these days when her breasts were still bigger than they'd been before her pregnancy. That a careful pinch against one nipple and a deep tug on the other made her clutch her legs tighter around him and ride him shamelessly, rubbing herself against him as wantonly as she could—

And then it slammed into her.

Like a train.

She cried out, but he was there, licking the sound of it from her lips, moving his own hips harder against hers, making it go on and on and on.

Making her shatter, then shatter again, then shatter once more.

Changing everything.

Changing the whole world.

Turning Sterling into someone new.

And when it was over, he let her drop her legs from around his waist and took a step back while she simply lay sprawled there on the table in a thousand pieces, trying to breathe.

It took a while and even then, it was a shaky thing.

When she sat up and pulled her dress back down to cover her, Rihad stood there above her, his dark face hard and his golden eyes glittering. He folded his arms over his powerful chest and considered her for a long, breathless moment, as if he wasn't still so aroused that she could see the proof of it pressing against the front of his trousers, hard and thick, and how could she still want him? Even now?

Even as the events of this morning flooded her, making her question a lot of things. Her sanity chief among them.

"Congratulations, Sterling," Rihad said in that low, rough voice of his that kicked up that fire in her all over again. "You succeeded in distracting me. How long do you think that will work?"

* * *

It had worked all too well, Rihad thought a few days later, as he sat in his luxuriously appointed offices and found it impossible to concentrate on matters of state.

Because she haunted him.

Her taste. The sounds she'd made as she'd writhed beneath him. The scent of her skin. The sweet perfection of her touch.

He found he couldn't think of much else. Especially during the meals they took together in his garden, where they both acted as if that scene *right there on the table* hadn't happened. They outdid each other with crisp politeness.

But it hummed beneath everything. Every clink of silver against fine china. Every sip of wine. Every glance that caught and held. Every movement they each made.

It was a madness in his blood, infecting him.

Or she was.

Because Rihad hardly knew himself these days. His entire relationship with his brother had been a lie. He was hung up on a woman he'd married while he'd believed she was Omar's mistress—and he had lusted after her while believing it. He was more enamored by the day with a tiny child who was not his in fact, but who felt like his in practice. He felt as if he was reeling through his life suddenly, unmoored and uncertain, and he had no idea how to handle such an alien sensation.

It was as if there was nothing left to hold on to. Or, more to the point, as if the only thing he wanted to hold on to was Sterling—as if he was as bewitched by her as he'd always thought his brother had been.

Maybe his enemies were not wrong to threaten invasion. Rihad was beginning to think it would be a kindness.

He was halfway through yet another inappropriate daydream about his wife when his personal mobile rang with a familiar ringtone.

Rihad dismissed his ministers with a regal wave and then swiped to open the video chat.

His sister gazed back at him from the screen, looking as defiant as ever.

"Amaya." He kept his voice calm, though it was harder than it should have been, and he didn't want to think about why that was, all of a sudden, or who was to blame for his endless lack of control. "Have you called to issue your usual taunts?"

"The quick brown fox always jumps over the lazy dog, Rihad." Her dark eyes were a shade lighter than the fall of thick dark hair she'd pulled forward over one shoulder, and it irritated him that she was both unquestionably beautiful and entirely too much like her treacherous mother. Smarter than was at all helpful and not in the least bit loyal to the Bakrian throne. It made her unpredictable and he'd always hated that—at least, he'd always thought he had. "I'm only giving you a much-needed demonstration."

"I feel adequately schooled."

"Obviously not. I can see you scanning behind me for details on my location. Don't bother. There aren't any that will help you find me." The light of battle lit her face, and he stopped trying to find any sort of geographic marker in what looked like a broom closet around her. "Are you ready to call off this marriage? Set me free?"

This was where Rihad normally outlined her responsibilities, reminded her that despite what she might have preferred, she was a Bakrian princess and she had a duty to her country. That it didn't matter how many years she'd spent knocking around various artistic, bohemian communities with her mother pretending she was nothing more than another rootless flower child, she couldn't alter the essential truth of her existence. That her university years in Montreal might have given her the impression that her life was one of limitless choices in all directions, but that was not true, not for her, and the sooner she accepted that the happier she would be.

He'd been telling her all of this for months. Years.

None of those conversations had been at all successful.

Today, he thought of the brother he'd treated as if he was a failure, the brother he'd claimed he'd loved when he'd never given him the opportunity to be himself. Not in Rihad's presence anyway. He thought of the way Sterling, the only woman—hell, the only *person*—who had ever defied him to his face with such a lack of fear, had flinched as if she expected him to beat her, all because she'd told him the truth.

He thought that perhaps he had no business being a king, if he was such a remarkably bad one.

"I wish I could do that, Amaya," he said after a long moment. "More than you know."

She stared at him as if she couldn't believe he'd said that. He wasn't sure he could, either.

He shrugged. "These are precarious times. The only possible way we will maintain our sovereignty is to unite with Daar Talaas. But you know this."

"There must be another way."

"If there was, don't you think I would have found it?" He sat back in his chair, his eyes on the screen and on his sister. "It does not give me any particular pleasure to insist you do something you are so opposed to that you've been on the run all this time."

"But...?" she prompted, though he noticed that defiant way she held herself had softened.

"But Kavian is a man who follows the ancient ways, and there is only one kind of alliance he holds sacred. Blood." He studied Amaya then, saw the expression that moved over her face, that hint of something like heat in her gaze. "And I think you know this all too well, don't you? Because while you were not exactly thrilled at the idea, you didn't run away until after you met him at your engagement reception. Did he do something to you?"

Alliance or not, Rihad would kill him. But Amaya only flushed then, though she tried to cover it with a frown.

"The reality of the situation merely impressed itself upon me, that's all. I realized that I'm not a Stone Age kind of a girl."

He didn't believe her, but that was hardly his business.

"I sympathize," he said instead, and the thing of it was, he did. He truly did.

"And I'm skeptical."

"Amaya, no one knows more about marrying for the sake of the kingdom than I do. I'm on my second such marriage."

"That doesn't exactly recommend the ordeal." Amaya's frown deepened. Her eyes searched his for perhaps a moment too long. "You're not the happiest man I've ever met."

And yet in comparison to Kavian, the desert warrior

renowned for his ability to wage war like an ancient warlord, Rihad was a nonstop comedy show. Neither one of them pointed that out and yet it hung there between them anyway.

For a moment they only gazed at each other, separated by their years, the screen, her continued refusal to surrender to the inevitable.

"Don't believe everything you read," he advised her. "My marriage is not an ordeal." He felt a sharp pang of disloyalty then, because he'd forgotten about Tasnim entirely. It was as if he really was a stranger, inhabiting the same body but utterly changed, all because of one lush woman and her artlessly addictive mouth. "And my first marriage might not have been a love match, but it was good. We were content."

Amaya's hand crept up to her neck and she cupped her hand there, then looked away.

"Kavian is not the kind of man who is ever going to be *content*," she said, so softly he almost didn't hear her. The old version of himself would have pretended he hadn't.

"I wish I could call it off," he told her quietly, and saw her swallow hard. Was he that harsh? That she had no idea that he wanted to protect her—that he would have if he could? "But you signed all the papers. You made your initial vows. By the laws of Daar Talaas, you are already his."

She shuddered, and when she looked at him again, he felt that great loosening inside him again, as if he'd lost this, too. This relationship with the only sibling he had left. This sister who clearly had no idea that he loved her, too.

He felt an unknown and unpleasant sensation swamp

him then and realized he'd felt it before. When Sterling had stood there before him with her eyes closed and her head bowed, visibly forcing herself to relax, the better to take a hit he hadn't been planning to deliver.

Helplessness.

He loathed it.

"Amaya." Her head jerked around and her eyes met his, and he saw confusion there. And something else, something a little more like haunted. "You are not a mere pawn. I care what happens to you. But I can't fix this."

"So I am doomed." And her voice cracked on that last word. "There is no hope."

"You can appeal to Kavian himself—"

"I'd have better luck appealing to a sandstorm in the desert!"

"Amaya." But he didn't know what to say. He was a goddamned king and what was the point? He couldn't save anyone. "I'm sorry."

"So am I." She shook her head, as if she was shaking something off. "I don't want war, Rihad. I don't want Bakri to fall. But I don't want to be Kavian's… *possession*, either. I won't."

And her screen went dark.

Leaving Rihad alone with his thoughts and his regrets, which were darker still.

CHAPTER NINE

THE SOUND OF the helicopter's rotor blades faded off into the distance, taking with it Sterling's halfhearted hopes that they might be called back to the palace to tend to some kind of governmental issue that simply couldn't wait.

And then the only sound—in and around and between the brightly colored tents tucked there between the towering desert sand dunes and arrayed around the series of tree-lined pools that shouldn't have existed in so arid a place at all—was the wind. It danced over the tops of the tents, making the hard canvas bend and stretch beneath the high sun far above, and then clattered its way through the palm trees.

Sterling was glad, because otherwise she was certain the only noise around for the miles and miles of uninhabited Bakrian desert they'd covered to get here would be the crazy pounding of her heart.

Rihad, of course, didn't appear to hear any of it. He was conducting a conversation in rapid-fire Arabic into the satellite phone at his ear, striding toward one of the larger tents nearer the water as if he expected her to follow along obediently in his wake.

Instead, Sterling stayed where she was. She tilted her

head back and let the desert sun play over her face. She liked the lick of heat, the tease of the dry wind against her skin and in the ends of the hair she'd scraped into a low ponytail beneath a wide-brimmed hat. She liked the murmur of the water from the nearby pools, the suggestion of cool, inviting shade beneath the trees and inside the tents. She would have been enchanted by the whole *desert oasis* thing altogether were it not for the fact he'd insisted she leave Leyla behind with the nurses, which was making her anxious.

And for what she suspected Rihad meant to accomplish here, which made her…something a lot more complicated than simply *anxious*.

"Maybe we can go in a month or two," she'd said when he'd brought up their perception-altering honeymoon again at another one of their dinners. This one had been more intimate, set up in his private dining suite with the wraparound balcony that opened up over the whole of Bakri City, where all she could seem to think about was his hands on her body, his hardness clenched tight between her legs. "When Leyla is a little bigger and will be better about me going away for a night."

Rihad had appeared focused on the food on his plate that night, not on her, though she should have known better than to believe that.

"It was not an invitation, as I think you know," he'd said after a moment. "It was an order. A royal command, even."

"Apparently, I have to remind you yet again that I'm not yours to command."

He'd laughed, and she'd started in her chair, because it had been genuine. The sound of it had cascaded over her, as if it was poured straight from the sun. "Do you think so?"

She tried to sound prim. Not at all like the sort of woman who would climax all over a man on a wrought-iron table one summer morning. "I'm not one of your subjects, Rihad."

"You are my queen." His gaze had risen to meet hers then and she'd flushed hot and red. His dark gold eyes had been alive with something like merriment, and there'd been hints of that laughter in his voice when he'd continued. "And in the spirit of transparency between us, which I know is your dearest hope—"

"What's wrong with murky?" she'd protested, aware she'd sounded as cranky as she had desperate. "I like a good swamp, especially in my marriage."

His eyes had gleamed, laughter and light, and she'd felt undone.

He would unravel her completely. She had no doubt. He'd already started.

"It will be more than a single night in the desert. I already told you it would be two weeks. And so it will." When she'd started to argue he'd only smiled. "I'd resign yourself to the inevitable, Sterling. Have I yet to promise you anything that didn't happen exactly as I said it would?"

She hadn't been able to breathe. But that hadn't stopped her mouth from moving.

"Are you going to command me to have sex with you, too?" she'd asked in that same absurdly overpolite tone, as if she was inquiring after high tea. "Consummation on demand?"

And she'd had no words to describe what his smile had done to her then, or how that lazy, predatory gleam in his dark gold eyes had made her feel. God, the way it had made her *feel*. How it had sneaked through her, tangling all around and making her hollow and needy, scared and yearning at once.

Did she *want* him to command her? *Reach up,* he'd ordered her that morning. *Hold on.* Was that why she'd asked?

"If you insist," he'd said after a moment, in a dark-edged way that had made everything inside of her feel the way he'd sounded. Like honey, sweet and slow. She remembered shattering all around him, again and again. She shivered just remembering it. "Is that how you like it, Sterling? Do you prefer to give orders on the street and take them in bed?"

It was as if he'd read her mind, and she'd told herself stoutly that she hated that. And that he hadn't, of course.

She'd sniffed as if she found this discussion crass beyond measure. "Not from you."

Rihad had only smiled again, harder and edgier than before, and it had banged through Sterling like a symphony of gongs. "We'll see. We leave in two days' time. I suggest you resign yourself to the torture."

And now she was far, far away from anything even resembling civilization. The helicopter ride had taken at least two hours and they'd left the city limits within the first twenty minutes. There was nothing for miles in any direction. There was nothing here except forced intimacy and, she thought while her stomach cartwheeled around inside of her, nothing at all to keep her from exploring the one man alive whose touch she didn't seem to mind.

"I've dismissed all but the most essential staff." His voice made her jump and she opened her eyes to find him propped up against the nearest palm tree, his dark gold gaze simmering as it touched hers. "There is no one else here but the two of us and, farther out, my security guards to keep watch over the perimeter."

"You mean, to keep me from running away from you."

He smiled again, and that other night at the palace hadn't been a fluke. It was devastating. It was almost as powerful as his kiss. It made her feel that same mix of weakness and wonder, and she didn't have the slightest idea what to do about it.

"I mean, my most faithful and devoted guards are there to protect you whether you like it or not." He'd let out a quiet sort of laugh. "But yes. Part of that protection would include returning you to my tender embrace should you wander too far from the oasis. The desert sands can be so treacherous."

"How thoughtful." But her mouth was pulling at the corners, as if her smile wanted to break free despite her own wishes. "Will you have men to guard the pools as well, in case I am tempted to drown myself rather than suffer your company?"

His laugh was deeper then. Richer. It was like drowning, indeed, in a masculine version of the best chocolate she could imagine, decadent and addictive.

She was in so much trouble.

"It depends which pool you mean to drown yourself in," he said, as if he was giving the issue due consideration. "This nearest one will take some work. It's barely knee-deep. You're more likely to drown in your wineglass."

"That can be arranged."

He moved closer. He should have looked like any

other man, the epitome of casual in nothing but a white
oxford shirt and sand-colored trousers, but this was
Rihad. He *was* the king. It didn't seem to matter what
he wore; nothing could conceal that low-edged hum of
power he carried with him wherever he went.

"Shall we discuss our agenda, now that we're here?"
he asked when he was much too close. When she
couldn't seem to do anything but lose herself somewhere between that look on his face and the pounding
of her heart.

"Our honeymoon has an agenda?" She fought to
keep her voice light and airy—and to keep from leaping away from him because she knew, somehow, that
he would know full well she wanted to do the opposite.
"Royal sheikhs in their luxurious oasis retreats really
aren't like us."

"Consider this nothing more than a statement of intent, Sterling."

She wanted to throw something back at him, to make
this interchange all about amusing banter and not about
the rest of the things that circled all around them, pressing in on them, as flattening and searingly hot as the
desert sun high over their heads.

"And what exactly do you intend?" she asked, but her
throat was so dry, and he was so close. He stood there,
much too near to her, so that she imagined she could feel
the heat of him. So that her palms itched to touch him
again—and that unnerved her more than anything else.

"I think you know what I want you to tell me," he
said quietly.

She didn't want to meet his gaze then, but she did.
And it shuddered all the way through her in a way that

made her feel raw and vulnerable. But not afraid. Something else that she wasn't certain she understood.

"No," she said.

And she didn't know what that meant, even as she said it. No, she didn't know what he meant? No, she wasn't going to tell him? No, in general?

But he smiled as if she'd whispered him a line or two of poetry and reached over to skate the backs of his fingers down the side of her face. *Undoing her,* she thought. He was tearing her down, pulling her apart, right where they stood.

"And I think you know the rest of what I want," he said in a low voice.

"I know this will be hard for you to understand," she said, trying to sound strong. Tough. Worldly and amused, in that way she'd perfected years ago. "But not everyone gets what they want all the time. Some people never get what they want at all. It's a fact of life when you're not literally the king of all you survey."

Rihad smiled, and the heat where his fingers caressed her cheek blossomed deep within her.

"But I am."

And still he smiled when all she could do was stare up at him, mute and undone and all those other things that tangled up inside of her and made her this shockingly susceptible to him.

Then he dropped his hand and stepped back, and Sterling felt that like a loss. She pulled in a breath, amazed she was still standing on her own two feet. Truly astonished she hadn't simply keeled over from all that intensity.

"I have some things I must attend to," he told her. "The sad truth is that the leader of a country is never truly on holiday, despite what he might wish. But you will join me for dinner. In the meantime, Ushala will lead you to your tent and see that you are settled in."

"What if I don't want to join you for dinner?" she asked.

She thought they both knew that she wasn't really talking about dinner.

And in any case, Rihad only smiled.

Sterling disappeared into one of the sleeping tents that functioned as a luxurious guest room out here in his family's private oasis. Rihad took a few calls as the afternoon wore on, impatient with this life of his that could not allow him anything resembling a real holiday. Not even a honeymoon.

He opted not to think too much about the fact that when he'd gone on a honeymoon previously, he'd welcomed the opportunity to work from the oasis, and neither he nor Tasnim had expected to see much of each other outside of their carefully polite meals.

But then, Sterling was different. Perhaps he'd known that from the first moment he'd seen her, so long ago now on that Manhattan sidewalk.

She did not emerge again until the sun dipped low and began to paint the dunes in the shifting colors of sunset. Reds and oranges, pinks and golds, and Sterling walking toward him in the middle of it all like another work of art.

Rihad sat in one of the *majlis*, a seating area marked off with a soft rug beneath him, bright pillows all around in the Bedouin style and a low table stretched out beneath a graceful canopy. It opened on the sides to let the evening in as he sipped a cool drink and watched the sunset outdo itself before him, as if for his pleasure alone.

After a glance to make sure she was coming to him—of her own free will, which pleased him, though he imagined he'd have sought her out if she hadn't and he wasn't certain what that told him about himself—Rihad didn't look up as Sterling approached him, didn't take his eyes off the horizon.

Almost as if he worried that if he did, his best intentions would simply crumble into sand and blow away.

He smiled at the glorious spectacle laid out before him instead, the colors changing and blooming as he watched. He never tired of the desert. How could he—how could anyone? The landscape was constantly shifting, yet always the same. The great bowl of the sky stretched high above with these magical, daily displays of fierce natural splendor. It reminded him who he was. It reminded him that Bakri was as much a part of him as he was of it. Just as the sky and the land were fused into this stunning unity twice a day as the sun rose and fell, so, too, was his family a part of this country. Twined together, made one.

That was what a marriage was, at its best. What it was *supposed* to be.

What he was determined this one would be, no matter what he had to do to get there.

Rihad did not choose to analyze all the reasons why his need for this burned in him. He only knew that it did.

She settled herself down across from him at the low table with that innate grace of hers that was beginning to feel something like addictive.

"Does your tent suit?" he asked her, as if they were

meeting at some or other royal exercise, where the highest protocols were observed.

"It's lovely," she replied in the same tone.

Rihad bit back a smile and waved to the servants. They appeared at once, filling the low table between them with various dishes, from perfectly grilled skewers of lamb to a pile of handmade flatbread, a generous pot of homemade hummus, assorted other dipping sauces and side dishes. Rihad took the opportunity to study this woman, this *wife* of his. She was nothing like Tasnim. He couldn't remember a single moment with his first wife that had ever felt like this—this seething thing, nearly at a boil, that thrummed along beneath his skin and made him feel predatory and possessive even when she wasn't in front of him.

And much, much more so when she was.

She wore another one of her dresses and a flowing pashmina she wrapped tightly around her like a blanket. More to continue to conceal herself from him as much as possible, he thought with no little amusement, than to ward off the night air. Her lustrous strawberry blond hair was pulled back into what was, for her, a merely serviceable ponytail at her nape, but then, elegance was stamped into her bones. She couldn't help but appear chic, even when she was attempting to look dowdy. She'd been haunting in those teenaged photographs that had taken the modeling world by surprise years back, all high cheekbones, world-weary blue eyes and that hooker's mouth of hers. More than a decade later, she was objectively, inarguably stunning, no matter what lengths she went to hide it.

And Rihad was merely a man.

He lounged there against his pillows and watched her eat her dinner with evident relish, this woman who could knock men flat like dominoes. Take down whole kingdoms. Wreck worlds.

Or maybe that was just what she'd done to him, when he'd been expecting something so much different.

"You're staring at me as if I'm an animal in a zoo," she pointed out crisply when she'd demolished a few lamb chops and several heaping spoonfuls of the grain and greens salads. "It's going to give me indigestion."

"I'm waiting for you to finish eating," he said lazily. "You're building up your energy, are you not? For the sex. Consummation on command, I believe you called it. A warning, Sterling. I'm very demanding."

"The sex," she repeated slowly. There wasn't a flicker of reaction on her perfect face, or even in those sky-blue eyes of hers when she fixed them on him, but he knew better. He could feel the air itself sizzle between them. "Am I to understand that you'll be performing a solo act? Right here, out in the open? How fascinating. You'll understand if I don't watch, I hope. I wouldn't want my stomach to turn at a delicate moment and throw you off your stroke."

He only watched her as the servants cleared all the plates between them and then piled the table high again with an array of tempting desserts—but Sterling was looking at him with that fire in her gaze and he couldn't have imagined any better treat than her.

"You're sitting here in silence, Sterling," he pointed out, playing up the languid desert king because he could see the way it got to her. He could see the way she shifted against her pillows, as if she couldn't quite get comfortable. "I assumed that you'd decided we should jump right into the sex rather than have a frank discussion." He smiled. "I'm perfectly all right with that, if it's what you wish."

She most certainly did not wish, Sterling told herself then. But she had the growing notion that she was lying to herself.

And worse, that he knew it.

"Do you ever have interactions with anyone in which you aren't threatening them?" she asked, mildly enough. "Whether directly or indirectly?"

"Most of my interactions are political in nature," he replied, a vision of male ease as he lounged there and watched her too closely, his dark eyes glittering in the light thrown by too many hanging lanterns to count. "So, no. I don't have any conversations that do not involve jockeying for power, or position, or status, or economic gain."

"You are aware that some people have conversations that involve none of those things?"

A faint crook to that perfect mouth. "I've heard rumors."

"I will have to decline your lovely offer," she said, and smiled at him in the polite-yet-distant way she'd perfected in New York. "I've never been to an oasis before and I think I'd like to take a swim in the middle of a desert. Your marvelous suggestion that we delve into my past and/or me, personally, while tempting, will have to wait."

She thought he would throw something back at her, but he only continued to study her with that small smile in the corner of his mouth. Sterling took that as acquiescence—or whatever it was when powerful men gave in, without seeming to give at all.

Sterling rose and walked past him toward the deepest of the three pools that shimmered there only a few steps from where they'd had their dinner. All the pools were hung with their own lanterns, each casting a dancing, mellow light over the dark waters. It made the water seem something more than simply inviting. Mysterious. Seductive. She stepped onto the mat that had been laid out there beneath the lightly rustling palm trees and kicked off her slides, then dropped her pashmina.

"You realize you are not fooling me, I hope," Rihad said almost conversationally, still lounging there beneath the canopy behind her. "I know exactly what you are doing."

"Swimming?" she asked over her shoulder. "You are correct, Your Royal Majesty. Your powers of observation are truly magnificent."

Then she pulled the floor-length, flowing dress she wore up and over her head, leaving herself in nothing at all but a very tiny, very provocative string bikini in a metallic, shiny gold.

She could feel his sudden stillness from behind her, predatory and vast, like an epic, nuclear implosion of the same hunger she knew beat in her, but she didn't turn back toward him. She didn't need to. *This* was the point. The tease. The distraction.

Getting him back a little bit. Making him pay.

And she'd spent enough time as a model to have rendered her nothing but practical, more or less, about her body. She might have given birth only a few months back. She might have a different shape now, and new marks like claws on a belly she doubted would ever be concave again. But she was well aware of the power of her curves. And she knew that standing there in a flirty gold bikini would make it as hard for Rihad to sleep at night as it had been for her since that morning in the palace gardens.

Sterling was very good at this after all. She'd made a living out of using her body like this, once upon a time.

But she didn't want to think about the past. She wanted to keep it behind her, as long as she could. Tonight, she only wanted to make Rihad ache the way that she ached.

She didn't look back at him, she looked at the inky black surface of the pool, lit with dancing gold from the lanterns, and it was like looking straight into Rihad's mesmerizing gaze.

She dived right in.

CHAPTER TEN

THE WATER WAS COOL, CLEAR.

It was like a silken caress over her skin, long and luxurious at once, and if she could have, Sterling would have stayed beneath the surface of that pool forever. She let herself sink, then float beneath the surface, and pretended she could remain there. But eventually her lungs began to ache a little bit and she kicked back up into the night air.

To find Rihad much closer, squatting there at the edge of the water, his dark gaze fierce on hers. It made her heart leap inside her chest, so hard and so high she was surprised it didn't make the water ripple in reaction.

"Do you think you are safe in the water?" he asked her, and there were stark lines stamped on his face as he gazed at her. As if need was carving into him, the way she could feel it in her, too.

Whittling away at her until she didn't know what was left, or who she'd be when it was done.

"I think that safety is relative where you're concerned," she said now, perhaps a shade too flippantly. She was more enthusiastic about swimming than she was skilled at it, so she moved closer to the side of the pool, reaching out a hand to hold on to the edge. "Kings are not exactly known for putting the needs of their wives before their own."

"You know a great many kings, do you?"

She slicked her hair back, as aware of the way his dark gold eyes tracked the movement as if he'd used his own hands. And his attention was like a live wire, ferocious and total.

"I'm aware of the entire history of the planet, if that's what you mean."

Rihad studied her in that focused, too-incisive way of his that made her want to *do things* to escape it. Before he could see every last corner of her dirty little soul.

"I have a modest hope that I am less bloodthirsty than many of the kings who predate me," he was saying drily. "And I know I'm better to my wives than most of those, given I've yet to execute one."

"Was that on the table here?"

"We're talking about absolute power. It's all on the table. Something to remember the next time you're feeling feisty." But his mouth was crooked into that small smile of his she was beginning to find addictive, despite that steady gaze of his that made her tremble deep within. "But I can't imagine you really want to talk about the powers of the Bakrian monarchy, or the march of kings throughout time, do you?"

"I don't want to talk to you at all. I wanted to swim."

He indicated the pool behind her with a jerk of his fine chin. "Then by all means, Sterling. Swim."

But she didn't move.

They could have stayed frozen there for a decade. She'd never have known the difference. Only that she couldn't look away from him.

This man who had far more power than the others

she'd known, who'd taken theirs out on her because they'd considered her so beneath them. Rihad was autocratic. He certainly used his power. But never like that. Never so viciously.

Eventually, he reached down and traced a lazy, sensual pattern from one shoulder, across the very top of her chest, all the way to the other. Then back.

And she still didn't understand why his was the only touch that made her feel like this, wrapped up in a blaze of need and outside her own skin. She didn't understand why she wanted him, wanted more, *wanted*, when she'd never wanted any other man in her life.

When she'd never wanted any *touch* in her life.

She didn't understand any of this, only that when he touched her she wanted to sob out, and not because it hurt her. And when he didn't touch her, it was worse.

He'd made her into a woman she didn't understand at all. Maybe it was that she felt like a *woman* after all. Not a punching bag. Not a clothes hanger. Not an ornament. Not a mother. *A woman*, for the first time.

"I hate you," she whispered.

Just as she had at their wedding.

But this time, Rihad smiled, and it was as if that, too, burst into her and pried her wide-open however little she wanted to let him in.

"I am so sorry, little one," he murmured, his dark gold eyes on hers, and that look of his slid straight through her, too soft and too slick. It made her shake and this time, not only inside. "It's not so easy to make me the monster you wanted me to be, is it?"

"Maybe not," she whispered up at him, filled with that same wild urge to *do anything* to keep him from seeing the truth about her. Before it was too late. "But this is very easy, actually."

And Sterling reached up, grabbed hold of the arm he had propped on his knee as she braced her feet on the side of the pool, and she yanked him off balance.

Then she hauled the King of Bakri straight into the pool.

He sank like a stone, in a cascade of bubbles while a great wave slapped at her, and she was breathing so fast it hurt while the adrenaline—at her temerity, at the fact she'd actually done it—spiked inside of her. She'd made the split-second decision to get the hell out of that pool *right now* when he surfaced beside her, and Sterling realized that she was frozen in place. Paralyzed, more like.

Why on earth had she done that?

But Rihad laughed.

He tipped his beautiful face back and he laughed, hard and long, and she was tempted to think it was all a great big joke to him, to have her throw him fully dressed into a pool like that—but then he dropped his head back down, fixed that edgy gold gaze of his on her, and there wasn't a shred of laughter on his lethally beautiful face then.

"That, Sterling," he told her, his voice a sensual growl she felt in her sex as surely as if he was already touching her, "was a mistake."

And then he reached over, hooked a hard hand around her neck and yanked her to him.

He took her mouth as if he owned it, and Rihad thrilled to it—because he did. She was his. The sweep of her tongue against his. The way she yielded to him so quickly, so completely, meeting him and spurring him on.

This was *his* woman. *His* wife. *His.*

She wrapped her arms around his neck and held on, and he thought he might drown them both as he feasted on her, taking and taking, so hard and so good he thought he might die from it. He thought he might not care too much if he did.

There was no time left then. Not anymore. He had to be inside her, now, and nothing else mattered. Not her secrets. Not all the things she still hadn't told him and had gone to such lengths to avoid telling him. Nothing but this mad fire, this perfect kiss. The heft of her gorgeous breasts in their little scraps of gold, the slick glory of her taste.

His Sterling. His queen.

Somehow, he moved them to the shallower end of the pool, where he could stand. When he did, he trapped her between the pool's bank and his body. He felt the wind against the wet shirt on his back, but he didn't care. He only cared about Sterling. About this. Her hands digging into the flesh at his shoulders. Her legs moving to wrap around his hips again.

And for the first time in his entire adult life, Rihad stopped thinking.

He fumbled between them, wrestling with his soaked trousers to pull himself free. Then, his mouth still fused to hers, he reached down between them, out of finesse and out of his mind as he pushed her little bikini bottom to one side and stroked beneath it, straight into her soft, scalding heat.

"Rihad…" she moaned, straight into his mouth, and it was the sexiest thing he'd ever heard.

He didn't think. He moved his hand, he held her

close and then he simply thrust straight into her, hard and sure, making her truly his at last.

At last.

She made an odd sound, and he pulled back to look down at her lovely face, the haze clearing slightly.

Sterling's eyes were too big and hinted at some kind of emotion he didn't recognize. Rihad held himself still, and she breathed hard. Shakily. Once, then again.

"Are you all right, little one?" he asked quietly, still so deep inside of her he thought it might kill him. She was so hot, so wet. Snug around him, as if she'd been made to receive him exactly like this. "Did I hurt you? Are you not yet healed from giving birth?"

"No…" she said, as if she wasn't sure. Her blue gaze was dark, slick, in the light from the gently dancing lanterns overhead. He frowned as she continued. "I'm fine. I'm healed, I… It's just… It's weird, that's all."

"Weird," he repeated, as if the word didn't make sense, and slid back a few inches, experimentally, just to see what would happen—

And then, impossibly, Sterling McRae blushed.

Bright red. As if, Rihad thought in total fascination, she was entirely innocent. As if this was her first time.

But that was crazy.

Still, once the thought was there, Rihad couldn't seem to keep himself from indulging it. He'd wanted to lose himself in her, pound them both into delirious oblivion with all the pent-up need that had haunted his every thought of her for months now—but instead, he slowed down. He took his time.

He treated her like the virgin she couldn't possibly be.

He kissed her everywhere he could see that flushed

red skin, until the rosy glow she wore was for another reason entirely. He set a slow, lazy pace, easy and wicked at once, making sure that each time he slid away she clung to him a little more, then pulled him back to her a little harder. He used his mouth and his hands, his teeth and his voice, until she was writhing against him, mindless and moaning, just the way he'd wanted her.

Then he reached down, pressed hard against the center of her need and sent her flying.

And it was the most beautiful thing he'd ever seen. So damned beautiful it hurt—and he wasn't done.

When she came back to herself, panting and dazed, he went a little bit faster, a little bit harder. He held her where he wanted her and took her until that made her cry out, then splinter all over again, and that time, he went with her.

But he was in no doubt, even then.

Sterling was a virgin.

Or had been one anyway, before she'd entered this pool.

And now she was his.

Rihad was unusually quiet when he climbed from the pool and then pulled her out behind him, but Sterling was still floating off in the clouds somewhere, too lost in the sensations still storming through her body to care.

He lifted her up and swung her into his arms, then carried her over the sands to his tent, not seeming to notice that he was still in his soaking wet clothes. He shouldered his way inside, where Sterling blinked in the softly lit interior until her eyes adjusted. When they did, she had to bite back a gasp.

Because it was like walking into a dream. Where her

tent was like a desert rendition of a high-end hotel room, Rihad's was something else entirely. It was a pageant of scarlet and gold, from the wide bed on its magnificent, kingly platform to the seating areas, some with pillows on the floor arrayed around what looked like a fireplace, some with wide, inviting couches, some set carefully around what looked like a personal library. There were jeweled chests and thick rugs, tapestries and ornate screens to mark off separate areas, and it felt like all the half-formed fantasies Sterling had ever had about distant harems and the harshly beguiling men who ruled over them.

And he was far better than any fantasy she'd ever had, she knew now. Even the ones she'd had about him, little, though, she'd wanted to admit that to herself.

Rihad still didn't speak.

He stalked across the room and disappeared behind one of the screens, into what Sterling assumed was his own bathroom suite. She stood where she was, dripping onto the priceless carpet like a drowned thing, and when he returned, his face was set into an expression she couldn't begin to work out. And his gaze was so fierce she couldn't look at him directly—though that was not exactly a hardship, she thought, as her eyes dropped from his. He'd stripped off his wet clothes and was starkly, proudly naked, striding toward her as if it was the most natural thing in the world for him to do so.

She supposed it was. Even she understood that nudity was commonly a part of the whole sex thing.

The whole sex thing *that you've now done,* she reminded herself, still more than a little dazed by it. The act itself and the fact that she'd slipped across a kind of internal boundary line while she'd been shattering apart in Rihad's arms.

It was over. Virginity dispensed with quickly and efficiently, and the best part was, Rihad was none the wiser. No awkward conversations filled with explanations and confessions, no accusations of being a great big freak of nature—all the things she'd always feared would happen if she ever got around to this hadn't happened with Rihad.

And she was still so turned on, still so hungry for him, that she shook.

He picked her up again, as if she was as light as a doll—or as if she was utterly his, a thought that was so electrifying it burst inside of her like pain—and she should have protested that, but she didn't. This time, he set her down on the high, wide platform step next to the bed and set about peeling her bikini all the way from her body, his hands like hot brands where the wet material had chilled her skin.

He produced a towel from somewhere and dried her off, carefully and thoroughly, and before he was done she was restless and needy all over again, moving from foot to foot when he crouched down before her—

And he knew it, she realized, when he glanced up at her, his eyes glittering darkly and that lush mouth of his in a crooked curve.

Her breath left her in a rush.

Rihad wrapped his hands around her hips and lifted her, then tipped her back so she sprawled out on the high bed before him. Then he folded up her knees and held her there with those too-strong hands of his, all of her aching lower body open to him. He looked at her for a smoldering moment, then leaned down and licked his way deep into her heat.

Sterling made a sound that could only be described as a scream.

And he took his damned time, all over again. He tasted every contour, every fold. He took her femininity as relentlessly and totally as he'd taken her mouth, and she was burning up for him so quickly, so deliriously, that she had the wild thought that she might not survive it.

He laughed against the core of her and it went through her like lightning, and then once more, he threw her off the side of the planet into that sweet, hot oblivion.

This time, when she came back to him he'd crawled up over her on the bed. He lined up that hard, proud length with her most sensitive flesh and, when she gasped out his name, pushed in deep.

It was different this time. Darker, hotter.

Harder.

She felt the wave snap back, then swell, and she tossed her head against the bed, as afraid of what was coming as she was desperate for it.

"Beg me," he ordered her harshly against her ear as he held himself over her, and it was like its own caress, rough and wild.

And she didn't think. She didn't argue.

She obeyed. She begged.

And it made it that much better.

Hotter. Sweeter.

Rihad pistoned in and out of her, making her a creature she'd never imagined she could be. She tore at him. She scratched him. She pleaded with him and he laughed, and that made her plead all the more. She writhed and she held on, she met each hard thrust as if she'd been made for this. For him. As if she'd waited all this time, as if it hadn't been an accident, because she'd been meant for him all along.

She wanted it to last forever. She thought she might die if it did.

And this time, when she fell apart, he shouted out her name like a hoarse prayer and came with her.

She didn't know how long she slept, or if it was even sleep—maybe she'd simply passed out from the enormity of what had happened? What she'd finally done? But when she woke again, she was tucked up next to him and he was playing with her hair, sliding the slippery strands through those clever fingers of his, that enigmatic expression still on his darkly gorgeous face.

That face of his she felt was stamped inside her, somehow, like a brand.

Sterling felt made new. As if he'd taken her apart and put her back together, and she would never be quite the same. She felt deeply and irrevocably changed. Altered, as if she might not recognize herself in the mirror the next time she looked.

She felt as if he'd taught her how to fly.

And she couldn't tell him that. He couldn't know. It was a slippery slope—

"Sterling."

She jolted back to him, to that curious light in his eyes and that little curve to his deliciously full mouth.

"Rihad," she said, and she wondered if his name would always sound like that to her now. Like a poem.

"I want to ask you a question."

"Anything." She meant it. Especially if they could

keep doing this. Just a few hundred more times, she thought, and that might take the edge off.

He shifted closer to her, propped himself up on one elbow and smiled into her eyes.

"Tell me one thing," he said, in that voice of his, so low and now intimately connected to something deep inside of her, as if he could simply flip a switch and she would long for him. She did. His dark gold eyes gleamed. "How is it possible that you were a virgin?"

Sterling went very, very still. He reached over and pulled a long strand of her hair between his fingers again, and this time, he tugged. Gently enough, but it seared through her anyway.

"That's ridiculous," she said, though her voice sounded faint—or maybe she couldn't hear it very well, over the clatter of her heart against her ribs. Because what else could she say? "Who's ever heard of a virgin my age?"

His gaze held hers, steady and direct. "I didn't ask you whether or not you were a virgin, Sterling. I know you were." His lips curved into something tender if not quite a smile, and it pulled at her. "Hail Sterling, full of grace."

"It's true," she whispered, because the thought hadn't occurred to her, really. Not fully formed anyway. "I accidentally performed a virgin birth."

"I asked you how."

"The usual way." She blinked when his eyebrow arched. "By which I mean IVF, of course. I did tell you that your brother was gay."

"Yes, thank you." His voice was as dry as the desert all around them. "I gathered that, as I saw no heavenly host hanging about the pool just now. How were you a virgin in the first place, Sterling? You're not a nun, virgin birth aside."

She had to clear her throat, because she couldn't get up and run. He would catch her in an instant and she'd end up answering anyway, just with a greater display of his superior strength to be awed by when she did. She had absolutely no doubt.

"Well," she said after what felt to her like a very long while, though he didn't seem to move a muscle throughout it, "it wasn't a plan. It just happened."

"How does such a thing *just happen*?" His gaze moved over her, and some heretofore unknown romantic part of her thrilled to that expression on his harshly beautiful face then, as if it really was tenderness. And oh, how she wanted it to be. "You were a beautiful girl on her own when you went to New York. A cautionary tale, really."

She opened her mouth to tell him another lie, but she couldn't, somehow. It was as if everything really had changed, whether she liked it or not. It wasn't only the sex. It was the baby. The way he'd saved her from herself when she'd been out of her mind on hormones and guilt. It was that he hadn't hit her—had seemed astonished she'd thought he would. It was his gentleness now. It was the way he'd taken over her body so completely and yet still left her wanting more.

Who was she kidding? It was *him*.

And Sterling didn't want to think about what that meant. She thought she knew—and that was truly insane. But she couldn't lie to him, either. And there were different levels of the truth.

"My foster parents were the nicest people," she told him, smiling slightly as if that might make these things easier to talk about. As if anything could. "That's what everybody always said, in case we weren't grateful enough. They were kind. Giving. They took in kids like me who'd been otherwise completely abandoned. They had their own kids. They were active and responsible members of the community. Everyone adored them." She couldn't look away from him, though she wanted to. "And why wouldn't they? My foster parents never left any marks. Sometimes they just hit us and other times they liked to play elaborate games, using us as targets. They practiced their aim with cigarettes, cans. Sometimes forks and knives. But there were never any bruises anyone could see." She saw that dark thing move in his gaze and smiled again, deeper and harsher. "They always told us we were welcome to tell on them, if we dared. That they'd enjoy ripping little nothings like us apart in public. Because no one would ever believe a word we said about the saints of the neighborhood, and they were right."

"Where are these people now?" Rihad asked softly. Dangerously, as if, were he to speak in his usual voice, he would raze whole cities to the ground with the force of his fury.

And it made something long frozen deep within her unfurl in a little blast of warmth.

"They're behind me, that's where they are." She smiled at him, a real smile that time, and when he slid his hand along her cheek, she leaned into it. "But after that I knew how evil people were, once they thought they had all the power. How vicious and cruel. So I made myself into an Ice Princess who didn't like to be touched and was always much too sober to have any fun anyway, so everyone left me alone. And then Omar came along, and I didn't have to worry about that stuff anymore, because everyone believed I was with him. And that's how I accidentally ended up a virgin."

Rihad didn't speak for a long time, and she would have given anything to know what he was thinking. What was happening behind that austere, ruthless face of his and that disconcertingly sensual mouth. She wanted to lick him until neither one of them could think anymore. She wanted to bury her face in the crook of his neck, as if he could keep her safe from all the things that swirled around her that she couldn't even identify. He would, she thought. He really would.

And God help her, the things she wanted then, that she was too afraid to name.

"But you let me take you." His gaze was even more golden than usual then, and it set her alight. "Twice."

"Yes." Her throat was so dry that it hurt when she swallowed. "I did."

"Why?" He traced a line from the tender place beneath her ear, down and around to stroke the line of her collarbone, as if he was trying to smooth the ridge of it back beneath her skin. "Why me?"

"We're already married, Rihad," she said, as primly as if she was lunching at some terribly dignified country club. "Your name is on my daughter's birth certificate."

And she saw that smile of his again, watched it light up his eyes. It filled her with the same light.

"Why, Sterling. That makes you sound traditional and old-fashioned, not modern and scandalous at all."

"It seemed safe enough," she told him, caught in that glittering gaze of his. Lost in the way he was touching her, so casually intimate, as if this was only the beginning. As if there was so much further yet to go—but she didn't dare let herself think that. "And also, to be honest, I didn't think you'd notice."

He didn't seem to move, but everything changed. Got way more intense, so fast it made her stomach drop. "I noticed."

She froze. "Oh. Was I…? Was I not…?"

Rihad laughed then and rolled, coming up over her and holding her there beneath him, that stunning body of his stretched out above her, so gorgeously male it hurt.

"You were exquisite," he told her quietly, sincerity in every syllable. "You are a marvel. But I am old-fashioned myself, Sterling, as you've pointed out to me many times. Deeply traditional in every possible way."

She was shaking, and it wasn't fear. It was him. "I don't know what that means."

"It means that you were far safer when I thought you were a whore," he said bluntly, his dark gaze seeming to burn through her, kicking up new flames and changing everything. Changing *her*. "Now I know that you are only mine. Only and ever mine. And I, my little one, am a very, very selfish man."

And then he set about proving it.

CHAPTER ELEVEN

THE HEADLINE A MONTH LATER was like a slap—the hit, perhaps, that Sterling had been expecting all along. She sat frozen solid on the balcony outside Rihad's suite, staring down at the tablet computer Rihad had left sitting there when he'd stepped inside to take a phone call. She felt sick.

Black Widow Sterling Lures King Rihad into Her Web! the worst of the European tabloids shrieked. And the article beneath it was even worse.

> Sex-symbol Sterling flaunts postbaby bod and enslaves the desert king! Starry-eyed King Rihad can't keep his eyes—or his hands!—off his late brother's lover. "But Sterling left a trail of broken hearts behind her in New York," say concerned friends. Will the formidable king be one more of heartbreaker Sterling's conquests?

It was beautifully done, really. Killer Whore. Vain Whore. Married Whore. Omar's Whore. New York Whore. So many clever ways of calling Sterling a whore without ever actually uttering the word.

The worst part was, she hadn't seen this coming.

She hadn't expected it, and she should have. Of course she should have. But she'd actually believed that now that she and Rihad were not only married, but also actually as intimate as that honeymoon had been meant to suggest, the awful paparazzi would leave her alone.

She'd been incredibly naive.

There are no happy endings, she reminded herself then, frowning out at the sea that stretched toward the horizon before her as if basking, blue and gleaming, in the sun. *Not for you. Not ever.*

But she'd been lulled into believing otherwise.

Their lazy days at the oasis had bled together into one great burst of brilliant heat, a haze of bright sun above, desert breezes over the cool water in the shaded pools and the desperate, delirious *hunger* that only Rihad had ever called out in her—and that only he could satisfy.

Sterling had learned every inch of his proud, infinitely masculine body. She'd tasted him, teased him, taken him. She'd learned how to make him groan out his pleasure, how to scream out her own. He'd taken her beneath the endless stars, in the vast softness of his bed, in the luxurious tub that stood in her own luxuriously appointed tent. He'd been inventive and uninhibited— and demanding, as he'd promised. She'd learned to be the same in return.

Sterling had given herself over to the exquisite pleasures of the flesh that she'd denied herself so long— all her life, in fact. Touch. Lust. Desire and its sweet oblivion. She'd eaten too much, drunk too deeply. She'd lost herself in Rihad, again and again and again. She'd told him the truth about herself, or a critical portion of the truth anyway—and the world hadn't ended.

She'd let herself imagine that Rihad was as powerful

as he'd always appeared to her. That he could truly hold back whatever nightmares threatened. That he would.

That she and Leyla and this marvel of a man could create their own truths and live in them. That they could finally be the family she'd always wanted.

But she'd forgotten who she was.

She always did.

It had been some weeks since they'd left the oasis and it didn't take a genius to figure out why the tabloids had latched on to her again. The article went on to make salacious suggestions about a list of regional leaders and some local celebrities, all of whom had been at last night's elegant function in one of the new luxury hotel complexes being built along the shore of the Bay of Bakri.

That meant that someone at that party had taken exception to the Queen Whore being paraded about on their king's arm and had taken to the tabloids to express their feelings.

"I'd prefer you not read that nonsense," Rihad said from the doorway, his deep voice like a flame within her, that easily. That quickly. Sterling looked over at him, still frowning, despite the little flip her heart performed at the sight of him, dark and beautiful there in the arched entryway. His mouth crooked as if he could feel it, too. "It will rot your brain."

"I told you not to take me to your events, Rihad." When his fierce brows rose, she flushed, aware that her agitation had sharpened her tone. "I knew this would happen."

"It is our job to ignore the tabloids," he said, mildly enough. "Or so you told me yourself."

But this was different. *She* was a different person

than the woman who had said that to him. And *this* incarnation of herself didn't want to let the tarnish of *that* one seep into what they'd built between them in the past month. She thought it might break her apart.

"It's only going to get worse." Sterling folded her hands in her lap and tried to remain calm, or at least to look it. "It always gets worse. They already call me the Queen Whore."

"Not out loud or in print, they don't." There was no softness on his starkly beautiful face then. No hint of a curve to his lush mouth. Only that dangerous light in his dark gold eyes. "Not unless they wish to explain themselves to me personally. Let me assure you, no one does."

"You can't threaten everyone on the planet, Rihad. You can't *decree* that people forget my past."

"Your imagined past."

"What does that matter? When it comes to perception, all that matters is what people believe." She shook her head at him. "Isn't that why we went on our honeymoon in the first place?"

"It was one among many reasons," he said, and his dark gold eyes moved over her the way his hands did so freely, these days. And she was still so astonished that she liked it. That she more than *liked* it. "The least important, I think."

He looked dark and forbidding in the gleaming robes he'd worn today for his meetings with some of the local tribes later on, but he didn't intimidate her any longer. Not the way he once had. Now all that power, all that dark authority he wore so easily, made her shiver for entirely different reasons. His dark gold eyes fixed on hers and everything inside her stilled in glorious anticipation, the way it always did now. Goose bumps moved sinuously over her arms and shoulders, and she wished she could continue to lose herself in it. In him.

But she knew what he didn't.

That her past was a living thing that stalked her. It always would. It always did, because it lived inside of her. No matter what she did, or how, the world thought the worst of her. That wouldn't change. It had never changed. She'd told herself she was immune to it for all those years with Omar, because that kind of notoriety had been exactly what he'd wanted and they'd courted it together.

But Rihad was different. Rihad wasn't hiding. The last thing Rihad needed was notoriety.

Rihad deserved a whole lot better than a secondhand queen he'd married only for the baby's sake, no matter how they fit together in bed. Sex might have been new to Sterling, but it wasn't to him. He could get it anywhere, she reminded herself brusquely and ignored the deep pang inside her at the thought. He was the King of Bakri. There would be women lining the streets of Bakri City should he indicate he was looking.

Sterling was the one who couldn't imagine anyone but him touching her. She was the broken one, all the way through.

"You married yourself off to stop a scandal," she reminded him lightly, though nothing inside of her felt anything like light. It was as if the moment she'd acknowledged the darkness, it had seeped into everything. Every part of her. "Not to perpetuate one every time you step outside the palace walls."

He considered her for a moment, his dark gaze unreadable. He was still standing there in the arched doorway that led into his rooms, where she'd spent the bulk of her time since they'd returned from the desert. They hadn't even discussed it—he'd simply moved her things into his suite. Sterling had been so spellbound by this man it hadn't occurred to her to maintain any distance.

For his sake, not hers.

And it was then, frowning up at him, angry at herself and worried about his future, that Sterling understood that she'd fallen in love with Rihad al Bakri.

It stunned her. It was a hit as brutal as that tabloid headline, swift and to her gut, with the force of a hard kick. She didn't know how she managed to keep from doubling over. How she managed to keep looking at him as if her entire life hadn't run aground right then and there, decisively and disastrously.

Love wasn't something Sterling could do. Ever.

How had she managed to fool herself all this time? A baby. A husband. *No one will ever love you, little girl,* they'd told her. *This is what you deserve. Deep down, you know it.*

She did know it. And she never should have let all of this get so complicated.

"What can possibly be going through your head?" Rihad asked quietly, jolting Sterling's attention back to him. "To put such a look on your face?"

"I was only thinking about how soon we should divorce," Sterling said, in a surprisingly even tone of voice. There were too many things rolling inside of her, making her feel unsteady on her own feet, as if she was a storm about to break. "That's obviously the easiest and best way to solve this problem. You remain the dutiful, heroic king who married me only to secure

Leyla's position and when they discuss the scandal that is me, it won't affect you at all."

He'd gone so still. His dark gold eyes burned.

"Do I appear affected now?" It was a dangerous question, asked in that lethal tone of voice.

"It will make me seem particularly heartless and horrible if I were to leave before Leyla is a year old," Sterling continued matter-of-factly, not answering him. "That might be best, then. I trust that once everything's died down, once you marry someone far more appropriate, we can work out a quiet way for me to stay in her life."

"Sterling." He waited until she met his hard gaze, and she could admit that it was difficult. That it cost her. "What the hell are you talking about?"

"Our divorce," she said, struggling to keep her voice light. To gaze back at him as if there was something more inside her than a great weight and a terrible sob breaking her ribs apart. "Leyla is now legitimate. A princess of Bakri, as you planned. There's no reason to drag this out if my presence here is causing you trouble. That's silly."

"Because it has worked out so terribly for you thus far?" he asked, a hard edge in his voice, like a lash, and she had to force herself not to react to it. Not to show him how it had landed and how it hurt. "My condolences, Sterling. When you came apart beneath my mouth in the shower this morning, *twice*, I had the strangest impression that you'd resigned yourself to the horrors of this marriage. Somehow."

She crossed her arms beneath her breasts and made herself glare at him as if she still hated him—as if she'd ever really hated him—her heart pounding at her as if she was running. She wished she was.

Then again, this was how it had started.

"That's sex," she said dismissively, and she felt something sharp-edged scrape inside her as she said it. As if she wanted to hurt him. As if she wanted to remind him that this had never been meant to happen between them. As if he was to blame for the fact she'd lost herself in sex and happy fantasies of happy lives she could never have. As if loving him was something he'd done to her. A punishment for daring to imagine she could love anyone without repercussions, when she'd been taught otherwise a very long time ago. "I've never had it before, as you know. It turns out, it's a lot of fun."

"Fun," he repeated softly, in a way that should have terrified her.

She told herself it didn't. Or that it didn't matter either way.

"And I appreciate you introducing me to this whole new world," she said, never shifting her gaze from his. "I do."

"Introducing you?" he echoed, and that time, a chill sneaked down her back. Her heart already ached. Her stomach twisted. But if she loved him, if she loved her daughter—and God help her, but she did, so much more than she'd known she was capable of loving anything—she had to fix this.

And there was only one way to do that.

Maybe she'd always known it would come to this. Maybe that was why she'd never touched a man in her life. Because no matter who he was, it would always end up right here. Face-to-face with the worst of her truths and no way to escape it.

There is no other man, a small voice inside intoned,

like words chiseled into stone. Deep into her heart. *Not for you.*

She knew that was true, too. It didn't change anything.

"But you're not the only man alive, Rihad, regardless of how you act," she told him then, before she could talk herself out of it. Before she could give in to all the things she wanted. "You were merely my first."

For a moment Rihad held himself so still he thought he might have turned to stone himself, into one of the pillars that held up this palace of his, smooth and hard and cold all the way through.

Which would have been safer for Sterling by far.

Because what shook in him, rolling and buckling, seismic and intense, was so vast he was surprised the whole cursed palace didn't crumble down around them where they stood. There was a clutching sensation in his chest, a pounding in his head and a murderous streak lighting him up like a bloody lantern.

"I am your first, yes," he said, in the voice of the civilized man that he'd always thought he was, before her—a king, for his sins, not this wild, fanged creature within that wanted only to howl. Then stake its claim. "And your last, Sterling. Let us make sure that part is clear."

"That's not up to you," she said, tilting her chin up as if she was expecting a wrestling match to break out.

Rihad could think of few things he'd like more than to put his hands on her, but he wouldn't do it just then. Not while he was still battling his temper, which was all the more unpredictable because he was so unused to it.

He'd never understood desire. Need. This kind of exquisite weakness. Now he was made of nothing else.

He tried to remain calm. Or at least sound calm. "I think you'll find it is."

"There's no need to get so emotional," she chided, and he was as astonished as that day back in New York when she'd started issuing orders. She stood, smoothing her hands down the front of the long dress she wore over her bare feet, a combination he found maddeningly erotic. Or was that another *emotion*? He seemed to be full of them where she was concerned. "I don't know why you're not seeing this clearly. The sooner we divorce, the easier it will be to rehabilitate your image."

"My image is fine."

Sterling inclined her head toward the table and his tablet and all those snide tabloid articles. "Evidently not."

She even smiled serenely in his direction as she walked past him into the suite, the long skirt of her dress flowing out and around as she moved, so lithe and pretty on her feet it was as if everything she did was a dance. Even the way she walked away from him.

And this was absurd. He knew that. He knew she was trying to needle him, though he couldn't have said why. He knew she wanted him as much as he did her—he hadn't imagined their morning in his shower, the way she'd cried out his name and ground herself against his mouth, and he'd seen that same hectic fever in her gaze now, too. It was always there. Always.

He hadn't imagined everything that had happened between them over the past month. This woman was his in every conceivable way. He had no intention of divorcing her, or even permitting her to sleep apart from him again. What did it matter if she admitted this or not?

Yet Rihad found it mattered quite a lot.

He stalked after her, catching her while she was still crossing his bedchamber and using her elbow and her momentum to spin her back around to face him.

"Don't you dare—" she began, but he was already touching her, and that was its own alchemy.

That fire that only burned hotter by the day exploded between them, the way it always did, wild and bright. He saw her pulse accelerate in her neck. He saw that white-hot heat make her eyes go glassy.

"You little fool," he bit out, but this wasn't temper, he understood. Not any longer. There was that bitter-sweet pang of jealousy at the thought of her with other men, but everything else was pure, sensual menace that he had every intention of taking out on her delectable body. Until she took his point to heart. "Do you think this happens every day?"

"I assume it must," she fired back at him, so busy fighting him she didn't seem to notice the way he was backing her across the room, to the nearest wall. "Or every popular song I've ever heard is a lie."

She let out a small, surprised noise when her back came up against the nearest brocaded wall, and then another when Rihad merely leaned closer and pressed his forehead to hers, holding her that simply.

"This is the sex you seem to think you can get any-where," he told her, and her mouth was a serious tempta-tion, but he ignored it, concentrating on pulling that long skirt of hers up and sliding his hands beneath. "This is the chemistry you imagine is so run-of-the-mill."

He felt that shudder go through her and then his hands were on her soft thighs, and it was his turn to let out a long breath when he found she was completely bare beneath her dress. There was nothing but the heat of her skin, the touch of her soft curls, and then that molten core of her, all his.

Only and ever his.

"Rihad..." she whispered.

"I don't want to fight with you," he told her.

He angled his head back so he could look at her, even as he plunged a finger deep into her heat. He watched a flush spread over her cheeks and knew that was the truth of things between them. The only truth that mattered, and it always would be. That dark, bewitching fire. That endless well of need.

"If you have something to say to me, Sterling, say it. Don't poke at me. Don't pretend."

She stiffened at that. "Pretending is the problem. It's what we've—*I've*—been doing this whole time!"

"I don't think so."

He pulled his finger from her depths, then held her gaze as he licked it clean, her taste as intoxicating as ever on his tongue. He felt his mouth curve as her lips parted at that, as if she was finding it difficult to breathe regularly. He reached down between them to handle his robes and his trousers, and then he stepped between her legs as he lifted her up, wrapping her around him and holding her there for a long, hot instant.

This time, he didn't carry her to a nearby table. This time, as he lowered her against him he slid deep inside of her, so deep they both groaned at the sensation.

Her hands balled into fists at his shoulders and she bit her lip as if she meant to resist him. But then she rolled her hips against his as if she couldn't help herself, and Rihad smiled.

He took control then. Her ankles were locked tight around his hips and he lifted her up, then brought her down, working her against him slowly. So slowly. Making her shudder and pant. Making it so good she'd forget all this divorce and separation nonsense.

Because she was soft and hot, a revelation around him with every stroke, and she was his.

All his. Always his.

It took him a long while to realize that he was chanting that out loud, like a prayer or a promise, and when he did, he laughed.

"Say it," he demanded.

But this was Sterling, his Sterling. So even as she writhed against him, even as her hips met his in this wild dance of theirs, she defied him.

And God help him, he loved it. He loved all of this more than he'd ever imagined was possible, more than he'd ever loved anything or anyone. Sterling was his, damn it. All of her. Her body and her heart alike, and he didn't much care if she thought otherwise. He knew the truth.

He wasn't giving her up. Ever. Even if his kingdom came down around him. Even if the world followed suit.

For the first time in his life, he didn't care about his duty. He cared about her.

"Say it," he told her again. "I can do this all day. And if I can, you will. But you will not come until you admit what we both already know is the truth."

She let out a sound then, half fury and half need, and Rihad laughed again, because he was as hungry as she was. As greedy for her.

"All yours," she gritted out, her blue eyes slick and warm on his, and he felt it like a caress. This was who they were. Caress, capitulation, it was all the same thing. It all led to the same place. "Damn you, Rihad, I'm yours."

He reached down between them and pressed hard against the taut center of her hunger, and she bucked hard against him, arching her back and digging her fingers hard into his shoulders, then screamed as she plummeted over the edge.

But Rihad was only getting started.

CHAPTER TWELVE

STERLING HADN'T MEANT to eavesdrop.

She'd been enjoying the gala, held in the grand art gallery that was one of the jewels of the new Bakri City, a testament to the country's bright new future. Or so Rihad had said in his speech earlier, in English, for the benefit of the foreign press. She'd allowed the phalanx of docents to lead her through the first great exhibit, on loan from the Louvre, and had honestly enjoyed looking at the collection of world-class, world-famous art.

It had reminded her of her favorite way to spend a day in New York City: wandering aimlessly around the Metropolitan Museum of Art and losing herself in all the marvelous things collected there for the viewing, from paintings to metalwork to Egyptian tombs. Except here in Bakri City there was the sea on one side and the beckoning desert on the other, reminding her that she was across the world from the things she knew.

It had been ten days since she'd realized that she loved Rihad. Ten long days and longer nights since she'd understood that she must leave him and, worse, Leyla, too. Every day, she'd woken up and vowed that it would be her last in Bakri, that she would find a way to leave the two people she loved most. Yet somehow, there was always another reason to stay.

And here she was on yet another night, dressed in beautiful clothes as befit the queen she still had trouble believing was legitimately *her*. She'd smiled prettily on command, quite as if she couldn't see the speculation in every gaze that met hers. As if she couldn't hear the whispers that followed her around the great courtyard.

As if she wasn't aware that at least half of the people who spoke to her were thinking the word *whore* as they curtsied and called her *Your Majesty*.

"Your daughter is the bright jewel of the kingdom," professed one Bakrian aristocrat whom Sterling had recognized from her wedding. Where this woman and her husband, both possessed of crisp, upper crust British accents when they spoke in their perfect English, had gazed back at her as if they couldn't understand a word she'd said.

"I certainly think so," Sterling had said.

"One can only hope she grows into her mother's beauty," said the husband, and Sterling hadn't much liked that look in his too-knowing eyes when he said it, or the way he'd leaned closer than was strictly appropriate when he'd continued. "What a blessing it is for a daughter to become like her mother in every way."

It took a moment for Sterling to understand that this person had, in effect, just called her infant daughter a whore. A *potential* whore.

She was going to ruin Rihad if she stayed. That much was obvious, no matter how he tried to dismiss it.

But aside from worrying over her biological limitations and the genetic propensity for ruining children she might have inherited from her own terrible mother,

Sterling hadn't really given a lot of thought to how her presence in Bakri would destroy *Leyla*. She'd thought that as Rihad's daughter in every way but her biology, Leyla would be safe. More than safe.

You should have known better, sneered that internal voice that she knew came from her foster parents, across all those years, as if she was still standing in the middle of that cold kitchen waiting for the next blow to lay her out on the linoleum floor. *You taint everything you touch.*

She'd ducked into one of the cordoned-off alcoves for a little breather after that unpleasant last encounter. She wanted to take a moment—only a moment—to let her face do whatever it wished. To drop her public smile. To simply not be on display.

Sterling pulled in a deep breath, then let it out. Then again.

And it was as she was preparing to walk back out and face it all again that she heard Rihad's deep voice from the other side of the pillar that concealed her.

"I have no worries whatsoever about the union between our countries," he was saying in his crisp, kingly manner. "Nor can I imagine that Kavian has indicated otherwise, to your publication or to anyone else."

That meant it was one of the reporters, Sterling understood, and that was why she didn't reveal her presence. She'd had enough of the press earlier, with their sugary smiles and all those jagged claws right underneath, sharpened on her own skin every time they asked her a pointed question.

"Yet your sister remains at large."

"The Princess Amaya's schedule remains private for obvious security reasons." Rihad's voice was so cold then it made Sterling's stomach clench tight. "But I can assure you that no member of the royal family is 'at large.' Your information is faulty."

"Neither Kavian nor Amaya have been seen—"

"His Royal Majesty Kavian ibn Zayed al Talaas, ruling sheikh of the desert stronghold Daar Talaas, is certainly not in hiding of any kind, if that is what your impertinent suggestion is meant to imply." Rihad's voice held dark warning then. "But he no more clears his schedule with me than I do with him. He certainly does not clear it with you. I would advise you to step away from this subject."

"Certainly, Sire." The man's voice made Sterling feel dirty. Tarnished. "My congratulations on your recent marriage."

Sterling winced then, at the thunderous silence that told her all she needed to know about the expression Rihad was likely wearing.

"Tread carefully," Rihad all but growled. "Very carefully."

"Certainly, Your Majesty, you must be aware that there is mounting concern among your subjects that a woman like that—"

"A woman like that?" Rihad's voice turned mild, which was her husband at his most volatile, even as that same old phrase knocked around inside of Sterling, leaving marks. New bruises to join the old. "By all means, enlighten me. A woman like what, exactly?"

That was when Sterling moved. She swept out from behind the pillar and hoped it would be assumed she'd simply taken herself off to the powder room.

Rihad stood squared off against a small, toad-like creature Sterling recognized as one of the paparazzi who had followed her every move in New York. She had no doubt that he was responsible for a great many of the horrible narratives that circulated about her to this day, as he'd taken after her as if Sterling was his pet project. He'd always looked at her as if he could *see* that truth buried deep inside of her. As if *he knew* how flawed and unwanted and *ruined* she truly was.

Part of her wanted nothing more than to leave him to Rihad's scant and rapidly eroding mercy, but she didn't dare. Not now, after all the recent bad press and a museum filled with more reporters. She was already enough of a stone draped around Rihad's neck, dragging him down. There was no need to add an assault-and-battery charge on her behalf to the list of her sins against this man.

"Sterling," the awful little man oozed at her. "We were just talking about you."

She didn't know which part of that offended her more—the way the man looked at her, the way he spoke to her with such unearned familiarity or the way he sidled closer to her with his hand extended as if he planned to put it on—

"Ancient Bakrian law states that if another man touches my queen without my permission I am not only permitted to rend him limb from limb with my own hands, but must do so to protect the honor of the crown," Rihad said conversationally, and the reporter froze. Rihad's smile didn't reach his eyes. "Barbaric, is it not? And yet so many of my subjects find comfort in the old ways."

He did not say, *myself included*, but Sterling felt certain she was not the only one who felt as if he'd shouted it from the rooftops.

The little man's eyes glittered with a sort of impotent fury that Sterling knew—she *knew*—would translate into yet another revolting piece about her in the morning papers. She could practically read the article now as it scrolled across the man's dirty mind.

To this man I will never be anything but a woman like that, Sterling thought miserably, but she only smiled at the reporter as she moved past him to take Rihad's arm. *The Queen Whore herself, parading around like so much pollution.*

"You shouldn't antagonize him," she said softly as Rihad drew her out onto the dance floor, the elegant crowd parting all around them to let them take its center, as if the tense exchange had never happened. "Not him or any of his little cronies."

"Must I introduce myself to you all over again?" Rihad's voice was arrogant, and his dark gold eyes still glittered furiously. "I am the King of Bakri. *He* should not antagonize *me*."

"You are the king, yes," she agreed, trying to keep her smile in place and her voice low, as befitted such genteel and public a place. "And you should not condescend to notice a man like him. That you do at all is my fault."

Sterling felt one of his hands tighten against the small of her back, and the other where his larger one gripped hers, and her curse was that she felt all of this like light. It was as if he poured straight into her, banishing all the darkness.

But she knew that wasn't true. She knew nothing could.

"Do not start this again," he warned her, his voice harsh despite his placid expression. "Not here."

"As you wish, Your Majesty," she murmured, so submissively that it startled a laugh out of him. Which in turn made her laugh, too, when she'd have said that was impossible under the circumstances. And still he spun her around and around that dance floor, as if they were nothing but beautiful. As if all of this was.

And some of the papers the next morning thought so, it was true.

But the others were vile.

There was a list of Sterling's supposed conquests, spanning the globe and including some countries she'd never visited and many men she'd never met. Another featured a list of her "raciest moments," which mostly involved skimpy outfits from her more outrageous modeling shoots held up as if she'd paraded around the streets of Manhattan wearing so little.

They didn't actually call her a whore. But then, they didn't have to call her anything. The comments section did that for them.

Sterling didn't mention the articles. Still, she could see the temper crack across Rihad's face and thought he tried to conceal it from her. Because that was Rihad, she understood now. Duty before all else. And he'd decided she was one of his duties. She cuddled Leyla on her lap and pressed kisses into the sweet crown of her head, and she only smiled when Rihad excused himself.

Because she knew what he refused to accept: this was never going to get better. *She* was never going to get better, or any less the subject of the repulsive speculation of the public.

And if she stayed here, Rihad and Leyla would rot right along with her.

Sterling might not have known a lot about love, but she knew—deep down she *knew*—that if she really, truly loved them, she wouldn't condemn them to that kind of life. Not when it took so little to save them.

So very little.

All she had to do was leave.

When his chief of security strode into Rihad's private conference room, scattering the gathered aides and the handful of ambassadors Rihad had been sitting with, he assumed it was about Amaya, at last.

"Has she been found?" he asked when the room was clear.

He thought the feeling that moved in him then was something far closer to regret than relief. But that made no sense. Amaya needed to be found and should have been found months ago. She needed to do her duty, no matter how Rihad might have come to sympathize with her plight. He hadn't lied to her when he'd told her there were no other options available to them.

But he couldn't deny the part of him that admired his younger sister for having stayed out of Kavian's reach all this time. Rihad liked the other man well enough. Respected him, even. But he doubted very much that any other creature on earth had led him on such a merry chase.

"We are tracking her, Your Majesty," his security chief said, standing at rigid attention, quite as if he expected a reprimand. "We have video of her leaving the palace an hour ago. It looks as if she's headed for the city limits."

Rihad digested that statement, and it took him longer than it should have to comprehend that the man was not talking about his sister.

But he couldn't make sense of what he was hearing.

He was aware that he'd frozen solid where he stood. He heard what his security chief was saying, but he couldn't seem to move. To react.

She had charmed her way into one of the palace's fleet of armored vehicles, because she was nothing if not persuasive when she wished. And because she was his queen. Instead of heading for the royal enclosure near the sea, a perfectly reasonable place for her to go without any guards because it was manned with its own, she'd had the driver change direction once they'd left the palace grounds and she'd headed for the far reaches of Bakri City.

There was nothing there, Rihad knew. Nothing save the border.

"My daughter," he managed to say, over the dark thud that was his heart in his chest. "Where is my daughter?"

His beautiful, perfect little Leyla, who he could not lose, and who, he realized, he'd never called *his* daughter before. Not out loud. He *would not* lose Leyla, no matter who her biological father was. She was his.

She and her treacherous mother were entirely his.

His security chief was muttering into his earpiece. Rihad was unnaturally still.

"The princess remains in the palace, Your Majesty. She is with her nurses even now."

"Excellent," Rihad bit out, and he started moving then, belting out orders as he went.

If Sterling had left the baby behind that meant he wouldn't have to temper his reaction when he found her—though he was sure he would have to think about that, at some point. That she'd taken off without her daughter, which was so unlike her as to be something like laughable.

He might have imagined, once, that Sterling was nothing more than a calculating, callous sort of creature. The kind of woman who would have a child for the sole purpose of tying herself to a man and, more to the point, his fortune.

That he didn't think that of her now, not even for a moment, told him things he was too furious to analyze just then. There was something seismic inside of him, bigger and bolder than anything he'd ever felt before. It was as massive as the desert, expanding in all directions, and he was not entirely certain he would be the same man when he survived it.

If he survived it.

But he had every intention of sharing the effects of it with his wife while he waited to see. Because he wasn't letting her go.

Not ever.

The helicopter landed with military precision on the dusty desert road, forcing Sterling's driver to slam on his brakes to a fishtailing stop—and putting an end to her escape fantasies that easily.

Sterling sat in the backseat and stared at the gleaming metal thing with its powerful rotors as if, were she to concentrate hard enough, she could make it go away again.

But it didn't. Of course it didn't.

For a long, shuddering moment, nothing happened. The helicopter sat there in the middle of the otherwise empty road. Sterling's driver, having lapsed into what sounded like frantic prayers as it had landed, was now muttering to himself. And that meant she had a lifetime or two to contemplate the leaping somersault her heart kept performing in her chest, no matter how sternly she told herself that *hope* was inappropriate.

She wasn't running away this time. She wasn't desperate or scared. She wasn't a fifteen-year-old kid and she was no longer afraid of her best friend's big, bad wolf.

This time, she was doing the right thing.

The helicopter's back door opened and Rihad climbed out, his movements precise and furious, and yet still infused with that lethal, masculine grace that made her mouth water. Maybe it always would.

But if so, it would happen from afar. In magazines or on the news.

She was no good for him. She was even worse for her precious daughter. Nothing else mattered

"Stay here," she told her driver, not that he'd offered to leap to her defense—the man clearly recognized the royal insignia on the helicopter's sides if not his king himself.

Sterling slammed her way out of the car into the hot desert sun. Memories assaulted her as the hot wind poured over her. Of facing Rihad much like this on a Manhattan street, in what seemed like a different lifetime. Of the dark look he'd worn then and the far darker and grimmer look he wore now.

Sterling didn't wait for him to reach her.

"What are you doing?" she threw at him across the hard-packed stretch of sandy road that separated them. "Let me go!"

"Never."

Short. Harsh. A kingly utterance and infused with all his trademark ruthlessness.

She was as instantly furious at him as she was pointlessly, traitorously moved by that.

"It wasn't a request."

"You do not give the King of Bakri orders, Sterling." He was closer then, and she could *feel* that edginess that came off him in waves, as if he was his own sun. "Your role is to obey."

"Stop this." Her voice was a hiss, and she slashed her hand through the air to emphasize it. "You're not being reasonable."

He was beyond furious—she could see it in every line of that body of his she knew better than her own now. He was practically vibrating with the force of his temper. And yet he only stared at her for a beat, then another, as if he couldn't believe she'd said that to him.

And then he tipped back his head and laughed.

He laughed and he laughed.

When he focused on her again, Sterling was shaking, and not from anything like fear. It was need. Longing. *Love.*

"I am renowned for my reason," he told her, no trace of laughter remaining in his voice then. "I am considered the most rational of men. My family is filled with emotional creatures who careened through their lives, neglecting their duties and catering to their weaknesses." He shrugged. "I thought I didn't have any weaknesses. But the truth is, I hadn't met you yet."

Again, she didn't know how to feel, so she ignored the great, swirling mess inside of her. She balled her hands into fists and scowled at him.

"You're making my point for me. I'm a weakness and you're a man who can't afford any. You need to let me go."

"Yet when it comes to you, Sterling, I am not the least bit reasonable," he growled at her. "Why the hell are you running away from me?"

"Why do you think?" she challenged, astonished. "I'm an anchor around your neck, weighing you down. You can't have this endless scandal and that's all this is. That's all I am."

"You left Leyla behind."

Sterling couldn't let herself think about that.

"She's better off," she gritted out. She swallowed back the anguished sob that threatened to pour out of her, to tear her open. "Divorced couples share custody all the time. There's no reason why we can't. And that means Leyla can grow up here, where she'll be safe."

"I can hear the words that come out of your mouth." His voice set every hair on her body on end. It prickled over her, harsh like sandpaper and a darkness beneath it. "Yet not one of them makes the slightest bit of sense."

"All I ask is that you find a good woman to help you raise her," Sterling pushed on, determined, despite the way everything inside of her lurched and rolled as if she was about to capsize herself. She couldn't let that happen. "Someone who is—"

"What?" Rihad asked brutally. "Not as dirty and ruined as you are?"

There it was.

It was shocking to hear someone else say that out loud after all these years. It was soul-destroying to hear it from him.

But Sterling wasn't running away from the only man

she'd ever loved like this, or ever would, because it was *easy*. She was doing it because it was *right*. Which meant she couldn't collapse at that. She couldn't let all that wild darkness inside of her take her down to her knees. It was too important that he accept this.

"You know, then." She couldn't process it.

He looked furious. Impatient. Darkly focused on her.

"I have an idea what those terrible people must have told you. It doesn't make it true."

"If you know," she managed to say, "then there's no reason for this to be so dramatic. I'm doing you a favor."

His expression shifted into something incredulous and arrogant at once.

"I do not want a favor, Sterling," he threw at her. "I want my family."

And that easily, he broke her heart.

"You can make yourself a perfect family," she told him, and she only realized as she spoke that her throat was constricted. That tears were welling up and pouring over, splashing down her face. It was as if he hadn't simply broken her heart—he'd broken *her* into a thousand tiny pieces and she couldn't keep them all together any longer. She wasn't sure she'd ever be able to do it again. "You can have more babies and a sweet, biddable wife who follows your commands and never shames you in public. You can—"

"*You* are my family!" he roared at her, and when she jumped back an inch he followed, taking her arms in those hard, surprisingly gentle hands of his. "You are my wife, my queen. We have a daughter. *This* is your family, Sterling. *I* am your family."

"Rihad—"

But her voice was choked and her words were lost

somewhere in a great, wild tangle that swamped her then. Far greater than fear. Far more encompassing.

"And I know that you love me, little one," he told her then, his voice lower, but still so raw it almost hurt to hear it. Almost. "Do you think I can't tell? When I do nothing but study you, day after day?"

"I don't," she managed to respond, though she couldn't stop shaking. "I can't. Nothing good ever comes of my loving something."

His hands tightened slightly on her arms, but his expression softened. He pulled her even closer. His dark gold eyes searched hers.

"Sterling." He said her name as if it was as beautiful as she'd thought it was when she'd picked it as a teenager. "I know that love for you means a hit must be forthcoming. I know you expect nothing but pain and misery when you dare to hope." He moved, rubbing his palms along her arms as if he was trying to warm her. Soothe her. *Love her.* "But I am a man of honor. My word is law. And no one will ever hit you again as long as you live. Especially not me."

She shook her head, hard, though shivers chased through her, one after the next as if she really was being torn apart. She could *feel* the tearing, deep inside of her.

"I'm your duty, nothing more," she said fiercely. "But your duty is to Bakri, not to me. And they deserve better. *You* deserve better."

"And you deserve to believe that you do, too."

She couldn't breathe past those words. She whispered his name again then, but she couldn't seem to stop crying. And then he let go of her, which was worse than a hit. Worse than a kick or two. She reached out a hand despite her intention to make him let her go, but then froze, because he wasn't walking away from her.

Rihad al Bakri, reigning sheikh, Grand Ruler and King of the Bakrian Empire, sank to his knees on the sand before her, never shifting that proud, stern gaze of his from hers.

He reached over, but he didn't take her hands. He took her hips in his powerful grip instead, as if he could lift her up if he wished. As if he could carry her forever, if she would only let him.

"I ordered you marry me once," he said in that low, dark, powerful voice of his. "Now I am asking you to stay with me. To live with me, love me, and who cares what the papers say. There are men watching us right now. Does it look as if that bothers me?"

"Rihad. You can't." But she didn't know what she meant to say and he wasn't listening to her anyway. His hands gripped her hips.

"I want to make more babies with you and this time, I want to hold them in my own hands as they enter this world. I want to make love to you forever. You are worth a thousand kingdoms, and mine is nothing but a pile of sand without you." His gaze was part of her, inside of her. "Be my wife in every possible way, Sterling. Not because it is my duty, but because it is my deepest wish. You are my heart. My love. I want you to be *mine*."

And she understood that vast, unconquerable thing that slammed down on her then. It wasn't fear—it was so much bigger. It was love. Real love, without conditions or qualifiers. Without lies. Love that might incorporate pain and darkness, as all life must in its time, but wasn't made of it.

She'd expected him to hurt her because that was all

she knew. She'd assumed she would ruin him the way she ruined everything, because that was what the people who'd hurt her had told her to justify their actions.

Terrible people, he'd called them.

But that was the past.

This man, here and now, on his knees before her in a way she imagined he'd never been before and never would be again, was the future.

She had to give herself over to the only thing she'd ever encountered that could beat back the darkness.

Love.

And within that, wrapped up so tightly it was nearly indistinguishable, *hope.*

"I'm already yours, Rihad," she whispered, fierce and hopeful at once. "I've been yours all along."

He wrapped his arms around her hips, resting his head against her stomach. She felt the press of his perfect mouth against her flesh and the deep shudder that went with it, as if she was accepting him into her bones.

"I love you," he told her, dark and imperious against the belly where she would bear his children. She knew she would, and not only because he'd decreed it. "Never doubt that."

"I love you, too," she said, her tears falling freely, but this time, they were made of joy. This time, she recognized it for what it was. This time, she believed it really would last forever. That they would, together. "I always will. And always is a very long time, I'm told."

"It had better be," he muttered, every inch of him the king.

And then she sank down beside him, and he took her in his arms, and for the first time in her life, Sterling let herself believe in forever.

CHAPTER THIRTEEN

Ten years later...

"HE IS VERY annoying, yes," Rihad told his furious daughter out in the private family garden that morning, and took care to hide his laughter from her. "But if you drown your brother in that pool, Leyla, there will be no party on Saturday and you may, in fact, spend your birthday in the dungeons."

"There aren't any dungeons in the palace," his ten-year-old replied, hotly. "Mama said you made that up."

He only smiled when she scowled at him. "There are dungeons if I say there are. I make the rules."

"Brothers are stupid," Leyla told him with a hint of imperiousness he thought she'd gotten directly from her mother.

Rihad thought of his own brother, lost so long now.

"I cannot forgive myself," he'd told Sterling on Omar's last birthday. As they did every year, they'd visited his grave on the palace grounds, together. "I doubt I ever will."

She had been wrapped in his arms, her back tucked against his front, his chin resting on her head.

"He'd already forgiven you," she'd said. She'd shifted

when he tensed. "He loved you, Rihad. He always loved you." She'd smiled up at him. "I was the one who hated you, for the both of us."

"Brothers might be stupid," he told Leyla now, "but you must love them anyway."

"Love sounds stupid, too," Leyla retorted, but she helped six-year-old Aarib continue to jump up and down on the wide lip of the pool near the waterfall anyway.

Though not without a very deep, long-suffering sort of sigh that did not bode well for her upcoming adolescence. Rihad repressed a shudder at that unhappy thought, given how stunning a child she already was, God help him. He returned his attention to the matters of state that awaited him on his tablet, a far more appealing prospect than his little girl growing up.

The papers hadn't always left them alone, but it was nothing as it had been. Rihad had seen to the dismissal of the particular reporters who dared hound his wife so relentlessly—just as he'd seen to the immediate exile of some of his courtiers when he'd finally seen the way they'd treated her.

The Queen of Bakri, by definition, was a woman without peer, spotless of reputation and widely beloved by all.

Ten years on, Rihad had the distinct pleasure of knowing that wasn't merely a decree he'd made, but the simple truth.

He knew the moment Sterling walked outside to join them in the garden. He always knew. She changed the air, he'd often told her, simply by breathing it, sharing it.

Those vicious, repulsive people she'd left behind in Iowa hadn't ruined her. She wasn't ruined, He thought that these days, she believed that without question at last.

His beautiful Sterling. His perfect wife.

He took a moment to marvel at her as she walked toward him across the stones while the world stilled all around him the way it always had. The way he thought it always would. She still dressed like the model she'd been, too elegant and so easily, offhandedly chic. That copper-blond hair of hers that still fascinated him beyond measure. Those long, long legs that had only this morning been draped over his shoulders as he'd driven them both to a hard, wild finish in the murky dark before dawn.

Ten years later and he was still hard at the thought of her.

"Are the monsters asleep?" he asked as she drew near.

"More or less." She smiled as she looked at Leyla and Aarib, as if she truly enjoyed the particular music of their young voices, scraping holes in the sky. He knew she did. Despite himself, so did he.

"God bless the morning nap."

Rihad thought of their younger boys, four-year-old Jamil and two-year-old Raza. Little hellions in every possible way, far louder than the older two combined, and they both demanded their mother's personal attention as only younger children could. "Indeed."

She moved as if to sit in her own seat but he pulled her down into his lap instead, nuzzling her neck until her breath caught. He pressed himself against the seam of her bottom, and she laughed.

"You're insatiable." But she sounded proud.

Content, he thought. They were content, and it was nothing like settling. It was like flying. Soaring through ten years and headed for ten more. Headed straight for forever.

"Only for you, my little one," he murmured against her ear. "Always for you."

They had not always had it easy, these past ten years. They had failed each other, hurt each other. The world was not always gentle and it was easy to lose each other in the whirl of children and responsibilities, even in a palace with fleets of nurses and around-the-clock staff.

But they had always had love. And love brought them back to each other, over and over again.

Rihad had learned to treat her less as a subject and more like a partner. Or he tried. She, in turn, had learned how to trust him.

This was intimacy, in all its complicated glory, of the soul and of the flesh. Lovers become parents, a king and his queen, a man and his woman. This was the magnificently double-edged sword of truly being known by another, across whole years.

In truth, he loved every bit of it.

And he still liked to show her how much.

"They're kissing." It was Aarib's disgusted little-boy voice, more piercing than usual, or perhaps Rihad wanted to be interrupted less in that moment.

"They do that a lot," replied Leyla, in her world-weary older-sister voice. "A *lot*."

"Why did we have more children?" Sterling asked him, laughing. "Whose terrible idea was that?"

But then she kissed him once more, and he saw moisture glistening in her lovely blue eyes. He ran his hand over her cheek.

"Thank you," she whispered. "Thank you so much, Rihad."

"For what?" he asked quietly.

"For everything," Sterling said, fiercely. "For giving me our family. For *being* my family."

She rose to go to the children then, and he let her leave, fully aware that she had no reason to thank him. She was the heart of this wondrous little tangle of theirs, love and trust and wonder, tears and scrapes and sudden furies.

Their heart. His heart.

His, Rihad thought. Forever.

And he was the king. His will was law.

* * * * *

MILLS & BOON®

The Chatsfield Collection!

Sheikh's DESERT DUTY
THE CHATSFIELD
MAISEY YATES

Princess's SECRET BABY
THE CHATSFIELD
CAROL MARINELLI

Style, spectacle, scandal…!

With the eight Chatsfield siblings happily married and settling down, it's time for a new generation of Chatsfields to shine, in this brand-new 8-book collection! The prospect of a merger with the Harrington family's boutique hotels will shape the future forever. But who will come out on top?

Find out at
www.millsandboon.co.uk/TheChatsfield2

MILLS & BOON®

Why not subscribe?
Never miss a title and save money too!

Here's what's available to you if you join the
exclusive **Mills & Boon Book Club** today:

✦ *Titles up to a month ahead of the shops*
✦ *Amazing discounts*
✦ *Free P&P*
✦ *Earn Bonus Book points that can be redeemed
  against other titles and gifts*
✦ *Choose from monthly or pre-paid plans*

Still want more?
Well, if you join today we'll even give you
50% OFF your first parcel!

So visit **www.millsandboon.co.uk/subs**
or call Customer Relations on 020 8288 2888
to be a part of this exclusive Book Club!

SUBS_2014